A Royal Quest

Mary Lide

A Royal Quest

WARNER BOOKS

A Warner Communications Company

Warner Books, Inc., 666 Fifth Avenue, New York, NY 10103

W A Warner Communications Company

Printed in the United States of America
First Printing: April 1987
10 9 8 7 6 5 4 3 2 1

Library of Congress Cataloging in Publication Data

Lide, Mary.
  A royal quest.

  I. Title.
PS3562.I344R6   1987   823'.914   86-22478
ISBN 0-446-51362-8

Designed by Giorgetta Bell McRee

TO MY DAUGHTERS AND SONS
Vanessa and Nellie, David, James, and Quentin
With love

A Royal Quest

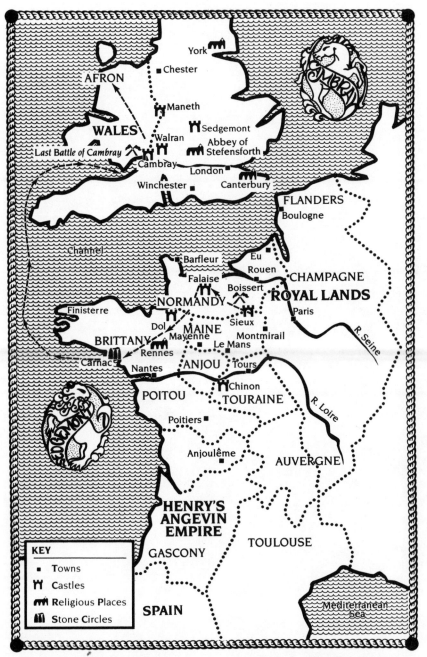

York

■ Chester

AFRON

■ Maneth

WALES

♯ Sedgemont

Walran

Abbey of
Stefensforth

Last Battle of Cambray

Cambray

London

Winchester

Canterbury

FLANDERS

Boulogne

Channel

■ Barfleur

Eu

Rouen

Falaise

Boissert

CHAMPAGNE

NORMANDY

ROYAL LANDS

Finisterre

Paris

Dol

MAINE

Sieux

BRITTANY

Mayenne

Montmirail

R. Seine

Carnac

Rennes

Le Mans

Nantes

ANJOU

Tours

Chinon

POITOU

TOURAINE

R. Loire

Poitiers

Anjoulême

AUVERGNE

HENRY'S
ANGEVIN
EMPIRE

TOULOUSE

KEY

GASCONY

■ Towns

Mediterranean
Sea

♯ Castles

ᛘᚽ Religious Places

SPAIN

𖠿 Stone Circles

◀--- Journey of Olwen to Falaise

◀--- Journey of Olwen & Prince Taliesin from
Falaise to Carnac - (by sea) Carnac to
Cambray - Cambray to Afron

Other Journeys (*Not marked on this map*)
Cambray - Abbey of Stefensforth - to the
coast - across the Channel to Paris
(Olwen, Robert & Urien)

Chinon - Poitiers - Falaise (Hue &
Queen Eleanor)

Chapter 1

, Urien of Wales, bard to the Celts, high poet of the old peoples of this land, record these things. Out of a long silence I write them down, not in my own tongue but in the fashion of the Norman priests, that men who come hereafter should read and remember. It is for the lords and ladies of Cambray I write—Lord Raoul, the Lady Ann, their sons—whom I have served faithfully all my life and on whose behalf I would die. And most of all it is for their daughter, Lady Olwen, fairest of her race, to whom my devotion has long been pledged as if I were a knight born, who since I saw her first has been my love, my bane. . . . It is a long story I tell, a story with many threads; who knows now how they will unwind? Ambition, hate, revenge, the dark side of this world are woven here, and honor, love, loyalty their counterpart. These are the things I speak of, and of deeds, great and ignoble, and of the men, ignoble and great, who achieved them.

Now I know there will be those who out of spite or ignorance will claim that I, of no account, have twisted these twisted strands still more to serve myself, that ever self-seeking, I have thrust myself to the front and have bound myself to this noble family to enhance my reputation. Not so. Such rumors grow out of enmity. For this story brings but little credit to me and certainly nothing of happiness. Yet, although it is true that most of the men whose names are known and remembered here are men of deeds, achieving great things, so it is also true that there are other men who serve as watchers, recorders of events, who sit and let the world spin by. Such a one am I. *You shall be my eyes, my voice.* So the Lady Ann once laid a charge on me, so now I fulfill it full-fold. And that was wished on me by fate. For since I believe nothing in this life stands alone, and nothing is done that does not come back sometime, like ripples from a stone thrown into a lake, so it is that I, the least part of this chronicle, live to write it, am destined to be its witness and its testimony. And that, too, fate has willed on me.

Now, it is no secret, and I am the last to deny, that I am not highborn as men deem wealth and rank, and chance alone brought me to the notice of these noble lords, overlords of the lands of Cambray, earls of Sedgemont in England, counts of Sieux in France, names and titles to make the head spin around, as mine did when I first heard of them. Son am I of a kitchen slut, a serf, here at Cambray, who claimed a Norman of the castle guard fathered me (a claim he never took much upon himself, at least not enough to wed with her, although if kicks and blows be proof of paternity, he left his mark on me). So those who sneer that I have no right to mingle with the great have some justice on their side. Yet I believe this, too, that although each man is born to his destined place, at our birth the gods give us gifts to create us what we might be. So it was that my mother named me with an improbable Celtic name, to give me hope of some future greatness after all. Where, poor wench, dredged she up that "Urien"? A Celtic name for a hero king, unfitting for a bastard churl. "Famed lord, land's anchor, boldest of warriors"—so the Celts sing of him and remember him. What possessed my mother in her birthing straw to give his name to her firstborn, except some equally improbable hope, some spark of prophecy, that hereafter it should also be said: Of all men the lords of Cambray chose to speak for them Urien the Bard, whose songs are known and loved throughout the land, whose name is known and remembered, even though he won no battles, nor fought in them. For are not bards counted as high in esteem among the Celtic folk as any king or prince, and are not poets the lords of this world, holding it and its follies in their hands? And in the end, are not words the only things worthwhile to last when swords are dulled and all those great warriors have turned to dust?

Cambray lies on the western edges of the Norman world, along the marcher lands between England and those Celtic principalities that men call Wales (although that is more like a Saxon name and not the one we use ourselves). It is a simple border castle, Cambray, with its great square keep and encircling walls. Built of stone by a Norman lord, it stands on the edge of a wild and spreading moor above the cliffs of the western sea. A quiet place was it as I remember it in my childhood, at the end of the sixth decade of the twelfth century after Christ, when he who is now England's King, Henry, second king of that name, also known as Henry of Anjou, claimed his island kingdom was at peace (although he won that title and that crown after many years of civil war so bitter that even today men turn pale at the thought of that anarchy, as it is called, and pray to God never to know its like again). But in my childhood, as a serf at Cambray, it seemed a quiet place. I knew nothing then of these civil wars and their aftermath, and might have lived out my life there in obscurity had not the lords of Cambray come back.

The first Norman settled there was Falk, who built the castle and married with a Celtic wife. Their daughter was the Lady Ann, only child of this union to survive, and Earl Raoul of Sedgemont was both her husband and her overlord. The story of the Lady Ann of Cambray you may know, how she met and loved and warred with that earl, and how at last they came to terms, made peace themselves, were wed to beget sons, after the turmoil and fret of their early lives. Lord Raoul had many lands and many cares. In due course these took him far from this western border, and by the time I was born, he and his family seldom came to Cambray but traveled, as is the way of great lords, turn and turn about to their other estates. Yet when that autumn they returned, I think, in their hearts his wife and children still thought of Cambray as their home. So that whatever else may be said of us, at least we share this in common, these noble lords and I: having Celtic mothers, Norman sires, and bound somehow to these moorlands, these wild cliffs, perhaps even against our will.

I cannot tell you exactly what year, what date the family first returned, except that Henry of Anjou had then been king for some twelve, thirteen years or so and we were all still children, the Lady Ann's two sons, her daughter, Olwen, and I. We do not keep records at Cambray, as do monks, whose quill pens are busier listing facts and numbers than hopes or fears or those other human thoughts that fill human hearts and give meaning to time. At Cambray we watch the seasons, note the shiftings of the tide, the phases of the sun and moon, as do all countryfolk wherever I have been. So I can tell you that these lords returned in the autumn of a year in which the harvest had been especially bountiful, the summer long and dry, the spring wet to set the seed.

That summer I had spent time with the other village lads in the foothills along the moors, old enough then to watch the sheep and goats (tasks I did so badly or so seldom as already to earn myself harsh names for laziness, incompetence, and worse). That summer a calf had been born at Cambray with two heads, an omen of great portent, and that spring twice the sea had receded farther than any remembered, to come surging back inland farther again than ever in living memory. And I was old enough to know my place, far beneath the notice of these fine lords. Yet old enough, too, to have a sense of something else, to feel . . . what? A promise, a questing, an improbable hope to take me from this kitchen straw and set my dreams above the clouds. And old enough to feel that same desire, that same quest, in other men, even before they knew it themselves. . . .

Well, then, to tell you of it for memory's sake, that September day, the young lords of Cambray had been hunting on the moors, not the first time they so hunted but certainly the first time I saw them return, those fine young lords and their guard, whose presence drew me like a moth to candle flame. That day I had been set to clean out the stableyard, had already taken my share of cuffs for loitering; so when they came clattering in with their huntsmen, I was nothing loath to lean on my fork and watch them to my heart's content. This was a Norman hunting party, sweating in their heavy leather coats, red-faced and important. Huntsmen shouted and cursed; hounds circled, whimpering about the horses' heels; servitors scurried to draw in the wooden sledges on which they had stacked the game, killed for sport, although the venison brought would grace the table in due course.

Lord Hue rode at their head, for all that he was second son. That was his way. His long hair flying red beneath the headband that he wore, dressed in the flamboyant style he liked—embroidered jerkin, bejeweled cloak, its material ripped and stained by the thickets on the moor he had forced his horse through. He rode the best hunter that Cambray could provide and pivoted it around to make the pages jump out of his path. That, too, was his style. I had heard of him; who at Cambray had not? He could ride anything that had four legs, was brave and generous in good humor, could fill a room with laughter when he chose. But he was also moody, so they said, full of black thoughts; and when he was angry, he was dangerous. I sensed at once his black mood that day. I heard the huntsmen mutter that he had ridden hard to outpace them all, had brought down more game than anyone; yet when he turned, I saw across his broad shoulders, along his horse's flank, the smears of mud that showed he had fallen. And marked, too, the way his head jutted out, his mouth was set, and how he beat with a whip against the side of his boots. I felt a shiver of fear run down my spine. Without noise, almost without movement, I dropped the fork and slid into the safest place I could find, behind the stable door in the bales of straw. I knew enough of anger to avoid it if I could; I knew enough to know it always looks for some scapegoat.

Behind Lord Hue came his older brother, Lord Robert of Sieux, a tall, quiet boy, as unlike his brother as chalk to cheese, taller by a head, fair-haired, gray-eyed. They said of him that in looks and build he was already his father's twin, although I had never seen the great earl himself. But even I could tell Lord Robert was tall enough to wear a man's hauberk and carry a man's sword. He was perhaps fifteen or so, almost a man, then, two years older than his younger brother, his lineage stamped on him from the long, thin face with its firm-cut mouth and chin to sea-gray eyes that looked out arrogantly over the high cheekbones, a Norman lord from head to foot. Seeing both brothers together, you would not have thought them come from the same stock. Even their voices were not alike—Lord Robert's curt and clipped, a Norman voice; Hue's a border accent with a border lilt, all Celt. Or so the castle maids declared, giggling together when he passed, eyeing him for all that he was young. They did not eye the older brother thus. Of Robert they said that he had a heart of stone and that, sometimes suffering in his limbs from some numbness, legacy of a childhood malady, his heart was numb, insensible to their charms. They never said that about Hue. And even they today had sense to keep to themselves, out of the way.

Lord Robert sat and smoothed his horse's mane. That was *his* way, to watch and think, to contemplate before he moved. They said that he could make a horse do whatever he wanted, without words, that he spoke but little, but when he did, men heard. They said, too, that he was a swordsman, steady as a rock, dependable and just, yet cold also, and dispassionate. But when Hue, on his horse, beat with his whip, saying nothing, that was a danger sign.

After a while, when the older men, the castle guard in the red and gold of Earl Raoul's household, had dismounted, had had their squires hold their cloaks and unstrap their spurs, then Robert, too, swung off his horse and took the whip into his own hands. He held it up. From the cracks between the bales of straw, I could see what it was—not whip at all, but a heavy, carved piece of wood or stake, curved in a strange shape, with a snarl of twine wound round it to make a trap.

Now wood is scarce at Cambray. The moors behind us are nearly bare of trees; only a few stunted ones, blown out of shape by the westerly gales, grow there. I recognized the wood at once. I had spent many hours searching for such a piece, had found it left by those spring storms, carved oak, torn from the prow of some ship, half buried in the sand, and had hidden it away behind the corn bins for a purpose of my own. Who had taken it and used it in this form? But there was worse. For as Lord Robert began patiently to unwind the string, coiling it carefully as he freed each knot, Hue leaned forward in his saddle in his intent way, as if coiled himself with rage.

"And who," he said, so low you scarce could hear and yet could sense the fury behind the words, "who took my own bowstring to bring me down?"

There was a sudden hush. The village boys were forever setting snares to catch rabbits and smaller game; such is permitted in a border fort, where food is scarce and ways are wild, although not permitted, even I knew, in most Norman households, where hunting is the lord's prerogative. But to set a snare where horsemen might be tripped, and to use a bow line to tie the net . . . what kind of madman would do that? And I had heard of Hue's bow, no ordinary hunting one but given him this year by a Celtic prince, a great longbow made of elm, as tall as himself. They said he already could pull it and send the arrow through a plank of wood. A special gift, then, a Celtic warbow from a Celtic warlord. To tamper with it alone would have been to risk punishment. To have used it in this wise to unhorse an earl's son was madness indeed. Again I felt apprehension prick my spine. I had never set a snare in my life, knew nothing of horses or horsemanship, had thought to use the wood sometime to fashion a thing out of it. Suppose now someone remembered that the wood was mine? There was but one whom they called "mad" at Cambray.

Lord Robert had finished separating line from stake. He balanced them both as if weighing them in his long, thin hands.

"A child's work," he said after a while, "some castle brat. Leave well alone." And for a moment he held Hue's gaze. Now much of what was said and done that day went past me at the time; it was only afterward, with age, that I could give sense and substance to words and looks, but there was nevertheless something in Robert's tone that made me remember who he was. The Earl of Sedgemont has many lands, but only one son is his heir, only one who should order us. I think Hue remembered it, too. A flush darkened his usually fine skin, a spate of curses burst out that matched poorly with those almost childish red, full lips. Perhaps it was the mention of a castle brat, as if his brother put him on a par with a child; perhaps it was that quiet voice, Norman-precise, that made his own outburst the more raucous; but I think it was something else, a tension between them, like blood running beneath the skin, so that suddenly, a word, a hint, could send the younger brother flaring wild. He snatched at the wood and hurled it with all his might. It crashed against the open stable door, showering splinters down upon the straw.

"If castle brat," he said in a hoarse voice, "I'll haul him forth, to trip me in a rabbit hole. I'll whip his half-breed hide, Celtic bastard, cowering in the dung."

The horses snorted and reared back; dogs jumped and barked. The older men, already on their way to guardhouse and keep, as I think Lord Robert had meant, spun around. Behind the bales I flinched myself, both at the noise and at the words. Most of the men at Cambray are half-bred; he was a half-breed himself, and usually proud of his Celtic heritage. Yet there was a loathing in his voice that day, when he spoke of things Celt, which I remember now and feared then, for it was turned in part against himself. I thought, sweet God, he'll kill someone yet, and felt fear start upon me like a sweat. As much as the outside world, a castle needs a whipping boy. That, too, was a role the fates had given me; I already anticipated my part. A figure half fell, half slid beside me in the straw, so unexpected I started up, but it pulled me down.

"*Jesu,*" it said, "stay still. He'll find me else."

It was a girl child, that at least I recognized, although in the half-light it was hard to tell. Her skirts were rucked up and knotted between her long legs, which were scratched with thorns. She was barefoot, her toes black with mud. Her hair hung in great snarls, and her breath came heavy, as if she had been running hard. After a while she leaned back, sighed, rubbed a dirty hand across her face.

"God's wounds," she said, still gasping for breath, "who would have thought the fool would leap his horse through a patch of gorse. Trip him! He almost rode me down. And ruined the best snare I have ever set. Praise God, he never saw me, too busy getting on his feet. But I have never run back so fast. And I'll be whipped in any case for going there."

Now I had not seen her before, though that was not so strange as it may sound. Cambray is small, but I avoided the castlefolk when I could, and castle children most of all. I had little liking for the castle maids, who take madmen for their own sport. If I thought anything at all, it would have been first that it served her right, more intent on my own misery than hers. Until the realization of what she had said came to me. It made me sit up again.

"You set the trap?" I said. "You took his bow?"

"Aye," she said briskly, trying to smooth her hair. "I found it propped behind a chest. I thought he had tired of it."

That, too, was Lord Hue's way, they said; done with a thing, he threw it aside carelessly, its value only what he found in it, its worth returned only when he wanted it again. But I had never known a girl to be so rash.

"*You* set the trap?" I emphasized the word.

She looked at me from beneath her mass of hair and crossed herself.

"*Jesu*," she swore, sounding almost alarmed, "the crazed boy, who croons to himself along the shore. What are you doing here?"

I was not offended by her, although her bluntness could have made me flinch. She had no worse phrased it than the other things said of me.

"The wood you used was mine," I told her, misery returning when I spoke of it aloud. "I thought to carve it into a lute stem someday." Once more I buried my face in my knees.

She observed me for a moment, head on one side, as I came to know she often did.

"That makes sense" was all she said. "I thought they said you had lost your wits. I'd hide, too, if I were you."

She crawled across me to the gap and peered out. She was about my height, my age, as thin as a rake and streaked with dirt, but there was a wildness about her, a freedom, that my poor pinched soul leapt toward. I had never seen her before, I repeat, had no idea who she might be, yet sensed the purpose in her spirit like a flame. For the first time a spark of hope lit up in me.

Lord Hue was on foot himself now, had seized a fork, the one I had dropped, had looped the bowstring about his knuckles in a double thong. He prodded with the fork, swinging the lash to make men jump aside. "Someone ran ahead of me," he cried. "Now will I find him out, the Celtic cur, to unhorse me and run." He began to advance toward the open stable door.

"Quick," the girl said. As she spoke, she had scrambled out between the bales, nimble as a cat. I saw her plan, to escape behind the lines of men more intent on watching before them than aware what went on behind their backs; but fear kept me rooted to the spot, although she knotted her fist in my hair and tried to drag me along. She was gone in a flash; too slow behind her, I lumbered to my feet, despair and guilt upon my face.

Lord Hue saw me at once. Head lowered like a bull, he charged through the men, shouldering even larger ones aside, and caught me by the tunic. I came limply enough, that little spark of hope already dead, anticipation already having made that guilt seem real. With a mighty effort he slung me on my knees across the broad steps that led to the granary above and stood, hands on hips, looking at me. I dragged myself upright, backed to the wall. "So, cur," he snarled, "where's my bow?" and he whistled the thong about my ears.

On foot like that, set on a step, I came almost to his height. His eyes, close to mine, were dark, flecked with gold, and in them I saw the specks of anger. When Lord Hue was wroth, they said, run for your life. But there was no place left to run; the girl had already disappeared, and I was left alone to take her blame.

I mouthed at him, words tumbling out without sense, but at least I had the sense not to mention her.

" 'His wood,' " he mocked me. " 'Found it,' " he said. " 'My wood,' " he said, each word a sneer, "as if a serf can claim anything, as if a serf has any rights, even to life. Shall you use my bowstring to kill me?" He brought it down across my arms.

There was a gasp. Now, looking back from my old age, I suppose all there sensed a truth. A serf owns nothing in this world, has nothing, except a master whose slave he is to do with as *he* likes. That is the first law a serf's child learns. And he who threatens a master looks for death. Yet I cannot truthfully say that if faced with death, I feared it as much as I would now, being either too young to know what was meant or, more like, too numbed with fear of what the next moment held. Or, as may be, already knowing that existence could promise little for me, so much at odds with it, so unfitted for this border world, I was already resigned to fate. Survival in a border castle is hard, and that is the second law a serf's child learns.

I stood huddled against the rough stone wall; beneath me a sea of faces, some with mouths agape, some all grins, a bear-baiting, a cockfight, no better pleasure than this. I heard a clatter of the castle guard, my father's straw hair marking him as he found excuses for his embarrassment; I heard my mother's scream, saw my sisters hiding in her skirts, the other castle brats wriggling to the front to watch the sport. As much against those sights as the blows I closed my eyes.

Before the third one fell, Lord Robert's voice made me open them. "There has been enough talk of rights," he said, "of things 'thine' and 'mine.' It is a poor, mazed thing at best."

In the pause that followed, I saw how the brothers faced each other, as if a current, red-hot, ran between them, fiercer than Lord Hue's wrath, such a wave of mixed love and hate, I almost closed my eyes once more against it.

"He is a singer." The girl's voice came out, clear and high, emphasizing the word. I knew her tone at once, although now when I thought of it, I realized, too, she spoke Norman French, as Lord Robert did. She stood beside him, carefully keeping him between her and Lord Hue. "This is Urien the Bard," she repeated, "the Welsh singer."

The tension broke. Men put their hands on hips and guffawed. Even Lord Robert smiled, the same sweet smile that she had. She had smoothed down her crumpled dress, pulled her hair back. I suddenly saw how the morning sun had brought out its color, bronze, like a new-minted coin, and her eyes were dark as Hue's own. She, too, smiled at me, the Lady Olwen whom I had not recognized. That smile gave me heart. "Head up," it said. And for the second time in my life came that flash of hope.

At the foot of the stairs, caught between his brother and sister, caught between his own conflicting thoughts, Hue bit his lip. I sensed the struggle in him, rage and reason, and thanked God that this time reason would win.

He threw down the cord.

"If bard," he said, his voice cracking, a boy's voice that slid from man's to child's, "if bard as you claim, then let him sing." He snapped his fingers—sent his page flying to fetch a lute. Now I had never held such a thing before, had seldom seen one, though in truth had saved that wretched piece of oak with the thought of one day turning its strange curved shape into the neckpiece of such an instrument.

Had I known the lute they finally brought (the men by now all squatted down to hear the rest of the joke played out, the children screaming and pointing underfoot), would that have silenced me, had I known it as belonging to the great earl, one he sometimes played himself? All I can tell you, when it was put into my hands, I felt it quiver with a life of its own. And when I struck a note, a chord, I felt the power running through my fingers to the shoulder blades, the way one feels on striking an iron bar too hard, a ripple, a shock. It was a sense of power I had never had before, although I have known it often since. And that, too, I cannot explain, save to tell you now that in that sorry world where I had found myself, the only things that ever gave me joy were sounds, words, noises, natural happenings, until, hearing them, I had to re-create them for myself.

In any case, then, ignorant of what a singer is, ignorant of my own ignorance, I sang. Since that day men have praised my voice, which in old age has not lost its tone, although I can no longer summon up the force that once I had. It has deepened, of course, and I have trained it to my advantage so that I can achieve by craft what then I did from the promptings of my heart. And the songs I sing are of my own making, that like a craftsman I put my mark on them. But I think I have never sung so well, or so fittingly, as then, untrained, for the first time.

And what did I sing? Somewhere out of memory, beyond thought (or did some god put it in my mind?), I heard my voice ring out, as if it were not my own, as if it belonged to someone else, above the noise of that castle with its watchroom, stable, and keep, as a lark sings exultant at noon.

> *And we shall rise, a mighty host,*
> *War bands, warriors, long-haired,*
> *Hardened by battle, one folk once,*
> *Out of exile and death returned,*
> *Ready in war to strike for our own.*

A Celtic war song, then, a defiant song to sing to a Norman lord to his face, a song of defiance, yes, and perhaps of prophecy. And when I was done, no one moved or laughed.

In the silence that followed, only Lord Robert spoke. "By the Mass," he said, as if drawing breath, "Urien the Bard, you speak the truth." He smiled at me. That smile made me his for life.

The little maid, Olwen the Fair, Olwen of the White Way, the white flower, she nodded at me as if to say, "See, I knew it would be so."

And beside them Hue stood, with bent head, and I could not tell if he wept.

That was our first meeting, then, how first I got my name. I have told you it for memory's sake. And for one other thing, that it will show you who we were, how we lived, how we came to be bound. Nor do I mean to suggest that afterward all things changed. Not so, not yet. I still was serf's brat, they still great lords. Nor did they stay long at Cambray that year. With the winter frosts they were gone again, they, their retinue, their busy lives. We sank back to our own small ways, small cares.

My mother perhaps had her moment of triumph, poor soul, to redden her wan cheeks with the youthfulness that once had made her beautiful to men. My father, that straw-haired soldier with the hard mouth and fist, he ceased his daily beatings; more from amazement than pride, I think, realizing that he could never whip me into a pikeman like himself. The other castlefolk ceased their jibes or left me alone; their children gave up their torments. Such respite at least was gift beyond price. And if sometimes in the night, when we had scrabbled for a place before the fire, I and those sisters, half sisters, clutching and whining by my mother's side (and whose get were they, dark-haired and fat? Not my Norman father's, I think), I lay upon my side, head buried beneath the sacking we used for warmth, and dreamed dreams of my own, why, that, too, was a comfort.

Time passed. The winter dragged its wet, weary days, and in the following spring the lords of Cambray returned again. And so they now did for several years. Why that was I could not have told you then, nor what had caused such a change in their lives, although in time that, too, would be made clear. But for a while it came about that in the spring we should expect them, that at the autumn's end they left.

Six months, then, of the year we had something to look forward to. I cannot say how much they remembered me, the boys of that noble house, fast growing into men. Hue certainly paid me no heed, although I often watched him, a bond between us, of thought and understanding, almost as if I could sense out his mind. And thinking back to those days, I suspect now he knew it, too, knew perhaps and feared, resented it. How else should he have known when to wheel his horse so that it almost crushed me against a wall, how to stalk past so that the point of his hunting spear struck the place where a moment before I had stood, how known in which direction to hurl his boots when his pages drew them off? I saw less of Lord Robert at that time; he rode with his father and the other men about those border affairs, as shall be told.

As for the Lady Olwen, she alone looked for me to give excitement, meaning, to each day when she was at Cambray. Our meetings were not often. I can number them upon a hand. She had spoken truth that she would have a whipping for having wandered on the moors. Among the castlefolk it was said she was forbidden to go there alone, although what danger, I would have scoffed at such a thought, not knowing then the care of noble maids, or the nature of that border watch. But the whisperers also said that when the mood took her, she would slip away despite that rule. And sometimes, I think now, knowing her, so unlike other maidens of her age and rank, her folk must

have let her go, when her spirit could not be denied. She showed
me how she set her traps. Not yet old enough to hunt with her
brothers, she was quick with line and net; her hands with their
broad fingertips were as steady as a boy's. She could find her
way through the thickets, brambles, and furze as stealthily as a
mountain cat. I had never known a maid who cared so little for
how she looked; and once when I showed her where the wild
fox denned, she lay for hours watching them with a stillness,
a silence, that I had never known in womankind.

I showed her where the birds made their nests, the speckled
thrush, the robin, and how the lapwing ran ahead with pretense
of broken wing to lead us away from its egg clutch upon the
ground. I showed her where the hare made its form. Once when
we came upon it, the soft gray down from its breast with which
it lined the shape was still warm. I took her among the rock
pools and showed her where the fishermen set their nets, and
in time I taught her the names and magic properties of flowers
and plants that we Celts know: primroses and wild roses and
the other sacred five-petaled flowers, and most potent of all, the
creeping white trefoil, from which some said her own name
was culled.

But best of all, I told her what I hoped and thought, words
coming slowly to me who now make my way by words, drawn
from me almost painfully. There was a place that I had found
that first summer I spent upon the hills, a kind of cave hollowed
out among the granite rocks, and there sometimes when a black
mood fell on her, I would sing to her to soothe her. For she
shared this quality with her brother, Hue; for all that she could
be so fair, as just and kind as Robert was, sometimes the dark
side of her Celtic self would make her change, run wild. Then
she could be fickle, inconstant, thoughtless, although never cruel
as he could be.

So the years passed, three, four; we settled to a custom that
gave something to hope for, to expect. Until the year when all
was changed. I know its date well enough, the year 1172, a year
to be branded in my memories. In that year many things occurred that were to change all our lives. Bear with me. I shall
tell you each in turn. It is not a question of forgetting, of not

knowing what first to say, but rather how not to say too much. In telling you I must tell all, all, as I still remember all: how Lord Robert came to be a man and took up man's cares, how Hue knew himself at last, how the outside world came to bear down upon us at Cambray. And how the Lady Olwen grew to womanhood to torment me. Each of these things then so interwoven that each in turn must be unwound. As a stone thrown into a lake, so the ripples spread. Bear with me, I say, now shall we come to them, with their joys, their pains. I told you how little happiness there was for me. Yet pleasure there was that, in the end, I should be the eyes and voice of these great ones.

Chapter 2

hat year, 1172 of Christendom, was to be a special year for us all. It began like any other one, except Lord Raoul returned earlier than usual to Cambray in an April full of storms, after a winter remembered for its severity. Snow had covered the hills for months that year, unusual for us, and there had been wolves sighted on the high moors—omens these, if I had understood them. And when the thaw came, it flooded the coastal fields until sometimes it seemed Cambray sat like a stone outcrop, an island in a brown and muddy waste. On hearing, then, of this early arrival of Earl Raoul's household (for he had sent messengers ahead to stir us all into our usual fret at news of them), I had watched for the family for days, going each morning to the moors to look for them; and when at last they arrived, with their noise, their bustle, their joyful cavalcade, the Lady Olwen greeted me in her usual easy way, as if we had parted just an hour before. But after that first meeting I seldom spoke with her, not even to pass the time of day and never alone as we used. In vain I waited for her—more than that, expected her—in all our usual haunts: behind the hayricks and cattle byres, and on the moors when I thought the mixture of April sun and rain would drive her, restless, out. She never came. For as I soon discovered, she had a new playmate this year, or rather, a new plaything, which they said her father had brought for her to await her arrival here at Cambray. It was a horse, a little moorland horse, creamy white, with long cream tail and mane, spirited, with a small, well-set head and long, springy legs, and most of the Lady Olwen's waking hours were spent in taking care of it. So although I saw her often enough, it was from a distance, with one of her father's men mounted as escort riding behind; and although she came up on the moors, it was to let her hound run (she had a new kind of hound, too, thin and gray, which could almost outdistance a hare) so she could race after it. She doted on that horse, I say, an interest I found hard to understand, for I must confess having little liking for horses, considering them unintelligent and dangerous. But Lady Olwen spent hours grooming this little horse, if she was not on its back; and when she could not coax the grooms into cleaning its red harness with the silver bells, she sat on the tack room floor herself, her skirts spread around her, while she polished and rubbed until the red leather and silver shone like new. Well, that was her way. Like Hue she could show an intensity, a purpose, and a will that could not be diverted from their path or changed. So now her full attention was settled upon her horse, and she had no time for anything else. Until that April day when someone else rode into her life. But I go too fast ahead. For first she had to turn to me for help. When she had need of me, she came to me again. And I did not fail her, not then, nor ever, as in time that, too, shall be told. But now she asked my help in a childlike, womanlike way, and boylike, manlike, I gave it unstintingly.

It was still April, and on an April evening that was closing fast (for the days had not yet lengthened and the morning had been gray with rain), with some of the other boys I had been leaning over the battlements on the seaward side. The boys were counting the fishing boats, which, having ridden out the storm in the shelter of the quay, were now going out for the night catch; I was watching the sea gulls, which floated like puffs of smoke, now sucked down by the wind close to the water's edge, now blown up above our heads, when a cry from the castle watch on the landward side gave the alarm. Already the lookout in the gate towers had sounded the warning bell, and down in the outer courtyard men came spilling out from the guardroom, half dressed, strapping on their swords as they ran.

Some rushed to double-bar the great gates, which had already been bolted up for the night; others came clattering up the narrow stairs to the battlements to overlook the moors. A border castle takes its duties seriously, never thinks itself safe, and never takes safety for granted; else it may not long survive. So our men peered over anxiously into the twilight, straining to see what threatened us. A group of horsemen it was, although they had left foot soldiers in plenty at the moor's edge; the horsemen, six or seven of them, advanced boldly behind their leader, who now rode up openly to the gate and hammered at its thick oak timbers with the iron rim of his round shield. Celtic horsemen they were, Celtic dressed in fine wool tunics and cloaks, leggings cross-gartered into soft leather boots, no chain mail, no iron helmets, their weapons Celtic round shields and broadswords set in wide scabbards richly ornamented, with gold interlaced. And when their leader lifted up his head in answer to our shouts, there was a gleam of gold about his throat; some Celtic warlord this must be, with his men, although it was difficult to catch all that he said, his voice half muffled by his cloak with its lining of red fox fur and his speech that border mixture of Norman and Celt. By then, of course, the Cambray guard was out in force. Dusk is a strange and dangerous time to be abroad, and no one comes knocking at a castle gate at that hour except for some reason best not known to honest men. Yet it was clear that these travelers were tired, their horses almost stumbling for weariness and their leader's gray stallion, a knight's charger this, no Celtic moorland horse, already lame. The men riding behind were small and dour-faced. It was clear, too, from the way they held themselves, not looking anywhere except straight ahead, hiding their anxiety beneath a stern air, that they had probably never been so far from home before but were too proud to let anyone else know that. They were older men, this escort, and there was something in their bearing, their looks and their manner, that suggested they were part of a personal guard to some older lord, someone whom they had served long and knew well. Yet the man who led them, when he showed himself, was young, too young to have such men serve him unless he had inherited them. And when he ordered them, it seemed sometimes they answered him in such a way, or anticipated his command, as if order and response had already been rehearsed. Their leader certainly was young, not old enough even to have the shadow of a beard, although in the torchlight—for our guard had bawled for pages to bring flares and hold them over the walls—in that light he showed himself proudly, for all that his face was lined with dirt and fatigue. Copper-colored hair he had, grown long and thick, and his eyes, dark and large, looked out over high cheekbones. It was his mouth most of all that betrayed his lack of age. For all that he looked decisive, firm-chinned, his lips were dry with apprehension or tension, too; and when he pivoted his lame horse to dodge the splutters of wax that fell from the torches, the gleam of gold at throat and wrist flashed an uneasy red-like fire.

Earl Raoul was the king's warden of the borderlands, and when the earl was in residence, Celts often rode in to visit him, sometimes to chat over old days. Many of them were friends, especially since the lady of Cambray had many Celtic kin. Often, too, the Celts came to complain about some loss incurred in a border raid or at some revenge the Norman settlers in these parts had taken against them, unwarranted, or so they always claimed. (They never came, of course, to make amends for the raids *they* made and the damage *they* in turn had caused.) But they never ever came like this, at night, in such haste, nor with such a fierce look of resolve. For that, too, was obvious beneath that young air of pride and weariness, and seeing it, other men drew back, sensing some feeling that made them ill at ease. So when the gates at last were unbarred and the seven horsemen were allowed to ride in, many Cambray men still stayed to watch, fingering their sword hilts nervously; and those on the battlements held their place and kept arrows notched to their bowstrings.

The young man, young lord, swung himself out of the saddle and bent to examine his horse with an air of concern that told better than words its worth to him. "By God," one of the Cambray guard whistled through his teeth, "that horse has been bred from a Cambray stallion," and he whistled again in disbelief. The Cambray horses are famous in these borderlands and

beyond, and sometimes it is true that Celts will bring one of
their small mares to breed either openly or in secret. But they
seldom ride up to Cambray gates on a horse so bred. Nor do
local lords often come with so large an escort, and seldom leave
so many foot soldiers camped outside. For now beyond the
walls the small pinpricks of flame could be clearly seen where
the rest of the men had settled down for the night, each in his
place out there on the flinty ground. These men would have
come trotting beside the horsemen all the way, covering distance with their long mountain stride, holding to the stirrups
as they ran. Now, weary, too, no doubt, they hunkered down
without complaint among the heather and the rocks, asking no
more than water to drink and a chunk of dry bread to gnaw
upon. I watched them for a long while myself, curious what
made such men run for miles at their lord's command, their
weapons strapped upon their backs, their big Welsh bows, such
as Hue had, tied to the arrow case. And when our castle guard,
still uneasy themselves, clouted us boys back down the steps,
driving us out of their way, I went alone to my own bed and
thought about those Celts long before I slept. Mine was a hard
bed, I grant, on the kitchen floor among the scraps, but at least
there was a roof over my head and a fire for warmth. These
Celtic soldiers could run for days, carry all their food with them,
live on air, and never willingly come inside Norman castle walls.
Yet so loyal were they to their lord that if he bade them, they
would try to tear down those walls with their bare hands. I
remember wondering what manner of men they were, loyalty
so strong in them that they would die at their lord's command.
I had not thought on such a thing before. Perhaps it was some
forewarning that made me ponder it, that made me shudder
even in the fire's warmth. And when I slept, I still dreamed of
those men. Their small flame points among the heather were like
their courage, determined and resolute. And it seemed to me,
in my dreams, that their resolution, whatever caused or nurtured it, would blot out all things else and would sometime
change our lives.

But I was to find out one day that when things grow bleak
enough to bring a man against a wall, then even the weakest

of us can show equal determination if we must. So I dreamed, dark, uneasy dreams, full of foreboding, until a sudden tug upon my arm sent me flaring awake.

I alone roused. No one else stirred. Around me were the sleeping forms of mother, half sisters, the other kitchen folk, a dog or two huddled inside for warmth, some men-at-arms, who, drinking late after the evening's excitement, had bedded down among the rushes, cloaks pulled over their heads for comfort. It was not yet light, lacking perhaps an hour until dawn. The world still slept peacefully. The time of trial I speak of was not yet. Another tug upon my arm brought me half upright. The Lady Olwen was bent over me, and it was her voice, urgent with command, that bade me get up and follow her. The time of trial not yet come by many a year, and yet a time of trial ahead, and she, childlike, womanlike, now set on it.

Half awake, I did as she said. It speaks much for my devotion, I suppose, that without further questions, without complaint, without hesitation even, I moved silently past those sleeping forms, pausing only long enough to hunt for my shoes. I slept, of course, in all my clothes, not like those noble lords and ladies, who, they said, and I have found out for a fact since, bed naked beneath embroidered sheets on mattresses of goosedown. Lady Olwen's shape was a faint blur in the predawn light, but she glided along in her quick way so that I had to hurry to keep up with her. She said nothing, turned back only once to ensure I was still behind her, and came out into the cold morning air, running before me over the cobblestones toward the stables.

There was no one about. The kitchen at Cambray stands apart from the rest of the keep with its guardroom and hall; the night watch had not yet changed so there were no men lounging to chat and stretch around the well and joke among themselves when the new guard took their place. Not even the cocks had crowed; the hounds slept on, heads on paws, dreaming of the morning hunt, and behind the stable was a silence seldom found in that busy place. Lady Olwen was waiting for me. She was enveloped in a long gray cloak that covered her from head to foot, making her blend into the morning like a wraith. She had not braided her hair but had tied it back into a snarl of red, and when she spoke and her head covering fell back, I saw that down one side of her face a long bruise showed blue across her cheek and along her chin.

Seeing I had noticed, she hastily pulled the hood into place, saying merely, "I need you to come with me. Those Celtic envoys will leave at dawn to go home. I must be there before them at the crossroads."

"Crossroads?" I know I echoed the word, still sleep-bemused, not taking in half she said.

She answered impatiently, unlike herself; quick she had always been but never abrupt like this, nervous and tense, as if something important awaited her. "They leave at dawn, I tell you, by the western road. We must get there before they do. It is a matter of," she hesitated, "honor," she said at last. I should have known from the way she spoke, the word she used, too serious, too solemn, that no good would come of such adventuring. But I gaped at her through the mist and, in my way, let her speak on. She hurried over the words as if she had practiced them, as if she had spent a long time thinking what to say. Now I suspect she had believed she would have to persuade me and had used all the arguments at once. "They came last night in haste," she told me, "to speak with my father; they leave in haste today. This will be the only chance I have to meet with them."

Now, there are obviously many things I should have asked, and anyone of sense would have asked them: Why is it so important that you speak with them at all? What is this honor? What this haste? But, catching a glimpse of her little horse already tied to the door, already saddled and waiting for her, I said simply, "I cannot ride so how can I keep up with you? And if they leave at dawn, when the gate is unbarred, how shall we get ahead of them?" Simple questions that only a fool would ask, and she answered them impatiently. "Their lord's horse is lame," she told me. "It has cast a shoe. The blacksmith will make him a new one, but the fire is out in the smithy. It will take time to heat it up. By then we will be far ahead. And under these sacks, look, spread like that, who will know me or my horse? As for riding," and then she did smile, "I'll ride. Your

strong legs can keep up with me, your strong Celtic legs. Besides." She was untying her horse, giving me the sacks to drape
across its back and down its flanks. "Besides, I've unstrapped all
their harnesses. That will delay them, too."

"But the guard will never let us through," I said at last. You
see again how she befuddled me and how I played into her
hands. Never a word I spoke of "impossible," never "no," only
"How shall it be done?" And she showed me how, her fingers
more deft than mine, and more skilled to quiet her horse when
it shied.

And so it was when the castle gates opened at first light, as
is the custom, to let men in and out—peasants to ride out to
the fields with farm tools, peasants to ride in with milk and
eggs, boys to lead out flocks of sheep or herds of pigs, grooms
back in with horses and grass—why, easy it was, as she had
said, for us to go out in their midst, heads down, trotting along
about our own affairs. And in truth who would care, what
harm did we, she like any castle wench on her small pony,
under her gray cloak and dirty sacks? And I, no need to hide
who I was. It was only when we were through the gates and
turned past the village toward the road running west that I came
to my wits at last. Like a blow on the head it was, to knock
sense back in rather than let it out. Swept up in the need for
haste, the need for disguise, rushed along in the midst of that
first bustle of a castle's waking up, the peasant's world (which
the lords of a castle never know about, although it is the world
that feeds and nourishes them), I suddenly woke up myself. As
I have said, the track we were following ran west and for a
while skirted the edge of the village fields along the cliff. On
one side were the fields, plowed into strips, each strip showing
a different color green; on the other side, out of sight, was the
sea, and below us, dimly through the fog, we could hear the
surf beating on the rocks. It had stormed all yesterday, and the
ground was wet, each grass blade and bush coated with rain;
and where the spiderwebs were stretched, face-high, great drops
of water showered down on us. I stopped dead, I say, one hand
still looped about her stirrup in the Celtic way, dug my toes
into the springy turf, and refused to move another step. En-

grossed in her plans, overwhelmed by her, I always came too late behind her in everything, but eventually reason had caught up with me.

"Why?" was all I asked.

She knew what I meant without need of any more words but would not reply, tried to spur on the horse to drag me along. Once out of sight of the castle guard, she had rolled up the sacking and thrown it under a bush, another explanation due, somehow, on our return. And now all those other things that she had spoken of poured over me in a flood as she still tried to urge me forward.

"Hurry, hurry," she said when I would not budge. "What's amiss?"

"You are," I said, for once blunt myself. "What are we doing? God's head, the smithy fire out, you say; who put it out? Their bridle straps cut? They'll cut our throats when they discover that. What honor? What lord?" And looking hard at her, as now I did, I saw how she had harnessed her horse, not with its lady's trappings of red and silver, but with a man's saddle or, since a man's saddle would have been too big, with a boy's gear (not Lord Hue's, I prayed), and although she rode astride, her skirts looped up, the dress she wore beneath the cloak was her best; green it was, with a silken sheen, although it was already torn and muddied about the hem. And there was that bruise on her face.

"God's teeth," I swore, for once resolute. "Not one step more until you explain."

At first she would not say a word either, pursed up her lips and grew balky herself. Then, sensing determination in me, too, she began to argue as only she could. "Not *cut* the bridles," she said, picking on one small point as if I had meant it as the most important one, "unstrapped, I said. As for the fire, I doused it; but anything can put out a fire, and we have had enough rain these past days to flood a hundred fires. And if you stand here blathering like a dolt," for she was not always nice in her choice of words, "we'll lose the advantage time gives us."

"Not another step," I repeated.

She grew cunning then, in the way of womenfolk, wheedling me. "Come, dear friend," she said, although I knew her fingers itched to whip me, "I cannot do without you today, and you would never fail me. I have a message to give those Celtic men. Or rather," she lowered her eyes at my look (she might not tell all the truth, but she never lied), "or rather," she corrected herself, "to their lord. You'd not want me to ride alone without a guard?"

"No." I thought. "But you've not asked your father's men to escort you because you would not dare."

"No harm in it," she next coaxed, "to watch my Celtic kin ride home. They came in friendship, and so they leave. My message is only a personal one."

And when I still would not move or let go of her rein, which by now I had firmly grasped, "Well, then," she said, between tears of frustration and rage, "I'll tell you all, if only, dear, dear friend, you will walk ahead."

Her anger I could deal with, I was used to that, but not her tears. And so it was, moving forward again, away from the coast as the path now began to veer directly west, she told me what had occurred to make her come here so much in haste. Hear it as she told me it, childlike, womanlike—which was which I cannot tell now and could not then. For I think she did not know herself, and the reasons that she gave, although spoken without guile, were true only in part.

"Last night," Lady Olwen said, "when those Celtic men rode into Cambray, I was in the stable myself and so was trapped there. I was not afraid," she said defiantly, "but I had gone to get a handful of grain, which the grooms will never let me have, swearing my horse should be out at grass with the other ones. So when I heard a man come into the stable, leading a horse that was lame, I thought it was one of the Cambray grooms and hid behind the grain bins down at the back. It is dark there, and I knew no one would notice where I was. When I realized neither man nor horse belonged to Cambray, it was too late to escape, and as ill luck would have it, he put his horse in the stall next to mine. So there I was with a skirt full of oats," she blushed again, "trying to tiptoe."

She tossed her head with its coil of red hair, much as her little horse tossed its mane.

"I was not afraid," she repeated, "but I did not want to be seen, so I crept along toward the door. There is no way to step through straw quietly. And as I moved there in the dark, I thought I heard a rustle on the other side of the partition, as if a man was following me. I sensed that every step I took he took one as well; when I paused, he paused. Then I did become afraid," she said, "and opened my mouth to shout out. Something thick and heavy dropped over my head. It smelled of wood smoke and damp and earth, and before I could throw it off, the man who had been tracking me jumped on me, too. He came so fast, so silently, so hard, he knocked me to the ground. I thought he would crush me to death; I could not even breathe, and everything went black. When I came to, he had propped me up inside the stall by his horse's feet and with both hands about my rib cage was forcing air back into my lungs. I hawked and spat. Sweet *Jesu*, what a way to meet, to be vomiting over his boots. If I'd had a knife, I'd have stabbed him for making such a fool of me. He stood up, brought over a bucket, and splashed water on my face and hands. The water dripped cold, ran in rivulets through my hair and down my gown. It gave me back speech fast enough. I swore at him, all the groom's oaths that I know.

" 'Christ's wounds,' I wheezed, the least of them, 'Christ's bones, I'll have you flogged or worse.'

"I tried to haul myself to my knees, but he pushed me back with his boot, stood staring down at me, legs apart, his hand on his sword hilt.

" 'Well,' he said after a while, 'you've not much look of a murderer about you, I admit. But the stableyard's no place for a girl. Has Cambray come to using maids to do men's work?'

" 'Murderer?' I gasped at him. 'Murderer yourself, to treat me thus. You've almost split my head in two, God's wounds. My father'll make short shrift of you.'

" 'No doubt,' he said. 'I expect little better from Normans or Norman keeps. But save your breath. You curse more freely than a fishwife. My father would whip any daughter of his for uttering such foul words. Be quiet or I'll wash your mouth out.'

" 'You'd not dare,' I said next, 'you oaf.' For I tell you he made me angry, such a mixture of impudence and jest. No one has ever talked like that to me before; no one has mocked me so.

" 'Then keep away from me and my horse,' he said, cool as you please. 'Plan no mischief against me and mine. And show me courtesy.'

"I could have lashed him for insolence, his mouth set in a straight line, his hair standing all on end where he had rolled me over, with wisps of hay caught in the curls. I guessed he was Celt by the way he spoke—Norman-French, correct enough, with odd words of his own thrown in—but it was too dark in the stable to make out much else except the flash of his teeth when he grinned at me. As now he did.

" 'Off you go,' he said, not even a hand to help me up, no word of pardon, no courtesy. 'Back to your nursery maids; over young to come rolling in the straw with men.'

"I rounded on him.

" 'I am the Lady Olwen of Cambray,' I told him. 'My father is the Earl of Sedgemont. Address me fittingly.' But it was hard to be dignified with water dripping down my chin and my mouth full of vile and bitter taste. And in truth, when I moved suddenly, my head spun around and my cheek flamed where he had caught it against a wall. I tell you honestly, I wished for once to be better dressed, among my mother's womenfolk.

" 'I beg your pardon, lady,' he said, but his courtesy was only another mockery. 'I am Taliesin, Prince of Afron, in the north. And if you are lady of Cambray, then act the part; offer me suitable hospitality, as is a traveler's due. And as is fitting to *my* rank. Warm wine I need, and food, and warm water for washing off a week's dirt. And fresh soap—and a quiet-mouthed maid to lather it.'

"I knew he laughed at me, but 'God's wounds,' I said again, 'if it's washing you need, there's the horse trough; stick your head in it.'

"Then he did reach out and drag me to my feet. 'Be careful,' he warned me. 'I've younger sisters and cousins of my own. I know what courtesies a maid should show. I've whacked bare bottoms in my time. If Cambray wenches are so ill-mannered, I'll whack some here!'

"He spoke as arrogant as a king. *Jesu*, but I bit my tongue. I thought he might. Prince, indeed. Whatever he was, it was clear to me that he was the oldest son, used to having younger womenfolk bow down to him. I almost told him so. 'You need an older brother,' I should have said, 'to knock courtesy into you.' But 'If you don't know the difference between murderer and maid,' is all I said, 'you've lots to learn. Go tend your horse and I mine.' He looked over the partition as I spoke. 'That white mousekin,' he mocked again. 'A lady's lapdog, more like. Why, lady, my hound would eat it at one bite!'

" 'That horse will best anything,' I told him, boasting, angrier than before. 'It can outjump any horse on the moors.'

"Then he did begin to laugh; he laughs like Hue does. I wished Hue had been there to have shown him how such laughter ends.

" 'Lady,' he mocked me for the third time. 'I've not come to run in children's games. I seek an audience with the Earl of Sedgemont, it is true, and although I have no trust in Normans, I will confer with him about business of my own. But having seen him, that is all I seek. And my horse outruns the world.'

"He straightened up. 'So since you have breath enough to curse me back home again, get you gone. I'll tend myself. Although were you older perhaps you'd not want asking twice!' And he grinned, that stupid grin Hue gives to maids to make them giggle as he comes near. 'The horse trough is good enough if that is all that Cambray can offer me.' "

She was silent then for a while. "Well," she said, almost apologetically, "I felt ashamed when he said that. For hospitality is due to all men, even those who swagger like a king. 'There are men to serve you,' I told him, 'and servants enough to tend your horse. And no harm will come to you within Cambray gates. Give you good-even, sir.' I spoke as calmly as I could. 'I hope we never meet again.'

'Oh,' he said, standing there, smiling at me in his arrogant way, so his teeth gleamed. 'I doubt it, else that mousekin of yours may be gobbled up. And so may you.' "

Again she paused. "So that is why," she said firmly, lips jutting out as she does when determined, "why for honor's sake I must see him again."

I almost choked. "But why?" I cried. "Dear life, you just said you hoped never to do so."

"Exactly," she said. "Because I lied. In truth, I believed we would. I thought to make him feel ashamed in turn when he saw me in my father's hall. But I never did. My father saw him alone. 'Too many important matters to discuss openly,' my mother explained. But I listened," she said. "I crept to the stairs and heard some of what he said. Not all of it. I am no thief to eavesdrop on what is not for all ears. And, Urien." There was misery in her voice. "He *is* a prince. My father greeted him with that title. My mother told me so herself; Taliesin spelled in the Welsh way, with an extra *e*. My mother had a brother who died young and whom she loved more than anyone. His name was Talisin, spelled in the Norman way, since her father and his were Norman. I heard this Celtic prince outface my father in his own hall. For he was angry, Prince Taliesin; his voice was stiff, more formal than any Norman lord I've heard. And although my father spoke him fair in his courteous way, the prince would not eat or drink with him. 'A bed I'll take,' I heard him say, 'more for my men's sake, since they have ridden hard. And I'll leave at dawn. But I break no bread; I drink no toast.' So you see," she repeated simply, "it is for my house's honor, as well as my own, that I meet him."

She looked at me, her dark eyes intent. "He did not have to mock," she said. "I know what he is. So now shall he know me."

I was silent, too, for a while as we went along. I did not dare tell her that perhaps she had met her match. I knew her pride. But then another thought struck me.

"*Jesu*," I said, "if he parted from your father, your noble father, in such cold wise, he'll not take kindly to seeing you again. Much less a fool's trip like this. He'll have your head if you give him such a message."

She looked at me sideways in her way.

"*Jesu*, Olwen," I cried again, for the first time in my life forgetting to give her name and title as I should, "*Jesus*, Olwen, then he'll kill me."

For her look said as plainly as words, "I'll not give the message, you will." I began to argue now in turn. "We are alone," I told her. "These Celts are armed. What you have told me so far leaves me to suppose they have little liking for anything at Cambray. Suppose they take advantage of us?"

"Oh," she said, dismissing my fears with a wave of her hand, "they'll not know we are alone. I'll hide in the cliff where the crossroads meet. And you, you will wait down there by the road. They'll think I have an army at my back. Besides, the message is a simple one. He is to come up to the cliff alone, that great Prince Taliesin alone. He challenged me; he insulted me," she cried suddenly, and her dark eyes sparked. The mark on her face showed blue against her fair skin. "He owes me that much recompense. But listen, Urien." As suddenly as that anger had blown up it was gone again; now she spoke calmly, almost subdued. "Urien, stay out of sight until they come level to you. Lie hid. There are rocks and bracken to wait behind. And when you rise up, say you will speak to no one but Prince Taliesin. He is to ride up to the cliff crest and hear news of import for him. Stand up straight now," she admonished me, "wipe your face. You have grown red with all this talk." An unfair remark, I thought, since she had talked far more than I, and I had been trotting along on foot through the morning sun that by now had come out full against our backs. "You speak for all of Cambray like a Norman he professes to despise. They'll not harm a boy, but if they insist, stay there with them, as hostage for him." She spoke kindly now, having got her way, but I felt abashed. My life in exchange for a prince's would not seem much, perhaps, but then it was the only life I had. But even though what she had told me was both strange and somehow painful, as if in telling me any of it she spoke too much, yet she had told it to me, as in the old days. And that offer of friendship contented me. Well, I was not used to women then. I did not know the way of maids. I did not know then that although they may say one thing, more often what they truly want or truly feel they leave unsaid. All those reasons that she gave to me why this, why that, why her "honor" (spoken as pompously as any Norman lordling) was at stake, as if she were a boy or man herself, were not complete truths, although not all lies. She left out the one reason that was to count the most. She *must* see Prince Taliesin because she *must*. And why she must, well, as I have said, perhaps she did not even know that yet herself. And such was her hold over me—God forgive me, I was so weak of will where she was concerned—that, when we came to these crossroads she had been speaking of, I did as she had bid me do.

The crossroads met at a cliff, although a better name, I think, would be a cliff fort, and so I call it, a Roman fort, built centuries long before, for where the road went under it, you could see how the path twisted and turned to avoid the many fallen stones and boulders tumbled down from the walls above; and the path had certainly been there since time began. The road divided at this point. One branch went north, past the foothills that separated Celtic lands from Norman ones. The other branch continued west. More like a track than road, it wound under the shadow of a fort that had been built on, or rather into, the cliff face, for in places the natural rocks formed part of the outer walls. Lady Olwen left me there, hidden in the cool, damp ferns, while she herself rode up to the fort along one of the many goat trails that threaded themselves through the rocks. I lay on my back, glad to rest out of the sun, and stared curiously at the strange walls cut in jagged outlines against the sky. Many stories were told of this fort. The men at Cambray claimed Lord Falk had brought the stones from here to build Cambray; had pried them out, great hewn stones of granite, and had had them hauled on sleds of wood, drawn by oxen or by men themselves when the wooden runners caught and stuck. But some said that the outer walls were older than Roman, carved by giant men who had lived in these parts when the world was young, and that once a battle had been fought here between those giants and their gods, and a Celtic king had outfought them all. Well, true or not, whoever built this fort and strung these walls along this natural outcrop of rock had chosen well. For the fort guarded the roads east, north, and west, and not one man alone, not a single traveler, certainly never an army on the march, could have passed without coming under its scrutiny. And looking about me curiously, I determined that even the open land at the foot of the cliff must once have been man-cleared, too, for all that it now was overgrown and stone-littered with great boulders stuck like white teeth among the gorse. Once this must have been a wide open corridor, with room for men and horses to pass freely up and down, and at the western end was still the outline of what must have been a separate watchtower. I marveled at what manner of men could have so built, so dug and cleared, to make this fortress impregnable. And what manner of heroes, or gods, could have overthrown such work to leave it scattered, gone to ruin under the winds and sky. The clatter of horses' hooves over the flinty ground woke me from my reverie. I almost bolted upright, until I remembered Lady Olwen's many instructions, so crouched down until the riders had drawn level with me. They rode slowly today, these Celtic horsemen, matching their pace to that of their foot soldiers, and they rode at ease, unbraced, their cloaks folded behind them, in their shirtsleeves, bareheaded, their weapons sheathed. I cannot say their air of fierce resolve was gone; rather, it seemed put aside, not forgotten but waiting to be remembered. At their head rode their lord, or prince I suppose I should call him, in Celtic style. Seeing him now clearly for the first time, I was struck again by how young he looked, with a fresh, open face, dark blue eyes, startling, almost black, against his suntanned skin. He should have been hunting with his men, I thought, laughing with them, not riding as he now seemed, alone with his thoughts. For the eyes that looked out from under that thatch of copper hair, curled and crisped with the heat, had a faraway look, almost sad, as if, off guard, he could give sadness a name. And there was a look, too, a shadow, behind that youthfulness. I had no words to describe it then, but now I think I would call

it a sense of purpose, a dedication, that makes even good men
dangerous. Such men can cause more harm than evil men, although they themselves be not evil and act for good. I do not
say I saw all these things written in his face, only their shadow.
And when I leapt up under his horse's nose from my bed of
fern, whatever dark thoughts had been troubling him vanished
into anger, real and immediate and certainly common to all
men, as he fought to subdue his horse. For that gray-black horse,
rested after a night's stabling, well fed, well shod, tossed its
head and reared back as if it had been frightened by a snake.
No mounted man likes to be made a fool, and I might easily
have been trampled underfoot, to say nothing of being broached
by a dozen spears, had it been any other man. As it was, his
guard knocked me down with the butt ends and held me there,
like a rabbit pinned, until their prince had controlled his horse
and could give his orders how to deal with me. Before he could
kill me, I gabbled my message out—not easy that, with a spear
at your throat and men's boots planted on either side your head.

"Greetings, Prince of Afron," I croaked, "greetings on your
house from the house of Cambray. If you will ride up to the
cliff fort," for so I thought the phrase elegant, "you shall find
a thing to your advantaging." A formal message, then, delivered
with as much aplomb as I could muster. Imagine my chagrin
when this great prince laughed. His laugh changed him, made
him a boy, and for a moment I could see what he would have
been if all cares had been laid aside.

"By Saint David," he said, when he could speak, "you need
a royal trumpeter, to say nothing of a coat of gold, to deliver
such a speech. No messenger sounds his best sprawled on his
back. But if you are trying to tell me that your mistress is that
quick-tongued brat of yesterday, tell her, if she would speak
with me, that she come down."

"She has many men with her, my lord," I lied with as much
dignity as I could manage. Then he laughed again and spoke
with his men, who guffawed.

"An ambush perhaps?" one mocked, pricking me to make
me squirm. "We've seen no men. We've followed your tracks
a mile long; a girl on a pony trotting all the way and a knock-

kneed boy. Here's the one, and the other has been peeping from the rocks at us this past half hour."

Then I did blush; all her carefully laid plans gone to naught.

"Get up, lad." Prince Taliesin was mocking me. I saw what Lady Olwen had meant at once, a mockery both good-natured yet sharp, to make you want to cringe. "If your mistress, your Norman lady, is afraid to come down, then we'll go up. But let me give you a word of advice. If you do everything a woman says, you'll be a dead man before you're grown."

"You must go alone," I cried, for that was a point she had been determined on.

He reached down and pulled me up by the slack of my shirt.

"You shall lead me to her, then," he said. "Climb up, master messenger." He forced me to scramble behind him, set off at a canter before I was firmly set. I hung around his waist for dear life, the first time I had ever been on a horse, and its great hooves and height terrified me. It bounded up the little track, striking sparks from the stones, and behind us his men stretched and scratched and laughed softly to themselves in the sun.

On the cliff top the Lady Olwen awaited us. She had thrown her gray cloak across her saddle bow, and her long hair blew freely in the wind. I was right; she had worn her best green dress with jewels stitched at neck and sleeves. And the little white horse that had been standing patiently began to dance and paw the grass as the bigger stallion came up, until she quieted it with a word. Unnoticed, I loosened my hold on Prince Taliesin's belt, slid to the ground, and scrabbled to safety, out of their way behind a rock. They paid no attention to me, prince and lady staring at each other. There was a strange immobility about them, a sudden stillness that I cannot explain. I knew very well who they were, yet as I looked at them, it seemed as if two figures were superimposed on them, a man and a woman, not a boy and a girl, and the woman waited immovable, like a statue cut in stone. There was a beauty about her that I have never seen in this world. I cannot say if she were old or young or what she was, but she was cut from time itself; and the man she greeted or bid farewell to was as old or young, as immovable, and as beautiful. All I can tell you, then I was frightened by what I saw, two things at once, one real and alive, one not real and yet not dead. I closed my eyes. But when I opened them, Prince Taliesin and the Lady Olwen were still sitting there silently. Yet it is also true that I had never known before how beautiful Lady Olwen was, as if I now had glimpsed for a second also the lady she would become, and in her eyes sensed the same sadness I had just seen in Prince Taliesin's.

Prince Taliesin spoke first, or rather raised his arm in salute, gravely, without a smile. The sleeve of his shirt fell back, and the gold bracelet glittered in the sun.

Lady Olwen bit her lip. I had never seen her at a loss for words. She was nervous, I think, and tense, as if what she said should be said well, as if she searched for both word and thought, as if—and this, too, I did not realize until afterward—as if this was the most important thing she had ever said.

Even her voice trembled when she spoke at last, and her hands shook on the reins until she clasped them tight on the saddle in front of her.

"My lord," she said, "I am come to ask your pardon for discourtesy. If you would not eat or drink in my father's hall, I hope I am not the cause." When he still did not reply, she went on. "But you, my lord, owe me a like apology." Then she did turn to him in her quick, eager way. "You did me wrong to knock me to the ground like a common man. You did me wrong to mock at me. I would show you honor as is right. So now should you honor me."

Prince Taliesin was taken aback. Of all the things he had expected, this was not the one. I saw he, too, searched for words to reply. "Lady," he began, but she broke in, in her impulsive way.

"I have not asked my brothers to right that insult, but, my lord, you owe me recompense, I think. One against one is fair and just. You told me your horse could outrun the world. Then let him run against mine."

He did not laugh, although I saw how his lip curled. "And the wager?" he asked, almost softly to her. "It would be theft to take it so easily."

"When you have won, ask what the wager is," she said. "But

since that horse of yours is half Cambray bred, it may be I'll ask for it."

"That was not the wager I had in mind," he said, softer still. "Nor you, I think." Perhaps she sensed what he meant, for she flushed. I had never seen her blush like that.

"To the ruined tower and back," she said, suddenly sharp to hide the confusion in her cheeks, to hide the fact that perhaps he had understood her thoughts, "unless you are frightened to ride against me."

Before he could guess what she was about, she took up her gray cloak and threw it over his horse's head, much as he had thrown his cloak at her the night before, and while a second time he fought his horse to a standstill, she took advantage of him and sent her little white horse scrabbling over the cliff, down to the path at its foot. By the time Prince Taliesin had disencumbered himself, she had already disappeared from sight.

"By Christ," he swore, and now he was all young man and angry, "she has tricked me after all." He watched her for a moment, swore another great oath, struggled to unbelt his sword, threw it and his shield aside, clapped spurs to horse, and bounded off. And now you saw indeed what he would have been had not some secret grief, some secret wrong, eaten his childhood, his boyhood, away. For he laughed as he rode, and shouted out his battle cry, the cry of his house, so that his men hearing it raised up a cheer. And when they saw him galloping along the crest of the cliff, they cheered again and began to stream up the little paths to the hill fort. For Taliesin's sharp eyes had spotted another track running along the top of the cliff, inside the walls, and although it was longer by far to the western tower, it was clear of stones and wider, so he could let his stallion race full speed. So, they say, ages past, another prince of our Celtic peoples at another time rode his thick-maned horse into a battle in this place.

Well, Lady Olwen's little white horse ran bravely, slipping neatly through the rocks along the lower path until it came within the shadow of the western end by the ruined tower, where it had to pause to make the turn. Along the crest of the cliff came the big gray-black horse, its ears laid back, charging down the cliff beside the tower so that when Lady Olwen turned, Taliesin was but three lengths behind. Now was the race more evenly matched, in that they both started at the same time and place, but nevertheless in one sense Lady Olwen had the advantage. For she was still in front, and although the little horse was tiring fast, it was able to twist between the stones and rocks more quickly than a larger horse could; nor could Taliesin pass it on the track, where there was room for only one horse at a time. Once the prince had to rein back so hard to avoid trampling that white horse that he almost threw his own. And, knowing this, and having planned it so, Lady Olwen turned and smiled in triumph at him. Exasperated, Taliesin suddenly threw his arm above his head so the gold shone and urged his horse away from the path across the moor itself with its treacherous litter of stone and rocks, where a misstep might kill a horse or a man who rode too fast. And now he laughed as he came, passed her on the last curve, and swept up in front of her before the cliff. The gods were with him; he did not fall. Only the little white horse, nudged aside, stumbled and rolled over like a cat. Before it faltered, Taliesin leaned over and clasped the Lady Olwen about the waist, plucked her into the air like picking fruit, set her before him, and galloped on. The Celtic soldiers leaned over the cliff edge and cheered, clashing their spears against their shields, as they do for victory. And presently the prince came cantering up, riding easily himself, the stallion snorting and stamping, still fresh, not even noticing the double weight.

He reined up when he reached the top.

"Now, lady," he said, and all men heard, "you have outchallenged me and outrun me and out-tricked me, and now fairly in the end have I outrun you. Thus was your wager made, and I claim my fee."

And he kissed her full upon the lips. Then he set her carefully down upon an outcrop of broken wall, so that she stood almost level with him, and wrestled off the golden bracelet. One of his men brought up her cloak and his sword and shield; he put her cloak about her shoulders and clasped the bracelet on her wrist.

"And now," he said as he took up his weapons and buckled them on, "go back home, Lady Olwen. This is no place for you. I have no quarrel with your house, nor with your father, nor with his sons. But as he is warden of the borderlands, so he speaks and acts in the king's name. My quarrel is with the king. I told you I had come on men's affairs. There is no enmity between your house and mine. But there cannot be friendship between us either."

Her face had grown white as chalk, except for the dark bruise. He must have noticed it, for he almost put his hand out to touch it, then drew back.

"I am not come in my own right," he said, and now I sensed the misery that drove him, that drove his men, "but in my father's name as well. Last and only son am I of an old lord, who has seen his other sons die before him. Three he had. Come of age, I have ridden here to avenge their deaths."

Lady Olwen's lips repeated the words; she did not say them aloud, but they hung like whispers in the air.

"My brothers," he said, the boyish smile quite gone, the face shuttered close, the dark blue eyes heavy with an old grief, "three older brothers were given to your king as hostages for peace in his last Welsh campaign. Dead they are, every one; King Henry had them killed for spite."

"Killed." She repeated the word aloud this time.

"Hanged," he said. "Gelded and blinded and hanged to force a peace."

The cruel and bitter words fell like stones and could not be unsaid.

"To avenge such death," he said, "a death for a death. For that reason I cannot eat or drink in your father's house, although he was not to blame. Yet he is the king's warden and is a Norman lord. For those reasons I cannot know his sons. For those reasons I shall not acknowledge his daughter, who, of all maids I have ever seen, is most fair. There can never be love between my house and any Norman one. So I bid you farewell, Lady Olwen. Do not look for me again."

He beckoned to his men. They turned, went silently down over the cliff, he and his six horsemen in front, the foot soldiers behind, and presently we saw them following along the lower path, westward beyond the ruined tower. And Lady Olwen stood and wept, twisting the bracelet about her arm.

After a while her tears were done. I do not think she wept for herself, although she might have, nor even perhaps for those poor dead sons killed in such shameful way, but for that young man who must bear the burden of their deaths all his life. Then she called to me, put her head upon my shoulder. Together we crept down the hillside as if her own strength were gone. We caught the little horse, cropping grass, its coat all flecked with dirt and foam; wearily she rode it back, taking turn and turn with me to walk and ride. For now I was so tired myself, I would have ridden anything. When we came within the safety of the village fields, she stopped and tried to smile. "Go your ways, Urien," she said. "You have done me service today. I had not thought it would turn like this. I cannot thank you for all that you have done, to reveal a story of such shame and woe. Never speak of this day again nor mention his name to me or anyone. Swear."

I swore, and so have kept my oath, never broken until now. She left me then at the field's edge, went slowly on to the castle gate. What she told, what was said within the castle walls, I never knew. Perhaps nothing at all. It is often only we ourselves who make great things or small of what we do. And no gossip has anyone ever had from me. But this I know. From that day on I never looked for her in fields or barn or on the moors. I knew she would never come. They said she had a maid of her own now, who, within the castle confines, walked a pace behind her and outstared all men to make them move from my lady's path. Nor did Lady Olwen ever ride alone again; the little white horse stood in its stable and grew fat. Its mistress braided her hair with strands of pearls, wore her silk dresses every day, and walked back and forth on the battlements in her silken shoes, gazing westward over the hills like a trapped bird. No word she said to anyone of Prince Taliesin's resolve or the wrongs done his kin; nor did I. But other men spoke of such things, a crime that had been committed many years before when he was still a child himself, and so had revenge lain waiting all this while until he had grown to take it up. And they said, too, that Earl Raoul had not even been in England at the time, affairs of his own keeping him abroad, although I noted that men were not easy speaking of that. But, becoming wiser in my own way, I saw now how seldom Earl Raoul and his older son remained at home but every day rode out along the border as if keeping watch, as if they looked for trouble from the Celts, as if they expected, one day soon perhaps, a young prince would return, leading an army from his northwestern lands. Lord Robert rode as his father's second in command, as was his right; a troop he led of younger knights, sons of his father's guard or vassals, young men of his own age. And among those young men now called to active watch was one whom I should mention here, since his name, too, must be known. A Norman lord he was, Gervaise of Walran, oldest son of a Norman baron whose castle stood east of Cambray. He often accompanied Lord Robert, riding with him on a big, rawboned horse. He was a big, raw-boned lad himself, Lord Gervaise of Walran, not yet grown into his strength, yet broad-shouldered, good-natured, well trained with sword and lance. The castlefolk liked him middling well, and he was loyal to both the young lords of Cambray and generous enough in his almsgiving to make him popular. Nor was he too particular in his own temperament, so that Hue's rages slid off his back without giving offense. Yet I did not trust him; he was boastful when he was alone, giving me sly kicks when no one was about, ogling the castle maids and pinching them, a typical Norman knight.

Hue was in a rage most of that spring, mainly because although these other young men rode with Earl Raoul, Hue himself did not. Judged still too young, he stayed at home to while away the hours in anger, pent up inside. So whilst his brother and his friend did men's work, Hue disjointed a shoulder climbing after an eagle's nest or lamed his horse by leaping every obstacle in sight, as restless himself as a caged-up hawk. And so, I think, it can be said that within the castle, tensions now of various kinds were rising like yeast in a cider vat, so fast that one day they, too, must burst forth. And one day they did—old wrongs, old griefs, mixed with new, together as bitter as those Taliesin of Afron felt. And so it happened by chance, or by fate, as you will, that I was again there to be witness of what occurred.

Chapter 3

he great hall at Cambray is not as large as other castle halls I since have seen, but to a serf at Cambray, it is the lord's own place, his own hearthstone. I had never dared enter it before. Anyone who goes there must first pass through the guardroom at ground level, a strong room with walls the thickness of an arm's length, then climb up a steep and winding stair, into a room, large, rectangular, with a vast stone fireplace at one side. A raised dais stands at the narrow end, set with table and chairs for the castle lords. Lesser guests, knights, and squires, sit below the dais on the stem of a T, at tables, which, when not in use, are kept stacked along a wall. Pages rush about to serve food brought from the kitchen on the outside. A kitchen serf has no place there, nor any serf, unless he be a bringer of wood, or water carrier, or one with specific duties to perform. And in the guardroom, my father would be on watch for me! Yet on a morning when the weather kept the younger lords and their friends dicing in the stableyards (I know, I left them there), when I knew the Lady Olwen safe at home, I braved the stairs and came at last into that hall, hoping for speech with her.

I had washed and tied my hair as I had seen Lord Hue do, in the Celtic style, and if my tunic was ragged and the leggings too large, at least they were almost clean. I was still small for my age, thin enough to slip between the trestle tables, not yet dragged out for the midday meal. I had counted on finding the

Lady Olwen immediately. What I had not then realized was
that above that hall was yet another flight of stairs. It led, as I
was soon to learn, to the women's bower, where the ladies of
Cambray kept to themselves, where no man but their lord
himself would go. And he, by ill luck as I first thought, was
not with them either today. He was sitting before the fire, with
his men, the castle seneschal and many of his guard. I turned
to slide out the way I had come. Too late, a squire had set
himself against the door, barring my escape. I slithered farther
along the outer wall in the shadows, hunched down, biding my
time in patience, hoping still she would appear. And since this
great earl was there, I watched him curiously.

He sat, Lord Raoul of Sedgemont, or lounged would be a
better word, before the fire, his boots upon the raised hearth,
long legs, like his elder son's, stretched out. Now, in all these
years I had seldom seen him unhelmeted, unarmed, close at
hand, certainly never at ease; and seldom would he have remained at home like this in his own castle hall had not these
last days turned all roads to mud, the moors to bogs, a mist as
thick as November covering hills and sea. There would be no
hunting, no patrols, on such days.

Well, then, Lord Raoul sat before the fire with his men,
nursing his old hurts, for he was slightly lame, they say, a
wound suffered in his youth, and the damp of these western
hills is hard on wounds. I had grown wiser in these past weeks;
I knew how to judge men. I liked what I saw. His voice I
recognized at once, clipped like Robert's, a Norman voice, and
when he spoke, men listened to him. And I noted, too, the way
he moved and sat; he had a habit I had never seen before in a
man, although his daughter had it, I think, of moving like that
mountain cat I had remarked upon before. Once I had seen such
a cat, high on a rock, where it had spied down on our flocks, a
great cat, which I had watched rather than giving the alarm so
that other shepherds or even I, if I could, would have rushed
in with spears to kill. He wore simple clothes, this great lord,
not like his sons, not even a fur-lined robe to keep out the cold,
and his hair was cut long in the fashion of former years, bound
back with a simple golden band as sign of rank; his hair was

thick and silver-gold like his elder son's. But his eyes were ones to watch, green-gray like the northern sea, Viking eyes they said.

He and his men were talking of old times, old campaigns, old battles. I think now that that day he had come down to do his comrades honor who had fought with him during those civil wars. He himself spoke but seldom, let his seneschal speak for him.

A grizzled bear of a man was this Dylan, who kept watch over Cambray in his absence and cared for it. Dylan, of course, I knew and was wary of. He was a reason of his own to avoid this hall. I would have run a mile rather than let him see me here; he was a man quick to fault stupidity, impatient with what he would construe as laziness, loyalty to Cambray and its masters his only standard for men. I slunk back still farther into myself, although not so far away that I could not hear what was said. For what they spoke of fascinated as well as appalled.

I am no soldier, for all my name; no warrior, although at the right time, I, too, have used a sword and been wounded. But I listened to their stories as one listens to the minstrels sing of hero kings. And even Dylan, the harsh-tongued, harsh-faced old man who ruled the castle guard at Cambray with an iron hand, even he could tell a tale: how he had accompanied the earl when, but a boy, Lord Raoul of Sedgemont had come from France and fought with Stephen, who then was king, against this Henry of Anjou who now held the throne. And when Lord Raoul himself stretched out his arm to throw another log upon the fire, I saw for myself the great scar that curled around his right wrist, a wound taken for the sake of that Stephen, who, when the earl was down and like to die, had straddled him, laid about with a mighty battle-axe, saved him from certain death, and won his pledge of loyalty. Of Stephen's wars they spoke freely enough, even with humor and, if I do not exaggerate, a touch of longing, for they were after all the wars of their youth, when they had served King Stephen well. But of their quarrels with the king who had inherited in the end, that Henry of Anjou who had hated Earl Raoul and hunted him down, they never spoke, at least not then. And although the cause must have been much on their minds, they certainly made no mention of that young Prince of Afron, whose determination to right the wrongs done his name was to shatter the border peace.

Nor was Earl Raoul impatient with his old seneschal, bearing with his boasting more modestly, answering questions for the younger men more tolerantly than many great lords would, and these border men hung on every word he said. I was entranced myself, I admit, to have these fables now made truth. Inch by inch, despite myself, I left the shelter of the wall and came closer to where they sat. I could have listened to them talk all day, almost forgetting the real reason I was there at all.

Suddenly there was a clatter on the stone stairs, a sound of feet taking the steps two at a stride. Into the hall of Cambray the lord's sons burst, with a disregard for propriety, a noise that was almost a discourtesy. And this time it was clear both sons were in an angry mood. Once again I felt that flicker of apprehension claw at me to make my hair rise on my neck.

Their anger puzzled me. As I have explained, I had left them dicing with their squires in the stableyards. They were both good at dicing and should have won, although the game is forbidden by Church law, and sometimes Dylan had tried to prevent the men from playing it. Earl Raoul did not comment on the noise, nor did Dylan himself, deep in some story that even I had heard: how once, long ago, his companions here at Cambray had been tricked into opening the castle gates to let in an enemy, a story often told but now so embroidered as to make us laugh. But from where I crouched at the edge of the table, I could see how Robert's hands were clasped behind his back and how he twisted the thick signet ring of Sieux about his right hand as if he would twist it off. Hardly had Dylan's story come to an end than he broke in, so unlike his usual self I could see all men were surprised.

"Is it true, my lord," he said, "that some weeks hence, in August, the Prince of England, young Henry, will be crowned as our next king?"

There was a sudden murmur at his words. I could not tell of surprise or displeasure or what. Who was this other prince they spoke of? It was only afterward it occurred to me, how strange

that for the first time in my life I should hear men speak so
freely, so casually, of kings and princes, as easily as I might
talk of Jake the miller or David the stableboy. And that I
should so quickly have learned to listen, unconcernedly, without
comment.

Earl Raoul did not at first answer his son, merely leaned back
in his carved chair and stretched his leg as if to ease it. And
when he spoke, he kept his face turned to the flames.

"Empty title," he said at last, "empty crown."

"And yet, my lord," Robert persisted, still unlike himself,
"will not you attend?"

"I had not so purposed."

"Nor yet your men, your vassals?"

"Nor them."

I noted now how Hue had stayed back, had let Robert come
first, speak first. Hue was in a royal rage himself, yet unchar-
acteristically, he held his anger curbed. I began to see the reason.
What Robert would come to by more subtle means, Hue would
hurl to your face. Better for Robert, then, to speak. And what
had angered them was equally clear. At such a time, such an
occasion as a crowning of a prince, should not the Earl of
Sedgemont be there, and they with him?

"Yet they say, my lord," Dylan intervened, in his border
way, asking a question instead of answering one, "is he not a
fair young man, this prince, one on whom to pin our hopes?
And has not his marriage with the Princess of France settled
affairs between King Louis of France and Henry, King of England? And will not he serve to smooth our difficulties here
among the borderlands that his father has stirred up?"

There was a pause. Until now, I think, Lord Raoul had let
the old man speak, humoring him as one might any companion
who wished, as do old men, to show the world he still lived,
show he still had thoughts worth listening to. But now the
earl's silence held impatience of its own.

"Hopes," he said. His voice was even, low, but held a trace
of what I sensed was a former bitterness. "Aye, hopes, as if
they could heal a kingdom's woes! Prince Henry is no doubt a
fair young man, but he is too young to play at king for all that

Henry, his father, will have him crowned. And I have heard
that although he bestrides a horse and carries lance bravely as
any man, it is his companion, William, who outshines him in
the tourneys he seems to devote most time to."

There was an appreciative rumble at that. The men at Cambray, both young and old, loved to hear such talk; it was the
sort of thing they craved, these border soldiers, starved for news
of a military world, living as they did upon the outskirts of it.
Not one of the youngest knights would have known what a
tourney was (I did not, of course); certainly few had ever taken
part in one, yet all of France played at them. Willingly they
hunkered down for an expert discussion by a champion on the
role and art of a tourney knight. I thought the worst had passed.

Hue said, too loud, "You, my lord father, did not scorn the
tourneys once to win land and fame for Sieux in France. At
Boissert Field you fought in one. Is not the turn of younger
men come yet?"

Once more the earl raised his eyebrows, waited for his younger
son to finish, then went on, "I have heard that the prince's
friend, that William, known as the 'Marshal,' is counted the
best of Europe's knights, downing I know not how many men
in a day, but it is also claimed that the prince's younger brother,
Richard, is already almost as skilled. Henry has the best horses,
best mail that money can buy, but I do not think he is either's
match—"

"Yet they say," Hue cut in again, "that all those lords, all
the nobles of England, will be gathered in Winchester, witnesses
to that prince crowned. They and their heirs."

This time the impact of his words could not be missed.

"God's wounds," the earl said. "All of England may seek to
throw itself off Cambray's cliffs, like lemmings intent on mass
suicide. I do not have to follow them. A gathering it will be,
but of fools. To what purpose will they come, these unknown
lords you mention but do not name, who will attach themselves
to young Henry's camp? His father still is king. King Henry
will not give up one jot of power to his eldest son, for all the
pomp and ceremony. He may crown his son, a crown is not
hard to find, but not one ounce more of gold, one rod of land,

no, nor one ox, one castle more will he give to satisfy further that young man's claims. I have been to crownings before. There was a time when each journey the king made abroad, a crowning was held at its end, a crown to be picked up at every churchyard gate. Henry himself cried a halt to that, so why now start again a custom he dislikes? He who holds power holds it, crown or not. Those friends of the young prince who think to edge their way into the forefront of the court may find themselves in the forefront of war. When they are caught between allegiance to father and to son, let them think then what this jaunt to Winchester will cost. Cost us all, God rot them, not themselves alone."

He swore a soldier's oath, roaring it out. I noticed how a faint scar on his cheek stood out, so tightly now he held his anger.

"By the rood, have not we had civil war enough that men must go running, pleading for it? Is not there trouble still in France—the French king digging at Henry's side, a maggot burrowing in upon his lands? Is not there trouble enough within the Church—an archbishop murdered, the Church fathers in discord? And here at Cambray we have sufficient unrest of our own to keep us more than occupied. Wherever Henry is, grief follows, for other men to bear. Leave well alone."

His echoing of his elder son's advice given that other time startled me. And Dylan—I saw now how his garrulousness could bridge a silence. "There's a truth," he said, wagging his white head, his dark Celtic eyes bright as a bird's. "My lord, you and I have marched knee-deep in blood, into a war that plagued us for a lifetime, before most of them here were born or weaned. Stick to border garrisoning. I remember now—"

"But, my lord father." Robert again was speaking. His father glanced at him quickly, looked away. In these past years Robert, too, had changed, grown broader, fitting into his height, seeming older than his years. Yet not wiser, I thought, if he challenged his father after he had so spoken. Lords do not like "if's" and "but's," especially not from their sons.

I marked how the earl's eyes darkened like his son's, and how his knuckles whitened on the carved arms of the old chair. The firelight gleamed for a moment on the gold ring he wore, the thick seal ring that once had belonged to Falk of Cambray.

"But, my lord father, will not King Henry expect you there?"

Before the earl's reply, Hue thrust forward, although Robert tried to hold him back. I think now Robert had spoken out to try to turn his father's wrath. He could in no way turn Hue's.

"But I am bid attend," Hue cried. "The prince himself orders me. Would you have me refuse a royal writ? See, Henry Plantagenet has sent me word; here it is with his seal attached."

He tugged beneath his tunic, pulled out a parchment; whether from the prince or not, I could not tell, but I thought so then, supposed it was a message that had alerted both young men, although how that message had been delivered, how it had reached them, I did not think of that. Nor why their father had kept such news from them. I felt a pull, I cannot say of sympathy, but at that bond, which I could not put a name to but which held me in some strange way to Hue's own thoughts.

"All of England and their heirs," Hue said, "except yours."

He stood alone now (or was it that the other men had drawn aside), legs thrust apart, head jutting belligerently. I remembered suddenly the way he had stood that day in the stableyard.

"What is here for me, my lord, but mist and rain? Shall I drag my life out in these barren hills? Are we so unwelcome, so uncouth, so unschooled in knightly ways as to disgrace an earl's entourage?"

Lord Raoul heard him through, although another man, my father certainly, would have clouted him to the ground before he uttered a third of it. At the end he said, almost patiently, I thought, in that rational Norman way, "Then act your part, not a spoiled child crying for the moon."

"I am no child," Hue cried, and then I saw that flash of rage men warned against, that and something more, some other thing that made me want to cringe away for nervousness, that other thing that bound us despite ourselves, a fetter, a chain to tighten and weigh us down.

"I can match swords with any man," Hue said, slow-voiced and cool now, as steel is heated white. "Give me horse. There is no man I cannot outfight, outride, no man who bests me on these borderlands. As you would know, my lord father, if you paid me any heed, if you would let me ride anyplace with you, if you would ever give me some part of your time. You would know then that I am no child. Is it not rather your past hatred of those Angevins that keeps you away? Must then I suffer for your hate?"

"That is long done with." Lord Raoul spoke as slowly. "But no son of mine goes crawling to the Angevins."

"No son of yours . . ." Hue spat out the words, and the men again moved back a step, uneasily, like horses scenting fire. "Then, by God and all his devils, hear me out. What son am I to what father, who treats me as no son of his? A by-blow perhaps, a bastard, to drag his way through life? Shall I be kept here penned up like some churl, never to know what is my place? When shall I know it and my rights? When will you grant me them?"

There was a murmur, the sound men make when old, strange tales surface from depths where fear has buried them. It sent alarm snaking along my skin. I seemed suddenly to remember whispers I had heard but not listened to, things not spoken, yet thought.

"Am I not a son, as this elder brother here? And he a five-months child although the elder by two years. If he were bastard, born out of wedlock, should not I be the older son? Should a scant two years be time to bury me? Time will not wait for me, my lord."

I felt the bitterness breaking out, flooding out. I felt it flow into my own mouth, like bile. I felt his energy, that coiled-up hate, that anger, running like blood beneath the skin. *A bastard half-breed*, so he thought himself. The accusation flew about us like scattered shot from a sling to cut and wound him, and the wounds were as deep as those scored across my own flesh.

"Or is it something else you would hide from me, some rumor that I should be privy to? If not your son, your heir, then whose son am I? Who is it that my mother's honor protects?"

That accusation, too, went echoing around the hall, into the rafters, flaring out along the old stone walls. I think it has echoed in my mind ever since. I think it had hung there all those years.

Lord Raoul gripped the edges of the chair, heaved it back. It grated across the stone floor, so slowly that it seemed to me we should see it forever fall. But even before it had landed on its side, he had leapt, like a cat, despite his lamed leg, and caught Hue about the chest, bunching his embroidered tunic to his throat so that, being shorter, Hue was swung for an instant off his feet, dangled against his father's tall frame.

"Unsay those words," Lord Raoul ground out, although his voice was almost too low for us to hear, a cat's snarl. "Never breathe a word against your mother's name to me. You are my son. That is enough."

He let Hue swing off his feet, tossed him to one side so that he crashed against the table where I was still crouched. He landed in a heap upon the floor. Even as his father turned his back and strode, tight-lipped again, toward the hearth, Hue sprang upright. I caught the glimpse of dagger blade as he plucked it from its sheath. His brother, Robert, saw it, too, cried warning as he ran between his father and its point. The blow struck down upon Robert's outstretched arm. And beneath them both, I, who had never made such a move in my life, I wrapped myself around Hue's legs to topple him.

All broke into confusion, which I cannot now describe. Guards ran and trampled and swore, stormed over me with weapons drawn. Hue butted and kicked upon the floor. Three men were needed to hold him down, and when they had bound his hands and feet, he still beat his head against the stones, thudding into benches, shaking like one gone mad. More men came running, the castle watch thudding up the stairs with drawn spears, snatching sword and pike from off the walls.

No man carries arms into his lord's hall; none lifts weapon against him and lives. But Lord Raoul was not harmed; the blow had not been struck at him. It was Robert who lay before the hearth, the blood pooled among rushes, between the stones.

I shut my eyes and willed them shut. I had never seen such

blood before. I wrapped myself in my arms, curled up against such a sight, crept back into a corner out of the way.

Amid this confusion only the earl himself was calm; a soldier, used to such violence, he had taken up his son, ripped back the tunic sleeve, knotted his own belt to stem the blood. Lord Raoul, then, calm; his son, calm. And so his lady wife.

She had come down with her womenfolk, hurrying down those stairs from the room above, alerted by those first cries of outrage, of panic. Thus I had my first close look at her, the Lady Ann of Cambray, who now, too, knelt by her son, and wrapped cloths about his arm, bade her women bring her this and that, soft-spoken, as if she picked flowers in her herb gardens. It seemed to me a long while before she leaned back and looked at her husband, her own gown all stained and crumpled. Her eyes were large, too bright in her white face; her hair fell like a girl's across her back, and her slender fingers trembled as they kept a pad pressed to the ugly gash.

"God be praised," she said, "a flesh cut. But great loss of blood!" The sobbing of her women quieted. At a gesture from Earl Raoul, the guards dragged Hue away, who still mouthed and rolled.

"Leave us," the earl said, "all of you."

His men saluted, drew back, stunned, shaken into a sullenness. I heard them clatter down to the guardroom below. The castle servants, pages, squires, withdrew; the heavy door swung shut; the women fluttered like birds back to their bower. I suppose the Lady Olwen went with them. Lord Raoul, the Lady Ann, their son, were left alone. And I, rolled like a bundle of rags in a corner, where I did not dare move, I waited with them.

"That was ill-done, my lord, ill-done." The Lady Ann's voice had our Celtic lilt, although it shook with anxiety. She knelt beside her son, wiped his face free of dirt, the firelight playing upon her hair. I saw how, from time to time, she ran her fingers across his lips as if to assure herself he still breathed.

Lord Raoul had begun to pace back and forth with his halting stride, and his wolfhounds padded behind him, their ears still pricked in alarm. She watched him, watched her son, both with the same face, the same silver-blond hair, the same high cheek-bones. But when she spoke again, it was not of her eldest child.

"You tormented Hue," she said. "You denied him his heart's wish before everyone. He is still a boy, and you hurt his pride."

"Pride." Lord Raoul's voice grated like winter ice. "I grant him his years. He boasted of using them as a man."

"What will you do to him?"

"What should I do," he said, "that I might do to any dog that lunged at me from the back?"

She was silent, her head bowed. I remembered what had been said of her. *Child of war, of woe am I.* She had known so many griefs, too many, that now her sons should bring her more.

"My lord, my lord." She might have been pleading for herself. "He is headstrong, wild. His temper tears him apart. At other times he is gentle, kind. Already he will be on his knees repenting what he has done."

"Thank God," he said, "that he did not strike deeper, then, to have murder to repent him of." He swung around on her. "Or will he repent that he did not strike deeper, harder, to rid himself of me? Or of his older brother at least?"

She sucked in her breath, such a gasp of pain that I felt my own breast twist with it.

"You wrong him," she said.

"Perhaps so, perhaps not." He spun back on his heel. "But this you grant. Rage, jealousy gnaw at him, some dissatisfaction I cannot name, like a beast that gnaws its own flesh. If I gave way to it, what would he next want, what next would satisfy him? Nothing would, nothing does. The more he gets, the more he craves."

"Because in himself he is dissatisfied," she said. "You wrong him. The only thing he craves is your love." She suddenly stood up, pulling a blanket from a heap of rugs they had brought to cover Robert.

"Raoul," she began. I saw her forehead, as white and delicate as a girl's, furrowed now with thought. She struggled with the words to make him understand. I felt the tension in her, stretched like cord. She said, "The only thing he wants from you is your love. Raoul, once in my childhood, I wanted love myself. My father, Falk, denied me it, and all my life, until I met you, I longed for it as a man dying of thirst longs for drink.''

"You did not kill to get it," he said.

"I did not have to." Her voice was suddenly very clear. "I had enemies to do that for me, to show me what my loss was. I beg you, before it is too late for him, show him you believe in him. Forgive him, before it will be too late for you.''

I heard the words, like stones dropped into a deep lake. They spoke of things long past, long gone, and yet as stones when they are dropped, they stirred up ripples that spread and spread. Who knows where at last they end?

He stood in front of the fire, rubbing his fingers over the scar that cut across his cheek. She suddenly reached up and took his hand in hers to still it with her own.

"My lord," she said, each word a caress. I had never heard women speak so to men before, nor yet men to women, soft, almost tenderly, although then I would not myself have recognized tenderness. "Raoul," she said, "for all the pains you have endured for my sake, for all those long-past griefs, so that it shall not be hate that wins.''

He said, almost to himself, "Sometimes I think all comes from that, spilled out because of it. Had Henry not hated me, he would not have looked to be revenged. Had Geoffrey Plantagenet, his brother, not hated him, there would have been no conspiracy, no Boissert Field, no Welsh expedition to trap us both. And had not I, for pride, for hate, fought against them as I did, we would never have been driven apart.''

They spoke of the past, names, people I could not know, almost felt I should not know. They were things, I sensed, that had not been spoken of in many years, things done, not done, that had been laid to rest until this day's events had dredged them up.

She said, "Hue is your son. Yet his birth has been a twisted thing, unraveled between us all these years. He senses it. Stephen's wars, Henry's malice, Hue's birth, they are all part of the same tale, and now your sons have inherited it.''

Upon the floor Robert stirred and opened his eyes. They were dark-fringed, purple-shadowed against his white skin, where the brown seemed to have faded. He attempted to pull himself upright against a chair.

"Father," he said. His voice was weak. I had never heard him use that childish term. "Father, are you hurt?"

"You took it all." Lord Raoul stood over him. "Now have you your first blooding to be a man." He tried a smile. "The other day you complained, I think, that you had never had a wound. They are not so pleasant, wounds, that I myself would seek them out. Even honor smarts." He was laughing, but I saw the firelight glint upon his face, catch at that faint scar. "My son," he said, "I thank you for my life."

"Father." Robert repeated the word almost childishly. "He did not mean to strike at you." He struggled as his mother had with the words. "He thinks himself older than he is, he burns to excel before you more than anyone. If I had held the dagger, he would have died for you."

I had never heard Robert speak so much. I saw his mother move beside him, uneasy lest he strain himself and start the bleeding again.

"Father." A third time that childhood name, although by nature he was much more formal, usually gave his father title, as was courteous. "Let him go with you to Winchester. You can give excuse now why I cannot. I wished for it, but there will be other times for me. Take him and show him to the world."

Lord Raoul said almost wonderingly, "You, too? Your mother already pleaded for it herself. But you? You are my heir, you are the older born. I cannot change that law."

But Robert was continuing, as if one point had been settled, as if he moved to a second one. "And let him know what lands are his inheritance: Sedgemont or Cambray, or even Sieux, if you prefer. But give him one."

His father stepped back as if stung.

"So," he said, "that also! By God, inheritance, is that what you have in mind? Is that the way these days, to carve your father's body before his death? I did not look to see my sons carve me up. When I am in my grave, ask for my lands, not before, snarling over them like dogs over bones. I tell you,

Robert of Sieux, what is yours is already bestowed. Ask nothing else."

"Not for me, for him." Robert's voice had weakened, but not his will. It came out suddenly strong, as strong and clear as his sister's, his mother's, as strong and implacable as that older man's.

"Acknowledge him and give him title to his inheritance. Let him ride at your side. Knight him. My turn at honor will come."

Father and son stared at each other, frustration, aye, and dislike, as palpable, as strong as steel. Yet love was there, too, and forgiveness.

Suddenly Lord Raoul let out one of his soldier's oaths and strode to the doorway, his hounds at his heels. He snatched at a hunting spear as he went.

"Where shall you go?" Lady Ann cried, running after him, her skirt flapping like a girl's, her unbound hair fraying into wisps.

"By the Mass," he said, not stopping in his stride or turning around, "by the rood, but I am bedeviled by your arguments, and by your son's. Let me forth. More pleasure lies in these mists and bogs than ever in your Celtic snares. Ann, I need time to think. I have said already more than I should. Events, places, people forgotten all these years—I would not remember them."

"Forgive me, my lord," she said, clinging to his arm. "We shall not harbor old resentments to make new ones. But we have said what we all know is truth, and you have said so yourself. Hue will never have peace without your giving it. Better to have left him with my Celtic kin, in those Celtic hills where he was born and half of him still lives despite himself, than to bring him back to be always a second to your first."

He put her aside, not ungently. "Peace!" he said. Then, "I shall think of it."

We heard him striding down the stair. The captain of his guard snapped to salute below. Presently there was a clamor as his men ran and clattered at his command. They crossed the yard, splashing through the rain, and we heard the thunder of their horses' hooves across the bridge, dying away. Then only the soft drip of mist, the distant sound of the sea beating on the rocks below the cliffs.

Robert said, with a sigh, "It is done. He will grant our request. But I could wish that it had been done in other wise. And that in granting it, he will not make a gap between us who else have been so close."

"And you, my son," she said, "who wished for as much, what then?"

He sighed again, almost smiled. "There will be time for me," he said, "but not, perhaps, for him."

She took his hand and sat beside him on the floor. I sensed the bond between them, without words, without thought. Aye, sensed and perhaps envied it, and knew again what Hue must feel, what envy, what longing it must rouse in him.

Then Robert moved restlessly, a second time tried to sit up. He said, as if remembering something, "Had Hue not stumbled as he ran, I would have been too slow. Who was it who flung himself around Hue's knees?"

He looked about him, painfully turning his head, even to the very corner where I was still hid. At his nod the Lady Ann herself rose up, took down a torch from the wall sconce, and fetched me forth. I came reluctantly, you may be sure, so stiff and bruised I scarce could move, great purple patches spreading where they had stamped on my ribs.

"Come up, come up," she said in her way, "no harm, no wrong." For perhaps she thought I was afraid of what I had done or expected some evil result. Afraid, yes, but not of that, *that* I count one of the best moments of my life, for me, for them, only to be compared with one other time—and that to be told in due course.

"Why," Robert's voice, too, was light, a ripple of laughter underneath, " 'tis a bag of bones in its kitchen rags."

He stretched out his sound arm and shook my shoulders to loosen the rushes and straw that were tangled in my hair, tried to brush off the dust. "God's my life," he swore, "Urien the Bard! What are you doing here, my fine cockerel, hanging on my high lord's table post, thrusting into our affairs?"

I opened my mouth to speak, but since no explanation seemed

to fit, I closed it again with a snap. The reason I had come seemed so far removed from what I had seen, had done, I could not even link them in my mind. And yet a sort of calm came over me, almost like that I had experienced when I had waited for Hue to knock me down in the stableyard. I knew this was the moment I had long dreamed of, yet I felt neither fear nor elation, not even hope. Numbness was all.

Robert was continuing in his precise Norman way. "Had you not moved when you did, I should be a dead man, or my father dead and my brother hanged for a patricide. We owe you much. What will you take from me in return?"

I answered, in as simple a fashion as if, being thirsty on a hot day, I needed a drink of water, or as if I asked someone to hand me a broom, as if this were an everyday occurrence, as if such question, such reply, were commonplace. "To serve you, my lord, and your house. Nothing else."

Then he did laugh, cut short when he tried to move his arm. "I looked for my inheritance. By the Mass, I did not expect so quick response. Well, if this be the first fruit of it, I take it willingly, although it be but a meager choice. Sir page, if you would be part of my entourage, go get yourself washed at the well, have the women find you better clothes. And take upon yourself your first duty, to wait on me while my arm mends. Thus shall we both be satisfied."

Afterward I marveled at my coolness, too. Afterward I thought, that is how it is, how in a moment, a flash, a life can change. *You shall serve me.* With those few words was my life made. So might it be that a dead man could look at the blade which would kill him, or a drowning man a wave which swallows him; that moment passed, a transition made, the live man dead. Or, in my case, what before was dead made to quicken and come alive.

But later Lady Ann drew me to her side and brushed back my hair with her long, cool fingers as she had brushed her son's. "Urien," she said, in her low, earnest voice, "do you truly wish this, or even know what it is you have wished for? Listen now. Long ago I had a friend, a squire. He was a serf at Sedgemont when I went to live there after my father's death. To be a squire was not within his expectation or thought, yet because he was my dearest, best-loved friend of those days, I believed, when chance gave him the opportunity, that he had chosen well. And rejoiced with him in his good fortune. He rose to meet with kings and ride with lords and fight a noble battle in the end. But death took him young, unexpectedly, far from the place and ways he knew as home. And so has death taken many men I have known who ventured beyond the confines of their own world. I speak not to alarm or dissuade you; the choice is yours. But beyond Cambray are many different ways, most of them harsh and cruel. I tell you this from my own heart. Cambray is where I belonged, too. Dearly have I paid to have left it."

I said, "Lady, never in my life before have I achieved anything. Even as a serf. But to honor you as best I can, that is something I can do."

She smiled. "Well," she said, releasing me, "you shall be my eyes, my voice. Aye, I think in those ways you will serve us well. God grant us all such loyal friends."

Thus it was I won my name, and thus in turn my vocation was given me. Neither has been a thing to regret. Although the Lady Ann spoke truth, that far from Cambray all was not as fair as in my youthful eagerness I would have believed.

And so it was, in due course, I also learned the arts of poetry, reading, writing, and their skills. And, as shall be told in its place, how to write and sing in Celtic style that I should be crowned at their festivities and be treated with more ceremony than any Celtic warlord. But as they tried also to teach me horsemanship, the art of sword and lance, and hunting skills, those I tell you plainly were a waste of effort, although for a while there was no greater swaggerer, in his new crimson tunic with the golden hawks of Sedgemont, than this new page set on the path to chivalry.

As for the Lady Olwen, since I had kept my oath and never spoken of what had befallen her and Prince Taliesin, and since it had long been obvious that good luck had kept it secret from her family (for which I for one gave thanks to God), who was I to mention it now? But I still sensed constraint between us, so that sometimes when we met unexpectedly, she would turn her eyes away as if she were afraid I had known too many of her thoughts. Then, too, when she sat with Robert, often that friend of her brothers, that young Norman lord I have mentioned, Gervaise of Walran, made a third. It seemed to me that although Lady Olwen used her brother as excuse, she was not loath to laugh with Lord Gervaise, so that I was forced to sit also and listen to them. And it seemed to me that the more her sadness grew (and I saw sadness in her eyes, her walk, her very expression when she thought she was alone), the more she smiled at Lord Gervaise. While he, poor soul, he smiled the broader that she smiled at him. My scowls—for it is not easy to sit and watch an older, certainly higher-born man usurp your place—my sulks became a thing of jest until, out of very shame, I hid my devotion. But I knew that she, in her secret thoughts, as I in mine, had not swerved one inch.

Robert stayed longer at Cambray than he meant, for although at first his wound healed clean, a sudden infection spread, a fever set in, and it was high autumn before he left. Much was to happen before that time, as you shall hear. Earl Raoul and his men rode away on a July morning, fair and mild, to lighten the heart and cheer the mind. They went to Winchester as I had supposed, to see a king's son crowned. And Hue rode with them.

Chapter 4

o Earl Raoul, his son, and their entourage rode away, to be gone for the while from our lives. I forgot my newfound dignity and hung over the walls with the other boys until the distant figures disappeared into the shadows of the whaleback hills. From time to time I ran down into the inner courtyard, where Lord Robert lay in the shade, for I felt he should be informed of all that occurred; that at least was his right. He was swathed in furs, albeit the day promised warm, and lay with eyes closed, face turned to the wall. I do not know if he heard half that I said. I panted out each new detail in my excitement, for it had dawned on me that next time there was a leave-taking from Cambray, we should be among those who left; farewell then, I thought, to ignominy. But for all my enthusiasm, which I could no more contain than a leaking barrel can hold back its wine, Lord Robert lay as languid as a sleeping dog and merely nodded from time to time to show that he was awake. This was the first sign that his wound had taken ill, but he bore its discomfort silently, in no way wishing to delay anyone.

First in line came the outriders, in scarlet cloth stitched with gold, bearing before them the flags of Sieux and Sedgemont. These riders were mounted on matching grays of the Cambray herd. The wind that always blows off the moors on hot days caught at the folds of cloth and stiffened them until the banners spread and snapped like sails. Following them rode the earl and his household guard, carrying the earl's own standard spread with its golden hawks. Today Earl Raoul rode a gray stallion, too, and around him his personal companions, veterans all, chatted together casually as the younger knights did not dare. They were of an age, these men, not old, not young, as comfortable in their high-backed saddles and their well-worn mail as in an old pair of shoes. I wondered how long it had taken them to learn to ride like that; they had been trained in childhood, of course. I felt my heart beat double-fast as the earl gave his quick salute and they clattered out the open gates and wheeled through the village, heading east. Each of these knights had brought his own squire, who led a spare horse, loaded with gear, and each had draped across his own mail the surcoat of red. And under their casual air they were hard and alert. I think I have never seen such proud display, a riot of color and panoply and strength.

Bringing up the rear were the younger knights, the squires, among whom rode Lord Hue. They spurred their horses to make them leap and cavort, prancing through the courtyard before they in turn thundered across the moors, which spread before them purple and mauve in the morning sun. But it seemed to me, who watched him, that Lord Hue looked pale and kept his eyes downcast. A few days' solitude in the Cambray cells had quieted him, a salubrious effect which, although I was sure it would soon wear off, had at least given him time for thought. I was both glad and sorry to see him go; I had the feeling it might be long before we met again. So even after the gates were bolted close, I stayed to wonder what the future held for Hue, for us, until I became aware that I did not watch alone. A silent, hooded figure stood in the shade, staring intently into the eastern haze as if she, too, were looking for some sign. It was the Lady Ann. I was suddenly embarrassed, as if I had intruded upon some secret watch. True, she planned to follow more slowly with her own mounted guard and her womenfolk within the week, but she stared after her lord as if at a parting that might never end. I had a vision, an insight, of all the other partings she must have known, the long waits, the loneliness.

Abashed, I crept silently down the steps so as not to disturb and took my accustomed place at Robert's feet.

The fever fit was on him, and he shivered under his rugs. When it was done, he turned painfully and asked, as if he had not yet understood, "Are they gone?"

"Aye, my lord."

"All, all?"

"My lord, your father, your brother, and all their guard."

"And Cambray?"

"Bolted up, my lord, the watch in place, its guard here left to Dylan's charge."

"Praise be to God." And he lay back, as if satisfied.

I stared at him. Jealous for him, zealous of his rank and place, proud—too proud, I dare say—of my own, I blurted out, "It is not just to leave you behind."

His gray eyes, like his father's, flicked open, and his gaze was such that I flinched. "My brother has rights as have I," he said. "If you would serve me, never speak of them again. Between my brother and me no quarrel is and, please God, will never be."

But later, when the castle leeches had done their best (or worst, for in their absence he still could jest, saying he thought an old Celtic hag with her potions and chants could cure him faster than their remedies), when they were done, regretting that anger flash or, perhaps, the fever abating for a while, he became conscious of where he was and what this day's work would entail, and he began to speak. It may simply have been, as I have noted since, that there often comes a time in the lives of men, even those most taciturn, when they feel obliged to say what is in their minds, as if out of their habitual silence a wave of longing overwhelms them to explain their plans, their hopes, their secret selves. Or it may have been that he felt that first touch of sickness or death that now threatened him and wanted, somehow, to make a testament of himself. In later years I have often met men, both highborn and low, who poured out their histories in a flood, as if through my words they could leave a record of themselves; but never, I think, like this, this time when Lord Robert entrusted his thoughts to me. For it was not only what he knew and thought but why, and what he believed would result, and I, although too young to understand, too callow, perhaps, to appreciate his confidence, nevertheless had the sense to remember it, so that in time it would be pieced together, complete. Although God knows it was not a confidence to give joy.

Nor did Lord Robert speak all at once, you understand; his words were laced through with fever's fret, sometimes making sense, sometimes senseless. I pick them out from memory, selecting those that are of most import. I do remember thinking at the time, how strange that he, who was by nature reserved, cautious, should reveal such a gift for words, to break the silence he had long imposed upon himself.

By now we had moved into the hall. The fires were lit; the restful sounds of castle life had closed us around; Cambray's great walls surrounded us within their arms. The fret of the sea was a distant sound, a background to all the other familiar ones: the hum of bees, the doves in their cote, the rustle as the hounds settled among the dry rushes on the floor. The air was warm with the scent of clover and mint, and the pale blue smoke curled about the open rafters overhead. Danger, treachery, revenge were far off, shadows in an empty room. Yet beneath all of Lord Robert's talk they waited, coiled to spring.

"Between my brother and this English prince," Robert began. He was lying on his side, his face pale, his hair matted with sweat. From time to time I brushed off the flies. *Wounds smart.* Now my lord learned that to his cost. "Between Prince Henry and Hue is a bond so strong that brothers they might seem beneath the flesh. They have known each other since boyhood, and through the years has their friendship grown. If anyone should attend the prince at his crowning time, it should be Hue."

He hesitated. "My father does not think so," he admitted, "although in his youth my father swore a similar oath of loyalty to his king and himself lived and fought, yea, risked his life and happiness for such a vow. He is the last man to break a promise he has made, or to condone unfaithfulness in his sons. Hue's oath was sworn to the prince as blood pledge, blood bond, that even Church law would not deny. What if it was made between the sons of bitter enemies? It still stands. Myself, I do not believe that quarrels should stretch so far to shadow our lives. For sometimes it seems they do. That oath my father swore has won him the enmity of the man who is now King of England. Yet one day, I think, there will be other kings, other lords, who will need our friendship and cherish it."

For a long while he did not speak. I thought he slept. Then he said abruptly, "But not in my father's time. For there is something you should know if you would serve our house. There is hatred, implacable, between King Henry of England and my father, Count of Sieux. Perhaps once, as children, it was not so. As you know, or do not know, poor Urien, never having seen the lake, the river, and the cliffs of Sieux, our lands in France and those of Henry adjoin, the river forming a natural boundary. When Henry was a boy, son of a count, and my father was a boy, grandson of an earl, they used to ride along the riverbanks. King Henry was younger; he wanted my father to notice him; he wanted, I think, my father's respect; he coveted praise as a blind man covets sight. Failing to obtain it in sufficient wise, he ordered it. No one, man or boy, puts a curb chain to my father's head; no one, lord or king, orders him. He and Hue are alike in that. The more my father ignored the boy who swaggered before him, the more the boy swaggered. Yet, I think, despite himself, Henry longed to model himself on my father, whom he secretly admired. Well, when both were grown to man's estate, and civil war broken out for England's crown, as you have heard, my father swore an oath of allegiance to one claimant to the throne, King Stephen, whom he loyally served. Henry, the Count of Anjou, who also claimed the crown, never forgave my father for not supporting him. So deep was Henry's resentment, in fact, that upon finally gaining the crown, he moved at once to declare my father's lands forfeit and my father a traitor, meriting a traitor's death."

For a while Lord Robert lay silent, contemplating. Then he smiled. "Outlawed, wounded, threatened with death, landless, my father was rescued by the Lady Ann." He almost laughed,

although pain cut the laugh short. "Ann of Cambray," he said.
"There was a gallant soul. Young, alone, unknowing of courtiers' ways, she fought to save her lands and his, outfaced the
king and outwitted him. And the only person at the time who
could give her aid was Henry's queen, Eleanor, Duchess of
Aquitaine, by whose efforts was my mother's wish obtained,
to restore Lord Raoul of Sedgemont and have him marry her."
He smiled again. "The king thought it a great joke to insist they
wed," Robert said, "my father being in truth a noble lord,
owner of many lands and titles, and my mother, of lesser rank,
his vassal and ward. The jest in fact lay upon the king, for my
mother was already great with child. The child was Earl Raoul's
own, and I was that child. You see how Hue spoke close to
truth. A few months' difference, and he indeed would have
been the first legitimate son. But so Earl Raoul and the Lady
Ann were wed and went to Sieux, where I was born. Yet, after
all, Henry had the last word. Previously he had seized my
father's castle at Sieux, early in those wars. Now he destroyed
it, tore it down, stone by stone. And the queen became an
enemy. The gifts of the queen are made in expectation of recompense; and having first supported us, the queen had counted
on my father's support in a new conspiracy against the king.
For it is commonly believed that Eleanor had allied herself with
the main conspirator, Geoffrey Plantagenet, her husband's brother
and her paramour." He suddenly looked at me. "You are too
young, sir page," he told me, "to know anything yet of par-
amours. But remember the name of Geoffrey Plantagenet. And
remember, too, the name of Boissert Field, where the conspiracy was planned. De Boissert and his daughter, Isobelle, sought
revenge against my family on the queen's behalf because we
would not join with them." These names I had heard before,
cried out in anger in this same hall. I had heard of Geoffrey
Plantagenet, now dead, cut off for his sins in his prime, the
man of beauty and vice, paramour to the queen, brother to the
king, and the man to whom the Lady Ann's reputation was
tied.

"That Geoffrey," Robert said, "lusted for my mother. When
she repulsed him, in his anger he used her to win his brother's

favor back, and so helped Henry capture her. That was at the start of the Welsh wars. She escaped, fled across the border to her Celtic kin, where she remained until Hue was born, but my father stayed to fight with the king. There are those who claim she gave away the Norman plans to the Celts, to my father's detriment. And Henry boasted to my father that my mother had slept with him himself." The silence that followed those words was again fraught with all those dark things better left unsaid. But Robert said them, broke them out of his deep thoughts as old wounds break and tear apart.

"They say," he said, "that Hue is not my father's son. And in his rage, Henry hurled these accusations at Earl Raoul. Yet I think, deep down, the king still admired my father and wished him well. Finally a truce was called between the two, which continues until this day. But with the queen never was peace so made. That is why, although my father will never bear arms against the king, there is no reconciliation possible, and neither he nor Henry could wish their sons friends. Yet friends they are, brothers of the soul."

When he had been silent for a long while, I ventured to ask, "And how began that friendship between those sons?"

A third time he smiled. I think his words brought to life that castle far away, those meadowlands, that lake, of Sieux. "Prince Henry and Hue met hunting," he explained. "My brother loves to hunt, as you know, and it is Prince Henry's prime occupation, as it is for all Angevins. One autumn day, when the river was in spate, when the meadow flats on either side were waterlogged, Prince Henry came riding with his hawk along the boundary of his father's lands in the region called Maine, far from home, whilst on the other side of the river, on Sieux land, Hue hunted alone with one old huntsman and his hounds. Prince Henry had ridden fast and had lost his way. He had cast off his hawk and lost her as well, and angry with himself had come galloping across those drowned fields in a spray of mud. The falcon was his favorite. She sat on his wrist on a gold-embroidered glove, and the hood with which he covered her eyes was scarlet, with small, bright threads caught in a tuft on the top. From time to time he caught sight of her swooping down from the sky in a great burst of speed. He might have stopped to admire her skill and verve had not those glimpses urged him to redouble his efforts to catch up with her. In the end, outdistancing his own guards, he, too, rode alone, until he came to a place where the river branched into several twisting threads. These he forded or plunged through, the horse's haunches almost enmired, until the main river blocked his path. And on its far bank, the northern one, he espied his hawk, held by another boy like himself.

" 'Stop,' Hue shouted, for Hue it was, as the prince spurred on his horse. 'You trespass on the lands of Sieux.' He paused to stroke the bird's breast—you know the way he has—making clear he would claim her as his own, and in truth she sat on his naked wrist, something the prince would not dare allow. Beside Hue the old huntsman muttered and tried to tug at his master's sleeve, and his greyhounds panted on their leash.

"Prince Henry was furious. 'Sieux be damned,' he cried, 'I'll take back my hawk.' He rode breakneck into the stream. Although his horse was a fine bay with long, thin legs, bred for hunting in the river flats, it was not meant to swim, nor was it easy to control in a fast-flowing flood. Losing footing it began to panic and fought the current, almost unseating the prince. Hue watched the struggle for a while, curious, I think, about the boy who rode so fast and carelessly against him. But realizing that the horse was being swept downstream, where there were eddies and pools and sudden rocks that could dash both horse and rider to bits, Hue sprang off his own horse and, first giving the hawk to his huntsman, leapt into the river in his impetuous way. Hue knows how to swim, and the prince did not. Not many men do who live inland, but Hue had been trained at Cambray. He judged instinctively when to go with the current or when to fight; he was not afraid to dive; he knew how to hold his breath and how to flail with his arms and legs. In short, it was not difficult for him to seize the horse's head and by tugging at the bridle turn it athwart the stream. Within minutes, by dint of pull and tug, he had brought Prince Henry back to shore, on the southern shore, that is.

"The horse heaved itself out and stood trembling, its sides

dripping with gravel and mud, its crimson trappings scraped and torn. The prince, still mounted, panted, too, wiping the water from his eyes. On foot beside them, Hue shook himself like a dog and prepared to swim back. But the prince prevented him, seizing his arm and drawing his hunting knife. 'Now, by Saint Martin,' says he, threatening Hue with the knife, 'this is the southern bank, my father's lands. You have my hawk, but I have you.' For the first time they sized each other up. They might have gazed into a glass. Each saw himself in the other's face—same red hair, same dark eyes, same fair white skin. They were of the same height, both shivering in their hunting coats, both blue with cold.

" 'By the rood,' Hue said with a laugh. 'God's wounds, you are churlish, sir, to give no thanks. I should have let you drown.'

" 'And you, young sir.' The prince could be lordly in his turn. 'What makes you speak so bold? You've but one huntsman with you. Bid him bring my hawk across, and I'll let you free. If not, I've a score of men behind me somewhere, enough to cut you down if you try escape.'

"Now Hue had noted at once the richness of the prince's gear, his embroidered saddlecloth, his gold sword belt, all signs of nobility. And he noted, too, the way the prince spoke, his voice of command, for all that he was young. A curiosity took him afresh to know who this boy was. At the same time the prince was curious in his turn, used, I suppose, to flatterers and surprised at not being instantly recognized. When Hue sang out his name and rank, proudly enough, the prince was equally startled.

" 'Hue, son of the Count of Sieux,' he repeated with a frown. 'God's breath, your father's name is known to me.'

" 'What should you know of him?' Hue asked.

" 'Enough.' The prince was curt. Yet he sheathed his knife, clambered down from the high saddle that alone had kept him in place, and began to remove his short Angevin cloak. 'Enough. My father is Count of Maine.' He did not need to add the other titles his father has: Count of Anjou, Duke of Normandy and Aquitaine, Duke of Brittany, and King of England.

" '*Jesu.*' Even Hue was speechless. He was standing on one leg trying to take off his boot, and he limped to a boulder and sat down. 'Then you must be Harry Plantagenet.'

"So that is how they met, Prince Henry and Hue. The huntsman, muttering beneath his breath (for huntsmen do not much care for hawks, venery being their only charge), gingerly carrying the prince's bird and leading Hue's horse and hounds, rode off to find an easier ford. On a stretch of dry sand between the banks of reeds, the two boys lit a fire from driftwood and hung up their clothes to dry. When the prince's guard came galloping up, beside themselves with anxiety, they found both naked before the fire, enjoying a goose roasting merrily on a spit, while nearby the huntsman, equally concerned for Hue, struggled to keep their gear from being scorched.

"But afterward that huntsman is supposed to have said, being an old man and free of speech, 'Lord love us, but you're peas of a pod. Whichever count fathered you, I'd swear you came from the same bed.' A remark that Hue has never forgotten, just as he has never forgotten the prince. They met henceforth whenever they could, although their fathers bade them keep away. And when last they met, they met as men and even greater mischief wrought. Three years ago that meeting was, at Montmirail. Yet I myself think both fathers wrong to try to keep the sons apart. Such brothership between men is rare, and I suspect that in Earl Raoul's heart, as in the king's, there is regret that never between them will such a bond be known. And especially for the king is that true, for that is what he most wished to have."

So spoke Lord Robert that summer's day at Cambray. And I have never forgotten either what he said. His words made sense, although I could not have myself put the sense into words. For such a bond I myself envied, longed for, and yet was never destined to know.

He was silent after, done with his words. Yet I was often to think of them and ponder their meaning to myself. For now the fever took full hold, and as it mounted and flared, so in his delirium he let fall other secrets, which, although at the time I did not know all they meant, I have kept secret ever since. For sometimes Robert called upon his father to rescue him. And sometimes, too, upon that Isobelle de Boissert who wanted to wed Earl Raoul, and having failed at that, plotted against the Lady Ann and against her newborn son. "They said I was too young for remembering," once Robert panted out, suddenly sitting up and grasping at my tunic with his free hand, "but I remember everything." His eyes were open, but he did not see anything in the room, and his voice was taut with a horror that was visible only to him. "Never woman passes but I do recall: the sickly taste, the cloying smell, the redness of that mouth whose smile hid death. Women stole me away; women's malice used me for vengeance. Poison was the curse they put on me, poison was my death they planned."

And such was the hold of that memory, I say, that all the rest that had gone before seemed a child's nightmare. And in the days afterward, when we fought to save Robert's life, and when he, such was his strength, fought us so that we had to tie him to his bed, then came forth those dark shadows in full force. They haunted me as they haunted him. Then knew I what evil Lord Hue's accusations had set loose. And when at last my master slept, and all about us lay still, save for the crying of the gulls and the distant wash of the sea, I dared ask the Lady Olwen, who, turn and turn about with the Lady Ann, kept watch. "Lady, what happened then at Montmirail? What is Montmirail and where is it, that my master remembers it?"

"Montmirail." Lady Olwen repeated the name thoughtfully, her eyes dark. "Montmirail is a castled town on the border of King Henry's lands in Maine and the lands of the French king, not far from Sieux. Two kings met there in 1169. It was January, the start of a new year, the start, they said, of a new peace between King Henry and King Louis of France." Her soft voice was soothing to my ears, as perhaps it seemed to the sick man, although the tale she told was of war and deceit and how the French king resented Henry's strength and Henry's lands, which almost hemmed him round. Yearly, she said, the English king laid claim to more of France, until, like a stand of trees, France had been reduced to a central core, hacked away by woodcutters around the edge. Finally, to placate the French and display goodwill, Henry had agreed to meet at Montmirail and, to show King Louis he meant no harm, had offered to divide his lands among his sons, who would pledge allegiance for them to Louis as their overlord. "A subterfuge, this," she tried to explain, "as all men know. Henry had no intent of making his sons independent of him; quite the contrary, he used them as puppets to convince King Louis of good faith. Now Louis, they say, dislikes King Henry, the more that Henry did him once great wrong by marrying Eleanor, Duchess of Aquitaine, who hitherto had been Louis's own wife. But in many ways King Louis is said to be naïve, simple as a child when it comes to state affairs, never deciding what to do until the last and then immediately regretting his choice. They say he wanted to believe in Henry's peace because he felt he should, and despite his councillors' advice, he welcomed Henry full-heartedly, believing everything said by a king whose deviousness is a commonplace." And the Lady Olwen told me how King Henry, on the other hand, was confident he could easily hoodwink the French, remembering how he had managed the sack of Andely and despising Louis for a weakling. "For the sack had been a scandal and a disgrace," she said solemnly. "Henry, advised by his mother no less, allowed King Louis to recapture Andely, a town in France. Henry himself had occupied Andely first, and Louis was discouraged by constant defeat. As a sign of contempt, Henry withdrew his troops so that the French king could advance and claim a victory. No wonder Henry had little respect for his host at Montmirail; no wonder he thought he could outwit the French."

Robert stirred and moaned. When he was quiet again, Olwen went on. "Among those present at the gathering, Prince Henry, the Young King, as he is now called, was most conspicuous. He came reluctantly, being easily wearied of diplomacy, and found means at once to send a message to my brother, Hue, just as he did recently to Cambray. Princes have such means. My father being already at Montmirail, Hue claimed there was no one at home to forbid him, so he set out. But Hue certainly knew my father's wishes and hopes. For my father was at Montmirail in dual role. In England, as earl and warden of the marcher lands, he sits upon the king's great council and frequently is called for advice. As Count of Sieux in France, he attends King Louis in a similar way and often gives advice to him, the more so because Sieux is important to the French, acting as buffer state between Louis's territories, east, and Henry's lands, west and south. Since Sieux also serves as a gateway between Normandy and Henry's other lands in Anjou and Maine, you can understand its importance to King Henry, too.

"But my father hoped for peace at Montmirail; he wanted to persuade both kings to come to terms, mainly because their wars threatened Sieux's neutrality. And he himself, preserving the careful balance he has long maintained, did not commit himself to either side. The last thing he expected was for his sons to intrude, to change that balance of power or support one faction above the other. As Hue now did."

She sighed and shifted on the floor by Robert's bed.

"I think the prince sent word to Hue because, being bored, he wanted company pleasing to him," she continued, "and because, knowing as he must have done how his father was using him as a sop to Louis's pride, he craved friends who cared for him in his own right. As for Hue, I am sure he went with no other thought in mind but to see Prince Henry again. Attended only by the messenger, Hue rode in secret to Montmirail, passed the outposts without restraint, boldly, as if he had every right to be there, wearing our scarlet coat with the golden hawks as proudly as a prince himself. Our colors are well known; the guards let him through at once, and skirting the town, he went straight to where the English court was encamped in pavilions outside the walls. King Henry and his men were settled at one side of a vast spreading field below the castle of Montmirail (which, within a month, Henry was to purchase in defiance of its rightful owner, the Count of Blois, one of Louis's greater lords). The day was warm for January, and the prince and his retinue were seated at the pavilion door with the prince's wife and his younger brother Geoffrey, all three in silence on huge carved oak chairs. The prince was idly pulling his hound's ears, while his little wife tried in vain to think of something to amuse and Geoffrey sulked. You did not know Prince Henry was wed?

God's breath, he has been married since he was a child, against all laws of Church and state, to a French princess, Margaret, one of Louis's daughters by his second wife." (Not Eleanor's daughter, she hastened to add; King Louis had three times been wed, but only one wife, his third, had given him a son, although daughters he had in plenty from his other marriages.) "They say Prince Henry is fond of his little wife and treats her well, but he prefers hunting and fighting, and he prefers Hue's company most of all. His face lit up when Hue appeared. Hue reined back his horse, its sides and legs foam-flecked where he had ridden it hard.

" 'Greetings, my prince,' Hue cried, and saluted him. 'You sent for me, and here I am.'

" 'God's teeth.' The prince bounded to his feet and ran to meet his friend, all unbraced, his shirt sleeves untied. His air of listlessness was gone; he laughed up at Hue, and his red-gold hair blew free where he had snatched off his cap. They say he has a smile as open and candid as a child's. 'By the living cross, you are welcome as the buds in May.'

"Overcome with pleasure at the prince's greeting, Hue flung himself off his horse, and he and Henry hugged each other like the boys they were, although later the prince complained that Montmirail had made him old. Having to sit all day and hear his father and father-in-law discuss eternal love (all lies) and listen to Churchmen preach on the advantages of peace (not likely to last long) would age any man, he said. In any case he was overjoyed at Hue's prompt response. 'I thought they'd never let you free from Sieux,' he said. 'I thought your father had bolted you up.'

" 'Not come?' Hue cried in his extravagance, never thinking of consequence; comes a thought into his mind, he speaks. 'By the Mass, my lord prince, you might as soon look for my death or order it than I fail you when you ask. Here I am.' And he dropped down on his knees in the litter of beech leaves, thrust out his hands, and took the prince's between his own. 'I am yours. All that I have is yours, and Sieux is yours. Before God I pledge allegiance to you, to be your man. Blood oath I swear.' And before the prince could stop him, he drew his dagger, pushed up his sleeve, and cut through the skin so that the drops of blood rolled down his arm upon the ground.

" 'Get up, get up,' the prince urged him, embarrassed, looking around nervously. He knew that Hue's 'all' was a nothing and that Hue had no right to swear such an oath. Hue has no lands of his own, and certainly Sieux is not his to swear away. The prince, older and wiser, realized that and saw, too, how his courtiers whispered and nudged, a new scandal to fuel the gossip already spreading like wildfire. Yet thus was the oath sworn, out of love, and cannot now be forsworn.

"Thinking fast, the prince drew Hue up and, keeping an arm around his neck as a friend, led him inside the tent, without a word of explanation to the other courtiers. Inside, he and Hue stayed awhile, at first arguing, then breaking into laughter at some joke, the little Princess Margaret left alone, she and Prince Geoffrey trying to pretend nothing untoward was afoot, the others of the prince's retinue straining to hear what was being said. Presently the prince called for wine, ordered his new horse saddled, had his falconers bring out his new falcons for display. He and Hue mounted up and rode off with scarcely a backward glance, hunted all afternoon and well into the night, missed a feast, and were so missed themselves that a massive private quarrel arose between King Henry and the prince, which only an archbishop was able to restrain. Such was King Henry's rage that he clouted his son to the ground when next they met; no worse, I warrant you, than the Count of Sieux did with his sons. But Hue could not be gainsaid. 'Such a day,' he afterward maintained, 'such a hunt; and such a vow, well worth the stripes I got.' "

"And how do you know all this?" I asked my lady at the story's end. For I was curious, too, with youth's curiosity. I had not yet learned that watchers do not always learn what they want; knowing does not always bring content.

"How?" Lady Olwen repeated my question slowly, then answered it simply. "How? Robert told me. The hunting party almost ran him down. And the whipping Hue received," she added, "not half the one that my father ordered Robert, on the grounds that he, being older, should have shown more sense."

She looked aside as she caught my expression. "How?" she said. "Because Robert had come to Montmirail, too, to see Prince Richard, of course."

The force of that "of course" remains with me still. And so now I heard another name that day, one that all men were to repeat, of the Prince Richard, Henry's second son, the prince I was to come to know best and most dislike, when he in turn became king, the prince that Robert of Sieux was to follow to the end of the world. Strange, I suppose, when you think of it, that the younger brother should cleave to the older prince and the older brother to the younger one, but so it was, and the ties were made. And Robert's devotion to that younger prince no less, and in some ways more, than the bond between Prince Henry and Hue. *I can wait.* I remembered Robert saying that to his father. Now I learned what my master waited for and for whom, proof of his patience indeed. And proof, if proof I needed, of how his heart was taken and his allegiance sworn.

My lady began to explain. "Four sons Henry has; Prince Henry is the first, he whom Hue will serve and accompany as part of his entourage. The second is Richard, whom Robert longs to serve and would have joined in Poitiers had not he felt his duty here at Cambray. I do not like that prince myself, like to an ox, with gold-red hair and big bones, strong enough to rip a man's head off; sweet-tempered, they say, until he is crossed, then violent as his father is. The third son, Geoffrey, is a sneak. He told his father where Prince Henry went; he told my father that Robert was there. The fourth son is John, his father's favorite, as yet too young to want or hold land but one day craving it. Those younger princes bide with their mother in Aquitaine, who loves her second son best of all."

Olwen suddenly gave me a smile, her eyes bright with sympathy, as if she had guessed what effect her words had caused. I saw her hesitate, as if she did not wish to cause more pain, as if she knew talk of this bond between her older brother and the king's second son would mean that even with Lord Robert I could not stand first. But I outfaced her and bade her go on, pride hiding what grief there was. And so after a while she did.

"Richard and Robert had also arranged to meet at Montmirail," she said at last. "They planned to hunt as their brothers did. Robert has known Richard longer than Hue has known his prince, although they do not blare it for the world. Richard's greeting to Robert was less than Prince Henry's, no doubt, but the pleasure was not less. Extravagance may be for show; there is still true sentiment in things unsaid. 'There's a herd of deer outside Montmirail,' Richard told Robert when he rode in. He was already mounted himself, twitching at the bare tree branches with his riding whip. 'You're late, but I will race you for the biggest buck.' And when Robert asked him how things went: 'I've had my fill of statecraft. They've given me Aquitaine, which already was mine, since birth, by my mother's gift. And they've given me a princess to be a bride.' Robert said that Richard laughed then. 'Alice,' the prince cried, 'Alice, by God, sister to that Margaret, Henry's wife, so already my sister-in-law, and a more whey-faced pair of wenches I've yet to meet. God's bones, I'd sooner bed with a wet fish. Brother Geoffrey has been sitting whining all day that no one pays him so much heed, his betrothed still a babe-in-arms, years until she's grown, and only Brittany to come with her. At least my Alice is more of marriageable age, and she is a princess of France.' He laughed again. 'But incest somewhere, I'll be bound, and betrothal isn't a marriage bed. Thank God for Holy Mother Church. Some Churchman will sniff out an impediment to save me yet. I shan't get my head stuck in that noose. In truth, I prefer my boarhound to a wife, clinging around my neck with a pack of wet-bottomed brats. And you, sweet friend' (for in private, when he is alone, they say, the prince speaks as affectionate as any maid), 'to serve as testimony to that, seeing you dislike womankind as much as I.'

"Off they went hunting then—the woods at Montmirail are famous for game—but being more circumspect than their brothers, they returned in time and heard the outcry when King Henry discovered his namesake was gone. Not that the king really cared, you understand; the whole performance was just a show, peace talk, oath-swearing, marriage treaty, son-beating, and all, to persuade the poor French king that Henry's sons were loyal allies. You see what games were played at Montmirail: King Louis convulsed with envy of King Henry for taking his lands, for taking his wife, for having four great sons by her; and King Henry expansive, overloud, trying to convince Louis of his friendship and loyalty, a lion persuading a jackal to dine. No wonder Prince Richard, too, was weary of the farce. Robert said Richard scarcely spoke to anyone, ate and drank a lot, belched mightily in the face of a French priest (for to avoid being seen, they sat at table, far from the kings, below the salt). Before the feasting's end Richard had dragged Robert off to listen in private to his latest troubadour, songs that we should not try to understand and you should not imitate even if you could. Robert was in disguise, you see, wearing a pilgrim's cloak with hood and shawl, not out of fear but to avoid unpleasantness, unlike Hue, who had blazed forth like a beacon in his finery.

"Now God alone knows where Hue and Prince Henry went that day or what they did that night, but come sunrise, when all the camp was still abed, the prince, having sent Hue back to Sieux, thank God, returned alone but drunk, reeling in his saddle with the haunches of a fat deer draped behind. He tossed the head with its branching horns to the startled guards as he rode through. 'Fit those horns on the newest cuckold,' he cried, and on reaching the center of the field, swaying in his saddle like a ship at sea, he began to bellow out a scurrilous love song like to match with anything Richard's troubadours could produce. Afterward he claimed he sang to please his wife; poor soul, I hope she never heard a word. But since Robert told me it was a song about a monk, thrice wed, whose third wife kept him on a leading rein, there was soon no doubt he meant it as a satire against the French king, whose nickname is 'Monk' and whose third wife is noted for her managing ways.

"At the end—God knows how he kept words and tune in mind—the prince laughed. 'I'm back,' he cried to the world. 'Here is the Prince of England returned, your future king. Where is your welcome for a king?'

"By then the French and English camps were both aroused and humming with intrigue. Men came flocking out to see the sport; so did Robert himself; so did the courtiers, whispering agitatedly, all news, they say, filtering first through their ears, their love of gossip being counted cause of many of our present woes. The prince's voice rose to a peevish note, loud enough to ensure there was no mistake, like to wake everyone from the dead, including the two royal kings. 'Henry the Younger am I, one day England's king, already proclaimed Duke of Normandy, Count of Maine, Count of Anjou and Touraine, overlord of Brittany, which I gladly deed to brother Geoffrey to cure his sulks, and Duke of Aquitaine by rights, although brother Richard's already set his foot on it, and now promised the service of the young Count of Sieux—by God, almost all of France. So why am I here, to do allegiance for what is mine? Rather I think King Louis should bow down to me!' "

She paused again to let me consider her words. "A scandal, then, of the gravest kind," she said, "threatening to undo all of Henry's work, certainly guaranteed to rouse all of King Louis's fears, and certainly no way to hush the matter up. King Henry, who is usually afoot before the dawn, lay abed, pretending to know nothing of the affair, while Louis's spies ran back and forth like ants, carrying tidbits of bad news. But when King Henry met his contrite son (for sober, the prince was abashed to hear what drink had claimed for him), Henry did not pause for speech, simply knocked him down, mad with rage."

Again she paused. "So that was how Montmirail came to an end," she said. "Robert rode away, not even bothering to hide what had been so publicly shown. After him, in a towering fury, came my father, thundering in pursuit. He brought both Hue and Robert away from Sieux, out of harm, then left them here at Cambray and tried to stop their meeting with the Angevin princes again."

Her words stretched into a silence that seemed to encompass the world. Almost without meaning to I found myself whispering, "Is the king's vengeance done? Cannot peace be made between us and them?"

She sighed, leaned back against her brother's bed, stretching wearily, spoke softly not to disturb.

"I cannot tell you that." Her reply was bleak. "It is not spoken of. Myself, I think it like to the mutterings of a storm heard a long way off, sometimes loud, sometimes soft, always there, underneath, the more bitter that our affairs have prospered. In France is my father equal to King Henry in that both hold lands of the French king, and never has Henry made a second move to harm our estates at Sieux. In England my father is bound to Henry as his overlord for the lands of Sedgemont and Cambray, although once in grief he repudiated them and threw away his title and rank. He took them back only because King Henry begged. I do not think Henry would dare harm him, yet my father is vassal to him." So spoke my soft-voiced lady, who in so short a while had grown to womanhood. Although her voice was gentle, her words were hard, harder because that night she gentler seemed. "But I think we are at the start of some enter-prise that may, in the end, destroy us all. Vengeance is like a poison, too, seeping underground, puddled where you least expect. King Henry has already killed an archbishop; he has murdered three Celtic princes to get his way; who knows what else his anger will do. Urien, you have changed your life for one that, in time, you may come to hate. We, too, are but pawns in the affairs of great men; they do with us what they will. But if you would survive, you should know this Henry and his sons, who one day will rule our world. Yea, I could wish my father wrong. Like Robert, I would not have old griefs rise. Yet they do, at every turn."

"And the queen, is her malice done?" Again I found I was whispering.

Lady Olwen shrugged. "She also has quarreled with the king and now lives apart from him," she said. "They say that when she discovered who the king's last mistress was, the Fair Ros-amund, she had her poisoned in her nunnery at Godstow. Poison is her weapon, they say, poisoned words or poisoned knife, what matter the method if she achieve her end."

Olwen put her lips to my ear, my lady who had never known evil or thought of it. "They say these Angevins are devil's brood. An ancestress of theirs, married to a count of Anjou, was proved a witch. A perfect wife she seemed, hating but one thing, to go to church. Urged by his councillors, the count ordered her to celebrate Mass, and when she tried to leave he had the doors barred by his men. She gave a great scream and, sprouting wings, flew out the window, never to return. They say her devilry has left its mark in the Angevin rage, which, in full spate, can drive a man to devil's work. And we—my brothers, that is—are bound to the Angevin by some bond, some allegiance, which I cannot explain. Call it fate or the will of God, but I myself think it born of the devil, too."

So there it was, all revealed, what I should not have known and did not want to know. Murder, poison, vengeance, these were things I had not looked to find. Yet, in truth, they were to be my destiny. For is it not writ in the Holy Book, let no man turn aside from what he has set his hand upon? Better death, I think, than such dishonor. And as the lords I served believed, so I, in my humble way, would follow them.

Chapter 5

ow while Lord Robert lay abed, some days seeming on the mend, others sunk to fever's lethargy, I would not have you think that all was despair. Looking back, in some ways I count this time as the happiest of my life. For once Lord Robert's convalescence was assured, though long, then had I free access to the people I most admired; and although there is no doubt they thought less of me than I of them, that did not change my state of mind. The Lady Ann departed at last to join her noble husband at Sedgemont; and since after a while Lord Gervaise came no more, for whatever cause, then in truth I could pretend I had the Lady Olwen to myself. Nor were absent friends forgot. News often came to us of Hue, how he was brought to Winchester to see a king's son crowned, the new Archbishop of Canterbury rendering that service, and the prince's wife being crowned with him. We heard of the improvements to the palace, long needed, for in Stephen's reign all of the royal residences had fallen into disrepair, the worse since Stephen's mercenaries had been quartered therein and had refused to move. The changes Henry made were the wonder of his time. There were even privies, set apart and carefully screened, and decorations on the state room walls, whose colors glowed with blues and greens. One painting afterward all men marveled at, that of the eagle harried by its young, their cruel beaks tearing the parent flesh. In future, men were to point at it and exclaim, "So are prophecies made truth

by time." And there at Winchester had Hue his wish granted,
his father knighting him, himself handing Hue the sword and
awarding him the accolade, no light tap upon his back but a
full buffet that sent the new knight asprawl, perhaps to remind
Hue again of all that knighting meant: not only war and warlike
deeds but obedience to his overlord, honor, and deference to
all men. And they say that Hue, scrambling awkwardly to his
feet, seized his father's hand and kissed it as token of his respect.
Knighted, then, reconciled with his father, who clasped him to
his breast in one last gesture of affection, and as part of Prince
Henry's household, Hue set sail for France, close friend of the
prince and companion in his future wanderings. Earl Raoul
returned to Sedgemont, joined there in time by the Lady Ann,
and thither were we to go ourselves come Michaelmas.

As for Prince Taliesin, neither was he forgot. For often I
sensed an air of expectancy in the Lady Olwen, as if daily she
hoped for news. And in later years they tell how that prince
and his men rode swiftly on from the pass after his parting with
us and came again at length to his father's principality, where,
in a fortress along the northern coast, the old man awaited him.
They say his father sat alone in an empty hall and greeted him.
A tall man the father was, bent forward in his great carved
throne, the skin on his face stretched thin across his high cheekbones, his gray-black hair grown long; but his eyes, dark blue
beneath their heavy frown, were bright with urgency. Four
sons he had once had, as did King Henry, who had killed the
oldest three. Now this one returned, his last born, his heart-
strings. Yet when he had heard his son relate the story of his
journey to Cambray, the old man, without a word, at the end,
merely raised his hand and pointed with his finger, east again.
As his father commanded, so Prince Taliesin must travel out
on vengeance's quest.

We were sitting, as was our wont, in the great hall at Cambray, and I was whiling away the hours of enforced inactivity
(for Lord Robert had not yet back his strength) by singing him
Welsh songs, which he and the Lady Olwen liked. He, in turn,
was teaching me Norman ones (although mine, I swear, were
more seemly for a noble house) when there came a clattering

at our gates. It was the lords of Walran, father and son, well armed, stern-faced beneath their helmets, weighted down as if by some mighty care. They came, of course, as friends, and we let them in but marveled at their warlike state and their air of anxious importance.

Lord Odo of Walran, father to Gervaise, swung himself off his horse heavily and strode toward the keep, his Norman sword swinging at his hip, his spurs grating on the stone stairs. Beside him, Gervaise, equally armed, almost ran to stay in step. And whereas in former days Gervaise had a smile for everyone, now, perhaps showing himself in more true light, he and his father shouldered a path through, without a by-your-leave, as if a thousand enemies were at their heels.

"Save you, Lord Robert." At least Lord Odo had the courtesy to greet my lord, although he did not wait to let the guard bawl out his name, merely pushed his way toward the fire, where Robert lay upon a couch. "Nay, sit you still, lad," he added patronizingly as Robert struggled to his feet. "No ceremony, I beg, lie back. I've come on border affairs, and it's an ill wind that finds your father gone and you still abed."

"Save you, my lord." Robert's greeting was also courteous, and he smiled at Gervaise as if to say, "Where have you been?" But by now I knew him well enough to catch the keen look he gave both lords and the almost imperceptible nod of caution to our men to take cloaks and swords, to serve wine and bring forth stools, all courtesies such as a lord makes for his guests. He had noticed, as did we all, how beneath their cloaks they and their men, crowding after them, wore full mail and, despite custom, did not render up their swords. Even Gervaise kept his sword belt on, although he had removed his helmet and thrown back his coif. Usually when he came to Cambray, he was decked out in new clothes, each time another embroidered shirt or coat to flaunt—he must have kept his mother's maids stitching day and night. But now he was plainly dressed in soldier's gear, and he scraped his feet in their boots and spurs and looked at the floor as if abashed, prodding at the rushes with his scabbard point. Yet I must admit he looked well in soldier's mail, better than in his velvet robes, his blond hair well curled, his shoulders broad in their hauberk of the latest style, made of fine chain linked together like a net of scales, hanging low about his knees. But he let his father talk, proof again if proof were needed that this was not a social visit, the more so that Lady Olwen and her maids were seated in the hall with us.

"I am glad, Lord Robert," Lord Odo of Walran was continuing, "that your father at least left Cambray well garrisoned. We shall need trained men. I am come to bring you warning, if you have not yet so heard. The cub of Afron is on the march. They say he is already heading south, gathering up malcontents to swell his troops; all of Wales up in arms, flocking to join his army's ranks. They say he will cross the border here, to march against King Henry's court. They say he plans to let the Welsh dragon loose."

There was a gasp, part surprise, part alarm. And part, I think, some other thing. A border castle is full of half-breeds. Some might have been there that day who, although loyal to their Norman lords, although well aware of the danger, would feel a twinge of pride that free Celts could so arm and could so rise. There might have been those, and such I confess was I, who thrilled to the image of a Celtic warlord on the march. Perhaps Lord Odo thought of that. His eyes narrowed, and his voice grew harsh. "The Celts last rose in sixty-five," he said. "You were too young, my lord, to have taken part, and your father was not even here. But we took part. No border castle was safe. Like locusts the Celts swarmed over our boundaries and walls. That year marked King Henry's second invasion of Wales, a bigger disaster than his first, eight years before. And in the first, I think, your father was engaged. He may not speak of it, but he will remember, as do other men, how he rescued the king from a Welsh ambush. We will lack his presence this time."

There was a hush. Lord Odo had blundered upon things better left unsaid, of which even Robert had not spoken, how the earl had been constrained to fight for King Henry against the Welsh and how, to his own risk, he had saved Henry's life. Aware of his mistake, the Lord of Walran hastened on. "No need to be caught like sitting ducks. I suggest we seize opportunity whilst we can. No sense in giving them advantage of attack; attack first. Advance across the border with all your men and mine. Hit them where they are most vulnerable."

Lord Robert eyed Lord Odo in his thoughtful way. "We have a treaty with the Celts," he said after a while. "Let us not be overhasty, my lord. It may well be that Prince Taliesin will not raise as large an army as you fear. It may well be he means no harm, merely seeks a passage through. In any case, in these last years King Henry has made overtures to the Welsh, especially since his Irish campaign. The Prince of Powys has already sworn a peace; the Prince of Rhys has already agreed to act as Henry's justiciar. Moreover, Henry has recently returned other hostages without harm. It strikes me that these gestures of peace will count more than ancient grievances."

Lord Odo of Walran heard him out impatiently, biting his lip and, like his son, fidgeting with his sword. "That may be so," he burst out. "The workings of the Celtic mind are not my concern, nor do I claim to understand what they might feel. But I do understand what they are capable of. You, Lord Robert, are too young, but there are Norman barons in plenty who, to their cost, can tally up their losses in that last campaign, when Olwain of the North and his men stormed our border in a rampage of loot and rape, killing, burning, and plundering. Thrice did he cross to our despite. No castle was safe from him, no Norman knight, no Norman wife. I do not speak to afright, you understand," he said, turning a little to where the Lady Olwen still kept her place, "but we marcher lords will bear the brunt. We do not intend to let invasion come while we sit idly by."

This time it was Dylan who answered, stepping out and making a gesture for silence. Old as he was, slow-footed, ponderous, when he spoke, there were years of experience in his voice. "Cambray has never shirked its duty," he said. "Since it was built have I served its lords. Their care, and thus the care of all men who serve them, is to guard the border and hold it firm. But, my lords, that treaty was agreed to in fitting way, made between the earl and Olwain of the North, swearing that neither side will cross the border in warlike array. If we break a treaty so signed, what should the Celts do in return? I agree with Lord Robert that the Celtic princes will not jeopardize a treaty they themselves sought." And there was a murmur of agreement from our men.

But still Lord Odo was not satisfied. His voice rose a notch. "Olwain of the North is dead," he cried. "His heirs dispute their inheritance; Wales lacks for leadership. Perhaps this Prince Taliesin has visions of filling the void. More to the point, did not your father recently receive this prince? What passed between them no man knows, nor what the prince came for or what he got. But if Cambray was to be spared, what guarantee was given that we should be spared likewise?" He paused to let that remark sink in. There was a rumble from our men, more open this time, and hearing it the lords of Walran backed a little toward their own men, closing ranks, so that they stood together in a compact group.

"It may well be," Lord Odo said, more conciliatory now, "that you think Cambray strong enough to resist attack. I hope you are right. But only a fool, I think, would trust a Celtic treaty, Celtic made and signed. I do not intend to be so foolish as to let them trespass without constraint. Tell the Celts so, and bid them be warned. One foot on my lands, then let them look for vengeance; first I claim my own. And those who survive I hang from my battlements, food for crows and kites."

Lady Olwen could not contain herself a moment more. She sprang to her feet, her eyes glowing, her cheeks flame-red. "I think," she cried, "there has been talk enough of hanging; was not a hanging the cause of Prince Taliesin's coming in the first place? Even you, my Lord of Walran, must admit he and his family were ill-used."

Lord Odo took another step back. "God's blood," he said, staring at her with his prominent eyes, "but you speak loud for a maid. Were I your father . . ." But recollecting, no doubt, who her father was and that he and his son hoped to make her welcome in his household one day, he swallowed hard and answered more softly, "Lady Olwen, these be not doll knights, playing with swords, but vermin, wild as wolves, trained since birth to treachery and attack. And burning hot for revenge."

"You believe then, my lord," Robert's voice was smooth,

"that revenge is a possibility? You claim it, I think, for yourself. You admit, perhaps, Prince Taliesin has some justice to his claim?"

"Justice, justice," Lord Odo began to splutter. "I know what Celtic justice means. I know what rights King Henry evoked and what those varlets forced him to. And I know, my lord," one last thrust this, his voice like steel, "that your mother is of their kin. Perhaps you think to keep Cambray safe because of her?" There was an open shout of outrage. I saw how several of our men shifted feet to give themselves room, whilst others eyed the distance to the walls where, by tradition, the weapons of Cambray hang. The castle guard at Cambray is half Celt, but to challenge the honor of their Norman lords is a direct insult, one to be repaid in blood.

"No offense, no offense," Lord Odo hastily insisted. "Take no umbrage, my lord. But were I in your place, wounded, my father gone, I'd look for help wherever I could. Your father fights left-handed, I am told, 'Two-Handed Raoul' his nickname. But you, my lord, lack that gift. . . ."

"I seem to lack several qualities." Lord Robert's voice was low, almost pleasant, but beneath I sensed anger, running like a riptide. "Or so you have now reminded me, with distressing frequency. Age, I think you said, and wits, added now the inability to fight. Three lacks, enough to undo any man."

"Now, now, no cause for alarm." Lord Odo began himself to be seriously alarmed. "I came but to offer advice and help."

"Which we will ask for when we need. Young or not, I know my father's mind. I know our responsibility for the treaty made. I will not attack the Celts unless they invade in full force, and then I fight only to defend. But I swear they will not cross our lands."

"Then on your head be that oath," Lord Odo cried. His hard slate eyes glared around defiantly, and for a moment I sensed a flash of hatred, distrust, envy, perhaps, quickly disguised. "But plenty of Norman barons think as I do. And as your father is warden of the marcher lands, then make sure his protection covers us. If not, we take the laws into our own hands."

To give substance to his haste, he snatched at his cloak, slung it around his shoulders without even bidding anyone farewell, and went stamping down the steps as roughly as he had come in, his men behind. His son hesitated for a second, glancing from his father's retreating back to the Lady Olwen's, for she had turned away after her remark, perhaps regretting it. A faint blush crept into Lord Gervaise's cheeks. For the first time I saw how alike he and his father were, Norman-eyed, broad-shouldered, and fair, both square-jawed and determined, fixed to some belief of their superiority that would dominate all their further lives. In the older man that narrowness of thought had turned to bigotry. I remember thinking that one day, in his age, Lord Gervaise would be his father's self renewed, and the thought disheartened me, not just another son inheriting all his father's lands and rank, but becoming heir, as well, to all his father's prejudice. Yet he spoke out boldly enough, although the Lady Olwen would not look at him.

"Lady Olwen," he began, "in truth my father came to wish you well and offer help. Especially in your father's absence—"

She rounded on him soundly. "Get you gone," she cried. "My brother cares for me. Seek out your Norman vengeance and call it justice if you will. I am glad to be part Celt. What treachery is here lies not with them." He could not blush redder, for he was caught between pleasing her and angering his father, not a choice he much enjoyed. Yet in the end it was his Norman thoroughness that prevailed; he revealed for a moment another side of himself, not the affable one he wanted us to know but something harder. Yet he still spoke well and certainly more courteously than his father had.

"I cannot be other than I am," he told her simply. "My father orders me. The words are his, but I concur; a Celtic band of wild scavengers is no sight for a lady fair. I would not have you harmed." But she had turned her head aside again and would not reply.

Down in the courtyard Lord Odo had snatched at his reins and with a Norman curse was hauling himself up into the saddle, wrenching around his horse's head, making straight for home. He roared for his son, who, after a moment's hesitation, left as well, running quickly down the stairs to mount and ride. And in the great hall at Cambray we looked at one another in consternation and fear.

Lord Robert had paled with effort, scarce able to stand, yet he had dragged himself to his feet and was leaning upright against the chimney, staring back at us.

"God's wounds," he swore, "bad news spreads like brushfire. My father hoped Prince Taliesin would have been distracted long since, before these border lords had frightened themselves into fits, but I see it is too late. Taliesin will be as tenacious as his father, who all these years has nursed his hatred in silence. Well, by the rood, 'tis true the prince asked my father—no, not asked, told, bold as brass—what he planned; that is, getting no help from Cambray, he would go direct to the king to make his demand. And in return my father told him what Cambray would do. And now that blustering idiot has made me swear the same, no Celt to cross our land when armed. Dylan, what for advice?"

Dylan came up to him, looking intently into the fire with his small Celtic eyes, as dark and glittering as a snake. He said, "Lord Odo is wrong but dangerous. If we do not turn Prince Taliesin somehow, he will. And a Welsh prince's death, however caused, even if he himself courts it, will undo that treaty faster than if the wind blew it away. Prince Taliesin's father is old, implacable, and he craves vengeance as a starving man craves meat, risking all, even his only surviving son. If that son dies, then the Celts, in truth, will have a cause. By contrast, Taliesin's little army may seem but a friendly expedition sent to pass the time of day."

"Then," Robert's voice was resolute, "a way must be found to stop the prince."

"My lord." Dylan also spoke briskly; for once he moved like a younger man, light on his toes; I think this appeal for help had rallied him. "A way shall be made, I swear. In the meanwhile, send forth the watch, guard the boundary to keep Prince Taliesin's men hemmed in and to stop Lord Odo's men from spilling out."

Before the day was over was this done: men thundering out

of Cambray gates, the watch within the castle on alert, warning given to neighboring villages and outlying farms, patrols ordered to scout the boundary length, north and south. But Robert, who scarce could stand and certainly could not ride, sat by the fire and beat with his good fist against the wall. "By Christ," he said at last, and suddenly he did sound young and vulnerable, "by Christ's holy wounds he bore for us, I tell you I cannot find it in my heart to hate a man who acts because he must. Nor can I wish to bury him because he avenges his own brothers' deaths. But my father and I are pledged to keep a peace. Prince Taliesin cannot cross our land." There was a misery in his voice, too, to make me sympathize; so do great lords pledge oaths to keep or break, either like to bring equal harm. For it was clear to me, and to us all, that my lord would not budge an inch from his stand. And if, as by all accounts, Prince Taliesin would not either, then stubbornness would clash with like stubbornness, head on. And at our backs the lords of Walran were poised to strike if we failed. No way out, then, for anyone, unless a quick solution be found.

So while all things at Cambray were battened down against attack, we pondered the impasse, arguing first this way, then that. Often Lord Robert and Dylan, deep in talk, disputed vehemently, without success. There were men who pointed out that Wales was large, a coastline dotted with good ports, a border running for many miles—why would there be a forced passage here at Cambray? The answer to that question, too, was known: the other princes had closed their lands or refused access to the sea; no support from them. And the choice of Cambray was a simple one; because the prince's intentions had been already told to us. No underhanded treachery here, no secrecy, simply the execution of a plan the prince had decided on, a determination, direct and hard. So with no time to seek advice from the earl at Sedgemont, with little hope of reaching a compromise, although all men hoped for one, we spared no pains to make ready in case of need.

The inner courtyards were stripped bare so men could run and climb the outer walls with ease. Armorers made their anvils ring as swords and helmets, not used in a score of years, were cleaned of rust and hammered straight. Space was made in the outer courtyard for villagers who, with their flocks and herds, soon came streaming off the moors seeking refuge in anticipation of the Celtic hordes. Every day women and children gathered up whatever grass could be found and wisp by wisp cut and tied it for foddering. What was left of the harvest was carefully guarded, to be put to the torch rather than let an enemy get it. Fishermen, surly Irishmen, were coaxed to launch their boats through the surf; salt fish makes good siege rations. But in truth a siege of Cambray's walls was not expected. Lord Odo at least knew Celtic tactics well; they take, devour, and pass on, not having in their strategy the patience or the skill to sit out a siege. But the danger of sudden attack was real, and against that danger Cambray prepared.

The early days of September continued hot. Hourly, it seemed, we scanned those dusty hills, and every morning safe we counted a day's more grace. But Celts can come like shadows, drifting in the night. And every day Lord Robert drove himself, back and forth across the great hall, willing his strength to return, until, dripping with sweat, exhausted, he was forced to rest. Sometimes he used me as a staff, I being just enough shorter that he could lean on me, back and forth, yet he could not use his arm nor wear his mail. And the first time he mounted his horse seemed like to be his last. But I could tell that as he paced up and down, so did his thoughts.

Meanwhile, too, the Lady Olwen watched, veering from joy to grief like an April day. Sometimes she thought that Taliesin would come and wept at the danger to him; sometimes she thought that he would not and smiled before remembering that then she would not see him again. And so it was that she was among the first to learn our wait was done. Although in truth all men could see the great pillars of smoke rising from the bonfires; the watch beacons standing ready these many years were now kindled to give alarm. And presently the outer guards came crying back, shouting their tidings even before they reached the gates. I myself had been keeping watch on the castle wall, on the seaward side, where the walk is narrow, scarce room enough for two men to pass, and the wall strikes down into the cliffs, stone and rock becoming one. Between the crenellations I could see the horizon's dip, where sea and sky become one, too. Both now were tinged with red, red sky for sign of alarm; and where the tide was out, the little line of boats bobbed gently against the jetty stones, built in recent years by the fisherfolk. I was playing softly to myself upon my pipe, the thin notes dropping like birds' songs in the translucent air, when I heard my lady coming along the inner walk. I have never known anyone so quick, so light, dressed now in her oldest clothes, which I thought she had put aside, her bare feet slipped into wooden clogs, her hair unbound like a servant girl's. The tears were running down her face, but she made no attempt to brush them away.

"They are coming," she cried, no need to say who the "they" was. "Robert's watch has brought the proof. Mostly foot soldiers, running fast; bowmen with their arrows notched, moving at a steady pace toward the pass." She paused for breath. "And Robert," she cried, "even now mounting up, sworn to lead out our men himself. Mother of God, they'll have to tie him on. And Dylan, like a block of wood, bowed to fate, no sense to him." She cried again, "It will be death for both, Norman and Celt. Either Robert or Taliesin will kill the other, or passing us, the prince will hurl himself upon Walran spears, already massed upon our eastern line. God save us from the villainy of honest men who will drag the world into its grave for faith.

"I tried to stop Robert," she cried out a third time. "I ran to Robert and pulled at his sleeve. I have never heard him speak like that before. 'Get you gone,' he told me; even his voice has changed, older, like flint. 'This is no time for you. I have no quarrel with the Celts, but Taliesin will not trespass upon my lands. I ride at dawn.' Mother of God," she cried, and now I knew she did not talk to me, had perhaps forgotten that I was there, such was the look upon her face, the tone in her voice. "I'll give him up; I'll close my eyes and never gaze upon him again; I'll shut myself into a nunnery, if only he and Robert will not fight." And there was no need to explain who that "he" was.

"Not even an army," she said after a while, crouching beside me in her familiar way. The twilight had come full upon us now. The bats swooped in and out of the cliffs; the line of foam where the waves were curled spread like silver threads across the bay. "Just a ragtag bundle of men, coming from nowhere, going nowhere, peddlers at a country fair, looking for a vengeance they will never get. Christ's wounds, were I a man to stand in Robert's place, I would find a way to turn them back." I had laid my pipe aside and was looking at her in the concealing dark as I never dared to face to face. For I had learned by now to endure not looking at her. I was older now; God forgive me, I had begun to shield myself for pride. Yet even in this dangerous time I took advantage of the chance. Her face was wan, tear-stained. More than ever she resembled the flower for which she had been named, its delicate blossoms spilled like stars for the winds to buffet. Back and forth she was blown, torn between her hopes and dread, torn between her sisterly care and her growing love. Yet her namesake plant is tenacious, too, clinging to the crevices of rocks, creeping over the roughest ground. Beneath her fragility was a gritted courage typical of her house, her inheritance, perhaps, from that first dour Norman lord who had had the will to carve his lands out of this wild western moor, who had won and loved a Celtic wife. Behind our backs the vast immensity of the ocean stirred as gently as a millpond. Presently there would be a moon, the large harvest moon in the autumn night, when the darkness would begin to race to dawn. And with the sunrise Lord Robert would lead out his men. I said slowly, the words forced out of me, like the songs I sing, not knowing whence they come, not knowing myself what they mean, "If not by land, then by sea."

Her hand, shaking me, pulling at my hair, brought me back. "What did you say?" She was crying in my ear and tugging at my sleeve as she had tugged at her brother's. "What did you say?" I stared at her bemused, not sure I had said anything.

"Sweet *Jesu*," she cried. She threw her arms about my neck. "Sweet *Jesu* be praised. By sea, he said." I felt vitality rise in her like sap. She was gesturing over the castle walls to where the fishing smacks bobbed on their ropes in the gentle surf. "Those Irish coracles have carried Celts throughout the world, have taken them beyond the edge of our universe to the ocean's rim. Missionaries, pirates, warlords have sailed in them. So shall Prince Taliesin."

"You'd never get an army afloat," I began to argue weakly, marveling how her thoughts had leapt ahead; she was always quicker than I was, sure of herself, when her mind was made up.

"Duke William of Normandy did," she argued back. "Horses and all he brought when he conquered England. But Taliesin can get the horses he will need on the farther shore. What we need now are fishermen willing to help them escape, gold to buy new steeds. And someone to persuade them to it."

She snatched up her skirts, jumped up, poised to run. I followed her down the steep winding stairs into the inner yard, where men were hurrying back and forth, and women were wringing their hands. Up more steps to the great hall, empty now, and up again to the women's quarters above. I had never been there before and watched in amazement as she scattered rugs and trappings on the floor, pulled open the massive wooden chests with their iron locks. Inside were clothes and jewels and other gear, which she threw aside in careless heaps until she found what she was looking for, the bags of coins, small and heavy, that formed the treasury of Cambray. She looped them around her waist, under her cloak, and stood up. "That for bribes," she said, "and horses' hire. Now who shall speak for us?"

"Dylan might," I said slowly, for while she had worked I had leaned against the door, trying to concentrate. I have never forgotten that moment: the streaks of moonlight against the stone floors, the Lady Olwen a crouched shadow beyond, the distant sound of the sea suddenly clear, and in the courtyard below the mounting hubbub of alarm. And I, like a sentinel, set to watch and observe. She looked up at me, her eyes moon-caught, her hair almost golden in its light. "Urien the Bard," she almost whispered, "this time your words have saved us all."

So down again those winding steps; across the night-dark hall, where usually by this hour all would have been drowned in sleep; down into the courtyard, bright as day. All seemed

confusion, yet, in fact, as military arrangements go, the organization was well done. Patrols were riding out and riding in;
the great gates open to let them pass, to let in the villagers who
straggled along with their goods in tow, women and children
scuttling crablike, their men stern-faced, armed with rakes and
forks that, before the night was done, would be exchanged for
knives or bows. Horses were being saddled and fed, the gray
stallions of Cambray prepared for battle; serfs thudded back and
forth trailing saddles, buckets, gear. Tired men swore and shouted,
weary grooms sweated as at midday, and in their midst Lord
Robert sat, waiting in his saddle, as contained and still as he
had been the day of Hue's hunt.

Dylan was at one side, arms crossed, his lined face, for a
moment caught off guard, drawn with weariness and concern.
He wore his old mail coat, leather-stitched, that had seen him
through a score of years, and his old border sword, its leather
strap worn and ridged but like himself worthy still, serviceable.
Even his helmet was old, a Norman helmet with its conical
shape and nasal guard, but his eyes were alert, and from time
to time he raised his head as does an old hunting hound, scenting
out the wind. Now, as I have often explained, I avoided the
seneschal of Cambray whenever I could, and of all men at
Cambray I most feared him. My blood could run cold just to
imagine facing him, with his tight-drawn face and knowing
eyes. But I, too, gritted my teeth and came on.

"The Irish fisherfolk are rough," I whispered to my lady as
we waited for the best time to approach, "but they are loyal to
their home." And as I spoke, suddenly, all these words I had
been thinking fell into pattern to make them clear. And the
thoughts that I had been fumbling with revealed themselves,
not vaguely possible but real. "These past two years King Henry
has been abroad in Ireland making war. Tell them that; show
them how Prince Taliesin will avenge their country, too, and
you have won them to your will. When their boats are in place,
then let Dylan persuade Lord Robert and the prince."

She looked at me, awed, I think, that for the first time I spoke
with authority. I tell you, I was awed myself. By now a groom

was leading up Dylan's horse. With an old soldier's caution he had stooped to tighten the girth straps, check all was in place. But he moved slowly, no heart in him.

"Now," I said. Together the Lady Olwen and I slipped through the crowd and came up to him. He straightened, saluted my lady in his old-fashioned way. "This is no place for you." He echoed her brother's words and shot a look of distrust at me. I let her speak. It was strange to hear her eagerness spilled out for him, and I was suddenly afraid for her, small and vulnerable in this world of men. I saw Dylan's dark eyes turn as he raked me with his brooding look. But I did not flinch, although another day, another time, had he cast such a look, I already would have taken to my heels. When she was through, Dylan softly said, "Well," and reached out his gnarled hands and jerked me clear, into the light where a torch flared and dripped upon the wall. "Well, well, Urien the Bard, by all the saints. I never thought to see you of worth." He almost gave a grin, showing blackened teeth. "Urien the soothsayer now, hotfooted after prophecy. What says Cambray's oracle? Or is it," and his grip hardened, biting into flesh, the grin quite gone, the hands rough and hard, "or is it some madman's trick you think to cram my lady with? Time's awasting, boy, what fool's plan?" And there was that to his tone to make me realize, if I had not before, that this, in turn, was no child's game, and death on guard, and so would he treat me accordingly if my arguments did not convince.

I said, "My lord," a salutation he does not merit, but which, at least, would mollify. "Lord Robert has sworn one oath, and Prince Taliesin one, and neither will be forsworn. I suggest an alternative. Let the prince take the old pilgrims' way, which the Church fathers took centuries ago. South they went, then west, carrying God's word to Brittany, following the sea routes south and west." When I was through, although how the words came to mind I do not know, "Christ's bones," he said, gawking at me in a way not exactly complimentary, not exactly hostile, "Mother of God. For once the fool makes sense. But how to get the boats in place? They must be there else the moment will be lost, and Walran troops be out in full force."

He observed us again, running a hand through his hair, thinking hard. "Go, then," he suddenly ordered me. He gave me a push for good measure. "If the guard stops you, say it is my command. Have the boats brought to the cliff closest to the pass. But hurry. Prince Taliesin's outriders have already reached the cliff fort; they, too, are ready to move at dawn." He suddenly struck his hand hard against his sword. "By Christ," he cried, almost to himself, "a hundred to one that it will not work, but a chance we'll take. Better it than none. But fail me in this, boy, I'll have your guts, if I live, which if you fail, I doubt. So run."

Not stopping for argument, I ran. But Lady Olwen ran with me. "Christ's bones," I swore when I had breath, when we had left the main gates behind and turned toward the shore, "he'll hang me for sure if you come."

"And stay at home?" She almost laughed, her spirits soaring like a bird's. "Besides, you need what I have brought." The sack beneath her cloak jangled merrily, the treasury of Cambray, which she had robbed, no guilt for that, although in aftertimes the thought made my blood run cold. "I'll talk to the fisherwomen, you the men. Together our arguments will overwhelm them."

As she had said, so we did. It lacked but an hour to midnight when we reached the fisher village. Yet within moments, it seemed, they had come streaming from their huts, pulling on their shoes and their bonnets, which even at night they wear out-of-doors, falling over themselves to help. Most people avoid the fisherfolk, 'tis true, for they have their own outlandish ways, their own pursuits, and sometimes, when you hear of their constant quarrels, their own God to make them so troublesome. They keep to themselves, apart from the Cambray world in their stinking huts at the cliff edge; and although their Irish speech is Celt, it is so unlike our own as to render them as unintelligible, as if they came from another world. Nor can I pretend to know them well, but being an outcast myself, I had come to appreciate them. And in my way, ever poking into things, I had often come to watch them work, their nimble fingers weaving back and forth along their nets, in this task neater and more careful than in their own lives. I had never helped them haul in the fish, the heavy, twisted ropes dripping with weed and the water suddenly boiling, bursting, alive, as the fish leapt and slithered in a silver mass, but I have sharp eyes and often had kept lookout for them from a cliff, watching for a long shadow, the deeper blue that marked a shoal drifting toward land. They are a restless folk, these Irishmen, never still, like the fish they catch, changeable, quick to pick up one thing and drop it quicker still. I did not know if anything would engage them long. But God was with us that night, I think. My words made impact, or rather the Lady Olwen's gold, which she dispensed freely, with promises of more when they returned.

We began to hurry toward the boats. They are small and round for the most part, like walnut shells, made of wicker and leather skins. Yet they sit down into the water almost uncapsizable, even when waves run high. We loaded up a few bigger boats with food and water jars, which Lady Olwen had had the women bring, and throwing overboard, in a jumble of rope and net, all their fishing gear, we had the men haul on the ropes to bring the boats in line, ready to cast off. Looking at them bobbing there like corks, I had a momentary misgiving. But it is true, no myth, that in such boats the Irish have sailed the Atlantic seas, going farther westward than any man before them dared. As long as they kept within sight of land, creeping slowly down our western cliffs, then west again to the Channel Isles, then south again to the Breton coast, they would not come to harm, providing that the weather held, which I prayed to God it would. As each boat in turn floated free into deeper water outside the jetty wall, a fisherman hauled himself on board and, taking up a oar, prepared to skull out into the bay around the promontory. Lady Olwen went with them, looping up her skirts like a peasant born, wading to ankle, then knee, then thigh. I followed her reluctantly, for the water ran cold and dark, its blackness even more uninviting than the cold.

"Set us loose," she cried, scrambling on board the closest boat. The wind caught it, twisting it. Ahead of us, the line of boats jerked and pulled like colts on a leading rein. The ropes

snaked past, falling in the water, out of sight; and seeing that
if I did not make haste, I would be left behind, I struck out,
flailing in the sea over my head until she reached down and
dragged me up by the hair. With her help I heaved myself over
the side; she took up the oar and fitting it in place began to
work it back and forth, following the line of foam that marked
the path of the other craft. A little flotilla we were as we headed
out into the open sea, where the currents spun us around and
drove us on the cliff point.

The current ran fiercer there, and the waves broke with a
sullen roar. It took both of us, holding the oar steady, to shift
our course so that gradually we in turn rounded the cliff and
turned inland again, hugging the contour of the shore, where
the water curdled like cream against the rocks. In between those
rocks were small, sandy coves, hidden from the cliff's top,
useless when the tide was full out or in, causing boats either to
be torn apart or left beached like helpless whales. But when the
tide was right, there was no better launching place. If only we
could catch the tide at its best. So we crept along, the leading
fishermen with flares, which they used to navigate, calling out
in their rough tongue the obstacles that lay ahead. Thank God,
I say, the night was fair. A wind or storm or burst of rain might
have caused shipwreck and would certainly have made the fishermen turn back. As it was, just before dawn, we came to the
landing, a strip of beach closest to the pass, and there we moored
the boats by tying ropes to large flat stones. And there the fishermen waited, shivering a little in the cold, dozing on their fish-
smelling sacks or drinking their foul-tasting ale. Leaving the
remainder of gold to their care, the Lady Olwen and I went on
alone, to climb the cliffs, which towered above us, forbidding
in their height.

There was a track of sorts, faintly visible in the morning
light. The darkness that comes just before day had lightened to
a gray and gritty tone, no color to it, all gray as if covered with
mist, and our hands and clothes, already wet, were wet again
by the heavy dew. We toiled up the cliff, searching for holds
among the heather roots, sometimes sliding down in a pile of
stone, moving as quietly as we could. Yet sea gulls, disturbed

from their resting place, screamed and fought about our heads and sometimes dived in furious attempt to dislodge us from their ledge. We hurried. The way, though long, once undertaken was not difficult, and presently as we crept on up, ear to the ground, we sensed rather than heard a drumming sound, a steady thud, the sound horses' hooves make at a distance. Lady Olwen gave me her hand. "Praise God," she said, and I felt her trembling, "we are in time." And so it was we reached the cliff top just as the Cambray men moved into place.

Unseen by them, or anyone, we settled down behind a patch of gorse, just out of reach below the cliff, and waited as they did. Our cuts and scratches burned and stung, and my flesh felt torn by thorns. But after a while, when the wind came up to blow away the mist and the gray began to lighten to rose and gold, we felt the ground shake a second time, a drumming again, a steady beat, as Prince Taliesin's men came through the pass.

The Cambray guard had stationed themselves openly, on either side of the main path. We could count a line of them, extending over the open moors, slightly uphill from where the Celts must come. They made no attempt to hide; this was not an ambush but a wall of men, and at their head Lord Robert held his horse in check with his left hand as it tossed and shook its head, scenting battle in the air. You could not have told, I think, that only willpower kept my lord upright. His squire had strapped his arm against his shirt, and his sword was belted against his thigh, but there was no way he could pull it and manage his horse. Yet he sat on that horse like a monument.

Down through the pass, under that ancient hill fort, just as those months ago I had seen men ride, the Celts surged on through. The sun caught at their armaments, glinting off their round, brass-knobbed shields and reflecting from their helmets' crests. Yet for an army it was in truth a ragtag sort, more foot soldiers than cavalry, although those foot soldiers could outrun a horse uphill and make a spear wall that bristled like a thorn hedge with spikes. In any case they and the bowmen outnumbered us two to one. Yet Norman cavalry, Norman knights, are trained to break through the stoutest wall; that is their weapon, the mounted charge. They can hack through spearmen like a scythe through corn. And I had a new vision, dark and hot, of how an army, years ago, was so cut down, this gulley running red and the air hot with rage and the cries of men. Beside me I think Lady Olwen felt it, too. She stood up, threw off her cloak, as if it stifled her, her hair blowing wildly in the morning wind. Her lips were moving, but she said nothing aloud. I think she was praying, and so was I. For we stood as at the edge of a tourney field, and death waited there in the lists.

Prince Taliesin rode in the front of his men, cantering easily along on the gray, theft-bred horse; two bowmen ran at his stirrup iron, holding the leather with one hand, and behind him but a pace away those six men of his household guard, if anything, smaller and more grim than before. The prince was dressed for battle in old-fashioned mail—small rings attached to a leather coat, an old-fashioned leather helmet, steel-plated and worn, which sat squarely on his red-gold hair—and his sword was drawn. Today you sensed that he alone was in charge; he knew what he was about, and those older men deferred to him, a prince who led out his war host. *Like wolves trained to fight.* Today I could believe it of him. Seeing Lord Robert and the line of Cambray men, he raised his hand to call a halt. In the silence that followed, no one moved on either side, the only sounds those faint ones of the clink of bridle where a horse shook its head, the stamp of hooves against the flies, the rasp of our own fear-filled breath.

"Greetings, Prince of Afron." Robert's voice was hoarse but calm. The wind that had come up with the dawn tore his words away, tossed at the horses' heads and tails, set the prince's hair aflame. "How do you come, in peace or war?"

Taliesin hesitated a moment in his reply. "Neither," he said at last. "My quarrel is with the English king. So let me pass."

"Not through my lands," Robert suddenly gritted out, as unbending as steel. "I am sworn to make a peace, not let a war band run riot through."

Taliesin nudged his horse forward another step. It danced impatiently across the grass. "I could take you hostage, my lord," he suddenly cried, and he grinned that boyish grin I remembered. "My bowmen are quicker than your mounted knights. Cambray would not attack me if I had you. Nor do I think you yourself could stop me." For he had noted at once Robert's bandaged arm. And it was true that his bowmen, armed with their longbows, had regrouped when he had paused, had their arrows notched, trained to shoot. Their arrows would pierce many a man before the horses in turn ran them down.

I felt my heart leap again, and Lady Olwen's nails cut through my flesh where her hand grasped mine.

"You still would have all of England to cross." Lord Robert kept his voice low. "Cambray has kept a border watch for longer years than you and I have known; it plans to keep it long after you and I are gone."

Taliesin smiled again. Young, far from home, he showed no trace of fear, although fear he must have felt, faced with an adversary he must have known would not retreat and Cambray, in any case, being but the first obstacle he must hack through. "You Normans are dog-mangered with land," was all he said, "that once, I think, was Celtic owned. It's not your lands I want. I come armed, 'tis true, but it is not with you I fight."

There was a stir among the Cambray knights; Dylan edged his own horse along until it stood at Lord Robert's side. "My lords," he began, his Celtic voice sounding strangely like the prince's own, his quick Celtic eyes darting from one young face to the other. "There is a choice, rather than fighting." He turned toward the lord he served, whose father, grandfather, he had served in turn. But what he said was also for the prince to hear—a Celtic trick, to say to one man what is meant for the second. "King Henry is no longer in England," he said. "He already is embarked to France and, come the Yuletide, will head south with all his court. France would be a better place to catch up with him, if it is King Henry who is sought." He paused again. "And since the Breton lords are up in arms, seeking but time and place for attack, they would be willing allies in an enterprise against the king." Lord Robert eyed him thoughtfully, perhaps having guessed his plan or already knowing it. But Prince Taliesin, who must have received a blow, unexpected, to learn his quarry had escaped again, he held himself as proudly as before.

Robert said in his considered way, as if he saw through Dylan's ruse, "But if the Celts make for Brittany, how shall they get there? The Welsh ports are closed, I hear, and they cannot swim."

"My lord." Dylan sat firmly in his saddle and straightened his back. His voice rang out so other men could hear him clearly; even we could. "There are fishing smacks anchored below, waiting for the tide. A fishing fleet could carry men to the Breton shore. But in any case I would have you remember the treaty's terms. It was sealed with the blood of many good men; to break it would be to undo the work of years and leave a legacy of hate that will last for centuries. But crossing by sea is not by land." And he laughed, a laugh that other men, hearing it, took up, as if it were the best jest they had heard.

Beside me Lady Olwen mouthed her prayers. "Do not throw your lives away," I heard her plead. "We are one kin, one race, not meant to fight."

Lord Robert had heard his old friend out; that was his style, cautious and just. Perhaps he had been forewarned; I cannot tell. I only know he inclined his head. "I shall not be forsworn," he said. "But if my lord prince will cross swords with me, then will my honor be satisfied. I swear no Cambray man will hinder him as he departs. So does he swear to leave afterward."

Whatever had been discussed between him and his seneschal, whatever arranged, this offer of combat, man to man, had certainly never figured in Dylan's plans. He almost groaned in despair.

Meanwhile Prince Taliesin stared at them both, his face pale beneath its brown, and for the first time laughter had died from eyes and lips. His dark blue eyes were narrowed against the sun. "I have never run from anything in my life," he began reluctantly, "I did not mean to start now. But I repeat, I have no quarrel with you. To avoid a greater wrong I will so swear. Let my men depart in peace. But I will not cross swords with you, Lord Robert; you are not fit. You . . ."

Whatever else he would have said died away as Robert gestured to his squire, who at his command drew his sword, clamped
it in his lord's left hand, and knotted the reins about his stallion's
neck. The squire jumped aside as Robert now, with voice and
knee, edged his horse toward the open moors. It moved slowly
at first between the two lines of men, then halted, turned, and
began a slow canter back. Lord Robert rode upright, and his
sword was held left-handed, as if he bore a lance pressed tight
against his chest.

Prince Taliesin had time for one quick look. He threw off his
shield, unclasped his belt; he, too, urged his horse on, while
unguided, unchecked, Robert's beast bounded toward him as
if on springs. The ground shook beneath the hooves, clods of
turf flew behind, and Prince Taliesin held his sword two-handed
above his head. I swear he laughed and shouted out the battle
cry of his house. And behind him his army clashed their spears
against their shields and shouted for victory.

Against my will I watched as he and Robert met with a crash
that shook the ground, sending both horses reeling upon their
haunches. Robert's recovered first. He urged it up with his
spurs, wheeled, and prepared to charge again. This time he had
dropped his arm, unable, I think, to hold the heavy sword
straight, and only brought it up at the last. Prince Taliesin, too,
had wheeled. Back he swooped, and now I know he laughed,
the joyous laugh of a man who feels his strength. His great
sword rose and fell in a swirling arch. But he did not strike
with it. Over Robert's head it flew, outlined against the rising
sun, and landed singing in a clump of grass at the cliff edge,
where he had thrown it. And as he swept past, he caught at
Robert's bridle with his free hand. The two horses galloped
side by side, until the prince could bring his weight to bear and
haul them both to a stop. Horses and men were panting, struggling for breath, and you could see the rip in Taliesin's mail
where Robert's sword point had slashed his arm. But Robert
himself was unhurt (although the force of that encounter might
well have opened his other wound); exhaustion alone had almost
done for him.

Taliesin said, his voice coming in great gulps, "Thus are we both unsworn; thus are we both released from oath. Permit me, then, to take my leave. In Brittany had I hoped to find my kin and march with them against this king who has destroyed my house and may yet destroy yours. I did not think to find a passage so easily. My thanks, then. I trust we meet again as friends." As he talked, his men had ridden up with his shield and belt; he took them up and, quickly looping a rag around his streaming cut, knotted it firmly with his teeth.

"Farewell, then, Lord Robert of Sieux," he repeated, sliding to the ground. "And for good measure I leave you my horse." He gave his grin, half boy, half man. "In truth it belonged to you in the first place."

Robert, with scarcely strength to breathe let alone talk, nodded to him, and Dylan let the horses be led aside. Many of the Cambray men, seeing what was planned, dismounted, too, and came to help the Celts embark. Apart from Taliesin's horse, the rest were mainly moorland bred, and we turned them loose, unsaddled, to roam. But the prince's stallion we kept. "Someday," the prince told them, "I shall claim it again." And he stood leaning against its side, pulling its ears as one by one his men, obedient to his will, like hounds, packed up their gear, saluted him, and started down the cliff path. Brave men they were to go like that. Yet such was their loyalty and such their trust, that Celtic honesty that the Lords of Walran had sneered at.

They were not long in their leave-taking, for as I have said before, they travel light and carry most of their goods upon their backs. It may well have been that the provisions we had packed would seem luxuries to them. And, in truth, the crossing would not take long if wind and tide favored them, as now seemed possible. Soon only the six bodyguard were left with the prince. He gave his horse one last pat, saluted Robert in his formal way, and threw his shield across his back. At the cliff's edge he stopped to pull loose his sword, sheathe it, unstrap his spurs, and come on again. Three steps below the headland, he suddenly stopped once more and bent, as if searching something out. So he moved sideways along until he came to where we were half hid, as if he knew we had been there all the time.

"Ha," he said. "I thought I sensed a spy in our midst. Here with your manikin, I see." (An unkind cut.) He reached through the gorse bush and catching hold of the Lady Olwen by the arms drew her out. Up she came easily, as a fish is caught, her wooden clogs slipping from her feet as they swung in air before he set her down upon the ground. There she stood, and he leaned toward her, resting his hand on his hip as he stared at her intently.

"And where's your mousekin?" he next asked, pretending to peer under a blade of grass. "Don't tell me it is left at home. Came you on wings?"

"We came by boat," she told him breathlessly.

"Without his knowing?" He jerked his head backward to indicate where a white-faced Robert still remained on guard to supervise from horseback the outgoing Celtic army. "Were you my sister, I'd have you whipped for venturing forth on such a madcap scheme. And without escort, too, except for this bag of bones. . . ." (Another cut, although, like the first, not ill-meant.)

"Who makes more sense than you do," she interrupted loyally, "especially since the madcap plan was first his to save your skin. Were you my brother, I'd have *you* flogged for tearing yourself to bits." She nodded at his bandaged arm, which still ran red. "You and Robert both, fools to fight when one cannot and one should not. That's madness in this world."

"A scratch," he said, "a nothing. But, Lady Olwen, do you mean you and your page" (which sounded better) "worked to save us? Why did you come? To see my discomfiture, to watch me lose? Was Lord Robert's anger worth that much? For angry he will be when he finds you out."

"Certainly not to see you win," she cried, his voice with its teasing undertone catching at her beneath the skin, "who beat me last time by a trick."

He suddenly laughed and threw back his head so his white teeth gleamed. "By Saint David," he said, "how you like to twist at words. Why, lady, I think that rather you tricked me. You thought then to win my horse by stealth. Better stick to your little mousekin. My stallion will never let you on its back."

"Perhaps," she said. "Perhaps not. You have been proved wrong before, Prince of Afron."

At his puzzled look, she ticked off the times on her thin fingers, one by one. "You said you would not see me again, who was of Norman blood. But I am half Celt. My name is Olwen, a good Celtic name, and I have another, given me at birth. Efa am I also called, Efa of the Celts, whom my grandfather took as hostage and afterward wed and loved. And you see we meet again. And a third time are you misspoke. You said you had no quarrel with my house, and yet you would have killed my brother had he stood in your way."

He flushed. "As to the last, lady," he said proudly, "I let facts speak for themselves. But do not always think you are right, mistress. If I am to bid you farewell, let it be properly done. I go to war, far across the seas, joining with my Celtic kin, and God knows how or when I shall return. I have never before left my native land." And for a moment, unaware, a sudden note crept into his voice, a wistfulness, gone in a flash, as if, a boy, he sensed the vastness of his enterprise, as if he guessed at its futility. "My father looks for word from me. Would you send that word? Say I am safely embarked. Say I am gone to France; say I will safely return."

"Aye," she said. She shaded her eyes to look up at him. The sun had come full out and was making a halo around her head; her skirts, salt-blotched and wet with dew, were moulded by the wind against her long legs, caught between them, flattened to her body curves. I could see right through to where her little breasts, like buds, strained against the wet cloth. I averted my eyes hastily, but not the prince.

He stared at her, as if the wet rags were gauze, were a film of mist, which the wind would blow naked away. "By Saint David," he swore softly, his voice husky as comes to men, "you have grown, little Olwen, from what you were. And were you alone and I alone, and this any other day, I swear I would not leave you here, nor I leave yet. You could make me forget myself, Efa of the Celts. Why did you come?"

She did not turn herself or straighten her skirts or try to hide, but never taking her eyes from his she fumbled beneath her

waist and drew out the golden bracelet he had given her. "This,"
she said. "You may need it again. I return it to you for luck."

He took the bracelet in his larger hand, cupping his around
hers, not letting go, both gentle and firm. His blue eyes were
almost black against the sun, but the smile that stole across his
face was the smile of a man who thinks on one thing. "Sweet
Jesu," he whispered in her ear, "you tempt me more than you
can tell. For the third time, why did you come?"

She still did not move, their bodies almost touching, line to
line, yet not quite, his hand still cupped about her own. With
her free hand she reached out and pushed back his sleeve. The
trickle of blood had almost stopped, but the rag was sodden
with it. She gently touched the edge of the cut so that her
fingertip was dyed red and lifted it to her lips. Out came her
pointed tongue like a cat's, and she delicately licked the smear
of blood. "Now are we sworn kin in truth," she whispered
back. "I share your blood. Now I shall not be forgot."

He said, "Efa of the Celts, you were stolen long ago from
us. Shall I bring you back one day? For the last time I ask, why
did you come?"

She made a little moue but still did not turn her body aside
nor modestly avert her eyes. But she would not answer him.

"I cannot tell," was all that she would say. "As for the future,
who knows it? But if you do not forget me quite, perhaps
somewhere, sometime, we shall meet again. And I shall send
my loving prayers with you. Those I gladly give." He lifted
her hand, palm uppermost, and spread out the fingers singly,
between his own. Still not taking his eyes from hers, he raised
her fingers to his lips. She began to shake, as if the wind would
sweep her away, her hair as red as flame to match his own, her
face afire, her lips red.

"I thank you for my life," he said simply. "Had you not
brought the boats, where should I have gone? I thank you, I
thank your page, and I praise you. One day, perhaps, you shall
be repaid."

There was a shout from the fisherfolk; the tide was running
fast. His household guard had come filing past and were waiting
silently for him. He released her hand, and with the golden

bracelet she had returned still firmly clasped, he strode after his men, his leather boots slipping from time to time. We heard his footsteps beating down the track, saw him gradually disappear, he and his six men like shadows at his back. In a while, on the beach far below, we heard the fishermen shout again as their boats scraped on the shingle when they dragged them out. There was a creak of leather, the rattle of sail, the rasp of oars. Within our view the little fleet began to move outward with the tide, going west until the mists came down and shrouded it.

"Praise God," I heard my lady say, the first words she had spoken since he left. "Praise God that he is safely gone." And she turned as if resolute. "Courage, Urien the Bard," she said. Her face was pale where before it had been red, and I saw how the blue veins stood out on her white neck and her heart beat fast as does a bird's if you trap it unawares. "Now come we up to pay the price." In truth, worn out with so much excitement, taut with emotion and some other strain, which then I could not name, my hands shaking, wet with sweat, I had not even given thought to how we were to get back ourselves. But she had. "Follow me," she said in her old way.

Up she clambered, out of the gorse bush, and began to walk along the cliff edge, where, far beneath us, in the blue-gray sea, the fragile walnut shells beat westward with their leather sails. There was a shout. "Walk on," she hissed, forcing the pace. "Do not look back. Stand firm." She threw up her head, proud as a peacock, and walked faster than before, openly now upon the path, until her brother himself, thrusting forward on his great stallion, blocked the way. He had looped the prince's reins around his own, and between the two great beasts the Lady Olwen stood her ground, almost overwhelmed by their height. I felt my legs tremble with fright, but not so she.

"What is that man to you?" Robert suddenly shouted at her, worn with effort and fatigue. I had never heard him shout so sharp, certainly harsher than she was used to. She never flinched. Hemmed in by Prince Taliesin's horse, which towered over her, snorting and stamping, she put out her hand and let the great head come down to blow gently against her palm. But she did not reply.

"By my troth." Lord Robert spoke more softly now, in much the same way the prince had done, the sort of voice men use to their womenfolk. "I hear it was your plan. I hear it was Cambray gold you used to bribe your way. By God, Odo of Walran was right, you speak overloud for a maid. No thanks you'll get from anyone, still less from me, if I find my sister lacking in the laws of propriety. When met you that man before? Where did you meet?" Now you saw her stubbornness in turn match and lock with his; you saw her refusal to answer him; you saw her scorn at his suspicion.

"By the Mass." Robert's voice had regained its habitual calm. "Lady, you do yourself more wrong. By God's wounds, my father shall hear of it. I'll have you betrothed myself, and wed, to keep you safe. There is no hope with that man, Olwen, no way for you. Disgrace, dishonor lie with him."

She looked at him, still smoothing the gray horse's head. "Then death," she said. "Do not put disgrace on me or on him. Those are words I do not know." And such was her look, he dropped his gaze, suddenly uncertain what to do.

"Take her up," he ordered one of his squires. "Lady, attend me when I bid." But to me he said, when she had gone, "I did not order you to my service to lead my lady astray. In my father's absence I speak as he would. Death should follow for a maid disgraced. I spare you that as I spare her. But take him away and have done with him."

They pulled me roughly along, past Dylan, who watched without saying yea or nay. Well, that, too, was a lesson learned. A fair lord in many ways was Robert of Sieux, and just, but conscious of his sister's rank, conscious of her name more than she was herself. And one of life's small ironies, I think, the whipping Hue had threatened, in the end Robert ordered it. Not such as Hue would have done, but enough. For Robert was a just man. I know I should not have let her come. As for my lady's confidence, well that day I served as her whipping boy. I did not regret it nor hold rancor. *I live to serve you.* So a second time, in my modest way, I did.

But from that day on Lady Olwen was shut up with her maids, almost under guard. Poor soul, I think she suffered longer and as hard in silence and alone. Dylan, having seen me whipped, to his satisfaction, no doubt (perhaps word having reached him of that earlier escapade), showed me, afterward, more attention than I merited, redoubling his efforts to make me ride. He himself had me mount, dismount, trot up and down, fall off and climb back up again until, as much from that as from any blows, I scarce could stand and thought to die. Yet there, too, I owe him my life. For if in the end I could straddle horse at all, or pull sword, it is because he drilled skill into me, although in future years he used to swear I almost broke his will, such lack of skill, such clumsiness, more like a bag of chaff or sack of grain than coordinated man. Lord Robert's wound did not break open or fester again; he received no hurt, praise God, nor did he show resentment once just punishment had been rendered. With every passing day he grew stronger, until he, too, was prepared to leave. But between his sister and himself hung those words that were to overshadow these last days. *Betrothed and wed.* Such was the punishment he had for her. Such is the fate of maidenhood, such I despaired of, and such the Lady Olwen now was forced to fight as best she could.

Chapter 6

ur leave-taking from Cambray, at the autumn's end, was all I had envisaged and more. Dylan oversaw us younger lads, suddenly as anxious as a broody hen. Each day he drilled us mercilessly, himself sitting motionless on his steed, his face a mask of gloom while he had us rehearse over and over again how to take care of ourselves upon a journey that he seemed to think would end disastrously. "A horse is worth a hundred *livres*," he used to say, "ten times the cost of a serf; a hundred times your cost, you gormless louts." And many other maxims of this kind, such as, "You'll find stable help wherever you go, but the care of your horse is yours alone." And "An unhorsed knight is as helpless as a hedgehog on its back; best way to get a throat slit." And "In surprise attack, mount first, arm last; a horse can carry you away faster than a sword can." He furnished us with a list of goods that should form part of our gear and a verse, God save us, to help slow learners with their memory. Since half of the things he named I had never owned, I could not imagine what use they were, but the verse I still remember:

> *A bodkin, a knife, a loaf of bread,*
> *A curry comb, saddle, stiff sewing thread,*
> *Shirt, and laces to tie its sleeves,*
> *A cloak, for shelter against the breeze*
> *Mail coat, sword, gloves of fine leather stitched . . .*

117

And so on and so on. And the equipment to be well taken care of, we being responsible for it to the Cambray armory.

"God's head," a youth next to me complained, "with that much stuff we could journey to the Holy Land."

Dylan heard him, reached from his horse, and plucked him forth by the ears. "God's head is it?" he whispered back, his black eyes glinting and his mouth curled. "More like I'll claim your own. Who knows in truth what God plans, or how long each journey takes? Prepare as if each day were your last, then perhaps you may survive." Well, an old campaigner Dylan was, and a wise one. I did not find his advice ill-placed, only tedious. My mother stitched for me a saddlebag to hang behind the cantle, and the castle women made me two shirts, which, since I had not yet begun to grow, were still too large when I put them on. My companions took that for a mockery, a jest upon my humble start, like an ill-planted herb stunted at birth, and wagered that I would never survive the trip, more like to slip between paving stones and be lost to sight or trip over a tree stump and break in two. I let them mock. Determination can be acquired by any man, and I have always found that wits are as sharp as swords. At least I had the will to survive, and even if I boast in saying so, I lived to see my mother housed in a hut of her own, and her daughters, those half sisters, grown to comely age, with husbands of their own (although in womanhood they still showed a tendency to whine that always made me grit my teeth).

But it is the parting with my father that I always recall. He must have been studying me unseen and doubtless took his share of jests to have revealed how inept I was, not new to him but now put on public display. But the part I played in Prince Taliesin's leave-taking he must also have known, and that may have convinced him I was of some use. The day before I left he appeared, red-faced, gruff, having no words to express what he meant. Perhaps it was a true father's concern (which coming unexpectedly took him also by surprise), or perhaps it was a sudden desire to have me think well of him now that we were to part and I had risen in the world. In any case, with many fits and starts and scrapings of the feet, he presented me with a gift. It was a sword. I had never seen its like before, too small and light for a grown man's use, too long for a dagger, yet honed sharp, its hilt carved in some strange shape, black with age, although the steel blade was bright from having been wrapped these many years in oiled rags.

"I got it off a French squire in a fight," my father explained, but I think he lied. For later, when I came to use it, the wax that had stained the hilt rubbed through, revealing gold beneath too valuable for any mere squire, and its markings, when I had time to study them, were more like Norse runes. Yet its steel was supple like a new-forged blade, and at the time I was touched by the gift (although had my father known of the gold, he might not have parted with it). So I strapped it on with pride, although it was clear, at least to me, that the path of squire and knight would never be mine.

Our cavalcade was not numerous, most of the men being left to guard Cambray. Lord Robert, restored by now to health, took only a handful of knights and squires, myself, and the Lady Olwen with her maids. I heard the older men grumble at riding nurse to a pack of womenfolk, deeming the care of women more onerous than a score of skirmishes, although I myself, and my friends, being young, enjoyed their company. And, in truth, these ladies seldom complained as older ones might do; never pretended to be afraid, never forced a knight to dismount on foot to lead them along, never pretended to faint for lack of food or rest, or made us fetch and carry for them like pack mules. Lady Olwen rode her white horse, but there was a look about her that made me think of Hue, the way she held her head and the quietness with which she met each day. But once, when we were beset, she showed her courage like a man of her house.

We left, then, on a day when autumn was full come. The very air of Cambray made one think of harvest and tranquillity. There was a good homey smell of peat smoke and salt marsh, and late heather patches covered the moors like a tattered cloak. Dylan and the Cambray guard accompanied us to the eastern border for courtesy and to ensure, I think, that we passed Walran lands without reprisal (for since Prince Taliesin's leaving, we had seen neither hide nor hair of those lords, who had slunk back into their fortress to sulk). So Dylan left us finally with many words of warning such as an old retainer is free to give and with few regrets on my part, although the sight of those familiar castle walls slipping behind the hills unsettled strange yearnings, which I beat down. The greater world was where I had set my hopes (although when I got there, I did not find it as great or as pleasant as I thought).

Travel with an earl's son makes for luxury. Each day messengers were sent ahead to prepare the next resting place; we traveled with our own gear, to the very feather pillows that we would use, and although I had never traveled anywhere before, and certainly never slept on goosedown, I soon became used to this new style of life. Comfortable beds, fine clothes, good food and wines: such were the delicacies of life as I had always imagined great lords enjoyed. I scarcely had time to appreciate these luxuries before we had to relinquish them—but I rush ahead. First, we came by slow degrees, no war party this, through a pleasant countryside, until, in quick succession, two events occurred to break our peace and reveal clearly that in the world we know, such comforts do not last long.

The first encounter had all the familiarity of an old friend. We had come by now to the end of the foothills, and before us stretched the woods that in those days spread to the boundaries of Sedgemont lands. I remember we were chatting in a desultory way about the last night's lodgings, talk in which I joined, by now as nice as the next man about a resting place, when there was a shout behind us and a tumble of rocks and dirt as a horse came breasting up through the underscrub. Even as we turned in our saddles, several more horsemen approached over the crest of a small hill. Their leader was in full armor, riding a bay horse, whilst beside him, on leading rein, his charger galloped along easily. An unknown knight, armed and fast, was a sign of danger, even I knew that!

"Ware arms." Lord Robert's shout scattered our men, a maneuver I had often watched on the practice fields, to form a ring around the women and the sumpter mules, enclosing the weakest of our cavalcade, while Robert and the rest of the household guard unstrapped their shields, unsheathed swords, and rode out to meet an enemy. Once in position they reined back, forming a shield wall, waiting to resist a charge. None came. Petrified, I had watched all this, and no man thanked God more gratefully than I when the leading rider identified himself, Gervaise of Walran, with a dozen of Walran men at his command.

Up he rode, young Gervaise, drew off his helmet, unlaced his coif. His Walran colors of blue and gray were smothered in dust, and his father's crest, a rough wolf's head, was almost hidden upon his shield, but his voice was cheerful when he hailed us.

"Save you, Lord Robert," he cried. "By the Mass, I thought you would never come this way. God's breath, I have been looking for you this past week." I noticed at once, as all must have, the red mark that scored one side of his round face, the mark of a mailed fist, and it was certainly true that he and his men showed all the signs of unseemly haste: straps left dangling, saddlebags jammed on, horses ungroomed, faults Dylan would have clouted us for. Gervaise noted Robert's quick appraisal and flushed. "I make request, my lord," he said more formally, drawing himself up, "leave to attend you on your march east. My men and I would make part of your company, at least until our paths diverge, you to Sedgemont, I to the coast."

On horseback, his fair hair tousled, his face pink and white with a glow of youth, he looked the epitome of a Norman knight, and I heard the women whisper so. I was jammed in among them, caught knee to knee, between another page and one of Lady Olwen's maids, and I felt the ripple of interest his appearance now aroused, like the stir in a carp pool when a piece of bread is thrown in.

"Lovestruck, more like," I heard one woman say. "Run off, with little of his father's blessings, I'll be bound," showing that she, too, had noticed the telltale sign of a blow, whilst another, more shrewd, muttered aloud, loud enough for our men to hear, at least, "Lady's delight, look how he craves it, poor sot." And she began to titter, as did all the ladies, behind their hands, poor fools themselves, besotted, if anyone was, by a handsome face and a strong back. Yet it is true Gervaise looked his best on horseback; afoot, for my taste, he had always seemed too broad for his height, as if his legs fitted better curled around a horse, as if he were more graceful mounted, the sort of grace that men acquire with learning to ride before they can walk. But he was his father's oldest son, heir to all the Walran lands; no border lord would let his son go skirmishing abroad without just cause.

Perhaps Lord Gervaise sensed the wave of sympathy his appearance had evoked. He certainly took advantage of it. He sighed. "God's wounds, Robert," he said in a more normal voice, "I thought you like to cut me down. I know we have had our differences, or rather, you and my father have, but since the incident is closed, I pray it may be closed for us. Your friendship is all I ask, I swear." And as he spoke, he glanced sideways quickly to where the Lady Olwen waited for the order to ride on. He did not address her openly, but his next remarks were meant for her. "I trust we meet as friends, as friends we have been this long while. And since I feared I should not see you again, I rode in haste after you. My father has permitted me to seek service with our lord king. I have his permission and his blessing." He had a boyish way of speaking, when he would, that also became him well, and now he added eagerly, "Or rather, he gave me them in the end. For is it not true a man must seek his own destiny, not sit meekly bawling for it like a slaughtered calf? I go to Canterbury, to the tomb of the murdered archbishop, Becket, then to join Henry in France and accompany him on Crusade."

There was a noticeable gasp at those words, several of our men crossing themselves, others muttering a prayer, and the Walran men looked smug. Even the women stopped their tittering and gazed at Gervaise more seriously. As did the Lady Olwen.

Crusading knights are the blessed of our times, those noble men who go to fight on God's behalf, over distant seas, against the infidel, and certainly excuse sufficient for Odo of Walran to allow his son to depart. For those who take the cross are deemed the favorites of God, to be accorded all honor and respect, and even at Cambray we had heard how such knights would sometimes up and take their leave upon the thought, abandoning their homes, their lands, their families, such a wave of enthusiasm sweeping over them as to drown all reason or sense—and few of them returned, poor souls, to reveal all the horrors that crusading entails, more horror than honor, I vow. But Gervaise was continuing. "When King Henry leaves, I leave with him; two hundred knights he swears shall go, and at Thomas Becket's grave will I offer my sword to be counted among those knights."

He spoke well, I do not deny, yet I felt uneasy; such words came too pat. Lord Robert perhaps sensed it, too. "I doubt," he said in his dry way, cutting through the general excitement, "that King Henry will make good that promise. He swore that oath because he was forced to it, as punishment for the murder of the archbishop."

"Just so." Gervaise's blue eyes burned; he missed entirely Robert's point. "Two hundred knights, I repeat, himself to lead them, within three years, a vow then to appease God for Becket's murder, for which the king was responsible."

Robert smiled his grave, sweet smile and gave an almost imperceptible shrug. All he said was, "Papal legates set Henry that task; my guess is that papal legates will help him find a way to wriggle free. My horse for yours, he'll never leave. But come," for he had noted how Gervaise's face had darkened with chagrin, "you are welcome to ride with us. And if not in the Holy Land, you may yet find action closer to home."

Now all this while the Lady Olwen had been listening intently. She and Gervaise had not spoken yet, and he had not looked at her openly, remembering, perhaps, their last meeting. Now, abruptly, as if she had made up her mind, she nudged her little horse out of line and spoke to him first.

"Save you, Lord Gervaise," she cried breathlessly, as if her decision had been so forced from her as to cause exertion above the norm. "Why, you give greetings slow like cheese curds. I swear you've never missed our company these past weeks. But your cheerfulness will enliven many a weary mile." She feigned a yawn. "It will be pleasant to have you ride with us and cheer my brother from his gloom."

I saw the look Robert gave her, surprised, so long a speech she had not made since we had left Cambray, and certainly not before. Since the parting with Prince Taliesin, as I have explained, she had kept apart, or was so kept by her brother's command, and seldom had speech with anyone. I guessed at once what she was about, but certainly Gervaise did not. He flushed and stealthily began to move his horse forward, closer to hers. But although he flushed, an expression of triumph, quickly suppressed, also crossed his face. I suddenly thought of a second argument he must have used to persuade his father to let him depart, for argument there must have been, that I do not deny. But the possible, even probable, loss of the Lady Olwen and her lands might also have been a decisive reason for Gervaise to pursue her, as well as pursuing honor in a far-off land. As for Robert, he was startled by his sister's effusiveness. He loved her well and was distressed that she might already have become entangled with Taliesin, a man he could not approve of, and certainly his father could not, a renegade prince, on the run, a fugitive with a hopeless quest; his sister merited better than that. Now Gervaise of Walran was someone Robert knew; comrades-in-arms had they been this past year; Gervaise would make a better brother-in-law than enemy. Since Robert was so little used to women and was afraid of them (and the story he revealed in his delirium certainly had showed he had reason enough to hate and fear), I believe he was quickly deceived. And that was exactly what my lady intended.

I knew her well. I could imagine what these past weeks had been like for her, shut up, almost a prisoner, with only her thoughts for company. *Betrothed and wed.* Maids have little choice, especially noble ones, and few defenses in this age we live in. She knew Robert well enough to recognize that he would stand to his word, and when she reached Sedgemont she would also have her father to answer to. Had she been another daughter, in another house, she might already have been married off at her age, to unite two families' worth or to give an heir to someone's lands. She must have been thinking these things, suddenly aware of them and dreading them. Too proud to dispute or plead for reprieve, she must have been looking for some way to escape a trap from which, within the narrow confines of her world, there was no way out. And she, too, was young. I cannot say I realized all this at the time, but now I do. How young she was, and innocent. She had not acknowledged yet all her feelings for Prince Taliesin, not their full force, nor yet the full force of Gervaise's own. And in her innocence, for she was innocent, as a young girl is, not knowing yet the extent of her own sensuality, the thought occurred to her of encouraging Gervaise in the hope of concealing her own dreams, in the hope of distracting her brother's mind.

Nor do I mean she "used" Gervaise deliberately; she did not know how to "use" anyone, but she must have seen him as someone she was familiar with, an old friend, an unexpected gift from the gods, behind whose attentions she could hide. And as they now rode forward, Gervaise secretly congratulating himself upon his good fortune to be so quickly restored to the lady's grace, she, in turn, seized upon Gervaise as a drowning man does any piece of rope. Beneath her smiles, her looks, I sensed a sadness, so deep that it was like to drown them both.

And one other thing. When at the day's end we waited in yet another courtyard for our horses to be unpacked, she, still on horseback, leaned down to me and whispered, "Urien the Bard," for so she always called me those days, "what will you sing at my betrothal feast?" She looked at me sideways with her large and luminous eyes. "Nay, never frown. In a world where babes are betrothed in their cradles, I am already too old. No great lord will bid for me, a crone. I should have been chosen long ago." She smiled, but her eyes were dark. In them I read what she should have said, what she herself perhaps did not yet know. "Alas, I was chosen, I did choose. No other hope for me."

From that day forth Gervaise rode with her, never left her side; he, too, had not much time to waste. And having sent word back forthwith to Walran to ensure Lord Odo knew his son came of his own free will (an easier message than the one we had sent to Afron), Robert allowed them to ride together, thankful, I believe, to see his sister's spirits revive, wishing her happiness. Gervaise was full of talk, mostly of Canterbury and the miracles there: three days after Becket's death, the first, a glowing youth with flaming sword, an angel, sent to guard the tomb; then, children cured of blindness and cripples made to walk, a sainthood promised for the holy murdered man. I listened, interested despite myself, the story of this Becket fascinating me although in my heart I felt envy's full bitterness that Gervaise could so ride, so talk. Yet jealousy is a sin that one day God will demand payment for, and so it was with me. And so with Gervaise when in his turn jealous rage led him astray. Yet it is strange, I think, that this Norman lord, solid as seasoned oak, plain-spoken, self-satisfied, should burn in his way with envy as he burned with crusading zeal. Yet that, too, was part of his Norman heritage. He was, after all, his father's son, showing all the virtues and faults of his Norman race— practical, hard, and yet at the same time visionary. Such a mixture has helped the Normans conquer half the world. And strange, too, that despite himself he should prove Robert a prophet. For he never went to the Holy Land, but Robert did, who had not looked to go there. But war Gervaise found, and fame of sorts, although neither the war nor the fame he sought.

Gervaise must have known of Prince Taliesin's leave-taking, and of Lady Olwen's intervention on the prince's behalf. He must have heard rumors of the scandal of their parting. As I have said, he was determined, shrewd, that mark of his father's fist but one sign of a hard upbringing, true to Norman custom. Now, as we rode along, he by the lady's side, breathing in her every word, weighing the nuance of her smiles, caught like fish on line, yet he was not held so fast that he did not hesitate to make good his advantage. He seized the opportunity to show her how the Norman world would judge the prince as a barbarian, half wild, without sense, whose actions were worthless (although, in fairness, a Norman lordling who had done the same would have been credited courage at least). With these criticisms Gervaise perhaps set his own fears to rest and gave Robert peace of mind. But one day he overstepped himself, and the lady dared to talk him down, revealing, to me, at least, what her real thoughts were.

Gervaise was speaking in his artless way, for as he felt himself more at ease in Olwen's company, he began to show himself as he truly was, a simple man, like many Normans I since have met, happiest with horses and hounds, more comfortable with warlike talk among men than in women's company, not over-nice in courtship, and given to harsh judgments, with which he expected the lady to agree.

"I hear this prince, so-called," he began, "is fled to Brittany. Let him look for help." (You see how he spoke disparagingly of Taliesin, "so-called prince" and "fled," as if both his title and his bravery were suspect.) "King Henry has beaten those Bret-ons to their knees. Only in one part, the far northwest, will those wanderers find someone to take them in, Viscount Guiomar of Leon, overlord of Finisterre, a monster of a man, a self-proclaimed murderer, who openly boasts of a bishop's death, his own uncle's no less. King Henry almost took his land once. What saved it was not Guiomar's skill, only the sudden death of the dowager Countess of Anjou, Matilda, Henry's mother, she on whose behalf civil war was begun, to make her queen." In his pleasure at revealing Taliesin's folly, Gervaise forgot that the house of Cambray had certainly not supported that lady in the civil war. It gave Olwen the chance to unsay Gervaise's words; even Robert could not fault her for that.

"That Matilda was a tigress," she cried, "who would have made a cruel queen. Mother to King Henry, you say; perhaps he learned his ways from her. And Guiomar no worse a man than that king you so openly admire. Henry ordered Archbishop Becket's death although he did not strike the blow. Why is the murder he planned excused and not the murder of a Breton priest? Or rather, to put things right way round, why should not both murderers be condemned? Why should Henry claim Brittany at all? It is not his. It had its own duke, its own laws, its own ways."

Lord Gervaise was startled by her outburst and did not know how to reply. He was not used to having women interrupt, and his lips tightened, much as his father's were wont to do. Yet being still a wooer, not yet a husband, he answered pa-tiently, "The Bretons asked for Henry's help. He merely gave what they asked."

"So say all conquerors," she cried. "And only the city of

Nantes did. They asked Henry's brother, Geoffrey Plantagenet, to rule them. It was after his death that Henry took the whole of Brittany as a gift from God, made himself duke, banished the reigning one, and betrothed his third son to the infant daughter of that exiled duke to make all seem just. No one asked what the Bretons thought or what the Breton lords wanted."

Each time she used the word "Breton" she might as well have said "Welsh." Both were Celts, similar in speech and history, and she defended them. And when, halfheartedly, Gervaise tried to reason with her, her logic defeated him.

"Razing castles, killing, seizing land does not make a conqueror true owner of the earth. Nor does it mean that Bretons have no rights left of their own." Unable to answer her, Gervaise clamped his mouth up tight. But, I thought, when she was a bride, such talk would win her a good clap, and I grieved for her in advance.

Presently, however, she turned back to him and spoke of more pleasant things, and so their tiff, if it could be called that, was patched about; and Lord Gervaise, in turn, to please her, spoke of *chansons de geste*, those old stories of heroes trapped by war and love, betrayed by treachery, killed by deceit. On the outskirts of their discourse I heard his voice cut, like steel, through the pleasantries, and heard him speak of such betrayal, such treachery, with a familiarity, almost a disinterestedness, as if one day they would become commonplace. And I grieved again for the Lady Olwen, who, having thought to escape one trap, was perhaps now more closely hemmed in by a second one.

And so we rode along, trying to avoid each other's dust, through an autumn sun that no longer seemed bright, already on the wane, harbinger of winter ahead. The forest floor was knee-deep in leaves, and the bare branches met, like ribbed bones, overhead. We seemed to have been moving forever like this, figures in a fresco that Henry might have had depicted on his palace walls, caught in a painted forest that had no end. And I thought suddenly, we all are suspended here, each of us making a little bid for escape; what will the future hold for us: for Lady

Olwen, grown now to womanhood, for Robert, hiding his thoughts, for Gervaise of Walran, lusting after fame and love, and for Urien the Bard, watching them all, helpless to alter anything? And already in France there were three other young men, each caught, too, by his own destiny: Hue, who would bind himself to Prince Henry, that royal prince aching for his own liberty, and from the western Breton lands, a western prince, Taliesin, chosen since birth to fulfill his father's revenge. What fates held their lives in hand, to make or mar?

At the forest's eastern rim we parted, Lord Gervaise and his men riding onward to Canterbury, we turning north, veering slightly west again, toward Sedgemont, still two days hence. The parting between Lord Gervaise and his friends was as might be expected, the lady with genuine goodwill, no more; he with many sighs, regrets—genuine, too, in their way, as he had been trained by some Norman tutor to show his chivalry. And between him and Lord Robert, their comrade's grasp that showed they had been brothers-in-arms and might, as Lord Gervaise suggested, one day come to closer kinship. Certainly the idea had been sown, perhaps too well; I could see that Lady Olwen herself began to realize that, and she lapsed back into silence again.

We were to spend that night in an abbey, carved out by the Benedictine monks within the confines of the forest, a rich and revered place, with its acres of land carefully plowed and its meadows, where fat cattle grazed, thick with clover. The abbey of Stefensforth was also large, well built of stone, with buildings that spread over many rods, both new land and deeded land, whereon had been built walls, stables, courtyards, and such, as well as inner quadrangles, cloisters, and refectories, to say nothing of the great abbey church itself, where day and night prayers were said for departed souls and candles burned and incense smoked and bells tolled for worship. Yet despite the richness, the luxury, or perhaps because of their excess, I felt an air of constraint, a lowering of the spirit rather than an uplifting. And here occurred the second event, more an exchange of news at first than incident, of great import to us yet also of such general concern that henceforth all men should remember it. There is no doubt it changed our lives, for ill, for good, who can judge which, but change it did.

We were well received, perhaps too well. As I have explained, an earl's entourage travels in style, and although the ladies were bestowed outside the walls, as was suitable, no luxury was spared for them or us. I cannot speak of the monks or their lives, but any comfort lacking where we were must not yet have been thought of, and when we joined the abbot at his feast, it was true he and his monks had a fat and comfortable air, well larded about the ribs. The Abbot of Stefensforth was a man of middling height and age, as richly dressed and richly attended as any lord. He had his falconer bring his falcon into the hall; each time she tried to fly, the falconer soothed her with loving words, the only female thing inside this place and she as illegal as any other one. Praise God, the falconer kept her well away from us, else she might have swooped to snatch the meat from our own mouths. Well, I speak the truth; I did not like that abbot, whose face was lined with fat and whose close-set eyes were pouched with it, and who was dressed in red silk like a veritable prelate.

As he ate his way though sixteen courses, both meat and fish, he grumbled without cease about his peasants, then his vassals (for he had vassals like any lord himself), and finally his neighbors, great lords all, who hunted over his lands without restraint. He never mentioned, of course, where he hunted with his hawk, and as it turned out, his anger had grown most hot because the barons, daring to flout the abbot's laws (by supporting some of Henry's own), had allowed a miller to build a mill to threaten abbey rights. The abbot took gulps of wine as he rehearsed this grievance, numbering his complaints aloud on his bejeweled fingers with each draft.

"Such insolence," he cried, "to defy me. Our mill has sole charge of grinding grain. God's face," his own grew red, "I swore on the holy cross, a portion of which I have in my church, that before a villein of mine would use the barons' mill, I'd tear it down, stick and stone. For who, noble, serf, or freeman, would use my mill when there was a second one? I soon brought them around, praise God."

He leaned forward and signed his thanks in another cup of wine. "I spread out all the sacred relics that we own—not all, that is, only those that have proved most efficacious: a silver cross with the thigh of Saint Boniface, a gold pax containing the ashes of Saint Cyprian, and other relics of purest worth. 'See these,' I told those proud lords. 'Look your last. If you rebuild your mill to my ruin, these holy objects shall be sold to pay my debts.' " He drank again. "And so I won. And so will God's justice be done, even against King Henry's greedy justiciars, who try to rob us of our rights and, worse than any lords, whom they defend, try to cheat and outrank us Churchmen by taking away those laws God gave us."

There was a silence at the end of his tale. The monks looked complacent, and those of noble birth, uncomfortable. Even Robert hastily speared another piece of meat and began to chew, at a loss as to how to reply. But the wine had loosened the abbot's tongue; he leaned forward, trying to grasp Robert's arm in a familiar way.

"Is it not so, my lord?" he insisted. "You and your father were present at Montmirail, at that last meeting between King Henry and our holy archbishop, Thomas à Becket, God rest his soul, who gave his life to protect the Church. You were witness how the archbishop tried to spare the prince from his father's wrath, when, for some boyish prank, the king had clouted him to the ground."

From my place where I did my lord service as a page, waiting on bended knee, offering him ewer and water to wash his hands, I pricked my ears. Here again came talk of Montmirail to plague our thoughts. And ever since I had heard of this great Becket, he had interested me, a commoner born, raised up from low degree by his wits to be the friend of kings and Henry's chancellor. Yet once he became Henry's chief bishop, all that friendship had turned to bitter enmity, and the archbishop himself had been cut down like an ox in its stall, murdered in Canterbury Cathedral before his own high altar. Robert was muttering almost beneath his breath, " 'Twas more than a prank, a drunken jest that went awry. . . ." when the abbot interrupted him, wiping his hand across his face, dripping with sweat and fat.

"Drunk or not," he cried, "the prince was but a lad, feeling his oats; no need for his father's pride to humble him. And was not Becket the only one who dared intervene, raising the prince to his feet and telling Henry that he should desist? 'This is no way to end a holy feast,' the archbishop is supposed to have said, 'a time when all men should be on their knees, praising God for his many gifts, even that greatest gift of all, His son.' "

Seeing his guests' blank looks, the abbot began to laugh, spluttering into his wine as he explained the joke (which being somewhat obscure did not make his listeners smile). "Becket meant," he wheezed, "that the meeting at Montmirail began on January sixth, the feast of Epiphany, when the three wise men brought their gifts to the infant Christ. But more than that, he rebuked the king for stupidity. For when the king had presented his three sons to his French host, to turn a compliment and flatter King Louis, Henry had likened the princes to those same wise men, bearing gifts to the 'King of Kings,' a blasphemy, since no earthly king can resemble our Heavenly one, and as any child knows, the wise men's gifts in no way brought the recipient joy."

When still no one laughed, the abbot hastened on. "In any case, a third rebuke, that Henry should treat his son in such shameful wise. And how did Henry answer Becket's mildness? With more anger, more blasphemy, telling Becket to pray rather to God himself to preserve his archbishopric. 'I've yet a second archbishop at York,' the king is supposed to have snarled, 'who will serve me better than you. He'll crown my son king in your stead.' As in truth this was done; but so much in haste, so contrary to holy practice and common law, that even the king's nobles were dismayed, which was why a second crowning was needed this year, performed by the new Archbishop of Canterbury, Becket now being dead. But consider this, my lord," and the abbot latched his hand in the folds of Robert's sleeve to draw him close, "consider how news of this open brawl has been received, with the young prince sprawled like a strawman between king and prelate. And more, think how the prince must have felt to see Becket again, his benefactor and friend. For Becket had been as a father to the prince, had reared him in his own household, lavished affection and praise on him as his real father has never done. Henry was not even present at his son's birth, as Becket was. Think, too, what that prince must have felt, two years later, to learn of Becket's dreadful death."

He paused to mouth another cup of wine while his monks crossed themselves. "All the world knows," the abbot then cried, "that Becket came to Montmirail to make his peace with the king and to forgive Henry for the malice that had exiled the archbishop in the first place and had hounded him from church to church, not even granting him the right to sanctuary. I saw Becket but once myself, a tall, thin man, who, they say, putting all splendor aside, wore a hair shirt beneath his robes and walked barefoot in sandals like a simple priest. But I remember his eyes, dark and burning with righteous zeal. And so, I think, both prince and king remember him at Montmirail, raising his hand whereon the golden ring of his office gleamed, to intone, 'You risk your soul, Henry of Anjou.' Our great archbishop is also supposed to have warned the king, 'Defying me, you defy God. There can be no crowning without me, nor holy writ nor church service. I uphold the laws of Mother Church, whose appeal is to eternity. Your rule is temporal and dies with you. God hears my just plea, not yours.' "

Once more the monks of Stefensforth paused in their munching long enough to murmur and nod. "And so God has," the abbot went on smugly. "For although Henry ordered Becket's murder when the archbishop returned to Canterbury, has not God found ways to punish the king? This May, at Avranches, did not the papal legates catch up with him, albeit he had skulked for two years in Ireland to avoid them? And was not that penance worse than what was done at Canterbury, where he was forced to strip his clothes and let the monks flog him like a common thief?" He gave a grin. "That has put the mighty Henry where he belongs," he cried, "at the mercy of the Church, which will show him little mercy in its turn."

He grinned again, and now across his face there crept a malicious smile. "As little mercy as others whom he has grievously wronged will show him—even that young son, the Young King, whom he has twice crowned yet never given lands or wealth fitting to the prince's rank and lawful inheritance."

His echo of Earl Raoul's words was startling, the more so that after ordering another flagon of wine, the abbot at last came to the point. "Your father," he said, "the Earl of Sedgemont, is one to whom Henry has done ill. No doubt the earl will join with us in showing Henry what our feelings are, a king who has usurped too much power, who has belittled all our ancient rights, and who has taken Church and noble lands for his own, with the help of his newfangled laws."

Lord Robert continued to chew slowly; a pheasant's wing had never tasted so tough. "It was a grievous death," at last he said, careful to avoid offense, but the abbot banged his fist, scattering dishes and making the table jump.

"A sin," he cried, "a sin, a sin. That we shall make Henry answer for. And his enemies shall take heart to see him tumbled in the dust." He lowered his voice and hissed in my lord's ear. "It will give excuse to many English lords who have been searching for a way to show their support for Henry's son, the new Young King. I wonder only that they have not risen before. Perhaps now they will."

At Robert's elbow, where I had been listening avidly, I shuddered at the abbot's words, so that the wine ran and dripped upon the white tablecloth. The abbot frowned.

"God's life, my lord," he said, sending one of his own servitors scurrying. "You are ill-served. Your state deserves greater respect." He paused again. "There are men who would accord it to you," he whispered, "great lords, princes, who think highly of you if you would but join with them. You are the older son, you deserve such courtesies. I hear you were not permitted to attend Winchester. I hear your younger brother was."

Robert set his goblet firmly down amid the litter of broken meats. "What my father does or does not do," he said, "is my father's choice. And between my brother and me is complete trust."

The abbot's eyes, under their layers of skin, grew hot, as

men's do when they lust for confidence, avaricious for it as a woman is. "We speak as friends," he whispered again. "Henry, the Old King, is doomed. God has given us a new one. The new Young King is already gone ahead to France and has promised to return after the Yuletide to meet with us. He will win King Louis to his cause. England will have need of men like you."

Robert suddenly stood up. "You speak treason, my lord abbot," he cried. Beside the abbot he looked tall and young.

"Treason, God's teeth," the abbot spluttered. His look, in a flash, turned venomous, his white hands, with their many rings, held in the air as if in supplication. "You speak too blunt. Treason is not a word friends of the Church would use. But since treachery is a label that the king would have put on Thomas à Becket when he said, as men report, 'Will no one kill that treacherous priest?' well, then, perhaps treachery is not so bad a thing. For what is treachery to a king already dishonored, deserving to be excommunicated, outside the laws of God and man? You talk with the naïveté of a child. As your father's heir you could speak for him."

"My father's advice is well known," Robert said, grave as a monk. "Long has he kept to his word, as he gave it last at Montmirail, neither for nor against. Neutrality he keeps, and so shall I."

But when we had withdrawn, Robert raged as only a young man can, striding back and forth along the silent cloisters, leaning on my arm as he sometimes still did from habit, although he topped me by a good foot, stopping sometimes to hurl curses that must have made those holy walls shake. "Play with me," he cried, "that abbot is a fool to try to make me ally to his treachery. For treachery it is, despite his devious arguments. Yet other fools will listen to him. But never the Earl of Sedgemont nor his sons. Nor am I so young that I do not know what he has in mind, to spread ill will between Hue and me. God's wounds, and all because the abbot nurses a grievance against the king as large as his belly and as full of chaff. For once when Henry spent a night here, the abbot, thinking to ingratiate himself, complained of the local bishop. It seems the bishop had taken offense at the abbey's riches and display, especially in the matter of food. 'Ten courses is all the bishop allows,' the abbot is said to have whined, 'whereas before I scarce made do with twice that amount.' They say King Henry looked at him, round and about as a man might do examining a horse's girth. 'Twenty courses,' the king exclaimed. 'At court, my lord abbot, we do with three. So shall the bishop order you.' "

I had to laugh. "But, my lord," I said worriedly when we were safely back inside, guards posted at our door, the Lady Olwen and her ladies, without the walls, well guarded, too, "that abbot may be a fool, yet he knows some secret, I'll be bound."

Robert looked at me keenly. "Urien the Bard," he said, much as his sister might, or Dylan, but without Dylan's mockery, "you have sensed what men older than you seem determined to ignore. Aye, I know what the abbot wants. War. Civil war, as we have had in the past, twenty years of it. You heard my father speak, you know what he thinks."

That word sank like a stone against my heart; I could feel its coldness like a weight, a coldness that is with me still.

"But the abbot is a holy man," I stammered. "Why should he want war?"

"Churchmen fight as well as knights," Robert told me shortly. "Duke William's brother Odo, Bishop of Bayeux, rode to battle at the duke's side and used a mace to avoid the curse of fighting with a sword, that way to keep within the letter of the holy law. So do all these Churchmen, who will use Becket's death to feather their own nests. They own lands; they have knights within their service; they will fight."

He said thoughtfully after a while, "That Archbishop Becket was a holy man, I agree. Yet stubborn, too. Henry chose him as archbishop because he thought he would help control the Church, not encourage it. I have a memory myself, once, when I was small, of seeing him pass, a tall, noble-looking man, at the head of a great procession, a line of sumpter mules, carts, carriages, stretched out for miles, with monkeys capering on strings like dogs, the wedding gifts, I think, for Prince Henry's bride. God knows, Becket put such riches behind him when he was made archbishop, more than this abbot does. But a crowning at Winchester does not really give us a new king; and Becket, who loved the prince, would have been the first to point that out."

Robert was silent for a while. Then almost to himself he burst out again. "For treason is what it is, to rise against a living king. And sin to rise against a father. But God's life, what shall I do if Henry's brothers rise with him; who then should I serve?"

Well, a strange messenger that abbot had been, spilling out secrets on a gust of wine. That night came worse. For as we slept, there was a scratching at our door. I had been sleeping with Lord Robert's squire, both of us in one pallet at the foot of our master's bed, and was awake myself, the squire being tall and strong, with long legs, which he thrashed about, disturbing my sleep. That scratching noise of steel on wood sends the senses flaring, awakes the nerves as no noise else. It roused the squire on an instant for his sword, whilst Robert as quick snatched up his, both mother-naked, advancing on the door. The squire, coldly professional in a way I was to admire, jerked the latch while Robert guarded him. The men who fell inside were known to us, although in truth no one might have recognized the second of them, his face a mask of blood, his mail coat streaked with it, his sword arm gashed apart. We hauled him to his feet and sat him down, whilst the other guards we had posted came crowding around. When he could speak, the wounded man told us news that struck a silence and a fear, such is the cost of treachery. He came from Sedgemont with tidings, simply told, an echo of the abbot's own. The castle was shut, the guard were left there in siege alert, and the earl and his lady wife were gone ahead to France, to Paris, departed already this past week, where we were bid to follow them. The cause? That war the abbot had spoken of was ready to break out, not only here in England but everywhere the Angevins ruled, even in Anjou and Maine, the paternal homelands. So came the warning that was to change our lives.

The Great War, so they called it of Henry's reign, as if war can be called great. And we, despite the earl's hope of neutrality, were caught up in its midst. For this was no small skirmishing, here now, there next, but one combined, united effort set off by the archbishop's death and led by the king's own son.

And our messenger, how came he to be in such a state? As his wounds were bound, he gasped out the rest: how hastening in the dark, hoping against hope he would catch us before we had left Cambray, a good month's ride away, he had stumbled on a group of men guarding the one road across the abbey lands. Who they were he did not know, nor what they wanted, but having blundered upon them in the dark, he blundered through, and they let him go. Wiser then in the aftermath, he had circled back and, seizing one of them in turn, had soon pricked the details out of him. Abbey men, they were, the abbot's knights, making a blockade to the north to stop us when we rode out at dawn.

"Now by the bones of Saint George, which this holy abbot swears he owns." Robert was angry, striding back and forth so his squire, half-dressed, could not begin to dress him. "By the holy Mass, which he will be too drunk to celebrate, he does not hold me captive to his will, nor attack my father's messenger. How are those churls positioned, where?"

Back and forth Robert strode again, his father's self, whilst we armed and prepared, listening to the messenger's assessment. He had blundered in and blundered out, but one man, even in the dark, does not easily fight his way clear. A Cambray ambush would never have let a man escape to reveal their whereabouts. And although the abbot's knights were more numerous than we, by everyone's guess they were soldiers who, like their master, had grown lax, unlikely to detain us long if we took them unawares. But break out we must, at once, before they began to think and came to close around the abbey to hem us in.

Now I saw for the first time how Cambray could arm and ride, what Dylan had prepared us for; an exercise become grim reality. It was the first of what, in after years, we would grow accustomed to. *You may regret leaving Cambray.* This was but the start, the format, of our future life. Yet as the horses were led out, having been saddled the evening before, and as the men silently mounted in the dark, not a whisper, not a sound, save the muffled clink of iron and steel, all gear previously loaded, everything muffled that could be safely so, I realized what a great captain Dylan truly was. Nothing was left to chance; the baggage train sorted through, all that could be abandoned was left behind (better to leave what was not necessary than be slowed down), and the Lady Olwen and her ladies were already similarly prepared. So that, although we left in haste, not standing on ceremony, we left in good array, not shoddily. And although we made a noise, as who could fail to hear when we stormed out of the main abbey gates, the abbot and his monks slept through, either because they thought it wise to pretend sleep or because, deep drunk, they never heard us at all. In any case, they must have relied on the ambush to stop us. That, too, was a mistake.

We let the wounded messenger lead us, he remembering which way he had come more by feel than by sense, for we left the road at once and cut across the open fields. In the darkness they all seemed the same, a mire of mud we floundered through and hedges like stone walls, with banks of turf and ditches on the other side that we had to break across. The women rode with us, top speed, their skirts knotted up, astride like troopers, not one word of distress from them. And when in the grayness of dawn we saw ahead the curve of the road (handsomely paved by the abbot's sweating peasantry), the women, those who could, rode on with us like men, with knives drawn.

The abbot's men had posted themselves against a hedge, with an open field behind their backs. It was still not light. The ambushers were lounging negligently, looking down the road, not expecting us, and in any event waiting for a leisurely group of travelers, not armed men spoiling for a quarrel. For Robert was angry, and although perhaps not wise in turn, he was determined to teach that abbot a lesson. Seeing the Stefensforth knights, he planned to charge right through their midst to teach them a lesson, too, and so he did. His voice rang out like his father's. "*À moi*, Sedgemont, *à moi*, Cambray." Our own knights took up the cry, not even having to urge their horses forward.

Downfield we beat, surged in upon the poor wretches, caught them looking the wrong way, caught them off guard as they had hoped to catch us. And with us rode the Lady Olwen, her dagger in her hand. And I rode with her.

What did I see? A startled face that crumpled apart; a sword arm suddenly flung wide; a hedge that blurred into a line of men, shifting and crumbling like the turf we kicked apart. When I could see again, we were through, and the Lady Olwen was shouting in my ear, "Draw, you dolt, draw," for although I had ridden in a charge, I had not even had the sense to unsheathe my sword. By the time I had struggled to free it, the fracas was already done, and whatever remained of the abbot's men had run howling back for sanctuary in their church.

Well, in the semi-dark it would have been as easy to ride round as break them down, but in this instance, I think, Robert was justified. So now, honor appeased, we wheeled back, rounding up the rest of the womenfolk; and if Robert saw how his sister rode, he did not blame her this once. But she said to me, as in more seemly way we headed toward the coast, making for the nearest port, the messenger sent back to Sedgemont, "Urien the Bard, I never thought to see you ride or fight." She turned to me suddenly, her hair fallen down, her dress ripped. She did not look like an earl's daughter now, more like the peasant maid I once had thought her. "So will you serve me, when the time is ripe."

"Lady," I told her, reining back so that we were out of earshot, "I cannot swear twice an oath that I have already sworn. But I repeat: I will serve you and your house as long as I have life. No more, no less."

"Well said, Urien," she told me. "And will you help me with anything I ask?"

"I swear."

"Good," she said. She suddenly smiled and stretched out her hand as she used to do. "One day I will hold you to that oath."

Thus it was that we heard the news of war and, escaping the abbot's attempt to force us to his will, came to the Channel coast, looking for a ship to France. And thus began the worst year of our lives.

Chapter 7

have made the journey to Paris many times since, seldom in weather so vile as then, a Yuletide spent in a dirty little port, in a fisherman's hut. And so it was that our journey, begun in leisure and grace, ended in a race for safety. A wise old fox was Dylan, no stranger to the vagrancies of the world; for in his cunning way he prepared us to expect the worst. And such were the whims of fate that all of us whose lives were entwined were destined to meet again.

Yet that cold December wait was one we might well have regretted. Cambray, with its homey amusements, kept up by Dylan, as seneschal, in traditional way, seemed in another world; the feasting for the villagers, the fires built with the Yule log, the spits for meat, the white bread for everyone, became things to dream about. This year we did not even have enough food, certainly no mummer's play or new suit of clothes, only the fishermen's huts and their smells were familiar. Well, this, then, was the other side of traveling with great lords; this, too, the consequence of greatness.

But when at last we were embarked on ships—better equipped, I hasten to add, and if not better built at least larger than those Prince Taliesin had journeyed on—I noted how the Lady Olwen kept watch beneath the forecastle, made of wood, as if looking for pirates herself.

"Courage, little sister," Robert said, coming up to her. He

looked at her, his brow furrowed. For there was no doubt that in these past weeks she had grown thinner and more pale than before. He had been seeing to the bestowing of his horses and men, fore and aft, making all as safe and comfortable as space allowed, and now he had a moment to think of her comfort, too. "Courage," he repeated. "The crossing will not take long. And he will already be there ahead of us."

The "he" was Lord Gervaise, of course, and the thought was kindly meant. But that was not of whom Olwen was thinking, and her gaze was fixed westward, not south; west to Brittany, not south to Paris, where we went.

But when we landed on the French coast, every day, every place, were signs of that general unrest, Henry's enemies springing up like weeds to thrust him off. And everywhere, men speaking, in tones hushed or shocked or relieved, of Henry's submission to the Church, as if that were the sign they waited for, the proof that God was on their side. And those who had most nursed their resentment secretly now were most open in defiance, most determined to be rid of a strange, cruel, and clever king, whose rule had been too long and hard.

In later years I have heard scholars, well known, dispute the cause of this Great War, laying blame here or there for this or that, as their own detachment allows. But they were far removed from the war and its start; easy to sit before a fire with warm feet and argue dispassionately among their books. Those of us who lived through it, this greatest, worst war of Henry's time, would agree upon two things. One was that the archbishop's death, a murder that had shocked all Christendom, was in truth the main reason for this war. The other, that the king's treatment of his son was the second cause. Myself, I will add a third, and it, I think, was equally strong: the claims of that young Welsh prince, who was to submerge his own personal wrongs in this general one, and yet whose personal quarrel was the most true, and most just.

We did not meet up with this prince (although presently we were to have tidings of him, as shall be told) but everywhere heard news of other rebels making their bid against the king. And as I took my duties of scribe seriously, I made careful note of their names (the more so since when we arrived at Paris ourselves, we found the earl but not the Lady Ann, who had been left behind to act as chatelaine at Sieux in these dangerous times). So much of what I recall was writ for her, a priest at Sieux serving as lector, since she could not read herself. That list of names, names heard of, names met up with, names dropped as hint, seemed to encompass the whole world, all men riding, like us, on the same errand, bent for a feast, to carve up King Henry's lands, determined to snatch their share.

Knights there were, small men with a squire or two and great lords with their retinues, hotfooted on the same quest, names I still remember, names to savor like honey, clinging to the tongue, sweet to roll around, the men who bore them less sweet. They came from Normandy; Gilbert de Tillières, the lords of Conches and Breteuil, Arnulf, the Bishop of Lisieux, the Count of Eu, ever ready for rebellion. They came from Maine and Anjou, well-known lords of Sarthe, Huîsne, and Mayenne, long restive under Henry's rule, spoiling for fight; and south again from Aquitaine, the border lords of Poitou and Angoulême. And from still farther south came lords of Toulouse, ever a thorn in Henry's flesh.

Some came alone, slipping along furtively; others rode openly as at a fair, dressed in their best, greeting each other as friends, although in the past they had not always been friendly; so does rebellion beget strange bedfellows. Yet all were armed; their forces, large or small, battle-keen, riding in haste, looking for allies or to be allied in a cause that was become common to all men. That Benedictine abbot was a fool, but not in this. If anything, he underestimated the rising against the English king and the strength of its leadership under the new Young King, Prince Henry. And where was that King Henry, where his son, in whose name this commotion was bestirred? Gone from Louis's court, gone south to the Auvergne, all this rebellion broken out in their absence, as now we heard.

Since then I have met nobles, more than my share, and have come to know the way of the world. I no longer gaze about me in that blank stare with which, like Prince Taliesin's men, I hid amaze under guise of nonconcern. So I will add that, to my taste, most of the lords we met on the high road to Paris that January of 1173, a wet and windy one, were a patchwork of ruffians. For every one who had genuine grievance, a hundred were like that fat abbot, puffing up a personal spite into a major claim, seeking to further their own ends. Yet had they been in King Henry's place, they would have acted exactly as the king had done. As we rode, for the most part through a mist of rain and sleet, I thought I had never seen such sodden fields, such rough forest stretches, such dreary plains, all soaked underfoot and gray above, portent of the times we lived in.

But one day we did hear of that Celtic prince, to make my lady's eyes shine and give her heart. It was the end of a long, wet ride, and come the evening we were all weary, hungry, cold. With a group of strangers (for as we traveled now through the French king's lands, we found we were often joined by these other lords and, whether we would or no, were obliged to make a company with them), at the day's close, then, when, in yet another villainous hostelry, we waited to see our horses stabled and fed, I began to wander, in my way, among the ragtag groups who made up the various lords' retinues. My lady Olwen and her squire (for she had a squire these days, Joycelyn by name, a stouthearted and strong young man who took his duties seriously) had come trailing after me, glad to stretch their legs, even through the mud. I had often before found things of interest in these nightly walks, heard strange tales, picked up more gossip than our betters did when they sat at meat; for this is the hour when men let down their guard and speak freely of their plans and fears. This particular evening my attention was soon caught by two men. They were afoot, yet their clothes were too fine, too elaborate, albeit stained with travel, for mere menials (although afterward, knowing better, I would have recognized their finery as old, outdated, belonging to another age). The French they spoke was different, too, and they had an air, not so much of secrecy as rather of reserve and haste.

The older man was tall but bent. He moved stiffly, as if his joints were cramped, yet had he been better attended or on horseback, I might have marked him down as a minor baron, come to offer his service at King Louis's court, for he had a look of nobility. But even a disgruntled lord would not travel so meanly, without escort, with only one elderly servant to wrestle with his bundles and one younger man, his son, I guessed, who at least was armed, as his father was not. They had the same dark hair, thin face, sallow skin, except that in the son the father's distinguished look had not yet emerged, or rather had been submerged into furtiveness, which the close-set dark eyes enhanced.

Such a sidelong glance the son now cast at me, then paused and nudged his father's arm so that the older man, too, turned slowly, with the expression of one used to looking and judging. Yet when he spoke, his voice was hesitant, and it was his son who told him what to say.

"Boy," the older man, prompted, now asked, his voice low with fatigue and some other thing, "boy, who serve you?"

Perfectly at ease in looking and listening, I did not like to be questioned thus, especially since my lady and Joycelyn had walked on. The younger man, irritated by my silence, gave me a push. "Speak up," he hissed, "answer with courtesy."

Since I meant my reply to be courteous, I gave the name slowly, and the older man repeated it as if he were savoring it, "Robert of Sieux, Robert of Sieux," until his son nudged him again and whispered in his ear.

"I did your master a service once." The old voice grew stronger, as if memory had come flooding back. "And his father, too, Raoul of Sieux. We met long ago." There was both pride and melancholy in his voice, and he smiled, a faint old smile, as he repeated a third time, "Robert of Sieux. I helped him and the Lady Ann, his mother; of all the ladies at the court I honored her."

He did not say anything then for a long while but picked at the edges of his sleeves, seeming to have forgotten why he was there and what he meant to say, like a man whose wits have been addled with age. His son gave him a despairing glance, whispered in his ear, meanwhile looking at me malevolently.

"Sir page," the old man began a third time, whatever thoughts had taken him away finally brought back to earth, "I know the lords of Sedgemont and recognize their colors that you wear.

Give your masters greetings. Sir Renier of Poitou am I, once high in the courts of France, when its queen was Eleanor of Aquitaine. And I served King Henry, too, ever since as a young man, full of grace, he came to marry Eleanor and bear her hence to England as queen again. As now I am come to act for that queen, with her first husband, the King of France."

It was hard to believe, yet I would not have contradicted him, an old man whose door of memory had suddenly opened wide. "I may not be as welcome as once I was," the old man went on. "King Louis does not hold me as dear as when Queen Eleanor and I kept all of Paris in our hands. Messenger have I been, and confidant of king and queen, listened to their secrets, heard their hearts' wishes. So shall I be again when war breaks out."

His voice, which had been fierce, almost jubilant, faltered. I held my peace. It does not do to tell a man who has been messenger to a king that his news is stale. But perhaps he guessed my thoughts, his courtier's instincts the last to go; some ingrained wariness kept him always on guard, alert to every nuance, every threat, in a world where danger lurks in smiles and malice is hid in ordinary talk. "I make no claim nor seek praise," he said, "but the real news I bring will startle everyone. Eleanor, beloved by all men, will raise up fire and sword against her husband. Then let King Henry beware."

Here was news indeed. This time the son did try to hush him, meanwhile giving me looks behind his father's back. I knew those looks. No son likes to hear his father boast, still less admit to bad luck, and least of all to reveal his frailty to a hostile world. "Listen to the old man's ramblings all you wish," that look said, "repeat a word of them, and you regret the day you were born."

Seeing that look, I felt kindlier to the young man and was surprised that when his father moved out of earshot, under the care of the servant, the son rounded on me. I tried to duck out of his way, but he seized and shook me hard, his black eyes snapping. His breath was hot and smelled of garlic, strange in a would-be courtier, and although at first I cannot say I was seriously alarmed—after all, my lady's squire, Joycelyn, was not far away—yet a man can take a dagger in his ribs between one breath and the next. But I will also say that, had I had time to think, I would have admired his anger. For it was on his father's behalf, and not all sons protect their fathers with such zeal.

"My father speaks the truth, boy," he was whispering fiercely in my ear. "Even if sickness has dulled his wits, he knows the court. News comes to him that no other men have access to. I tell you, page, with your fine clothes and swaggering ways," for he had noted, quick as his father once must have been, how proudly I held myself, "there are plots afoot that would frighten you out of your skull, had you any brains to put therein, such a gathering of noblemen not seen since the world was young. Many lords will attend my queen, not only from Aquitaine and Poitou, but also from Normandy and Brittany, from—"

His list ended suddenly when Lady Olwen turned around. Perhaps it was this last name that caught her ear, or perhaps it was the sound of his voice growing louder than he meant, but she and her squire suddenly realized the scuffle I was in. Quick as Joycelyn was to draw his sword, my lady was quicker still. "Leave my page alone," she cried. "Pick on someone your own size." And she rushed toward my assailant, prepared to use her fists.

At her voice, the youth let go my arm and stood gaping at her. "Holy Mother," he had time to ask before both she and Joycelyn bore down upon him, "who is that lady, what is her name?"

I told him, dusting myself free, not overpleased to have been rescued by a maid, but a sudden surge of pity for the old man and for the son overcame my misgivings. "Sir," I said, in my way a courtier, too, "I bear you no ill will, nor your noble father. This lady is Olwen, of the house I serve."

"Daughter, then, of the Lady Ann." A slow, painful blush overspread his cheeks. Before my lady and her squire could reach us he went toward them, cap in hand, with a courtier's bow that revealed him in a better light. "Lady," he said, and now you saw how he had been trained to address a highborn lady of rank with skill and taste, "lady, tell me how I shall serve you, and it is done. My name is Bernard from Poitou. With my father I am come to court about state affairs. Sir Renier is he, cousin to Queen Eleanor, long her councillor, a man, I think, not unknown to you."

She knitted her brows together. "Aye," she cried, "I think my mother has spoken of him. And you, what do you do, Bernard of Poitou?"

"Lady," he replied, "if you remember that name, you will know my father and I wish you well. But there may be others," he hesitated, "who will not be so kind, who, conjuring up old enmities, will look to do you harm."

"But who would harm me?" she asked in her forthright way. "Not with my brother, not with my squire, Joycelyn, not with my faithful watchdog, the Celtic bard." And she smiled at me and bid Joycelyn put up his sword.

"Perhaps so." Bernard of Poitou sounded dubious. "But my father is wiser than you think. In his day no man was more skilled to scent out danger and intrigue, a wolfhound on the trail not more quick. He knows what spies Queen Eleanor has called out, and where put them, in high place and low. He knows what old friends she relies upon to give her fresh access to Louis's court. Be careful, I beg." He flushed again. "Perhaps I speak out of place," he said. "I shall be new in Paris myself." He gave a sudden rueful grin that made him seem less surly, gave his ill-favored face a certain charm. "This is my first venture into the high world of courts and kings, and I must seek out service where I can. My father believes, nay prays, that he will find his purpose in life again, and I am come to give him comfort and support. Better, I think, we should have stayed at home. However, since we are here, we must survive as best we can. And if there is any way I can be of service to you, ask and it is done."

"There is one thing." Lady Olwen's face grew pensive; she bit her nether lip, and I saw how her fingers played with the streamers from her wide sleeves, winding them into little knots. "You spoke of Brittany. Tell me, what do you know of Prince Taliesin?"

"The Welsh prince?" Bernard of Poitou did not blink or show

surprise, his father's training standing in good stead. "Lady, I think all men will know him soon. He brings half of Brittany with him." One look at her face convinced him to go on. Gesturing to the servant and his father that he would follow them, he hunkered down beside my lady there in the stableyard and began to tell her what he knew, while I, in dismay, stared at her, not believing she would so openly speak of the one man she should not. And so we heard Prince Taliesin's tale, pieced together in later years from what Bernard of Poitou now told and the prince himself remembered.

"In Brittany," Bernard now told us, "the prince landed in Finisterre. He did not lack for friends, it seems, but what he lacked at first, to Breton eyes, I mean, was experience. A Welsh prince, not used to fighting in Norman battlefields, might well prove more of a hindrance than a help, or so the Bretons thought, even though they heard he had brought an army with him, and Welsh bowmen are an asset to any cause. Viscount Guiomar of Finisterre is rough, a giant of a man whose lisp belies the ferocity of his character. His open contempt toward the young prince, when first that salt-drenched band appeared on shore, has become legendary. I tell you what I know, lady," Bernard added apologetically as my lady's face clouded at this news. "Take heart, it ends well. 'Damn his eyes,' the viscount is first reported to have said, 'I'll not play wet-nurse to a Welsh cub scarcely dry behind his ears.' And he is supposed to have added in an aside, which, since his broken voice carries as well as a loud one, was easily heard, 'On foot, no less, like all those Welsh bowmen they brag about.' Viscount Guiomar meant that for an insult, of course, being Norman-influenced enough to despise any soldier who walks. Not my opinion, lady, you understand," he added hastily, as Lady Olwen began to protest. "I merely report what was said, and I know the prince rides as well as the next man. For listen now. When the prince and his Celts arrived at the viscount's fortress, a windswept, dilapidated affair, I hear, not so much in need of repair as of being finished (a Breton fault—they seldom stick to one task long), on seeing the prince, the viscount was obliged to change his mind, for Taliesin took the last remark as a compliment. 'If I could walk

or run like my bowmen,' the prince is supposed to have said,
'why, my lord, then would I, as soldier, be content, and so
would you, since no men run or fight as well as they do. Myself,
I prefer a horse. My legs are long and get in my way afoot.' "

This was a clever and wise reply that made Guiomar smile,
although he hid his amusement. And indeed, they say that lord
of Finisterre is like the place where he lives, as fickle as a summer
sea, one moment smiling fair, the next running to storm, and
no man knowing the reason for the change. 'Ride, then,' the
viscount is supposed to have said to the prince, and beckoning
to his grooms had them lead out secretly a black stallion, a
great, heavy, hard-mouthed beast, which in fact was already
deeded to the Church, having, like its master, killed a priest.
It had not been ridden in a while and was stable-wild. It fought
and reared, throwing the grooms about like twigs. But when
Prince Taliesin saw it, judging its temper and noting, as the
grooms had failed to do, that its mouth was a mass of sores
where the curb chain had cut too tight, he vaulted into the
saddle without touching the rein and, when the grooms let it
go, brought it to a standstill, using knees and spurs. Watching
him, Viscount Guiomar is said to have sworn by God's legs,
his favorite curse, and lisped, 'Christ's balls, but the lad speaks
truth.' Leaping from his chair, he embraced the prince whole-
heartedly in Celtic style."

Bernard looked down at the Lady Olwen, who had followed
him, her eyes bright, her head on one side, as she holds it when
engrossed. "And so they say," he finished simply, "thereafter,
riding on that black horse at the head of his men, Prince Taliesin
helped the viscount in a local quarrel and so proved his worth
with battle skills, a bonny fighter, so they claim, quick and
clean, a swordsman as well as a horseman, certainly trained in
all knightly skills. And when the word was given for the Bretons
to rise, place was made for the prince under the viscount's
banner. All through these months they have been skirmishing,
the prince and his six horsemen, who, they say, like shadows,
follow him wherever he goes (having sworn in their turn never
to leave him), together showing themselves a match for any
Norman cavalry. And in the taking of the castle at Dol, a fortress

that lies on the western boundary of Normandy and that has been the scene of much bitter controversy, the prince himself led a sortie that drew out the castle guard and so enabled the Bretons to break inside. Afterward the viscount is said to have thrown his arms about the prince's neck and called him son, and knighted him upon the spot."

As the Lady Olwen clapped her hands, Bernard added dryly, "Not that the prince welcomed it, but Viscount Guiomar explained that to the Norman mind, a man unknighted is not considered of noble birth, and since he is shrewd in all his dealings with a Norman enemy, he pointed out to the prince that if Taliesin was to deal on equal terms with them, best to prepare in a way they would understand.

"And so it is, the favorite of the Breton lords, their honored friend Prince Taliesin, has left them quartered for the while along the border near Dol and has himself struck across Normandy, he and his six companions. They await Prince Henry, to make a claim of him. And that, lady," he said with a bow, "is all that I know about Prince Taliesin."

"God be praised." My lady threw her arms about Bernard and embraced him in her carefree way. "Master Bernard, you are truly my friend. I thank you for your courtesy." Gratitude rendered in such wise was enough to make his very ears burn red.

But when he had gone, promising to tell her when Prince Taliesin arrived, my lady turned to me and thanked me, too, for making a new friend for her. I hung my head. She guessed at once what my thought was—my expression gave me away—and rounded on me, suddenly fierce.

"And should I forever be silent?" she cried, and there was a note in her voice that was new to me, a resolution, I think, an acceptance of things. "Shall I nurse my grief, not daring to confide in anyone, not even in you, my best friend? Must I sit here, go there, do this, be that, as if I have no will of my own, and never know how Taliesin fares? And should I forever listen to someone else bleating in my ears, such lustful words I do not care to repeat? Oh, Urien the Bard, I thought you cared for me more than that. Robert's punishment thrust me into a living tomb. What shall I do if even in my thoughts I cannot escape?"

She was taller than I by now, and looked at me, her dark eyes piteous, like a hart struck by a spear. Her words were like wounds in my own flesh. What could I do or say who must also be silent in front of her? She took my hand and held it so tight that her knuckles turned blue and white. "Urien the Bard," she whispered, "rejoice with me. I shall see him again, I feel it, I know it to be so. But I swear I want nothing from him, only to see his face. Nor shall I look at him except as one friend may look at another one after a long and dangerous absence. I swear I will ask for nothing else."

I could not resist her blandishments. "If you do everything a woman says," so said the prince, "you'll be a dead man before you're grown." Aye so, but in his time he was as helpless as I. No word was ever spoken of Sir Renier or his son to sound alarm, and so it was, as God willed, we came by slow degrees to the greatest city of the world, and once again I held my peace. Not my lady. Now she chattered like a magpie, pointing out all the sights, although they were as new to her; forever begging Robert to make haste; all for hurrying night and day, happiness spilling from her like effervescent wine. But when we came to the city gates, she, too, was overwhelmed. In later years I was to see this mother of cities many times, in fair weather and foul, but never like this, now, as a boy, fresh from the Cambray border, wide-eyed and curious. The impression remains from that early February day when we finally clattered through its streets, of towers, houses, churches, bridges, all mixed together pell-mell, with a muddy, winding river in full spate to bind them in. That jumble of buildings, the filth in the streets, and the herds of pigs allowed to roam as scavengers I shall never forget, most of all the pigs. Indeed, they said a former king's son, brother to the present one, was killed when his horse stumbled over a herd of swine, and sure enough the pigs that day looked sufficient big and sufficient tusked to kill a man. In later years, when Paris became again the center of Crusade, with walls and towers and turrets and new battlements to transform a small city into a citadel, I came to know it well, certainly better than this first time, when we seemed to spend most of our days either waiting for someone to arrive or planning how we were ourselves to leave, when, in the midst of this upsurge of war, Earl Raoul hung grimly to his hope of peace.

One other thing I also recall. In those days many great lords had built small fortresses of their own, like small castles, set within and without the city walls, with vineyards and garden plots scattered in between. Most of these were grouped about the central island, Île de la Cité, one end of which was dominated by the king's own fort, the other by the bishop's palace, with stone bridges linking both to the mainland. Earl Raoul, true to his own idea of things, had chosen lodgings for himself away from this more noble part and close to the center of a different world, which, again in later years, was to interest me more than any noble one. This was the University of Paris. For if there was one thing Paris was famous for it was its scholarship; and although scholarship has never been my prime concern (a poet studies men, rather than their brains), yet even I, from a rustic backwater, could not fail to notice the excitement that the university generated, almost palpitating, as we wound our way through the crowded streets where the students lived.

The house roofs met over our heads, making a tunnel, if not a tower of Babel, in which every tongue was spoken although none, I swear, was ever listened to. At every doorway students, in their long black gowns, came surging out, like squires bent on quarrel, with tongues as sharp as swords and wits like weapons to beat each other down. And as we tried to make a passage through, like to die of suffocation if not from stench, I thought I had never seen such a violent, gesticulating, shouting, laughing, crying, arguing mass of men, alive with thoughts to their fingers' ends. They reminded me of a shoal of fish, leaping and sparkling in the sun. I could have watched and listened to them for weeks.

To tell the truth there is little else I recall of that first time in Paris; nor, in the end, was our arrival as pleasing as it might have been. For when, by dint of force, using the butt end of their spears, the flat of their swords, our weary troops pushed a way clear, I found Earl Raoul's quarters were not so grand as

I had hoped, a palace being the least of my expectations. Although the building was stone-built, with guards in plenty and a great open meadow to the rear, and although afterward I realized how well the earl had chosen, close to the students' section, where any armed men would seem intruders and certainly would have as much difficulty in passing through as we did, I had hoped to be at the center of the world of court and kings. Nor was I happy, I suppose, to find us stranded here, without the Lady Ann, my mentor and my guide, who, as I have explained, had stayed behind at Sieux. And least happy of all to discover, in her stead, the smiling person of Lord Gervaise, dressed in the latest Paris style with long furred gown against the cold, waiting before the thick iron-studded gate to lift the Lady Olwen from her horse. Nor, being ever alert where she was concerned, overzealous on her behalf, was I pleased to catch the look the earl at once exchanged with his son. For the earl gave his nod, that half-shrug of his which asked as plainly as words spoken aloud, "Is that the man? Will he do?" Aye do, to turn a noble lady into a noble wife. I scowled, limped off, saddle-sore, and would have given my right arm to have been back safe with my lady at Cambray, far from these noble lords and all their schemes. Sunk deep into my own personal misery, I never thought at first what the lady herself would feel, to see the man she had played with now standing there, waiting for her to fulfill her debt.

Chapter 8

ell, Gervaise was there in the flesh; nothing could be done to change that. And full of himself, telling us at once of his visit to Canterbury, where he had prayed for service in God's holy cause and "for other things." What they were he would not say, but from my lady's blush I guessed she knew.

"So much for Crusade, boy." The earl interrupted him to take his daughter's hand, looking at her with troubled eyes. He noted at once, as others should have done, her silence, her trembling stance, her downcast eyes. The earl knew women better than his son did. His own eyebrows drew close. If this were love, then his daughter loved like no woman he had ever known, and sharply he bid Lady Olwen's maids take her indoors at once, to bring her to food and warmth. His look was thoughtful when he turned again to his son and threw his arm around his neck as a sign of affection. "There'll be no Crusaders here this year," he told us. "A pack of wolves with Louis as huntsman leading them. I hope they will not swallow him whole first. And Henry, about to let his empire crumble apart in his absence. But come, lads, a cup of wine. I am glad, at least, to have you here."

The earl, too, had grown thinner, I thought, in these past months, his limp more noticeable; and although he showed his son his usual courtesy, it was clear to me he had many cares on his mind. Which, as soon as he had gone about his own affairs, Gervaise of Walran did not hesitate to reveal.

"You should have come earlier," he cried to Robert when they were alone (and as Robert's page I followed, as was correct, although Gervaise glowered at me, more openly showing his disfavor now that he was so well entrenched, holding grudge, I suspect, for the affair at Cambray and disliking the Lady Olwen's protection of me). "I had not seen King Louis before," Gervaise now went on, settling himself and his intended future brother-in-law in a comfortable niche against the broad staircase steps, which were wood-wrought, with a carved balustrade, a nicety I had never seen and found less comfortable to lean against than our old stone pillars at Cambray. "I had not thought King Louis so old. I thought . . ." And for a moment he was silent, musing perhaps to himself on what he imagined a crusading king would be, as he saw King Henry, or even perhaps himself, a perfect knight, in burnished mail, surcoated in white, a soldier of God.

"Louis rode on Crusade almost twenty-five years ago," Robert told him in his wry way. "He is no longer young."

"Aye," Gervaise agreed, "and he looks his age. His face is thin, and on it are engraved deep lines, signs, they say, of the illness that has begun to plague him since Montmirail. They say," he hesitated, "they say in the midst of some discourse he goes apart and, wrapping himself in his cloak, falls asleep as peaceful as a child. They say," and now he did lower his voice, "his words are husks of grain, blown here, now there, by the wind. I myself heard Earl Raoul praise God that the king was still in Paris since he was more like to have turned tail and fled back to Reims or retreated to some monastic cell."

Again he mused. "But there is another thing," he said after a while. "King Louis is proud. Illness, defeat, three wives, and the son who was born at last still too young to rule if Louis dies, his kingdom all but lost, and he himself prepared to risk the rest in one desperate throw; nevertheless, he still believes in his undisputed right to be God's envoy on earth. His most faithless words are spoken to air, as if he expects God to take them and firm them up, as if God's voice speaks through him. Yet he was not even born to be king. His older brother should have reigned and Louis been placed in church choir or monastery, where he is happiest. He showed his worst side when he saw Earl Raoul, or Count Raoul, I suppose, as I should call him here. I wish you had been there, Robert," he said, and now his voice was all respect; he spoke as becomes a man of sense in the face of nobility. I admired him then, afire with an enthusiasm that honored him as well.

"Were I King Louis," he was saying, "and had invited such a count to give advice, I'd think up ways to placate him first. Count Raoul is not the man to speak softly to your face and say another thing behind your back. For when we came to Louis's court, an old, damp sort of place, with corridors so wet they seemed to soak up the water from the Seine—hard to believe that from such spongy walls a king of France hurled defiance at the invading Norsemen two centuries ago—the king's guard led us along in haste, showing us no courtesy. Ill-groomed, ill-favored, ill-mannered are they, slouching and spitting, making show of force only when they think it will not be returned. I wonder King Louis permits their disrespect. The king was standing with a group of men in an anteroom. He reminded me of my father's old boarhound that growls with toothless gums and fawns and whines all in one breath. So was the king, pretending fierce, pretending sweet.

" 'Save you, my lord count,' he says. His tone was mild, but underneath his thin eyelashes, his pale blue eyes darted looks, the shifty glance of uneasiness. 'God preserve you, Count Raoul, and grant you peace.'

"Earl Raoul came straight to the point. They say of him he grows more like each year to his grandfather, your great grandsire, of blessed memory. I like his way. He speaks his mind; men know where he stands, and where they do. Not many men dare that these days. 'If God wills, we shall have peace,' Earl Raoul said. 'We mortals seem intent to kill it at birth. Angels, we need, to disperse these war clouds, and seraphim with flaming swords to defend us from these warlords I see

gathered here today.' For he had noted at once that many of
the nobles were full-armed, to their hauberks and shields, and
all wore swords in defiance of courteous custom.

"The king cringed; his courtiers, gathered around him, hissed
in outrage and whispered suggestions as to how the king should
reply. Presently King Louis pushed his courtiers aside. 'Ever
quick with advice, Raoul,' he said. 'Hotheaded like your son.'
He raised his thin hand, where a red ruby gleamed like a drop
of blood. His voice was bleak but had a curious undertone,
almost triumphant. 'There are other lords who do not agree
with you. They would dispute that remark.'

"He drew aside, holding up his robes like a monk, so Raoul
could see who stood behind him. Earl Raoul knew them, I
think, four English lords, who advanced, all smiles. A moment,
I shall remember their names. One was the Earl of Leicester, a
bitter, hard-faced man who resents that his family's power has
waned since Henry's rule. He was followed by the Earl of
Derby, angry because Henry has confiscated his northern estates. The third man was the Earl of Chester, fat-faced and
merry with wine, and, I think, of the four most dangerous, too
young, your father said, to remember the civil war, not old
enough, or wise enough, to consider its consequence. The fourth
and last man was Hugh Bigod, Earl of Norfolk, from whom
Henry has taken East Anglia. All four, then, with grievances a
mile long, all four hot with resentment sufficient to make them
willing to act as one.

"Count Raoul's greeting to them was terse. 'So, my lords,'
he says, 'come begging for scraps? What do you offer to the
feast?' They laughed as at a joke, trying not to take offense,
fingering their dagger hilts. They were in full armor, I tell you,
beneath their robes, and although their belts were gold-laced,
the swords were not for show but were real. King Louis seemed
not to mind. I think he felt their battle gear was a compliment,
meant to remind him of his martial youth. He laughed and
rubbed his hands, a miser counting over his gains. 'These great
earls,' he emphasized the word 'great,' a whisper of satire almost
as quickly swallowed, 'these lords have promised their support.
In England their vassals will rise at their command, and they

themselves have offered certain English lands to whatever French lords pledge their help in return.'

"At this thought King Louis's jubilation did break out. He laughed so heartily that he choked and spat and allowed the earls to beat him on the back in a familiar way. 'Dover and Kentish lands,' he spluttered, when he could speak, 'a gift that wins the Count of Flanders to our cause; the soke of Kirton in Lindsey for the Count of Boulogne; and to the King of Scotland, ready to overrun the northern border at our command, the whole of Northumbria.'

" 'Which is, by right, already his,' Hugh of Chester broke in. When he spoke, the smell of liquor on his breath was like a pothouse.

" 'A veritable feast indeed.' Earl Raoul's voice did not rise, but his color did, and his hands whitened along the joints. 'England quarters up well to your huntsman's knife. Which of your vassals do you destroy to supply the game? What French lands are you promised in return?'

"King Louis's face grew long; the thin nostrils flared, and his mouth grew hard. It made me think how he must have been in his youth, when he himself lopped off the hands of rebels who defied him and set fire to a church of frightened villagers. Their screams, they say, so haunted him that he was driven to go on Crusade. For a moment even King Louis showed himself as a man who would not brook the slightest interference with his will.

" 'These English lords do as their king commands,' he whispered, the long *s* sounds making him seem more ominous. 'Their former king, Henry the Older, is deposed by a younger one; the son has taken the father's place. And you, Earl Raoul of Sedgemont, with holdings of your own in England, which king will you serve?'

"Earl Raoul took a step forward, and the king drew back. 'Do not look for me to divide my lands,' the earl said. 'I covet no man's estates, but I keep my own. Sieux has been ours for more than three hundred years, and Sedgemont and Cambray since my grandfather's time. No man touches them.'

"The king made a tushing sound. 'Come, come, Raoul, we

shall never have a chance like this again,' he began, when the
Earl of Leicester broke in—a tall, haughty man he is, not one
to cross. 'But King Henry took your castle once,' he cried. 'You
owe him naught. Do you know where Henry is? Gone south,
to treat with the Count of Maurienne, who in return will open
the mountain passes through the Alps; all of Italy defenseless
beyond, within Henry's grasp. A monster we have supported,
Raoul, an ogre, who looks to swallow the world.'

" 'And what in return for that ride south?' Earl Hugh of
Norfolk took up the tale. He certainly is old enough to remember the anarchy of civil war. 'A marriage between the Count
of Maurienne's infant daughter and Henry's youngest son, John
Lackland, justly called, for lands he lacks. Except his father now
grants him some, as marriage settlement, three castles, three
border forts. And where did they come from? Why, they were
ones the king had given first to his oldest son and now takes
away. God's breath, you'd think with all the world his to give,
Henry could find some better way to bestow gifts than to rob
his heir.'

" 'Who will no longer support such injury, such insult.'
Now the Earl of Chester spoke, smiling the while at news that
must have struck a blow to Earl Raoul's hopes. 'And your
son rides with the Young King. What will you do when they
come here?'

" 'When they come.' Count Raoul echoed him. 'Between that
when and now much may happen. King Henry may be a monster, but he is no fool. Nor is the prince so young, so foolish,
as to defy a father who is stronger than he. Prince Henry should
be advised to go back home, not hustled into a rebellion he will
regret. And you, my lords of England, should bid your prince
make his peace with the English king rather than let the French
one tempt you into war. You play with fire. Take care it does
not burn.'

"By God, Robert," Gervaise went on, "that was blunt. The
Earl of Chester's round face drew down into lines older than
his age, and Hugh Bigod fingered his sword hilt. 'Mayhap,
mayhap,' the Earl of Norfolk said finally, his pig eyes small,
'as sound advice as your grandfather gave in the last war. Much

good it did you. Henry tore down your walls at Sieux fast
enough!'

" 'And forced you to marry with your ward.' This last from
the king, whose voice could not conceal his malice.

" 'As much sense as your older son when he let a Welsh army
through. Such advice will cut you off from everyone, my lord,'
William of Derby piped up.

" 'Well,' Count Raoul answered them. He wore no sword,
carried no weapon; his voice was cold and rang like steel. 'You
speak of old wrongs,' he said, 'put aside if not forgot. Before
you dismember the present world we live in to create new ones
to satisfy your own revenge, think first. Faith is sworn to vassal
by overlord, by overlord to king, a binding oath on both sides
sworn before God, not easily ignored. Faith is the cornerstone
of our world, not only faith in God but faith in man, face to
face, land in return for military service, land in return for protection. How will you protect your vassals when you give them
to another overlord? Destroy the faith between them and you,
you plunge us back into a darkness such as the heathen Norsemen brought. Remember that, my lord king, when you wreck
the peace of Montmirail.' "

Gervaise paused for breath. "Christ's wounds," he swore,
"how your father quieted them. But, Robert, they say those
English earls spoke truth. Prince Henry waits but a chance to
break away from his father's guard and will make his escape to
join King Louis here. And not only that prince." He hesitated
again. "They say his brothers will come with him."

Robert's face, which had grown still and quiet at Gervaise's
news, suddenly brightened, as if a lamp had been lit. But he
made no move, asked no question. It was Gervaise who told
him what he wanted, hoped for, yet at the same time must have
despaired of. "Prince Richard will ride with his brother. Prince
Geoffrey, too. All the eaglets, then, who are old enough to fly.
And when your father heard that, he smote his hand against
the wall, just as you are doing now, and swore, just as you are
thinking of doing, 'God's breath, all the eaglets from the nest.
But the king eagle is still aloft. And not even Paris will be safe
until he gets them back.' "

Such were the tidings that Gervaise gave, told part in admiration, part in awe, and part, I think, out of curiosity, to know how the house of Sieux would stand. But he did not dare ask what Robert had already asked himself, "When Richard comes, whom will I serve?" Nor did he ask, what of Hue? How would the house of Sieux stand? Rather, how would it divide? Those were questions that must have racked the earl, afraid for both his younger and his older son. Although between Robert and the earl all continued as before, the earl as affectionate, generous, and tolerant as a father could be, the son loving, respectful; underneath, that current, sensed at Cambray last spring, began to tug and tear. For the earl held firm to his conviction that in the end reason would prevail, while Robert, who longed to see Richard, King Henry's son, almost hoped the prince would not come, to avoid quarreling with the earl. But both father and son knew that sooner or later a decision would have to be made.

Then, too, there was the current flowing, full force, between Gervaise and the Lady Olwen. For Gervaise was not backward in his wooing, and to tell the truth, I suppose there could not have been many maids who would have looked at him unfavorably. Young, ardent, he was not bashful in his suit. It was only that Olwen did not respond as he had hoped or felt he had been led to expect. What was said between him and Earl Raoul, or what between Earl Raoul and his son about Gervaise's claim, what asked for, what promised, what laid aside, I cannot say, nor what messages were sent posthaste, of war and love, back to Odo of Walran. Gervaise remained with us, guest of my lord, friend of our house, as before at Cambray. And while he waited for King Henry's return (for in this also he held firm, that he would support the king, come what may), he used the time to advance his own cause. I do know that, like many of the young men of his class, Gervaise was confident. He was used to harshness, no milksop, his father's parting blow no doubt the last of many before he came to manhood; what he was not used to was defeat. And so, expecting victory, acting as if the prize were his, the more he pursued, the more the Lady Olwen retreated from him. I saw him not once but many times, walking with the lady in those gardens that backed upon the earl's house. Gervaise often seemed to crowd upon her, almost thrusting her into some quiet alleyway bordered with vines, and once taking her hand and pressing it to his lips, actions enough to make me snatch for my sword, had I worn one. Nor was he patient in his wooing, making no secret of his lusts. I know he often visited the whores in the stews, Paris being crammed with them, like all cities I have been in, and, like many other young lords, he boasted of his prowess there. Yet strange, although such habits were common to most men, and I am sure Prince Taliesin was no prude, such talk would not have offended me coming from the prince. What seemed vicious in Gervaise might have been normal in another young lord, the main difference being, I think, that Taliesin would never have had to boast.

As for the Lady Olwen, why was it now she turned away from the man she had tried to hide behind? Why felt she safe to do so? Her mother's absence must have been a blow to her, but her father proved an unexpected ally. For the earl was wise. Gentle, too, I think, in a way not common to many of his rank, he would neither give his consent to a betrothal nor allow Gervaise of Walran to pursue too hard until the earl had returned to Sieux, there to consult with the Lady Ann. Time is what the earl gave to Olwen, and time is all she had ever bargained for. But once, when I heard her plead with Gervaise to let her be, there was an understanding in her voice new to her, as if she pitied him, making her seem older than he was. His stern reply frightened her. "I am not one," he said, his Norman harshness very clear, "to be fooled with. Nor do I bend and sway as is the fashion of this court. Your father does not frown on an alliance; your brother welcomes it, and so does Odo of Walran. If you say so, we could go back to Walran now. I could give up Henry's wars," he said, "but not you, Lady Olwen. That I shall not do." Feeling she had only herself to blame for his intent, despairing then of dissuading him, the lady withdrew in distress, avoided him, and found solace suited to her needs and place.

Now, although Earl Raoul had verged on quarrel with King

Louis, that did not mean he and his son, or daughter, were denied the court. I had the impression that the earl had frequently been at odds in council with this king, yet like King Henry before him, Louis relied on the earl's advice. And even if King Louis had shut his doors, I think Earl Raoul would have remained. He waited, as did all of the court, for the return of the King of England. And whichever king it was, young or old, Earl Raoul wanted his son, Hue. For again, whatever messages had been sent to Hue, wherever he was, ordering him to return to Sieux forthwith, I do not think that Hue's obedience was something the earl had counted on. So while the earl waited, and Robert waited, and Gervaise, Lady Olwen took her place at court with the Queen of France.

The present French queen was young, the third of Louis's wives, and of the three, perhaps, the happiest, in that she was the only one to have borne him a son. Philip Augustus was then eight years old, a strong and clever child, they said, round and plump, as his mother was. And such rejoicing at his birth as never before, the city alight with bonfires, bells tolling all night long, that Louis, in his age, might at last have an heir, a *don de Dieu*, God's gift. The happy mother of this gift was Queen Adela of Champagne, and such was her triumph that there was little that Louis would not give her. Since her son's birth she had put on weight; there were some who said she was as complacent as a cow with calf and that when she strolled abroad upon the green meadows of her country estates, she looked as if she had been set down to graze. For it was true she did not like Paris, a city of smells and disease, and was happiest in her own rich lands of Champagne, where, like any country lass, she could dance and flirt and feel at ease. But she was also deeply religious and when in Paris spent much of her time in church (not in the great church of Notre Dame, being rebuilt these many years, but in one smaller, nearby, set about with grassy walks, which reminded her more of the churches in Champagne), where she prayed for a speedy return to her home. She seemed easygoing in those days, but it was said that underneath that placid air she had a will of steel, and of all the people in the court, she could bend Louis's will to her own and, what was more, keep it so bent. She took a liking to the little maid from Cambray; she nurtured her, and learning soon, in a motherly way, of Olwen's plight, she made a pet of her.

So it was that my lady often went with the queen to Mass, in the great abbey church, and afterward walked with her along the riverbanks, where, as the spring now advanced, chestnut trees gave signs of bud and the grass grew almost as green as in the queen's own lands. I never saw this queen close to myself, but Olwen often spoke of her, and once, when Gervaise remonstrated with her, she told him that the queen was kind to her, making the court alive with jests and song. "Many ladies of note attend her," she told him, smiling suddenly in her old way. "As demure as in a nunnery, not a man among the flock. Those ladies crowd her hard, I think. Some praise her skin, all pink and white; some her hair, the color of her Champagne wines; all use flattery to win her support. I think she likes me because I do not ask her for anything, as those other ladies do. But when they beg, she opens her large blue eyes and says, meek as a mouse, 'The king, my husband, must decide,' although everyone knows she tells him exactly what to say. For so, they whisper, she controls him in his bed. But they say, too, that in secret King Louis still mourns his first wife, the love of his youth, that Eleanor of Aquitaine who left him to marry with King Henry of England. I think it sad that such love as once Queen Eleanor commanded should be lost."

"Not I." Gervaise was adamant. "On the Crusade Queen Eleanor openly consorted with the Count of Antioch, a *chevalier sans reproche*, so strong he would ride his horse beneath a bridge and stop it short by reaching up and grasping the keystone. A holy war is not the place for carnal love." So spoke Gervaise, who, the night before, had slept with two jades at once, who would be a Crusading knight himself!

"That may be so," my lady said thoughtfully, not willing to annoy him, "but, Gervaise, there are old ladies at the court who remember Queen Eleanor well. And one of them, who listens to me when I speak, often talks of her." She suddenly bit her lip. "I do not know if I like that lady or not," she confessed. "Sometimes soft, sometimes hard, but she is old and must be

revered." So she spoke, my lady, and so spoke Gervaise, who
one day was to see that queen against whom he had spoken so
roughly. Better he had not seen her to change his mind. But I
leap ahead.

Talk of Queen Eleanor worried me; I began to wonder if my
lady's father was at fault, to let her walk abroad. But the earl
was preoccupied, and had any dared question him, as no one
could, he would have said, with justification on his part, that
his daughter was well attended (true, she had both maids and
squire) and that in the queen's own company what danger could
approach? What indeed? Vipers can be found curled in the qui-
etest place. But one thing was fact: Queen Adela's demands
kept Olwen at least away from Gervaise, and that seemed de-
sirable. And my lady seemed more at ease, perhaps finding in
those older women she had spoken of a replacement for her
mother's comfort, or perhaps, mingling now with other young
ladies like herself, she felt she could let down her guard and feel
free of cares. I was wrong, on all accounts. She went with one
thought in mind, and danger was lurking there. As by and by
shall be told.

As for Sir Renier and his son, they dropped from sight, swallowed up in the city's maw, the father at least. Bernard of Poitou
I saw from time to time, when, as he had promised, he brought
us news. But from the day of our arrival, a rumor spread like
wildfire through the city streets. If in truth Sir Renier had revealed this story (and perhaps he did), it was certainly of general
worth and showed there was skill left in that old forked tongue,
even though he spoke so haltingly. It might well have earned
him and his son places in the new court that Prince Henry would
establish in his own right. All this, of course is surmise. I know
only that the tale was told and ran on wind's feet, in the way
rumor has. And since it had all the marks of our Lord Hue
stamped on it, from start to end, it may well have been true.

All knew, of course, that Prince Henry planned to come to
Paris when he could; the question was when and how. Since
Christmas his father had held him trapped; the more he raged,
the closer was he kept under watch. And we had heard that the
prince's entourage had been halved, more than one hundred

noble youths and knights sent on their way; we knew that those who remained had hung on, unwanted appendages, neither allowed to serve the prince as they should nor granted honor as was their due. It was whispered openly that King Henry, jealous of their influence over his son, would have dismissed them all had he dared, and those he left in his son's household he treated like a pack of serfs, beneath his contempt.

All this was known, I say, and also how, since the conclusion of the treaty with the Count of Maurienne (that treaty which had so enraged Prince Henry with its terms), King Henry had kept the prince by his side. The prince was forced to eat and sleep and ride with the king. If the story be not denied, they even sat in the same privy side by side, were shaved by the same barber, bathed in the same water, a devoted father inseparable from his son. Such attentions drove the son wild. He strained to break away as does a colt, new-bridled. The chance now came. And this was the tale that engaged the Paris world, agog for gossip of the most scurrilous kind.

The king and the prince had traveled slowly northward from Savoy, the king no doubt aware of all these stirrings throughout his land; his son determined to unite his father's enemies under his leadership. They had reached Chinon, one of those forts of which baby John had just been made the proud owner. It must have galled Prince Henry to be lodged thus in a castle he had thought his own, a castle he had been forced to surrender without a fight; to have been led there like a child, by the hand, must have seemed double insult. Chinon is a large and formidable castle, one of the appanages of the house of Anjou. It was said of it that only King Henry himself could have brought it under siege, so strong it was, and certainly King Henry must have felt safe enough there to relax his watch upon the prince. That was his mistake.

Weary with a long ride and hunt, weary perhaps of having to keep one eye upon his surly son, that night the king went early to rest, fell asleep, and slept soundly and long, a man who boasted that he scarcely needed sleep at all but could ride and hunt and feast and ride again, always on the move, without sign of strain. (And in his youth such a boast was just. Many men had disappeared from Henry's court, worn thin, worn away by Henry's constant energy.) Imagine the king's chagrin next day, his choler, his disbelief, on waking, to find the bed cold, the room empty, where the night before the prince had seemed to sleep, the prince fled and all his companions fled with him.

The story of how all this was done is tinged with mirth, even though the consequences were grim. During the evening meal, when the king had shown signs of fatigue, or at least what would have been interpreted so in an ordinary man, such as nodding of the head, blurred speech, rubbing of the eyes, the word was passed among the prince's remaining friends to prepare for a royal flight. In the dim hours before midnight, when in truth all honest men might justly lie abed, one of the prince's close companions crept to the king's own door and scratched at it. The guards saw him, of course, but since he came in all innocence, taper in hand, dressed only in his shirt, without his boots, seeming half asleep, they thought him a simple young man anxious to speak on some innocent matter with his master the prince. Unarmed, young, with a face as guileless as his lack of beard, no harm in him, he persuaded them to let him in. That young man was Hue.

Inside the chamber the prince, who was waiting for him, slid out of bed, where he had been lying motionless as a block of wood. Together, ignoring the royal snores, they knotted the bed covers, slid down from an embrasure to a nearby wall, and hoisted themselves over its battlements. Whence a quick run took them down the outer steps, through castle corridors, snatching food and clothes as they ran.

"Dear Christ, I'm starved," the prince is said to have complained, his mouth full of capon. "My father is as niggardly with meat as he is generous with companionship."

Hue, who had not eaten or drunk all day, such had been his efforts, his mouth equally stuffed with a ham bone, is reputed to have replied, "Aye, my prince. One you need to live, the other throttles you." And they had both roared at their jest, as young men do.

In a smaller courtyard the prince's horses were standing bridled. Squires were waiting to strap on his armor, his spurs. While he armed himself, Hue, anxious that no delay mar his plans, sprang half naked onto his horse and urged it forward into the outer yard, where the castle guard, already alarmed, as well they might be, were gathering uneasily. Determined not to be gainsaid by them, Hue rode against them so furiously that they were obliged to retreat toward a gatehouse. From that safety point they argued, swore, and prevaricated, hoping to gain time until someone of importance should be roused to give them orders what to do. Angered by their insistence, when the prince appeared on horseback, Hue took matters into his own hands. One fast move, for which he was already famed, carried him from his horse onto the back of the captain of the watch, bearing him to the ground. The captain, although in full mail, was taken by surprise. With Hue on top of him, threatening to take off his head with his own sword, the poor man gave the order to wind up the portcullis, the inner gate, and let down the drawbridge beyond.

This was done. Easy was it, then, for the prince and his entourage to gallop through, the road to Paris beckoning ahead. But easy also for the king and his men to follow in due course. That, too, was something Hue had thought about, and he had devised a plan. With the help of another of the prince's companions, William, known as the "Marshal," Hue had kept the exit clear while the prince and his companions had thundered across. Then, as some of the prince's men hacked at the portcullis ropes, Hue and William together held up the heavy gate with its spiked bars until everyone had scuttled clear. Hue is not as tall as William (who is dubbed a giant, capable, 'tis said, of carrying a horse upon his back), but he is agile and quick. Together, then, he and this William heaved up the gate one last time, let it slip off their shoulders, rolled underneath before it came crashing down. Their squires had already led their horses through. They ran across the drawbridge to the other side of the moat, where the prince still waited for them.

Hue now began to struggle into his hauberk, while the prince and his men mocked at him, accused him of fleeing from a maiden's chamber, where her father slept; what maid had Hue seduced this time? His mail half over him, Hue's head emerged in a mass of curls. He gave a great laugh and, seizing a spear, tied on a strip of red torn from the end of his Sedgemont coat. "This to remember me by," he cried, "the rape of Chinon." And he hurled the spear with all his might. It struck the end of the bridge in front of the jammed portcullis gate, and stayed there quivering, with its strip of red. Still laughing, he threw his arm about the prince, and they smote each other on the back like the boys they were at heart; then, spurring hard, they vanished in a cloud of dust.

By the time the king's retainers, arguing violently among themselves whose right it was to inform the king, had gone en masse to the royal chamber, huddled together like limpets on a rock, the morning was already come; the prince and his companions were long gone, riding at a gallop across the placid countryside toward the safety of King Louis's lands. King Henry, rudely awakened, unwashed, unshorn, threw his cloak about him without a word, took the stairs three at a time, and running as lightly as a boy himself, vaulted into the saddle of his horse before his startled groom realized he was awake. But Henry is forty years old; his fresh youth is gone. He has not his son's laughter or light jest. Grim-mouthed, in royal rage, he whipped his horse toward the gates, those of his guard whom he had not already booted from his path trying to saddle their horses to follow him. The cut ropes, the iron bars of the portcullis, thwarted him, as Hue had intended they should. It is claimed the king was so angry he almost tried to ride the bars down, as if energy alone could hew steel apart.

On the other side of those bars lay the open drawbridge, spread across the quiet moat, the dusty, empty road, and there, as if still on guard, the spear with its arrogant scrap of red. Well, youth has advantage over age, and plan over surprise. But these were the things Henry could not forgive: the boys' youth and their careful arrangements, insults these, which Henry's revenge one day would repay. The third thing was Hue's laugh. When told of it, the king must have remembered another boy, Hue's father, Raoul, who years before had laughed in the same way. So although the king did not then know Hue, recalling only vaguely that young hothead who had led the prince astray at Montmirail, and having ignored the prince's retinue deliberately these past months (a decision Henry was to regret), henceforth Henry was to remember Hue and mark him down. The more so when at last the portcullis ropes were repaired and the king could issue forth, he realized he was too late, not only to get Prince Henry back but to stop his other sons from escaping as well. The revolt of three sons, already rumored by Gervaise, was now substantiated, as was the more serious defiance of his queen. For these reasons alone Henry would not forget the red-haired lad who had laughed at him, especially as in consequence he now had to fight for his life and for his empire, which his sons were trying to break apart.

I tell all this in detail, although then I do not think all details were known, only enough to set the city ahum with excitement. Not many men fooled Henry of England and lived to speak of it. But, I repeat, such was the rumor: that Prince Henry was already safely on his way to Paris, to be expected within the week, his two brothers and his mother, the queen, close on his heels. But how the prince did arrive, and how Earl Raoul looked in vain for his son Hue, that story will be told in time. For there was one other thing that was news, and true to his word Bernard of Poitou sent us notice of it: how, in anticipation of the arrival of the new English king, another prince came spurring in, the Welsh one, with his six men behind him. Unheralded, unlooked for, he was come to demand a new king's justice. And that was the message my lady dreamed upon.

Chapter 9

hatever King Louis might have felt about Celtic rights or Celtic wrongs (not much, I presume, since he let Henry take Brittany without raising a finger to prevent its loss), and however far off Wales might have seemed, a misty land cowering beneath a mountain weight, Louis was certainly not insensible to the effect of Breton help nor yet disposed to ignore a prince who was reported to have the ability to hold those fickle Bretons in line. Nor, in the final count, was Louis insensible to the promptings of his queen. For Queen Adela's view of the matter was also heard, and she, like all of Paris, was to become enchanted by the prince, a sign of favor not lost upon the king (even less upon Gervaise of Walran, I may add, whose jealousy now began to reveal itself, perhaps with good cause). Nor was it lost upon Prince Taliesin, who would have scorned to use such favor and certainly never looked for it.

I tell this part of our story from hearsay, since I was not present when Prince Taliesin came to King Louis's palace, and in our household neither Gervaise of Walran nor the Lady Olwen spoke of it. Nor yet Lord Robert. Although in later years he did mention it, suddenly laughing and saying, "God's wounds, man, Taliesin swept those silly demoiselles off their feet, in more ways than one. If I had thought a fox cloak and a pair of boots would have done me so much good, I'd have put them on myself." But silence in the earl's entourage, a new scandal brewing, did not mean silence in the rest of the world. Talk of Prince Taliesin became a commonplace, as the Paris citizens took him to their hearts. He himself used to say, with a shrug, "Better any prince than none," meaning that in the general uproar of those times he may well have been mistaken for Prince Henry; when all was said and done, one prince was worth as much as another one. But certainly for a while Paris was abrim with gossip so that even honest citizens, who perhaps had never heard of Wales, and certainly never of that little principality of Afron, now spoke of both familiarly as something all men should know, as one might say "as handsome as a Taliesin" or "as proud as Afron," both expressions that passed into general use.

All the world was at Louis's court that day, I think. Affairs of state, those long and heavy council meetings, had been put aside, and lords great and small, all those who could cram under the royal roof, had come to celebrate the news of Prince Henry's escape. (Not his arrival yet; that still was looked for. For some strange reason Prince Henry, having reached King Louis's lands and safety there, had begun to dawdle along, although good sense, if not policy, should have dictated to him to make haste. This large, uneasy confederation was not like to last in any coherence for long.) And presiding over this noble gathering, King Louis sat, jubilant. Not since he had set out on Crusade had he felt so much in command nor been accorded so much respect, and he reveled in it. As did his queen.

Queen Adela was also present, with all her ladies, for once well content to be in the capital city, on this day of her husband's triumph. She viewed the court with her self-satisfied, placid smile, seeing, at last, her husband accorded true esteem. In her heart she believed that in the future he would be regarded as a monarch of skill and resource, who alone had found the courage and ability to crush these all-powerful Angevins. And she, at his side, was determined to preside with him, revealing the brilliance that her secret rival, Queen Eleanor, once had known. So while she waited for her stepson-in-law, to ensure her husband was tendered all due appreciation and thanks, she was determined to enjoy herself. And it is true that since the time of that other queen (whose name was never mentioned in the presence of the current one), the ancient court of the Capets had never shone with such splendor and grace.

Into this gathering Prince Taliesin strode, expecting to find the king in council with his men, prepared to negotiate in martial terms. He was obviously surprised to find what was, for him, a serious affair decked out instead as for carnival. He was dressed in his homeland style: his red-fox cape swung about his shoulders, clasped with a golden pin; his leggings were of worked doeskin, and he wore soft boots to his knees. His shirt was white, of the finest stuff, not silk but embroidered in wonderful stitchery, and his sword belt was wide, fastened with a buckle of Celtic design, also in gold. And at his throat and wrist, those golden bands picked up the gleam of his copper hair. Now these were clothes more of hunting style and as such were familiar to the Norman world, as elsewhere, but never worn like this, on ceremony. Had the prince been anyone else, alone, he might have seemed a country nobody, unschooled in court etiquette, out of place, and the other courtiers could have found a way to laugh him down. With his six bodyguards, also so dressed, their spears and round shields held at salute, he suddenly appeared as exotic as perhaps a Moor from Spain or a bird of different plumage, a hawk among a gaggle of geese. He made those French courtiers, with their long silk gowns and their slippered feet, look womanish, even effeminate, and those of them who wore their mail coats beneath their robes began to curse that they had not worn them above, at least to show the world they were men.

Taliesin had come, I say, expecting to have discourse with a king, and finding he was mistaken, he had made a quick retreat toward an open doorway, where he stood watching, hands on his belt, his dark blue eyes coldly appraising the multitude. He could not have chosen a better spot if he had so planned to set off his accoutrements, his person, his furs, outlined as he was by the light behind his head and the play of torch flares from the walls. He did not even notice Queen Adela's interest until a scandalized courtier approached and nudged him. And when he spun around on his heel, his cloak flaring, to look at her, his expression of startled disdain so intrigued her that she is said to have leaned forward, in her breathless way, and whispered to her intimates, "*Jesu*, who is that god?" and beckoned to him to approach.

At that period Queen Adela was still young, a vigorous and lusty matron, albeit plump. When she wished, she could be as haughty as any queen alive, and such was her piety that her honor was never in doubt, a situation that makes for marital bliss. But there was no mistaking, as she sat there beside her husband, who had already fallen into a doze, that she revealed herself as a lady full of energy and well-being, appreciative of men.

The prince made obeisance in proper style in a slightly old-fashioned way, his men clashing to arms behind him. Together they made a perfect foil, wild-looking, masculine, a contrast to the queen's gentle pink and white, which she could not fail to note. And when the prince answered her, his voice, with its Celtic lilt, neither hard nor soft, having in it all the sound of the western sea, his slightly foreign pronunciation of French enchanted the queen again. She beckoned to the servitors to bring him wine, asked him many questions about himself—his name, his rank, his standing, whence he came. All questions having been replied to in his correct and old-fashioned way, he prepared to take his leave, a state of affairs that scandalized the queen's courtiers anew and intrigued her.

She suddenly leaned toward him again and asked in her gentle voice (for when she wished she could be as gentle as a maid), "Do we seem so strange to you, Prince Taliesin, that you would turn your back on us? Are you so bored that you are ready to leave so soon?"

"My lady," he said, confused by her question and yet courteous. "I should indeed be unchivalrous if I turned my back on so fair and rich a gathering. It is only," he hesitated, "that these festivities are new to me."

"Did not you have feast and joyous society in your house?" she asked.

"My lady," he replied, "for as long as I remember, our house has known nothing but grief."

There was such a genuine sadness in his voice, such sudden

and direct appeal, that the queen's good nature was touched. She gave him her hand; he took it by the fingertips and handed her down from her throne. "I insist," she cried. "This once, in my house, today, you shall find joy with us." She beckoned to her musicians with her free hand and bid them strike up a tune.

Now there are not many men, I think, who, expecting discussion, politics, strategy, council of war, find themselves instead called on to dance, or at least, being so obliged, do not themselves look foolish. Realizing what the queen had in mind, neither fawning over her nor showing bumptious disregard, the prince stood back a moment and let the queen dance by herself, to show him the steps, which, being neat and quick on her feet although so plump, she was not loath to do. He watched her for a moment dance the galliard, long enough to shuck off his cloak and unbuckle his sword, which he threw deftly aside before taking her hand, hesitant at first, following her, then as he understood, laughing down at her and joining her. The tune was vigorous and the dance complicated, such as the queen loved; her feet in their violet silk kicked and swirled, and her long blonde braids beneath her elaborate headdress bobbed about. She seemed as nimble as a girl half her size. Her blue eyes sparkled to match the much darker ones of the prince, and her cheeks glowed red; she danced as heartily as any country woman might in Champagne. And Prince Taliesin matched her, step for step.

The courtiers had cleared a space so that they danced in a semicircle before the throne, where King Louis nodded in his sleep and smiled, and where a third throne stood vacant for the new king. Prince Taliesin was quick and lithe, as I have said. He did not dance as courtiers do, with sweeps and airs, but, taking his clue from the queen, began to execute steps of his own, complementing hers, deferring to her yet sometimes leading her. And being young and, I think, fond of music, like all Celts, he did what no courtier would dare, he began to hum in tune, whistling under his breath and smiling at her with sudden pleasure that lit up his face. And all this, too, enchanted the queen, so that when at the dance's end he would have led her back, with all due respect, she stopped him and said in her calm voice, which at times makes one think of honey and cream, "Well, my lord prince, you have danced with me, dances of my homeland. Show me now what, in happy days, you would do in your own."

It was a royal command, and a royal favor, not often so openly shown by a queen who was always discreet. They say Prince Taliesin nodded, retrieved his cloak and sword, and snapping his fingers, had his men step forward. All this while they had been standing apart, at attention, as if on guard. Now two put aside their armaments; one drew from beneath his cloak a kind of pipe; the other unstrapped from his back a harp. With a shout that startled everyone, the remainder broke into step, a true Celtic dance, as intricate as the windings of their ornaments or the interweaving of their art. Their soft boots beat a rhythm faster than the French dancers recognized, to the sound of music none there had heard before, wild and haunting, like birds' cries. Their cloaks flared, and at each turning in the maze traced by their footsteps, they beat their swords upon their shields. In truth, they say, their dance was so fast, so intricate, that for a moment King Louis's court caught a glimpse of another world, which hitherto they had despised and which now revealed itself, as mysterious and as strange as it was unknown.

Some men sweat when they dance and have to stop to mop away the heat; others lumber heavily, thumping on their heels; others put on sheepish grins as if they expect to be ridiculed. These four men with their prince to lead them were grave and dignified, and their dance so old, it seemed to have been created before time was thought of. And at its end there was a hush, more gratifying than any applause.

Afterward, applaud the court did, taking note how the king, awake again, smiled genially, how the queen whispered eagerly in his ear, realizing that here was a new favorite to be reckoned with. The queen was certainly delighted. They say she cried eagerly, "Bravo, Prince Taliesin. You put us all to shame," which she did not believe but liked to hear contradicted. "I beg you to take one of my younger ladies and teach her such gracefulness."

Prince Taliesin had begun to round up his men (who, although obviously not understanding all that was being said, had allowed themselves the luxury of a grin or two). He turned at the sound of the queen's voice and listened intently.

"My lady queen," he said, in that tone that made the ladies sigh. "I think no one here needs to be taught anything of grace." A fine-turned compliment, which was a crowning touch.

The queen clapped her white hands. "I insist," she cried, "to please me." For the first time the ladies who attended her pushed forward, some thrusting themselves eagerly, others hanging back for shyness. He scanned them carefully, his blue eyes narrowed in concentration, his brown, clean-shaven face with its strong jaw and sensuous mouth causing many a maid's heart to beat fast. Slowly, deliberately, he looked them over, one by one, hands clasped behind his back, his legs in their supple boots apart, as much at ease as if he were indeed standing on his own hearth, a prince who there was free to pick and choose as he desired. And when he found the lady he sought, he made no sign to her, spoke not, simply flicked his fingers again to start up the tune, never taking his gaze from her, waiting for her to join him, his eyes suddenly as blue as the summer sea.

Lady Olwen all this while had been standing between her brother and Gervaise of Walran, still as a statue, in her green gown, her hair caught back in a net of pearls. They say she had not said a word either nor made any sound since Prince Taliesin had appeared but had watched him dance with the queen, silent as she had promised, sight of him enough. So had she said, and so she did. But she had not promised what to do if he sought her out. Before her brother or her lover could protest, Gervaise already paralyzed with rage, she came through the crowd, which parted on either side to let her pass, and took the hand that Prince Taliesin offered her.

He held her in Celtic style, not a Norman one, arm about her waist, and as the music again reverberated through the hall, step by step, foot by foot, hands entwined, bodies molding together, swaying apart, the lady and the prince began the dance. She knew the steps, of all the ladies there the only one who did; she knew the tune; she knew its meaning, a courtship dance, danced only at betrothal feasts or weddings, yet she danced it with him openly. Hair floating free, for her cap of pearls had fallen off, waist caught in border style, bending and dipping at his touch, she danced, never looking at him straight. But he looked his fill and held her tight.

"Mother of God," Gervaise of Walran is supposed at last to have spluttered out. "I'll kill him first. *Jesu*, to put such shame on me." He struggled with his sword.

It was the earl who caught his wrist in a strong grasp and would not let it go. "Be still," he said. "We are here, no cause for alarm. No need to spread more gossip." But they say also that afterward the earl watched his daughter through hooded eyes, watched as her hair floated loose from its bands, as she smiled; saw the glint of the prince's quick smile in return, and was suddenly silent, remembering days long past, when a maid had so smiled at him, had so danced before him, at Sedgemont.

At the queen's behest other dancers began to join the prince, following the music as best they could. Soon the empty space was filled with courtiers eager to prove how much they liked this new style. Under cover of their noise, the prince drew his partner to one side.

"So, little mistress," he is supposed to have said, standing back to observe her, although he kept his hands about her waist. "Here is strange sight, in all your new gewgaws; where are your bare feet these days?"

His teasing confused the Lady Olwen. Willingly had she come to dance with him; eagerly had she hoped for some sign from him; long had she wanted to see him again. The moment arrived, she hardly knew what to say, she who had a word for everyone. When she spoke, so indistinct was her mumble that the prince had to bend his head to catch what she said, for an instant both copper curls meeting as one.

"But glad to see you certainly," the prince was continuing cheerfully. "Dear God, in a world full of strangers, true comfort to find another Celt, even if she must be bewitched to fly here so fast. How come you here, dressed up so fine?"

Again her reply was low. "I thought you would never find me among the crowds."

"Not find!" He laughed, a man's laugh, full of confidence.

Prince Taliesin, too, had learned things these past months. "Why, lady, did not I promise never to forget you?"

His laugh, his words put Olwen on her mettle. She suddenly looked at him, her eyes bright. "So you say," she said, almost in her old way, "so you promise, no doubt, to all the ladies you have met in their courts. I know what promises men make to maids, broken before they draw a second breath. I know what trust to put in you."

There was something in the fierceness in her tone that made him pause.

"Now, by Saint David," he began, taking a step back, "you do me wrong. These past months have not been a royal progress through royal beds. In a world of war I've not had much time for pleasantries, to say nothing of ladies, maids or not, which most, I suspect, have not been. You speak harshly, Olwen of the Celts. Rather, I thought you might have been pleased to see me." When she did not reply, her eyes downcast once more, he went on, "Prayers you promised for my safekeeping in God's hands. Is that all it meant, to scold as soon as we meet? I think other ladies would be more generous."

"Then choose another," she cried, tears almost starting with chagrin. "I do not hinder you. Take all the time you wish; there are plenty to choose from, and the night is not yet begun."

"Nay, Olwen," he said, contrite, "do not fight with me. Rot my tongue, why be so cross? I looked for you from the start, having heard the earl was already here. And now we have met, cannot we find a place apart from all this throng to sit and talk? I would hear your news, give you mine."

"Is that how you woo, Prince Taliesin?" she asked, putting her head on one side and looking up at him, slantways, beneath her long eyelashes. "Is that how you please your other ladies, just sitting, talking in the dark? For shame, to deceive poor souls with such lies."

Under the eyelashes her eyes still gleamed, and her lips trembled although she spoke so valiantly. Beneath his touch he felt her body shake, so slight he could have spanned her waist, and again the intensity of her voice and looks caught him off guard.

He suddenly swore a great oath, took her by the hand, and

as the dancers swirled and spun, shouldered a way through them
toward a side wall, where there was a deep embrasure cut into
the thickness of the stone. It was more like an alcove, with an
opening giving to the river far below, and he set her at its end
and stood in front of her, shielding her with his body. When
she shivered against the cold wind that blew through the window slit, he took off his cloak and wrapped it around her, for
the first time letting his hands brush along her skin.

"Lady Olwen," he began, "if this is the best we can do, listen
a moment. Tomorrow or tomorrow's morrow will my quest
be done, when this new king arrives. Who knows how it may
end, for good or ill as God decides, or how that king will hear
my demands, who is not used to having any demands made of
him. But today, this night, I can be free." He suddenly gave a
smile, his teasing smile, his teeth white against the color of his
skin, his eyes deep blue as she remembered them. Where the
opening of his fine white shirt showed, the column of his neck
was smooth and brown, and a pulse beat against the skin, so
that she longed to put her hand upon it to keep it still. "Even
the Queen of France has given me leave for joy tonight," he
said. "I thought you would share it with me."

She gazed at him intently, aware, perhaps, more than he knew
of the sudden spilling of his own thoughts and fears that he had
unwittingly revealed, realizing that he was not yet truly aware
of hers.

He took her silence for concern. "I would not hurt you," he
whispered. "God's breath, why look so feared? I would only
take speech with you." But once more his hands stole around
her waist beneath the covering of his cloak.

"Aye," she said, still fierce, "so say all men. And if I came
with you and spoke with you in the dark, what should I be on
that morrow's morn? How should I be different from those
other women you have known? What would men say of me?"

Again he let her go. In a tone that was meant to be reasonable,
he said, "Come, lady, I did not swear to be a monk to please
you. You sing to one tune. And what should a gentle maid like
you know of men? You still speak like a child—"

"Which I am not," she cried, vexed by him. "Nor did you

think so at Cambray, Prince Taliesin." She smoothed the folds of her dress. "At the queen's court men look at me," she burst out. "Would they look at a child?"

He stared down at her for a moment, his eyes hidden, and stepped back. "No, no." His voice came out muffled, almost against his will. "I grant you your years, if you will have it so."

"Nor was it a child who helped you once," she was continuing, but he caught her arm and bid her hush.

"What would you have me to do?" he asked her, trying to keep his voice light, trying to tease her into smile, although what he said was not exactly jest. "If I were to ask you, as woman, to come with me this night, would you come? True, a man does not woo at his best before the world, nor do I look to make love openly, but as man to woman, would I please you?"

"Love." She interrupted him. "Aye, that, too, is a word to bat about, to speak of as casually as you would the time of day or the turning of the tides. You speak too carelessly, my lord."

"But if I asked you, if I so begged?" he insisted.

She was suddenly racked with indecision, rocked with it; her little breasts panted with it. "Oh, God," she said, almost to herself, "it is not easy to be a maid. How could I come? I am watched. I am the last child of my house, the only daughter; shame cannot come from me on them. They would not let me even if I would."

Her intensity took him by surprise a second time. His eyes narrowed in thought, and he almost whistled below his breath. It was on his tongue's edge to mock at her. "You have thought of it, then," he wanted to say. "In truth, you have not forgotten me." But he held back the words. He sensed, I think, suddenly, that this was not a time for jest; for a moment he caught a glimpse of her uncertainty, even as she tried so hard to disguise it.

Perhaps it made him realize how young she was, how vulnerable, despite her playfulness; how innocent, despite her quick talk. It caused him to cross his arms about her, under the cloak, gentling along the spine as he would any young and tremulous thing, his fingers warm through the thin silk, his breath soft against her cheek. She hid her face against the broad expanse of his chest, suddenly burrowing against him as if to find safety, as if together they could hide from all the world of Louis's court, spinning past, with its listening ears and spying eyes.

"We are blood brothers," he reminded her. "See here, the scar." He smiled at her. "It reminds me of a day when you had time for me."

She shuddered. "Forget that day," she told him in her forthright way. "But do not forget the friends who helped you."

"Sweet *Jesu*," he protested softly. "Of all men here I have most need of friends. Do you not think I know that? Whatever else you think of me, grant me at least some sense. And if not tonight, at least sometime soon, I shall look for you."

The dance had ended, the dancers scattered, their little moment together done. Reluctantly he put her to one side. "As friends," he said, almost formally, as he had spoken to the queen, "that I swear." He clasped her face in both hands so that her hair framed it and she was forced to look up at him. "I swear," he repeated, and kissed her full upon the lips.

It was her brother who brought her away, led her to his horse, set her before him, rode with her out from the peering eyes and wagging tongues, another source of gossip for the court to savor in full.

It was Gervaise of Walran who, almost mouthing in rage, shouted, "Marry me she shall or be cursed before all men as strumpet to lead me on."

And it was her father who told both of them, his eyes dark gray, the scar on his cheek white, "Let her be. I order so. Her mother was such, as I know to my cost." His eyes were dark with remembering. "Loyal are these ladies of Cambray," he said, still thoughtful, "true to their word, true to their loves. Fair is my daughter, and virtuous, and I keep her so. But to force those ladies to our will is to break them, for they will not bend. I shall keep my daughter safe, not destroy her."

Gervaise heard him out in silence, heard the earl's order for silence to be kept. But in private, they say, that Norman knight clapped his hand to his sword hilt and swore by the cross it bore that never should the lady see Prince Taliesin again, such was his rage and jealousy. And further, in private, he cursed, ugly-tongued, vowing that had the lady been his, he would have had her flogged; a whipping would soon bring her to her knees. And Gervaise vowed also that whereas her father and brother were weak where women were concerned, he would not be; married to him, the lady would know her place. And other such oaths, which young men swear when they feel thwarted in their love affairs, but with a bitterness twice as deep that although he offered marriage in honorable wise, she dared look at a man to whom he felt superior and who was not even able to offer her that much. Well, Gervaise pitted himself against opponents worthy of his idea of himself: a lady whose will was to prove as strong as his and a rival who certainly was an honorable man. And he pitted himself against a worse enemy than both of these: against himself, love against honor, love against pride, and in the end, pride against envy. Such were the conflicts that burned in him, such were they to destroy him. And from that time, there began to grow in this young Norman lord a hatred and desire for revenge (feelings foreign, perhaps, to his younger self) against this Welsh upstart who, he felt, had publicly put him to scorn.

But not all his curses, his oaths, his prayers, could dismiss his rival out of hand. Nor could his hatred of Prince Taliesin diminish that prince nor prevent the prince from seeking out the lady whom both men desired. For Prince Taliesin was in like predicament—not able to show all that he felt, perhaps not ready to consider it, a man committed to a certain course and unable to turn aside. What he truly thought I cannot say, myself being neither warrior nor prince, nor yet embarked upon a hopeless task. Yet had I been, and had I held that lady in my arms, I'd not have let her go. And so, perhaps, was he as reluctant. And because he was the man he was, and knew her, he may well have decided it was not right that he should allow time to pass without seeing her and trying to explain. But mostlike, as now I believe, it was none of these thoughts (which come with age and are heavy with logic rather than desire). The prince was young and eager, riding, for that moment, on a crest of hope. He could no more prevent himself from seeking out the lady than keep iron from running molten through the flames. He saw her because he *must*, as once she had him. *I shall keep my daughter safe.* Of course, Earl Raoul meant so to do, but in his youth what daughter had been safe from him? Prince Taliesin and the lady were destined to meet again; as soon dim the sparks when a sword blade beats on anvil steel as keep them apart. But when the prince heard, in his turn, of a rival for her favors, jealousy, too, may have spurred him on.

As for my lady, what said she, what felt she? For the first time in her life, I think, she began to know what all who love must feel, the complexities, and the restraints that love imposes, whether we will or no. That she cared for Prince Taliesin with more than a child's infatuation I have no doubt, and that she sensed its force and perhaps feared it. *Her mother was such.* And her mother's mother, Lady Efa of the Celts, who against all odds loved her enemy and found happiness. But if my lady may have been shaken by these conflicting ideas (she who before nothing in this world had dismayed), again, she had nowhere to escape. Wherever she turned, iron bonds closed her round, of convention, custom, and her own respect for family ties. Aye, pity her, my little lady, who now began to know true love and had neither means nor words to express it, ripe to be tricked by a hostile world into revealing it.

Since I was privy to the second time she and Prince Taliesin met (I mean the second time in this new state, on the verge of things, not yet committed, cautious, testing out), let me speak of it. It reveals, better than my words, the lady's mind and the prince's own. It shows him for what he was, bound by honor, caught also in a trap in which he could neither speak nor not speak, move nor not move. Yet he sought her out (although afterward he was to claim that she had so sought him). And she was more than willing to be sought.

There was no waste of time. The following day brought them together again. For feeling free to walk with my lady, and her squire and maid, on their way to church, to humor her, I had made a detour along the riverbank. By then I had come to know this part of Paris well, and being always curious, and small enough to slip in and out and find things to amaze, I had long wanted to show her the wharves and piers and boats, where traders from all over the world plied their wares. The Seine had been a route for merchants since Viking times, and doubtless before, and to these large warehouses, or *halles*, that Louis had built came traders from all over the known world, each bellowing out in his own tongue the goods he had for sale. The mixture of noise, sounds, smells, tastes delighted my lady, as I had hoped, almost as much as the students did when I had showed her them. "One day," she cried, standing on tiptoe, stretching out her arms, "we shall be carried out to sea, far, far away. You, too, Urien." And she had laughed, a prophecy of her own, I suppose.

That morning, then, the Lady Olwen and her maid had seated themselves on the verge of a pier that jutted out over a sandy strip. She wore a blue dress, I remember, golden woven, etched with flowers, but had pushed her skirts out of the way and rolled up her sleeves, dipping her hands into the water to attract the schools of small fish that darted around the wooden piles. She had a happy look that I remember also, as if for a moment all troubles had rolled aside, and her laugh was the one I loved to hear. Myself, I was seated carefully out of the dirt at the wharf's edge, parchment in lap, diligently practicing my writing craft, when a sudden shadow blocked my page and slanted across the bleached wood boards. Startled, I looked up, ready to shout alarm, when I recognized those same Celtic guards, stiff, like trees edging a dusty road. I opened my mouth to give them greetings, to warn my lady, I was not sure which, when the prince swung off his horse and, putting his fingers to his lips, strode out lightly upon the wharf, moving with his quick tread, which I would have recognized anywhere. Even full-armed he walked like a man used to picking a path through the undergrowth, light on his toes, a walk a true Norman knight could never hope to imitate, used as Normans are to having their horses do their walking for them.

On reaching the end of the pier, where the lady and her companions were bent, intent on their game, still in silence the prince threw aside his cloak and sword belt, drew his gauntlets

off, and pushed back his steel coif so that his hair blazed in the
sun. Then, in one easy movement, he leaned down beside the
Lady Olwen and dipped his hands beneath the water alongside
her own. Lady Olwen started back in fright as he knelt close
to her, his shoulder in its mail coat touching hers, her gaze
attracted by the golden glitter from his bracelet as he thrust it
into the stream.

"Hush," he told her, not looking at her, his eyes fixed upon
the riverbed. "If you would play at fishermen, you must be
patient." His brown hands had caught hers beneath the water,
brown skin against her white, and he opened and shut her fingers
with his own, carefully trailing them with the slow current.

Nearby, Olwen's maid and squire peered into the clear depths,
where the fine sand glinted and where, midstream, large trout
lay, speckled gray and black, among green beds of weeds.

"See." The prince spoke, soft-voiced, as a fish, attracted by
the slow and steady movements, began to stir. "To catch fish
you must copy them; lie calm, watch, wait." And more urgently
now he began to play with her hands, pressing them back and
forth upon his own palms, luring the fish out from its hiding
place.

Suddenly Lady Olwen pulled herself free and tried to stand
up. She was panting, her lips soft, and there was a bead of sweat
along her brow. "Let me go," she said, almost incoherently,
"I must leave. I shall be late."

He did not ask "Late for what?" nor did he move, but lazily
continued to kneel and trail his hands, as if in truth he had come
here expressly to fish. "Look." He pointed after a while, as the
largest of the fish began as lazily to swim toward the pier,
fascinated by the steady movement in the water, the golden
gleam. "In a moment you'll have a fat trout to grill."

Almost angry with herself, both afraid to show what she felt
and yet feeling deeply for him, she scooped up a pebble and
threw it into the water with a little splash. "No," she cried.
"I've done with trapping living things. I'll not be used for bait
for anything.

"Not even for me?" Taliesin showed no surprise at her sudden
change of mood, no resentment, merely rocked back upon his

heels and began to roll down his tunic sleeves beneath his mail coat. But his voice was grim. "I thought now you like to angle for men."

She said, biting her lip in that familiar gesture, "What do you mean?" She hesitated again, not sure what words to use, went on, "Last night you swore to be good friends. . . ."

"Am I not now?" he said, as if surprised, still not looking at her, still staring in an abstracted way across the river into the heat haze.

She tried again. "You were more gentle last night," she said.

He interrupted her. "Aye so, but last night I had not heard of Lord Gervaise." There was a silence then between them, hard and long.

"Gervaise." She repeated the name almost stupidly.

"Just so," he said. "Nor had I then heard your name mouthed aloud by him in the Paris stews, as freely as that of any Paris whore." He paused. "What gives him right to speak of you? How is it you are so named and no man to smite the speaker dumb, as he deserved?"

The violence of the expressions he used, in contrast with his almost casual tone, struck her full force. She almost recoiled from it as from a blow. She turned pale a second time, tried to pull away, then forced herself to gather her courage up. "And what were you doing in such a place," she asked, "that you should hear those things spoken of?"

"I slept alone last night," he told her bluntly, "as did you, I trust. As did not that Gervaise of Walran." At the repetition of the name, he began to frown. "That Norman knight is not for you," he cried. "In the city streets they say that you will be wed." He paused again. "What is that man to you?" He rapped the question out.

"Nothing," she answered him passionately. "Nothing, nothing." When he did not reply, she went on, "Gervaise has made a marriage bid for me. Can I help that?"

He said slowly, "In the city streets I also hear your father spoken of. They say the earl will consider first your happiness. What joy for you!" There was an edge of bitterness to his voice. "Had I daughters," he went on, "I'd not give them such liberty.

Freedom always brings responsibility. Have a care, Olwen of Cambray, as you walk abroad so freely, pause so freely, talk so freely with any passing knight. Harm may come to you."

She tried to recover her composure, tried to laugh his words off, all the while struggling to release her skirts where he stood on them. "What harm?" she challenged him as she had Bernard of Poitou. "You remind me of our old seneschal, Dylan, more full of danger than a gorse bush thorns. What harm in a queen's court? I have no enemies."

"Your father does," he told her harshly. "One day in Paris, and a man senses the city like a forest, ringed with wolf traps, and courts abrim with mischief, envy jousting there with hate. Your name is spoken; that alone is a danger sign. And were I in the mood, what would stop me now, here, from having my will of you, as that Norman lordling boasted of?"

She flushed, tried again to drag herself away. "A silly boy," she cried, "wine-drunk, not meaning half he says."

He caught her by the arms and pulled her up, almost shaking her so her head rattled. "By Saint David," he gritted out, "you talk like a maid possessed, as if you were still wandering at will, safe in Cambray. I am not a silly boy meaning half I say. I suppose you'd run to hold *his* head in the gutter if he moaned loud enough, although yesterday when I asked an hour of your time, you refused. Am I a nothing, too, less than a nothing, perhaps?"

Her skirts were still hooked about his spurs; his hard grip left marks along her arms. The harder he held, the more she seemed to slip between his grasp, like trying to catch a moonbeam or a snowflake. He could have shaken her apart, and yet she would not yield to him. "What gives you the right," she dared him, "to order me? No one hurts me, save you."

"By God," he breathed, "no woman I have ever known challenged me as you do, or treated me with such disdain. . . ." An indiscretion she was quick to note.

It was his turn to flush. He held her more closely than before, so that her hair floated against him, releasing its scent of lavender and rose water. Her eyes were dark with something he could not put a name to, and her body bent under his like a reed. He started to say harshly, "Were I in the mood, Lady Olwen," when he broke off, began instead to curse beneath his breath, oaths such as men use when perplexed, goaded out of their usual ways of thought, the sort of uncertainty men of action seldom feel. "By the holy wounds, by the head of Christ," the least of them, "by God, is that the Norman faith you brag about? So much for friendship, then. I know what trust to put in you."

His words in turn goaded her. "Not so," she cried in her passionate way. "If you were in any sort of danger, if you were wounded, sick, in need, would I fail you then? You would but have to send me your message and I would come. Nothing would stop me if you asked for me."

"Well." He pounced on her words, his tone more dry now than angry. "Let us hope not that bad, else would I be of no use to you or anyone. I thank you for your offer, lady, nor would I seem to lack in gratitude, but if you would give so much for friendship, what would you swear for love? You told me I did not know what love was. Do you?"

Cleverly he darted a look at her, his raking look. "What would you do for love, little Olwen of the White Way?"

Confused by him, she said in her quick fashion, "If I loved and were loved, I would follow you to the ends of the earth. There is nothing I would not do for you . . ." She stopped, bit her lip, would not continue, aware too late that she had also given herself away. She tugged at her skirts so fiercely that the stitching ripped. "Move, move," she almost cried, "I cannot free myself."

"Do you want to?" Prince Taliesin had begun to smile; he moved toward her, and his arm came about her shoulders as at the royal court. "What if," he whispered, and his mouth was against her cheek, her neckbone, searching along her ear, "when my quest is done, I should come again, what then?" And light as thistledown his lips touched the fine skin, tracing out the curve of chin and cheek, touching the long eyelashes that hid her eyes from him. Caught against him, her mouth like a bird's, slightly opened, waiting to be fed, her heart beating against his like a trapped bird's, too, she said what she truly wanted to say, "Do not let me go. Only with you do I feel safe."

She reached up her arms, the wet and trailing sleeves leaving damp patches on her skirts, and clutched him around the neck, her body arched against his, her fingers twined in his thick curls.

"Hold me," she cried.

Her heart beat like a trapped bird's, I say; her breasts rose up against the fragile cloth; her delicate mouth felt for his along the sunburned edge of his jaw, where the faint marks of a beard had begun to show. Breathing together they clung each to each, while the city hummed and throbbed and the old river beat its track to the sea.

But when again she began to pant, this time it was he who disentangled himself. "Let be, little Olwen," he said then, betwixt laugh and groan, "although what I would do would be no hurt, yet hurt it would be. Go you to church and pray for me. Pray that soon the end of my quest be come. Pray for all honest souls—wait for me."

"Do not leave me," she cried. "I cannot bear to lose you again."

His face tightened into lines that made him seem older, resolved. "I must," he said. "I am not yet free to make a choice, but I will not leave this city without seeing you again."

And with that promise she had to be content, a promise both made, openly, to all who cared to hear.

When he had mounted his horse and ridden off, after a long while she, too, drew herself upright. "Come," she said simply to her maid and squire, and she took my arm in her old way. In silence we all went along with her, no need to swear a silence; all knew it must be kept, although still not silence enough. Yet when we came to the queen's church (in which, since the remaking of Notre Dane, the greatest sermons in the world were preached by men whose fame is universal), where the ladies of the royal court kept state, with their long headdresses of silk, their embroidered robes, their jewels, I was abashed to think of evil amid such graciousness. And seeing how those ladies strolled, by pairs, along the riverbank, swinging their missals bound by thongs, their soft leather shoes swishing through the grass, I realized, for the first time, that my lady shone among them like a jewel herself. I knew then a pang of fear and of regret, as sharp as a spear thrust, that she had gone too far from me, into another world, where I could never save her if I would.

In heavy mood I walked back slowly, not interested in the city gesticulating on every side, to be welcomed by a clout for leaving so many chores undone. But as I sat and polished my master's boots and straps, trying to comfort myself with heroic thoughts that one day, perhaps, even I would excel before my lady and rescue her from her enemies, so that she would thank me as she had thanked Bernard of Poitou, so that she would cling to me as she did Prince Taliesin, I knew my imaginings in vain. Like Gervaise, I had my little hopes of fame (alas, when they occurred, they were very different in reality from dream). For enemies there were, and danger abroad. And help needed. As now was proved.

Chapter 10

ernard of Poitou it was who warned us. For although silence was kept in the earl's household, loyalty to the earl and his daughter being paramount, yet no such silence was kept in the city of Paris itself, rumor running there rampant and unrestrained. Paris was alive and quick in those days. Craving excitement as a drunkard craves wine, its citizens remembered other lovers who had found shelter beneath their roofs, and although not caring which lover a lady might choose, they were not indifferent to the choice: between a man whom all the world would praise and one who, having nothing to offer, perhaps never would have more than that. Such open talk, such gossip, frightened me, too, when I heard it, as it had alarmed the prince. I sensed disaster ahead. It seemed that such a display could only encourage hostility and be useful to an enemy. As now was proved.

I was sitting the next day, or the one following, I forget; time seemed to blend, one day much like the next as we lived in this suspense. My lord and I had come along the riverbank. Soon this day, too, would come to its close, another long day, another long wait. And all day had Lord Robert been quiet. Concern for his sister struggled with concern for Gervaise, with concern for the earl and for Hue—so many cares upon his mind. The nonarrival of the English princes was both blessing and curse. For between my master (and by now I knew his heart like my own) and his father especially a silence had arisen, composed of many things, of which the most important was dislike of disappointing the earl. Neither father nor son would openly discuss his plans, each not trusting the other, fearful of forcing confidence, unwilling to be the one to cause pain. Yet pain there would be, inevitably, and every day the thought must have crossed both their minds that when Prince Richard came, Robert would be lost, not to the rebellion itself but to one of the rebels, at least. Between the earl and his older son was a bond, more strong, I think, than between most men: this son's birth had almost caused his mother's death; his vulnerable childhood had been a reflection of the earl's own vulnerability. Wounded, betrayed, his castle in ruins, a wife and infant to protect, the young Raoul had had a bitter homecoming to Sieux. His son's rescue from the treachery of a Boissert plot had seemed a miracle. To break the bond, so formed, so strongly made, would tear both men apart. And Robert knew it as well as the earl. So, then, I was playing on my pipe to soothe my lord, to soothe myself, the Lady Olwen gone to church, her prayers not likely to add to our peace, the earl still in council with the king, Gervaise repaired grumbling into the city to sulk, when Bernard of Poitou's voice hailed me.

Since our first encounter we had met from time to time, he to ask news of our household, particularly of the Lady Olwen, and I to listen avidly to his stories of the great world he skirted about. But he had never come openly, and I gestured to where my master lay with his head buried in his arms, supposedly asleep.

"Is that Lord Robert?" Bernard said, abruptly rough, more like the man I had first met. I was surprised. In the intervening weeks I had come to know him well. I liked him; his plain face and ill-favored features hid a warm and loyal heart. I did not like to hear him speak so sharp. I looked at him more carefully; he was dressed today in silver-gray, black, and white, colors that did not flatter him; he seemed like a raven in his yellow boots, with a yellow feather in his cap. But my jests were stifled as he said hurriedly, "Dolt. You are a fool to let your master sleep while all the world falls apart. Where is your mistress, where Prince Taliesin?"

I tried to hush him, glancing nervously where Lord Robert lay, and whispered that my lady had gone to Mass, as was her custom, with the queen.

"Fool," he cried a second time, even louder. "Will the queen be absent from the court today, when her son-in-law is expected? I told you to take care. Surely you have heard of Isobelle de Boissert?"

Thrust out at me like that, suddenly, unexpectedly, a name I had heard but once before, it surprised me out of memory. Yet there are those who have told me since that the very sound of that name sets the senses flaring awake, a hint, a taste, of evil, like ashes cold from a peat fire, smoldering in the damp.

Bernard could scarce contain his impatience. "Who save you has not heard of her?" he cried. His fingers twitched to shake the knowledge into me. "Isobelle de Boissert, who once was betrothed to Raoul of Sieux and broke her troth when his fortunes fell, who tried to woo him back when her father planned a rebellion in Geoffrey Plantagenet's name. She played for high stakes then, did Isobelle, hoping to become Geoffrey's wife when he took the title of Count of Anjou from the king. Countess of Anjou would have suited her. And when Raoul refused his help, she plotted to kill him at the tourneys of Boissert Field. She had already tried to kill the Lady Ann when Raoul's son was born. As one last revenge, from the nunnery where she was imprisoned, she tried to capture the child. When your master wakes, who sleeps disaster away, ask him what he remembers of De Boissert, what of the Lady Isobelle whose plan it was to poison him."

As if this bitter litany finally reached my master, he started up, his hand already reaching for his sword. "Who speaks that name," he cried. "Who dares?"

"I do." For once Bernard of Poitou had lost all pretense of calm. I think he meant to make his presence known. He ignored my protestations and advanced toward Robert. "My lord," he said without preamble, "get you hence to find your sister. I tell you that Isobelle de Boissert is here, sent ahead by Queen Eleanor to pave the way, let out from the prison of her nunnery, God knows why. Ask not how I know. But so I do. And I know that she-witch has made a rendezvous with the Lady Olwen after Nones. What she will do then I give you leave to guess. But she knows of the lady's promise to meet with Prince Taliesin if he has need of her. And she knows of Prince Taliesin's promise to see your sister again."

Since I did not know most of this, I could but gape, while Robert, rising in full wrath, seized Bernard by the scruff of his new clothes and threatened him. "By the living cross," he roared, "I'll cut off your ears if you speak false. Who are you to have news of such filth as that she-wolf, that bitch?" I had never heard such loathing in his voice, and with his free hand he jerked at his sword as if to make good his word.

Bernard said steadily, "My lord, you may fight me if you want. I warn you I shall defend myself. No doubt you will win in the end, but my death may not be so quick as you could wish. I have been well trained as a swordsman, and in seeking to kill me, you delay yourself. Rather, listen to me."

A brave man was Bernard of Poitou to outface my lord, who, seeing the sense of his words, let him go and bid him speak. As best he could, he did, in hurried tones, what he said enough to dismay anyone, that uneasiness now become a fact.

"My lord," he said, "who I am is not important. But my father, Sir Renier, who came here on behalf of Queen Eleanor, has heard this very morn that she will never enter Paris again, anathema to the French queen, distrusted by King Louis himself. Ask me not how or why, but so it is, and we, as consequence, must leave forthwith, withdraw back to our southern lands, which I for one wish we had never left. But I am come to warn you. Since the Yuletide, when first the prince's rebellion was planned, has your family's old enemy, Isobelle de Boissert, been here, too. She came in secret, of course, under assumed name; but she is housed and equipped with revenues from Queen Eleanor to act as spy. A hanger-on at the fringes of the French court has she been, seeking news and sensing change, waiting to see if the wind blows fair or foul.

"Beneath pretext of piety, which her sojourn in a holy place enhanced, she has tried to ingratiate herself with Queen Adela and the other ladies and has often met your sister in such guise.

Realizing today, at last, that any hope of success can never be achieved, Isobelle has let her disappointment spill anew to hate. And ever between her and your house has been death."

Robert sheathed his sword. "Aye, no one knows that better than I. Death is her second name; she would have killed me, father, mother, all. Ask me sometime where hell is. She is writ therein. So, what shall she do?"

Bernard said, "Since every day she walks with the ladies of the court, after Mass, there today she awaits your sister, whose very beauty rouses jealousy. She will lure the lady Olwen to meet with Prince Taliesin. But the means, the place of rendez-vous between your sister and this prince, what skill has been used to get them there, I do not know. Nor what she plans for them when she has them in her grasp. Those are things you must find yourself. But quickly now."

He had scarcely finished speaking before Robert was striding back, shouting for his horse, the household guard, calling upon his own men to arm. Before following him at a run, I snatched a moment to bid Bernard adieu, suspecting we would never meet again. He clasped my hand in both of his. "Farewell, Urien the Bard," he cried. "Do not think ill of me." There was a sudden misery in his voice, of regret and shame. "The way of courtier is hard, and I am not hardened to it. I had not thought to sell myself as whore to bring you such evil news. I had not thought to serve a lady of that ilk, nor find such wickedness condoned by my father's queen." Well, long it was indeed before I saw him again, Bernard of Poitou. Back he went to his vineyards and crops, better country life of simple country lord than this dark and dangerous underworld of spies and courtiers. But without him hope would have been lost.

In the yard all was haste, yet calm. Urgency ran like a forest fire beneath a peat bog. The captain of the guard, four men, myself, my lord, we mounted in haste, thundered out of the courtyard, taking the paths along the riverbanks toward the abbey church, the startled cries of the rest of our own men, of the honest citizens we scattered from our path, following us. Now again I saw what discipline means, to knights who mount and ride when so bid. "Ride," said their lord, and so they did,

their swords bared, their shields unslung, their helmets locked
in place. Lost in the saddle, stirrups gone, I bumped helplessly
along in their dust, by some instinct long-drilled into me by
Dylan, looping my finger through the mane while my free hand
fumbled for the hilt of my own sword. And when we came to
a more crowded thoroughfare, Lord Robert still did not give
the signal to slacken speed, instead wheeled down an alleyway
that led to those small strips of vines and garden plots with
which the city still was laced, like green silks threaded among
dirt and stones. And always on our left we kept the riverbank.
The river flowed on as it has done these thousand years; the city
spilled about us with its fair towers and green trees and mighty
church steeples, smiling in the late afternoon. Beneath that water,
where the sun sparkled low on the horizon, beneath that smiling
face, death and treachery waited for us. And fear rose and knotted in my throat.

The ride to the queen's church was not far, the route faster
than the one we had walked that spring day. I recognized its
spires even before it came into sight. It stood beside a huddle
of houses, set apart, quiet at this hour, never filled as it used to
be in the days of Abelard and Saint Bernard, and empty now
of the court—the ladies all gone to watch for more interesting
sights with the arrival of the English prince. Robert did not
pause to dismount. Up the wide stone steps he urged his horse,
and hammered on the huge wooden doors with the hilt of his
sword, until two of our men beat their horses forward and
thrust with all their weight to break the doors apart. Together
we clattered down the dim-lit aisles, where a great rose window
of stained glass caught the western sun, sending splashes of
yellow and crimson across the uneven stones. The aisles were
empty, only a few monks praying in their hoods, who started
up at our impiety; a lone priest with a pax dropped it in alarm.
Up one aisle we cantered, scattering mud and dirt, knocking
underfoot the tapers that stood in the oratories, startling an altar
boy to screams so that the censer he held spilled its hot scent
into the air. In front of the altar we turned to gallop out again,
down the steps by bounds toward the grassy walks where I had
seen Queen Adela take my lady's hand and embrace her. Noth-

ing, no one, emptiness, the river running deep. Only underneath a distant stand of trees a few serfs closing the leather
curtains of a litter resting on the grass. Even as we wheeled to
ride back, these men heaved the poles into the horses' traces
and prepared to whip up the beasts. Beyond them an expanse
of meadow and empty paths. In a short while the sun would
set, already low, time for feast and merriment, time for ambush
and intrigue.

Again we wheeled, passing closer to that group of serfs. There
were not many, their gear old, their coats worn. But it was the
color that struck me—gray, tarnished silver, rusty black, the
colors Bernard of Poitou had worn, the colors I had mocked
him for. So I knew he had spoken truth, how he had come to
learn it and from whom.

"Hold." Lord Robert's voice had aged, too, this past hour.
It was his father's voice, heavy with command. The old men
gaped at him. But there were a couple of younger men among
them, coarse-faced men with bullying looks, who had the air
and stance of cutthroats. One of our knights, riding up to them,
brought their horses to a halt, beat all the men to a stop with
the flat of his sword so that our master could snap his questions
out. Their quavering replies conjured up my lady for me, with
her sparkling eyes and her flame hair and her merry innocence,
a simple maid, walking with the great ladies of this land, their
pet, no harm coming to her.

"Stand aside, young sir," the spokesman said, rubbing his
toothless gums with a sort of glee. "We have no truck with
knights. Nor maids, worse luck." He made to urge his companions on. Nonplussed, our men might have fallen back had
not Lord Robert spurred forward himself, right up to the bier,
making the horses shy. With a hand that visibly trembled he
pulled at the heavy leather curtains so that the rings that held
them clattered apart.

A voice within screeched in protest, fingers jerked at the
thongs to hold them fast, a head came out to peer around. At
first it was difficult to tell who it was, such a froth of headdress,
so many ribbons, coif, gold bands, as if a dozen young maids
were hid beneath those fripperies. And the voice, which orig-

inally had been shrewish, shrill, mellowed into honey as she saw she was surrounded by men.

"Young sirs," she chirped, tremulous, almost flirtatious, "we are a lady all alone. Unprotected, helpless. Chivalry demands your defense. Pray let my men go forth. We have seen no one." She peered around the corner coyly, almost beckoning, as a young girl is supposed to do.

"Lady." Lord Robert again thrust his horse alongside, although it snorted and pawed. "I beg leave—" Whatever else he would have said was lost to her screams. Terror was in them, terror, stark and raw.

"No, Raoul," she cried, throwing up her hands. Like sticks they were, stuck out from her thin wrists. "No, Raoul, I meant no harm. Holy Mother, preserve me, no harm, no harm."

She began to gabble, prayers, perhaps, vows, mouthing in a frenzy of fear. Robert observed her for a moment, silently. When he saw her like that, I think, his own fear began to evaporate; what but skin and bones was left of that dark image who had haunted his nightmares, what was there to fear from her who was fear personified? He suddenly sat back in the saddle, gathered up the reins, and waited for her fit to pass.

"So, Isobelle de Boissert, your sojourn in convent has done some good," he said, and with the tip of his sword he dragged the curtains full back. "Yet you mistake me for someone else. Not Raoul of Sieux. Robert am I, his son."

Within the shelter of her litter, exposed now to the full light, the old woman, for such she was, rocked back and forth upon her cushions, also embroidered in black and white. She reminded me suddenly of something that scuttles forth when a rock is overturned, something pale, unused to light. Her hand clutched a crucifix, and her headdress was knocked askew so that underneath, the heavy coil of hair, gold-tinted, padded out with sheep's wool, began to slip. Her face turned palsy white where it was not rouged with paint and crumpled into an old mask, dissolving to grease and sweat.

"Christ save us," she whispered, "from the dead returned, from the past reborn. Not Raoul of Sieux? Then you are his ghost, his twin. What do you want of me?"

"My sister."

"Sister, sister," she muttered as if her wits were gone; her head shook like a chicken, and she clawed at the cushions with her nails as if searching for escape. Lord Robert did not give an inch, although seeing her fear exposed he might have. I saw how his hip jutted forward so that his sword swung within easy reach. With one gauntleted hand he seized her wrist, like to snap a bone.

"Forgive, forgive," she wept. Her tears, whether real or feigned I cannot say, made tracks across the painted cheeks. "False were you to me, Raoul of Sieux, whom once I loved and thought loved me. Yet you abandoned me, married with that Celtic whore, and left me to wither all these years, Henry's prisoner. Should I wish you joy in a son?"

Her voice suddenly became cunning, low, as if she were recalling where she was and to whom she spoke. "And should I let such a pretty maid die of grief? Should I refuse her aid? I only gave her the help that she begged for; I only told her where to meet her lover; what harm in that?" Her voice whined as does an old woman's, such as she was beneath her powder and paint, that whine, that appeal to age, the last of her tricks. "Child of love is she," she cried, "child of joy, born when Raoul returned from exile. I only told her where happiness is to be found tonight; I only told her lover where to find her. Come, Master Robert." She gave him a grin, a caricature of what once her smile might have been. "Have you no sympathy for lovers? Have you no heart of your own?"

"Nay." Robert's voice was bleak, and there was suddenly such a nakedness in his look, such an old despair, that I turned away. "You have already had your will of me. Numbed am I by your poison's curse, never knowing love's charms. There is your vengeance, Isobelle de Boissert. I give it to you again, full force. Savor it as you will. But tell me where my sister is."

He let her go so violently that she collapsed and lay whimpering to herself, her eyes bright as a snake, cradling her head in her hands.

Robert heeled his horse aside. With his back to the litter he summoned the captain of his guard. "By Christ," he said through whitened lips. "Enough of games. Bring forth those men; question them. Deal with them as you will."

Well, the order was rough, confession not a nice business. Our men were quick and thorough. It did not last long, one of her ruffians ready to throw himself upon his knees, ready to scream her plans away for mercy. "I heard it all, the place, the time, the lady you seek already gone to meet her prince as was planned. And word sent to him, in her name, to meet him there, a lover's tryst beside the old western gates, in the Church of Mary of the Holy Cross, new named, new built. In the crypt will they meet. And there lie our hired men in wait for them."

Thus will a sword prick make cowards of the meanest villains. When he was done, my lord ordered, "Take them away. Witness to a crime; have done with them." But when they came to drag the old woman forth, "Let be," he said. "She and her waiting woman have paid a price for one crime they did; the one is dead, hanged after death as a poisoner. This one has lived out her life away from the world back in her convent, so let her finish it, cold as the hell wherein she lives. She and I were bound before my birth, and by my death she hoped for revenge against my parents' love. Her mark is on me, bleached by poison's touch. I have no further use for her."

So we left her beneath the trees that soon would bear new fruit and rode on, two men remaining to finish the hangman's work and to warn Earl Raoul of what had been done; the remaining two, the captain of the guard, my lord, myself, riding along the riverbank, taking the fastest way to the western gates. And as we rode, as never before or since, hoping against hope at every turn we would see my lady's quick figure ahead or pick out that of her sturdy squire, I managed to gasp out, "My lord, what of the prince?"

Robert, still taut-faced beneath his helmet, said only, "We do not know if he will come, or what he intends, or by what means a message was given him, only that he would take my sister as his own. For that alone is he suspect."

By now the streets had begun to clear; the long evening shadows were athwart our path. I imagined my lady walking fearlessly forward, earnest and quick, joy and anxiety struggling within her. I thought of the dark crypt where murder lurked to cut short her joy and would have ridden on ahead had not now my master held me back. "Gently, gently," he said, as if recollecting himself, "we cannot rush in unprepared. We will find her, never fear. And when those murderers come, we will be waiting for them." And for the first time he smiled to give us heart.

The square where the church stood was small and mean, although once the church had been well known, sacred to the saint of travelers, now renamed in honor of the Virgin, mother of God. We came cautiously up the one street that led to the square. The evening had begun to chill; a wind had risen to scatter the winter leaves that had blown in heaps, and across the river ripples spread like a film of ice. This part of the city, I think, was so old that it had almost been abandoned: the buildings fallen into ruin; the western gates, once a main thoroughfare, long blocked; no people in sight, just a stray dog or two. The square ended at the church door. All was quiet, undisturbed, no sign of life, no marks of horse or men; and where the steps ran down beneath a new facade, the iron links that blocked them had not been unhooked, the moss that covered them had not been touched.

We swung ourselves off our own mounts and gazed around. I heard one man mutter a prayer of thanks. But where was the Lady Olwen, where her squire, where Prince Taliesin? And what should we now do, since it was clear we were here first?

A little stir of wind came again, like a breath. The bank of clouds that had begun to mask the sun would bring an early dark, and beneath them a thin red line shone rustily along the water's edge. From the church undercroft rose up the smell of age, ruin, death, so strong that my hair stood on end. And while above ground the men worked quickly and efficiently, one to lead the horses aside, tied out of sight behind the church; another to sweep away all our traces; these two left to guard the entrance to the square, out of sight themselves, with orders to detain the lady when she came, but to let all others pass, we—Lord Robert, the captain of his guard, and myself—tiptoed down into the vault. "And if the prince comes," Lord Robert's instructions were clear, "let him pass as well. But look alert. Whoever and whenever, the assassins will be more numerous than we and must not see you to spring our trap for them too soon. Below ground, in the dark, let's pray their numbers hinder them."

Down we crept, in furtive haste, treading carefully in each other's steps to leave no mark. The stairs were old and slippery, broken at the sides, so that a man, lacking care, could tumble there and break his neck. They led to a dim, short entryway—empty, no place there to hide; beyond it a larger vault, already dark, held up by six squat pillars that seemed to bear all the weight of the upper church upon their backs. I sensed an oldness there, thick and foul, like a taste or smell. Whatever Christian church had been reared above those pillars, this was no Christian church beneath; the very darkness cried out with heathen sound. Since then I have heard that in ancient times there never was such a building made without its offer of human sacrifice, and it seemed to me that the air around us was heavy with the stifled cries of men whose eyes and mouths were stuffed with earth, so did those victims' deaths clamor about us, unavenged. I felt the skin on my hands grow cold and the hairs on my neck rise up like a dog's. I could have thrown back my head and howled.

Lord Robert steadied me. Like his father he was rational in danger's face; like his sister he went about dealing with it in a practical way. With one hand he thrust me back against the farthest wall, he on one side, the captain on the other, this last a man noted for his courage and skill, myself a weak third between. They drew their swords, tested the blades, the edge, then held them loosely, tips pointed down, so that there would be no light reflected from them. We waited. The air grew cold; the little rectangle of light at the steps' entrance dimmed. A sudden bird's call, fluting through the pillars, made us start. Once, twice, thrice it fluted through the vault, and I felt Robert stiffen suddenly—the cry of the Cambray guard, their secret call, repeated three times. One was to let us know that the lady was safe; the second told us that the ambushers had arrived; the third, after a slight delay, alerted us that the prince had come.

Then all were here, and Isobelle de Boissert's game was to be put into play.

We waited, holding our breath. The little patch of light we had been staring at so intently suddenly was blocked as a figure crossed in front of it. There was a whisper, magnified by the echo in the undercroft; a form came stealing down the stairs, hand outstretched against the wall to steady himself. No man on honest mission creeps like that. Five more times the patch of light was dimmed; six times in all we heard the drag of mailed feet, the quick curse as someone's spurs caught, the shuffle as each figure fumbled in the dark against another, taking a place beside one of the thick pillars. There was a grunt as one man's sword rattled from its sheath, then silence, save for their panting breath.

I felt Lord Robert's arm tense again, his shoulder grow taut beneath its mail coat. This time a single figure darkened the rectangle of light, paused, looked down. I recognized its height, its shoulder's width under the cloak of fur, yet still the figure hesitated, puzzled by the place, and we heard him speak softly, perhaps to one of his men, although they could not all have been with him. Then he turned and took a step forward, peering intently into the dark, and a ripple like a sigh satisfied moved below, as imperceptible as the wind's stir, yet to us as palpable as a shout.

Now I cannot say what would have happened next. I do not believe Lord Robert would have let Prince Taliesin walk unknowing, unarmed, into that trap. Nor do I think he would have waited until the ambush had closed the prince around. Nor do I think Prince Taliesin was completely unprepared. But I felt I could not take the chance. My father's sword was in my hand, somehow, although I do not remember drawing it; I felt my hand move of its own accord. My body lunged forward almost as if drawn on strings; the sword tip slid between a pair of shoulder blades even as beside me Lord Robert and his captain moved also in step.

There was a gasp, a gurgle of breath, worse than a scream. It funneled out into the passageway, into the open air above

Prince Taliesin's head, and the prince, hearing it, leapt back and drew his sword. As he now leaned down, intent, every nerve alert, Robert gave the cry of his house. "*À moi*, Sieux, *à moi*, Cambray," he cried, and stormed forward. There was an answering shout, my own, as I, too, leapt, as I, too, thrust, the three of us moving as one, each aiming at a different post.

The effect in that constricted place was chaos. The sound echoed and rolled like a wave which, caught in a cave, rushes against a rock and rushes back. The ambushers, taken off guard, were attacked from behind as they had planned to attack; they ran in circles in the dark, stabbed at air, stabbed each other, threshed on the ground. Those who were not cut down at once fought each other or, throwing aside their weapons, raced for the stairs, where Prince Taliesin waited for them. Within seconds of his arrival the ambush was done. Our charge carried us to the foot of the steps, where already one body blocked our path and where the prince, one of his companions now backing him, held the entrance.

"We meet again, Prince of Afron." Robert's voice was calm for a man who has just broken out of a death trap. "Hold back your men. We come as friends."

At the head of the stairs Prince Taliesin pointed his sword menacingly. "Who are you?" he snarled. "Who shouts, 'On Cambray, on Sieux'? Where is the Lady Olwen of that name?"

"And who are you," Lord Robert told him, cold as ice, "to name that lady to me? With what right?" He came up the steps stiff-backed, still holding his naked sword, and we followed one by one until we stood level with him.

It was the prince's turn to give ground. He bit his lip, indecision in his eyes and voice. What could he say that did not implicate her? And so you saw he realized, even as he frantically thought of where she was or what might have happened to her. "I am here," he said at last, "because I was bid. The lady—"

"Is safe," Robert told him, "with my men beyond the square." He looked at Taliesin full, without blinking. "She should not be here," he said, "nor you. Malice brought you here, a trick, to lure her and you. Last time we met, lord prince, she came between us, between your oath and mine. That, too, was ill-done. My sister is not for you."

Taliesin began to sheathe his sword slowly. Behind him in the gloom, two of his men, his constant shadows, were, as ever, silent, watchful. "I think," the prince began, but what he was about to say was lost. There was a scrabble at our backs, a cry, the thud of feet. Across the square, running, her squire in hot pursuit, our two men hot after them, came the lady, skirts looped up, dagger drawn. Mistress and squire, between them they seemed ready to take on all the world, and so I think they might have had not she seen us in time to stop. Or, to be precise, I do not know if the lady saw us at all, but she did the prince. She passed her brother without a word, straight toward Prince Taliesin; the dagger went clattering to the ground as she ran upon him, beating at him with both fists, crying out her mixture of relief and fear. And he, regaining balance where her leap had almost toppled him, seized her by the wrists and swung her off the ground, almost laughingly trying to defend himself. Yet still she fought him, using feet and teeth, all the while, I hate to admit, berating him with curses that would have made a trooper blink. Finally catching her about the waist and uptipping her, backhanding Joycelyn, who now had come rushing up, Taliesin strode off toward the church, her legs flailing at air, her hands still pummeling his broad back.

We watched them go until suddenly Lord Robert gave a grin. He took a draft of the clean evening air as if he were breathing for the first time. "Mother of God," he said almost to himself, "who am I to interfere? Whatever I could do or say is about to be done or said by someone, I think, with more experience and who has more right. At least in this instance," he hastily amended. He watched for a moment, his usual tolerant look replacing the harsh, unforgiving one. Perhaps for the first time he began to feel some sympathy for the lovers as the prince set the lady down, dodging her blows and in the process giving her a good whack or two, as I have no doubt she well deserved. For now my lord turned his back, shouted for his men to quiet the horses, straining at the smell of blood, ordered out the body count, a

grisly business not fitted for women's eyes, conferring quickly
with the prince's men, keeping us all well occupied away from
the church door. I worked with the rest. But I am what I am.
A watcher does not always have choice over what he sees. He
watches and records because he must, not because he wishes
to. So this:

"All set to kill me, then, if they had not." Prince Taliesin's
voice was dry with relief, too. He had pushed aside his cloak;
his tousled hair had crisped into curls, and his face had grown
suddenly lean in that half-light. "Christ's bones, lady, were you
a man as you once wished, I'd put an end to your meddling.
Why are you here in this forsaken place? What fool business set
you to bid me here? To watch my death? Who were those men
in the crypt; who ordered them? Were I the earl, I'd have you
in a nunnery straight, not run amok to do men harm. Six dead
men there, five of your own, how many more of mine would
you have risk their necks?"

He had dropped her almost randomly upon the upper steps
of the church, inside a kind of portico, and stood in front of
her, staring down at her. It was almost dark now, a dim glow
in the sky, an evening star low down across the river's edge.
His voice was soft, but underneath it ran an anger's streak. "Ill
luck dogs you. Whenever I see or hear you, disaster follows as
night day."

Lady Olwen heard that anger. She sat down suddenly, as if
her legs had given way, and against her will her hand stole to
her ear, where he had given her a clap as she fought with him.
He saw the movement and pulled away her hand. "That for
biting me," he said, and for a moment his fingers gently touched
her skin. "And if you curse me again, I wash out your mouth
as I once promised."

She struggled to keep her own voice low, to match his calm-
ness with like calm, knowing her brother was within earshot,
knowing his men were a few paces off, and determined not to
show him any fear.

"And you," she said, "why did you send for me?"

"I send?"

His astonishment must have been clear. She reached beneath

her cloak and silently drew out a gold band, so like the one he wore, the one he had given and she returned, it was difficult to believe it was not the same. "I told you I would come," she said simply, "if you needed me. Someone told me there was danger, you wanted help. So I came as I had promised. I did not know it was a trick. In a nunnery, you said; that's where plots are hatched these days, my lord prince; that's where court ladies are trained to lie and cheat. Nowhere safe." Her voice was suddenly sad, betrayed. "I thought one of the old ladies of the court was my friend," she said in a child's voice, bewildered by treachery. "I thought she spoke to comfort me, not to use love to trick me. I did not know who she was; I did not recognize her as that Isobelle de Boissert who has long been an enemy of my house. And I thought you wished me well, not come here to threaten, too, because you live."

"A trick," he repeated. "Then one to catch us both. I also received a message, lady, sent from you, from someone who claimed she spoke in your name, a lady of the queen's court, to tell me that you had need of me in turn and would wait for me here. Is this lady the same as the one you speak of? Who is this Isobelle de Boissert?"

When she had told him, falteringly, what in the interim she must have learned, as she waited with our men, stopped by them as she and her squire came hurriedly through those streets, he almost groaned, balled his fist, and smote the wall with such force that the plaster on the stones crumbled in a shower and a line of blood started along his knuckles, down to his fingertips. "By Christ," he cried, "I did not think to be the means to kill you, Olwen the Fair. Christ's blood, but that must be answered for." He stood fighting his anger and regret. Then, as his thoughts cleared, "But lady, God forgive me, the malice, the revenge, those I make sense of although condemn; God forbid that any vengeance should fall on you. But why me, as its instrument?"

Lady Olwen began to speak, bit her lip to silence. She could not say, "Because I spoke of you with love; because that woman guessed and used my love; because she used my hope of yours as bait. And for her, to know that moment of false happiness would be turned to death, yours first, perhaps, to torment me, or mine to torment you, anticipation of that would have crowned a lifetime of De Boissert malice." Nor could she say, more simply, "You, my lord, because all the world knows what I feel, save only you yourself."

But he was quick. "Love." He was repeating her word. "You spoke of love? Was that what set the trap?" She could not answer him. To tell him would throw away her last defense.

"If it is love," he said, softer still, "if that was the reason you came, have not I right to know? But say the word. There are my men. They and I could bear you hence, far from here. Then would you know what that word means; then at the morning's end would it be you who would cry desist."

She turned her head aside, a blush started in her cheek. "What should I know of that sort of love?" she said, almost painfully. "I am a virgin, not yet a woman wed."

"Wed?" he said. "There is a word women are overfond of. I do not know of wedding, but what is so special in marriage vows to make a loving flower between man and maid? If love it is you want, Olwen of the White Way, I could love you. See how your stars shine tonight, so should I love you all night long." She was silent, her head still turned aside.

"But do not wanton with me, lady," he cried, and suddenly his voice was grim. "Three times to my loss have you played with me. Who else have you wantoned with?"

"Wanton?" she said. "That is a harsh word."

"Aye," he said. He was silent for a moment. "In the city," he said, "men still claim that Gervaise of Walran, that 'wine-drunk' boy, that Norman lord who is 'nothing' to you, will give you the marriage that you want. Will not that satisfy you? Remembering him, I almost did not come tonight. Having him, what do you want of me?"

"Arrogant," she cried suddenly, "proud, who thinks all women run to his beck and call. Go back, then, and crow on your own dung heap."

"Perhaps I shall." His voice was thoughtful, but he did not move away from her. "One day you may find it a refuge. But remember, Olwen, words are like blows, they leave hard marks. They can say things that later you may regret. You cannot marry two men at once, nor love two, nor wanton with two. You must choose.''

"Your words harm not me," she cried, proud now herself. "I do not care . . ." But she lied, and he showed her how, his fingers suddenly warm and soft, tracing down the cheek that he had bruised, tracing softly with his bloodied hand the silver shimmer from the contours of her long eyelashes, down the rounded cheek, along the trembling chin.

"Take care, Olwen of the White Way," he whispered softly against her ear. "A child may wanton and do no harm. A woman's wantonness can ruin the world. I did not come to Paris looking for you, but now I have you, should I let you go? Is that an answer to please you, Olwen, who would be my bane?"

"One day," she said, "of your own free will you have promised to seek me out. When that day comes, ask me then."

He suddenly smiled, his teeth white in the starlight. "Is that a curse," he whispered again, "your curse on me, a Celtic curse for the Celtic part of you? Hear mine. Three times have you of your own will sought me out, and never told me why or how. For the first time, then, I shall claim your lips, a hundred times like this, like this. And for the second time, your skin, white and delicate like the name you bear." And his hands were already slipping between the lacing of her gown, seeking out her little breasts that seemed to rise of their own accord.

"And for the third time," his voice was urgent with desire, "but one thing, and that the best, your maidenhood, which if I have it not, no man shall."

And with each word his hand flicked along her body length, tracing out the curves, the peaks, soothing her breasts beneath her gown.

"You'd not dare." But her lips scarce could open to speak before his own had covered them, his tongue caught between.

"Dare not me," each word a whisper, a caress. "I am a man so sworn to deeds." And now one hand was firm against her back, its print dark with blood along her spine. "If I were to hold you thus, ride up your gown, and touch you thus, tell me now you did not come for me."

One hand caught about her waist, the other drew her down

upon him; she seemed to sink upon him, caught between his knees. "There, there," each word a touch, she surged against him, soft as wax, her young flesh pliant and warm, her breath against his lips, her body lustered with a new warmth. "When my quest is done," he said, "until then, to set my mark on you, no room for any other man."

Behind them the stars rose, the river flowed, the wind stirred among the drifts of fallen leaves. In the darkness there he showed her how a maid may be first gentled by a man.

Lord Robert's voice seemed to come from a mile away. It rang out loudly, ordering his men to untie the horses, making sure Taliesin and his sister heard, discreetly making his presence known. After a moment or so of grace, he called again more urgently, "My lord, your men await you, and so do mine. Lady Olwen, we must return before this night's work also be spread abroad to be a shame and a regret."

Prince Taliesin gave a start. I think he had forgotten where he was. He let the lady slip between his fingers, almost as water does, glimmering in her silver gown, and he hesitated for a moment over her as does a man who sees illusion or a dream fade before he has completely grasped at it. Then he turned half aside, remembering, I think, the world of men. And after a while he strode down from the church porch to where Robert awaited him.

"My lord." Taliesin at first still spoke hesitatingly, as if his thoughts had not yet cleared. "My lord, I have not thanked you for my life. A second time I owe you it."

Robert smiled his sweet smile, so much like his sister's that it always astonished those who saw it. "Nor I thanked you," he said as simply, "at least not with as good a will. So are we quits, Taliesin. But I believe you would do well to walk warily. You have other men with you, I mean other than these your bodyguard? I would suggest you lodge with them outside the city, only enter when Prince Henry's arrival is confirmed; then let my father present you at court, ensuring your claim be given just hearing. But do not," he hesitated, "expect great things."

Prince Taliesin inclined his head. One of his guard led up his horse, that black charger of whom stories had been told. But

Robert set his hand upon the bridle to halt the prince. He said, hesitatingly again, "Nor would I be just, my lord, not to tell you, man to man, frankly, that were you any other than what you are, I would welcome you to my heart as a brother, especially after this night's work. I did not think so before, and that I also freely admit. Not because of you yourself or any fault in you but because of circumstance. My sister is the only daughter of my house, my father's last born, child of my parent's love that endured so long apart. It would break their hearts, I think, it would break mine, to have her go far away from us, into a world she does not know, into a future that may not even exist."

Again Taliesin inclined his head. Seeing his gesture Robert suddenly put a hand on his, that gesture of friendship he often used. There was genuine regret in his voice. "In my foolishness," he said, "I advised my father wrongly, I think. When I can, I will undo that wrong. I shall look for you again, Taliesin. I shall tell my father you were here. I will guard my sister well. And that also I will tell my father."

It was a fair speech, honest, and, in its way, not unjust. And so Prince Taliesin accepted it. Had the lady been one of his own house, he would have said the same. He nodded, took up the bridle, vaulted onto his horse's back. His hand lifted in salute, he led the way, and his men followed him in line, cantering easily back along the road they had come in on. And when the drumming of their hooves was gone, we brought the Lady Olwen home.

Well, I am but a chronicler. These are the things I write in later times, what I saw and what I knew, no more, no less. It is God's will that makes us what we are although we weep for it. I told you there was little joy in this for me. I would not wish to remember it, this day that my love was lost to me.

Chapter 11

ather I will tell you instead how, the next morning, Prince Henry and his entourage finally reached Paris and, having dawdled their way along for whatever cause, now made amends by holding full council of state in the open courtyard by King Louis's fortress. There, under an ancient tree (which men claimed had been standing when Louis's ancestors had ridden out at their army's head to drive back the Huns in the early days of Christendom), benches were put along the sides, as if for a tournament. And on a raised dais, two thrones were set, for the King of France and the King of England. Below this upper dais were two other chairs, apart, for Prince Richard and Geoffrey, brothers of Prince Henry, who on this occasion had been well instructed to play their part with more respect than at Montmirail. Below them, according to rank, were arrayed the lords and barons of France and England, a great and impressive crowd, in which my masters were certainly conspicuous, both by their height and their noble mien. Today they were dressed accordingly, not exactly in Norman style, rather in their border one, their mail coats covered in red and gold, golden chaplets on their silver-blond hair. But they kept their hands clasped on their great long swords. Around them stood their household guard, dressed also in Sedgemont red, and in front of them, pushed forward so I could see, was I, Urien the Bard, the earl having heard of my part in the night's affray and being pleased to notice me. So it was that I, son of

217

a serf, witnessed royalty in all its glory, both English and French, and saw three royal princes in their prime. And saw, too, what befell when Prince Taliesin came to make his claim.

Well, first King Louis greeted his son-in-law as once he had greeted his father, effusively, lovingly, offering to knight Prince Richard immediately. On learning that English royal messengers had been sent by the Old King to persuade the prince to return, Louis listened to them impatiently and broke in with a phrase that has become famous. "Messages from the King of England?" he cried. "Impossible. Here sits England's king. Whoever bade you come must be an imposter." A fine start to a council that might have reconciled father and son instead of driving them further apart. Worse, when these bishops—for King Henry had sent bishops to plead with his son—when they reminded the prince he had no royal seal to sign his papers with (the one his father had previously prepared for his use being left behind), King Louis triumphantly produced a replica, which he had had made in advance. In this way he ensured there should be no further delay in having the prince sign treaties with his allies, who gathered around avidly, wolves indeed snarling for bones. And in this Earl Raoul had but spoken truth: the king who in his own lifetime crowns his son cuts off his own head with his own hand.

Since this was the first and only time I saw Prince Henry, I will tell you truly what I thought. He was handsome, charming, not so like his father as his father's father, that Geoffrey, Count of Anjou, who was called the fairest knight in all of France. And to my eyes, Henry was strikingly similar to Lord Hue. In many ways he was affable, good-natured, generous, as exemplified when once he had summoned all the knights in Normandy who bore his name to wine and dine with him as friends. Yet if King Louis was indecisive, Prince Henry was like wax, as charming as an April day and as unreliable. He it was who, finding that his servants had packed one bottle of wine for him alone, unstoppered it and poured it on the ground, not willing to drink if his companions went athirst. But he it was also who, after his first crowning at York, being served by his father and being rebuked for insolence, that a prince should allow a king to wait on him, had replied, even more insolently, "Not so, for should not the son of a king be waited on by the son of a count?" (A play on his father's rank before becoming king, which although true was not courteous for him to comment upon.) A charming man, then, endowed with that Angevin charm, which no man knows how to define but all men recognize. And in rage, cursed with the Angevin temper, as hot as ever his father's was. And, this I guess at, not always as loyal to his friends as he would have them be to him. And when he beckoned to his young wife to join him on the dais, he almost seemed a child, playing at royalty.

However, he had the sense to show respect to King Louis, sufficient to keep that monarch pleased, nor did he neglect those English earls, clumped together in a solemn group, who, of all men there, were least inclined to acknowledge the charm and first to look for ratification of the new reign.

The one lord who did not acknowledge him at all was Earl Raoul. What the earl had said to Louis he said as bluntly to the prince, whom he alone addressed by that title. Well, the attempt was useless and only made the prince scowl, the more so that the earl admonished him almost as if he had been his son.

"As you are young," I heard Earl Raoul say, "you should be guided by wiser heads. Your father will not brook this flight."

"Nor I more admonishments," the prince said with a pout. "When we need advice of this kind, we'll ask for it. But have you no other favor to ask, my lord?"

"None." The earl was firm. "Only news of my son."

"Hue." The prince laughed. "Why, my lord earl," he said, as if he did not know his remarks would provoke, "he is gone to Poitiers to escort my mother to our side. Not here to Paris," he hastily added, as King Louis looked bleak, "but I still have hopes she will join us. Then look for Hue." But the earl continued grave, his dislike of Queen Eleanor almost as great as hers of him. It did not please him to think of his son in her company.

"Well," said the prince in a more expansive mood, "if Earl Raoul has no further business of me—"

"But I do," Earl Raoul broke in. "Leave to present a border

prince to your majesty's notice. Taliesin of Afron claims the right to speak with you."

From the back of the courtyard there was a stir, and the prince now advanced. He was new-shaved, so that he looked even younger than he had the other time. The sun shone on his golden torque, on his brooches and clasps, and although he, too, wore a Norman mail coat, booty of war, I suspect, he still looked different from a Norman in it; he wore it, walked, held himself differently from those lords. "Lord king," he said in his foreign way, in his slightly broken French that was to set new fashion in Paris that spring, "for so are you now called, and so I come to address you, three things have I in mind: to right my father's wrongs, to claim vengeance for my brothers' deaths, and to find restitution that is just."

Puzzled by this form of speech, which although not exactly offensive was certainly not what he was used to, being too decisive and overproud, Prince Henry bent to listen to King Louis's councillors whilst the ladies of the court, for there were ladies sitting in the upper tiers, again as at a tournament, smiled and waved their hands at him. (All save the Lady Olwen. What she did I will tell you presently.)

The French councillors buzzed like a beehive, and the young king, grimacing at their suggestions, rubbed his hand across his forehead where the gold crown of sovereignty had left a red mark. "Now, prince," he said, in an easy way that had often won him friends before, "a title I know full well, having but recently given it up for a new one" (a remark which brought a laugh at the thought that this Welsh prince could in any way compare with him). "We are both inexperienced at this, you with request, I with judgment. But this I know. My father's wrongs are not mine. Ask him to right your claims. But since you speak of things done before our birth, certainly before we were old enough to remember them, I suggest rather that they be forgot in the general amnesty of this day."

"I remember my dead brothers." Prince Taliesin's voice was cold. "I am not so young that I do not remember them alive, nor the day they rode out willingly to be hostages to your father's peace. Nor so old that the news of their death did not cast its shadow across my boyhood."

There was a silence then, a great intake of breath. Prince Henry tried to laugh it down. "Well, then," he said attempting joviality, "as compromise, why not join forces with mine, combine your claims into those of the general weal?" A nice touch that, which made his companions clap their hands and nod their heads, pleased at the prince's sagacity. "Here is a prince of worth," they seemed to say, "here a king worthy to follow."

Prince Taliesin took a step forward, and his sword swung dangerously. "I am not come to join in rebellion," he said, his voice low but with that note in it that made men take care. "What you do is your affair. But justice I claim, as your father has proclaimed his justice to the world. Your father unlawfully slew my brothers in shameful wise for a war that was not theirs. Three brothers I had, my father three sons. This, then, is his complaint; these are his three demands:

"One: Give back the lands he has lost, all those borderlands that were seized by your father's men.

"Two: For his sons, give him three hostages of equal birth and rank to do with as he will.

"Three: And for the part of a faithless king, penance, as was done for another shameful murder, public penance, before the world." The court was stunned. No wonder Earl Raoul had dismissed the prince's suit last year! The Prince of England was flabbergasted, certainly never having heard its like, nor having been spoken to in such a way, and left with no doubt that had Henry the Older been there in his stead, the Prince of Afron would have made exactly the same request, not changing it one jot.

King Louis gaped; his mouth worked like a fish, and the English lords snarled like cats. Only one man threw back his head and laughed. That man was Earl Raoul. He had been standing at one side, having, true to Robert's promise, presented Taliesin, and perhaps of all the men there, he was the only one who had guessed in part what the prince might say. "Come, lad," he said, and no one was sure to which prince he spoke, but the words were kind, not meant to offend. "Come, lad, you are mad. No man, least of all a Norman, would do penance for a crime he did not commit, although crime it was. And no Norman would put his head into a noose to be hostage to three murdered men. But the lands along the border, that's a different case. As warden of the marcher lands, I think those could be restored to make some fitting recompense."

His laughter was kind, I say, not only tolerant but even approving, that of an older man who applauds some feat of daring by a younger one. And his words were clever in that, by seeming to address the Welsh prince, he gave the English prince sound advice how to answer him. Advice Prince Henry again ignored. He leapt up, so suddenly that his crown rolled off under a chair, an omen that many men were quick to note. "By Saint George and all the English saints," he shouted, "you speak out of place, Earl Raoul. As for you, Prince, what you are, never mention that holy martyr in the same breath with your Welsh scum. Run home before my patience snaps. I've men here who would whip your insolence."

The worst thing he could have done was threaten Taliesin; pride thrives on scorn. The prince leaned forward so both hands rested on his sword, and his eyes darkened. He said, even more stiffly, as if he sought now for words in a tongue not his own. "That was my father's message; that was what I was bid to say, and so it has been said. Now hear my own. I am sworn to uphold his claim, and with my sword and shield so shall I do. I offer combat to you or your champion." And again there was a sudden hush.

"Get you gone, Prince Taliesin." Henry's voice cracked with anger. He had come off the dais and was pacing back and forth in front of it as if the earth constrained him, that royal gait. "Tell your father I grant you your life. Let him have that for recompense. Never come near us or our court again, on pain of death. Never set foot on English soil. Go back to your Celtic moors and stay there. Outlawed are you in all my lands. None of my lords will cross swords with you."

Prince Taliesin heard him out in silence, too. When he was through, "Then I bid you good day, Prince," was all he said, not even a trace of anger, only contempt. He clashed to salute as did his men. "We shall never meet in converse again. Look for me on the battlefield. And when you and your lords do, by God, let them call for help upon their English saints."

He was about to stride away when there was a rustle from the seats where the ladies sat. Now Olwen had come with us, her father permitting it, partly I think to keep her where he could see her, partly to show the world that all was well. And she, she came partly from pride and partly because she knew already what she would do. She stood up then, her face pale except for that faint bruise along one side, reminiscent of the one he had given her at their first meeting in Cambray. "God speed you, Prince of Afron," she cried. "God keep you safe from harm and prosper your enterprise." The ribbons from her dress, gold and red, fluttered down toward him. He caught them midair, held them up, and saluted her. So was her open admission made, before the king, before the court, before her father, before her brother, and before Gervaise of Walran. And made, too, to Prince Taliesin, that he should know her choice.

What a rush of noise in the wake of that, what stampede, everyone busy making his view heard, the earl and his son caught off guard by her defiance, the queen trying to smile, protesting at the same time, King Louis suddenly furious in a way not seen since his vindictive youth. He began to whisper hasty instructions to his guards, while the English prince, mottled with indignation, his eyes hot-flecked as his father's, seemed almost ready to mount and spur after the prince, had not his companions held him back. Those English earls, who thought on policy, were grave with concern, seeing the Welsh support that they had relied upon suddenly disintegrate. And from the back of the courtyard, where Prince Taliesin's men had been holding his horse, a great cry rose up. Together those Celts shouted, breaking their long self-imposed silence, one mighty shout that struck terror in all the English there, and in many a French lord. In Welsh they cried and beat their spears. "Men of the western seas, the flames are rising, the rivers run red." It is the cry of our race to war and death. And from my lowly place I echoed them.

Well, the earl's men, snapping to salute, made a shield wall to batter our way out. The earl already had reached his daughter and brought her forth; Lord Robert, grim-faced, hauled me along. "Father," he cried, "leave now, as best we can. Prince Henry, in such mood, will strike at friend or foe, indiscriminate. He knows he has not answered this prince as he should; he will be mad with rage at having thrown away Breton help and with having another man outshine him. He will blame you for putting him in such a quandary. And he will not forgive Olwen's speech."

And true enough, as we left, the prince howled at us, his face twisted into a sneer that was frightening to see. "God sod you, Raoul of Sieux; look for Sedgemont when I am in England. Tell your daughter to hold her tongue. Were Hue not your son, I'd have your head. And if Hue fails, I'll have his." Another indiscretion his supporters tried to hush. So did the first council of the new reign begin, so did it end; not much hope of patching up a compromise after that.

We broke through to our horses, mounted quickly, rode forth, lances set. At the bridge across the river we came to a check. Prince Taliesin and his six men were already halted there on our side of the bridge, and on the other, a group of King Louis's cavalry was massed in battle array.

Prince Taliesin turned to us, bareheaded, his eyes dark with suppressed anger. "My lord," he said, "you gave good advice last spring. I did not expect overmuch from this new king, got even less. But I did not think to have myself held to such small account."

"As little as I got." Earl Raoul suddenly smiled. In the open light you saw his age. He was older than King Henry, whose sons had already defied him, and these weeks of inactivity had left their mark. As ever when he was weary, the thin line on his cheek showed clear, a scar he had received in his youth for honor. But he did not hesitate, and when he spoke, his voice was young. In his just way he offered the prince honorable amends.

"Paris has become too hot for us," he said. "Best that we both ride clear."

"If we break through that." The prince jerked his head toward the French soldiers, peering over their lances. He turned slowly to face them.

"Well." Earl Raoul was cheerful. "There is but one way to try. Will you join me, my prince? A handful of Celts, a border lord, his son and daughter, we should be a match for any French army today." And he laughed as a young man might and drew his sword. Beside him without speaking Lord Robert drew his.

Prince Taliesin understood. A great smile broke across his face. He did not hesitate. Behind him his men fell into step, the lady in their midst. And ahead of us, those three lords rode, the three of them abreast, side by side, knee to knee, advancing steadily, first at walk, then trot, their horses tossing their heads against the bits as their hooves thudded hollowly on the wood, those three heroes of my youth, pace to pace, their swords steady as rocks, their shields unslung into a line of red and gold and the green of the Welsh dragon.

"Sa, sa, sa," cried the Celts. They raised their spears and clashed them. "Sa, sa, sa." And they clashed again. The drumming quickened, edged to a gallop as the lords advanced. Before their onslaught the French line broke, splintered into a hasty rout, all looking for the fastest way to escape. Some leapt into the river; some turned tail down the narrow streets; some threw themselves off their horses and crawled under the bridge; all ran without a blow being struck. Over the bridge we rode, down the streets to the city gates, to the white tree-lined road, the dust spiraling beneath our feet. Sa, sa, sa, rang the shields.

At the parting of the ways Earl Raoul reined up. "Farewell, Taliesin," he said. "We may not meet again. Or if we do, it may be that we shall serve on different sides, in a conflict that threatens to overwhelm us. But I am proud to have ridden this once in your company."

"And I in yours." Prince Taliesin responded to the earl's courtesy eagerly. "Although, my lord, if I can, I shall rob you of your greatest treasure." The earl did not pretend he did not understand. "As to that," he said, grave on the instant, "I cannot answer. I thought the lady bespoken."

Before he could say anything else, Lady Olwen replied herself. "Father," she said, "since I am here, should not I have a word to say? Should not I talk on my own behalf?"

"God's wounds," her father swore, "you have already said enough, sufficient to lose me my head and perhaps this prince his." But although he sounded gruff, his eyes were kind, and he smoothed his scar as he did when perplexed. Yes, I think the earl was overfond where his daughter was concerned. That fondness, perhaps, made part of her difficulty.

She said, "I would not claim anything more than custom allows, nor good sense; I am sensible of my place as daughter to your noble house. But, my lord father, I do not wish to be wed to Walran lands."

"But you would be wed to Taliesin?"

She suddenly blushed and hung her head. "He has not asked me," she whispered.

Prince Taliesin had been listening to this exchange. He broke in upon them, very young and stiff. "I do not boast of my estates," he said. "They are large. Although not so wide or fair as these about us, yet I hold them fair. I am my father's sole heir, as well born as any of your sons," a delicate way of referring to the Lady Ann's Celtic kin. "In all ways a Norman counts worth I think that I can show mine. But I am still not finished with what I must achieve. If, at this war's end, when I have met the English king (I care not which one, young or old), when I have fought and bested him, then shall I come again. Will the lady wait for me?"

"Nor can I answer to that." The earl's reply was again grave. "In the end she must chose; I trust her to make the right choice."

"That I do not debate." Prince Taliesin gave a smile. "Nor will I in the end discuss merit or rights. Only what I shall do. If I can achieve it, I will."

He saluted the earl and his son in his formal way, a salute, I think, of the old times, inherited perhaps from Roman days. But he saluted the Lady Olwen in his own style. Riding up to her, under the earl's very eyes, he held out his arm. "You threw me these ribbons," he told her. "In my country a gift like this could mean only one thing. If you tie them on, then I shall wear them until you untie them yourself."

She struggled to loop them over his mail, her fingers cold and trembling and slipping on the knots, such was her haste, her nervousness. "Now," he cried, "am I bound in truth to you, Olwen of the White Way. Let no one else be so bound." And he took her hands and kissed them slowly, as he had done that other time, wheeled his black horse once, and rode on. Back he went to the borderlands, where his Breton allies expected him. Waiting no longer for a general call to arms, they refused to help Prince Henry's cause, instead struck forward on their own, almost achieving the victory that would have ended the war, as shall be told.

We watched him leave. Earl Raoul sighed. After a while he said almost to himself, "That, too, is a man I could have as a son; he, too, is a man I could trust." Beside him the Lady Olwen stared ahead, said not a word, as proud and tearless as if her heart had been turned to stone. Years of breeding and endurance showed in her look, her head unbowed even if her hopes sank low.

So we in turn took our leave of a city that under all its smiles had shown us little more than treachery, murder, and intrigue. Back we rode to Sieux, that castle I had heard so much of, all thought of persuading the royal council to make a truce come to naught. But only the earl and his daughter rode together in the end. We had scarcely gone another league when Lord Robert slowed his pace and faced his father squarely in the path. He had been quiet, Robert, since our leave-taking of the court, not the ending he had hoped for, certainly, an end, then, to his plans. Now he told his father what they were. *How will Robert choose?* So made he his choice.

"My lord father," he began in a formal way; then, his voice breaking a little, "father, I will not deceive you. Around that corner," for we had come by now to a place of winding paths, between deep stands of trees, cut by many pretty streams, which I think we had all ridden through lost in our thoughts, "by that oak copse wait Prince Richard and his men. He has come out hunting for the rest of this day and has asked me to join with him. Moreover, he has asked me to stand sponsor for him when he is knighted, and that I, too, intend. I shall ride no farther with you this day." He allowed his father time to answer, his horse twitching and fidgeting against the flies.

"I do not ask for your leave, my lord," he said after a while, in his quiet way, determined and resolute, "not even for your blessing, although I would willingly take both. Only your farewell."

"And if I order you to stay?" The earl and Robert faced each other squarely.

"Then, my lord," Robert spoke slowly, every word like a drop of rain falling slowly on a dusty road, "here is my sword." He clapped his hand to the hilt. "I have used it to keep my word, as you, in your time, have done. Do you think I would not use it now if I were forced to?"

Around the line of trees we saw a group of riders approach, a band of men, Prince Richard at their head, a giant himself although still but a boy, his hair, like his brother's, deep red. He and his guard were dressed for hunting, so must they have left the council when we did; they must have arranged to meet Robert here. This meeting was no sudden whim, the choice had already been made, and Robert now prepared to implement it.

Earl Raoul was thoughtful and stern, his arms folded about the pommel of his saddle. Nor did he reply again, but gazed steadfastly with his sea-gray eyes, like a man who has received a violent blow, the second in so many hours. They looked alike that day, these two men, both honorable, both unable to give way, but not like brothers, for the earl suddenly seemed his age, his face set into lines. Although he had long expected some misfortune of this kind, I do not think he had felt it would come so soon, nor yet knew how to answer his son. In the end he sighed, as he had when Prince Taliesin rode away. "Go then," he said. That was all; no word of reproach, none of encouragement, no kiss of peace exchanged between two men who were as close as men can be.

To his sister Robert was more open. "Farewell," he said, taking her in his arms, "sister of my soul. I did you wrong to wish Gervaise upon you, and I do you a wrong to wish that you would not leave us, since that is what I do. But if in the end your choice falls on the Prince of Afron, I shall grieve to have you gone so far, nothing more. As I leave now, so should you then." And he kissed her cheek.

But to me he said, through my ready tears, "I leave you to the Lady Olwen, Urien the Bard, in whose employ I think you have been since the start." He smiled. "One day will I send for you again; until then cherish her." He suddenly held me close. "I could have loved you well, Urien the Bard," he said, low-voiced.

He rode away to join with Prince Richard and to take his part with that prince in King Henry's Great War. Ah, pity father, sister, mother whom he left behind; pity him, noble heart, who could not have a woman that he could love; as pity him I did, who knew the reverse, unable to love the woman I would have.

"Pitié, pitié," *we cry to the vacant sky,*
"Nowhere, no place," the implacable gods reply.

Since his story is one not for the telling here, I will only add in brief that Robert went with Richard as he intended, saw that prince knighted by King Louis, the only good thing to last from those days. And when in due course news came of the Old King's revenge (for all this while King Henry the Older had not sat idly by to let his realm disintegrate), hearing then of Henry's ravages in Aquitaine, Richard rode there to protect his lands, and Lord Robert rode with him. They say Prince Richard, hearing of his father's attacks, swore a great and solemn oath and, banging his hand against a tabletop, bade his older brother a scant farewell. "Aquitaine is mine," he cried, "my inheritance since birth, doubly given at Montmirail. Our father shan't deed it away to brother John. By Christ, I keep what's mine. And if you want to keep yours, brother Hal, then fight for it, too." Off he went with Robert by his side. How he and Robert rode and fought and conquered their enemies, inseparable as broth-

ers, is another story, I say. And how in the end they rode to
the holy wars, as long ago the Lady Ann had prophesied, and
how I went with them.

One other parting I must explain, before our arrival at Sieux.
At least a parting it was, although by proxy, not in person. For
it must be obvious that Gervaise of Walran, too, had dropped
from sight, ever since that day of Prince Taliesin's triumph at
King Louis's court. Now he sent a message, greetings to the
earl, written with a flamboyance that he could not have produced
himself, often boasting like other men of his rank that he could
not read or write, such employment fitted for priests, not knights.

"My lord earl," he had dictated, then, full of flourishes and
fine words, most of which were misspelled. "I go to fulfill my
oath sworn in Canterbury to King Henry. I join with him. I
honor you in your neutrality; I cannot accept your sons' choice,
but I do not fault them. And with full right, I make formal
request for your daughter's hand. I am my father's oldest son.
All of Walran is mine, together with more lands north of Leeds
and two other manors as my father decides, to be mine now
while he still lives, as well as gifts of jewels, armor, horses, if
I require. And for bridal gift I offer 3,000 livres, and so many
bushels of corn and barley, fresh from the mill, and the keys
of my largest manor at Chepelhurst.

"In token of this I set my seal and send her, as gift in advance,
a handkerchief of worked silk, a wreath of gold, and, for her
girdle, a purse of fine embroidered leather . . ." And so on,
very properly writ out, as if he had been an estate clerk listing
a master's wealth. But the earl read it, I think, as it was intended,
for he, at least, could read, and tucked it away in his sleeve after
showing it to the Lady Olwen.

What said my lady of these events? I think she was stunned
by them. Suddenly our world dissolved to fragments; brothers,
lover, friend, all gone; she alone as solace to her parents. And
she certainly had to weigh Prince Taliesin's offer with her father's just reply. That was a charge upon her, the last child of
her house. I think she ached to share it with someone, and of
all of us on that ride south to Sieux, she must have longed most
to see her mother again and feel her comfort. Yet I think secrecy

had begun to work on my lady, too, giving her endurance beyond her years. As shall be shown.

Sieux is a noble castle built in Norman style upon the edge of a spreading lake, perched on a cliff top like to the prow of a ship. It has the feel of age and strength. Its foundations stretch down into granite cliffs, with inner and outer baileys and a keep, overlooked by battlements that command the countryside for miles. The walls are still white with new stones, where the damage Henry II once caused is still being restored. Even in the brief time I was there that year, it seemed that workmen were constantly about, forever busy with plummet, windlass, and pulleys, adding layers of stone, extending them, building them up. And workmen there were of various kinds, constantly on the move, reinforcing here, digging there, chipping here. In the spring season each year, they say, these masons return full force from their winter headquarters at Saint Purnace, and the noise of their work is constantly heard, a background to the other sounds of castle life.

But I speak the truth. I have never liked Sieux well. For many dreadful deeds have been done there, and in its undercrofts there are deep passages winding under the cliffs, used now for storage space, kept clean and aired by currents that seem to pass naturally through the rock—to me they had a feel of age so old I did not want to consider when they were made or by whom. Nor, despite its size and strength (those things I do not deny), was Sieux noted for its wealth, much of the earl's resources always having been used for defense and to rebuild the fortress after Henry's men had destroyed it, little left for rich furnishings or display, no fine tapestries or rugs or wooden carvings such as other castles had begun to boast of. Yet the Lady Ann had given this grim place touches that would have made it homey to anyone who knew Cambray. A herb garden had she built within the walls, where grew all the flowers she is famed for, with many plants of use, such as fennel, coriander, and parsley. And fruit trees of apples, quince, and cherry were trained against the inner walls. Among these pleasant walks the ladies spent much of their time, and I with them, while the earl, at a loss, I think, without his sons, spent his hours hunting along the

borders of his lands or rode, as once Hue had done, beside the
banks of the lake. And here in these pleasant walks we heard
the news of Lord Hue and his fate that was to shatter the earl's
last thought of peace.

For beyond us, in the great wide world, how fared the war
of Henry's reign? While we enjoyed a brief respite here, a joyous
one in some ways, in others sad; whilst the spring advanced on
all sides, this is what occurred elsewhere.

First, as to King Henry the Elder. After leaving Chinon in
haste, Henry wasted no energy crying over his vanished sons.
He had no time for that. His sons had lingered long and carelessly, and even after their arrival at Paris, still did not act as
quickly as they should have. Henry, wiser in war affairs than
they, took advantage of their inactivity and himself, like a mael-
strom, a war god with eight arms, a thunderer, struck at several
points at once. He had no choice. Any appearance of delay on
his part would seem admission of defeat, and even a hint of
defeat would encourage his enemies to achieve it. And he must
have known, as it seems his sons did not, that the war would
be won or lost in those very lands his oldest son, Henry, first
claimed, namely England and Normandy.

So first, after the disaster of Chinon (although among his
enemies it was always called the "rape"), Henry made a lightning sweep back to England, so quick that Louis complained
that like his ancestress, he must have flown. Returning to France,
he reappeared along the borders of Anjou, whence he sent out
troops under seasoned captains to harass his enemies on all sides.
He understood that to enhance the impression that he was everywhere at once would not only demoralize the opposition but
make it doubly difficult for them to concentrate. (And since his
plan succeeded, it should be explained that when at last the new
king and his allies did march to invade Normandy at Rouen,
their troops were so disorganized, their plan so ill-advised, that
their attack came to a grinding halt. A disaster, then, that the
death, by a crossbow, of the Count of Boulogne, Louis's brother-
in-law, made complete. This count was heir to the Count of
Flanders, and his death so distressed his sister, Queen Adela,
that she begged King Louis to retreat. This ignominiously he

did, leaving the way clear for King Henry the Older to fall upon the remaining troops and tear them to shreds. But to Sieux, which guards that gateway north and south, Henry never came. He circled Sieux lands but never thereon set foot himself. At first, that is.)

In two other regions, also, Henry made great effort to regain control: in Aquitaine and in Brittany. Thus, in Aquitaine. Once he had accepted the fact that his sons were gone, Henry must have made a reassessment of his advantages and weaknesses. The greatest danger, he felt, was in the south, where his queen, Eleanor, had long held sole control, the more so that between him and her was a deep rift. As gossip smirked, once she was past childbearing age, he had quickly replaced her in his bed with a host of mistresses, of whom the Fair Rosamund was but one favorite. King Henry rightly now blamed Eleanor for his sons' defections, especially the younger sons. His anger was intensified when, sending priests to admonish Queen Eleanor at Poitiers, where for many years she had lived, he found her gone. And Hue gone with her.

This is the way it was. After the escape from Chinon, the prince and his companions had ridden toward Paris, but Hue, as had been planned from the start, circled south to act as escort to the queen. At first the queen was gracious and welcomed her son's messenger. She had long been holding court in Poitiers, that graceful southern city which pleased her more than any other and which she had always called home. She had been glad to return to its charming streets, its churches, walls, and towers, to a climate mild and sweet, away from that cold, damp English one. Eleanor was proud of her ancestral domain with its new-built palace, which Henry had tried to imitate, and she received Hue in the great hall beneath the line of new windows, a luxury that even Henry could not boast of. Gossip has it that although she hid the thought, she dreamed of making a grand entrance in Paris once more, scene of many of her former triumphs as Queen of France, and hope of it made her sparkle with pleasure. That day she had dressed carefully in blue to complement the blue of the spring sky framed behind her in the long arcade. Her gown was edged with small seed pearls, simple jewels for a lady of her rank, and her maids had woven a chaplet of spring flowers for her hair, so that, from a distance, tall and slender, she still looked like the girl whom once two kings had vied to have, the maid of whom poets sang praises in every European court.

When she beckoned to her guards to let Hue in, it is said he fell upon his knees, smitten with her beauty and charm. Perhaps that was true. Hue had a Celtic flair. Certainly it is true he did cry aloud, "God preserve me, my lady, I am blinded by your grace. Your royal son sent me to escort you hence. He did not tell me I should be messenger to the gods." A nice beginning to his new assignment. His own person in its workaday clothes (for, you remember, his departure from Chinon had been hasty), his cloak hem ripped, his boots mud-splattered, his red curls matted about his cheeks, seemed proofs of his devotion and zeal, and enchanted the queen. At first. For when the queen, flattered as she could not fail to be by his open admiration, bade him rise, herself served him wine, herself had her maidens prepare a bath (and if gossip be believed, herself tested its warmth, its fragrance, herself unbuckled his sword belt), there was no doubt of her favor to him. It was only afterward, when the tale of the escape from Chinon was revealed, that her favor died. You would think that a tale which had so much of romance and high adventure would appeal to her, at whose court the *chansons de geste* had had their start. But in the telling of the tale, Hue revealed who he was. His rise in the favor of the queen, faster than any other man had known, ended there. Her current favorite, Raoul de Faye, who overnight had seen his own fall from grace, was responsible in part for Hue's fall. This Raoul had long been close to the queen, one of her southern nobles, her kinsman, as were many of her favorites, as if she felt most at home with men of her own race. Raoul de Faye had been captain of her guard, master of her revenues, and, rumor had it, so close that even at night she could not bear to part with him. He did not intend to let a young upstart, half his age, supplant him long, certainly not the son of Earl Raoul of Sieux.

"What?" The queen is supposed to have started from her chair so violently that the string of pearls her ladies were fastening around her swanlike neck broke and cascaded over the floor, an unfortunate memory of another time when the Lady Ann herself had come to Poitiers to beseech Eleanor to be her friend. Her white forehead furrowed, her eyes shadowed with thought, the queen paced and paced about the long-columned porch. "Not that son, not son of the Lady Ann, born in Wales. Not Hue." Never had been the queen so fierce, they say, like a tigress balked of her prey. The book she had been holding was torn in shreds where her long nails had ripped, and she ground her pearls underfoot. "Not the bastard Hue, who was said to be Geoffrey's get."

Hearing her say that, Raoul de Faye dropped his second hint, his second shaft, to damage again. "Geoffrey Plantagenet's bastard," he is supposed to have whispered in her ear, "or the king's?" Of all things he could have said, that wounded most. In a fury the queen sent him away, too, and seating herself before one of those windows that gave a view of the placid countryside, she wept such tears of rage not known since the end of the Crusade, when King Louis had ordered her ignominiously home. From that time her hatred grew against Hue, although he knew it not, for she hid it in cunning wise, pretending still to favor him, although she never again led him into her inner rooms nor let him lie with his head in her lap while she herself combed his hair. There are those who claimed it was because of Earl Raoul that she turned her hatred against his son; others say it was rather his mother, the Lady Ann, whom the queen most envied, the more that her own lover, Geoffrey Plantagenet, those years ago had abandoned her to woo that lady instead. The truth was somewhere in between. For although Henry had taunted Raoul that the Lady Ann had slept with him, afterward he admitted that he had lied and ever since had testified to that lady's integrity. Seeing Hue, the queen began to feel a jealousy never so strongly felt since Henry had taken his last mistress, the Fair Rosamund, to Woodstock and installed her in the queen's favorite hunting lodge, where her favorite son, Richard, had been born. She began to think that Hue's resemblance to her son (which many people were whispering about and which I myself have commented upon) could not be explained otherwise. She had always believed that in Henry's youth he had been faithful to her. As a young man, much younger than she, he had been besotted by her, trapped by her beauty, numbed by desire. He had looked at no other woman, so she had claimed, and such had been her hold over him that although he admitted to fathering two sons before being wed, in those early days of marriage he had been loyal to her, a gift not many kings bestow upon their wives. Seeing before her each time she looked at Hue proof positive in the flesh of her husband's perfidy, Eleanor felt the knife cut deep.

I do not mean to say that the queen need have believed all of this (there are other reasons for men's looks, and many men have red hair, gray eyes, white skin), but she let herself believe. It gave her an excuse to whip her hate; it gave her reason to explain Henry's neglect of her; and, in the final instance, it gave her cause to justify her own acts. If Hue were not Geoffrey's bastard, she must have argued to herself, then Henry's own; if not Henry's, then his brother's, in either case a Plantagenet, illegitimate heir to Angevin lands, a threat, then, to her legitimate sons. And that thought, too, was a weapon to keep at hand.

But she was clever. She did not dismiss Hue entirely, nor did she show her hostility. In secret her malice grew, the more her spies revealed how much her oldest son had relied upon this young man as friend. She let Hue prepare her departure; in haste they were supposed to ride, so that when Henry's messengers appeared, in truth she was already gone. But gone in such a wise, in such disarray as to make success almost impossible. And this she did, too, deliberately, as if she wanted to have Hue fail, just as a wild creature rends its own flesh rather than let a huntsman take it alive.

It seems that Hue (and so he himself later explained) had planned to ride to Paris with a large armed escort, one of the ways to placate King Louis being a full mustering of southern lords who would follow the queen's lead anywhere. Instead, the queen had her lover, Raoul de Faye, take most of her men. She, with but a few, and herself in disguise, forced Hue to ride north toward Anjou. "Our only hope," she told him, cold, in her way of showing displeasure, "is to ride fast. A big convoy will alert Henry's men, will slow us down. Let Raoul de Faye order the rest on ahead. Instead we shall slip along the borders of Sieux, which you must know well enough."

To this plan Hue agreed reluctantly. For Hue was also in love, I think, the romantic love of the young *chevalier* for the older lady of the *chansons*. Smitten by the queen, having tasted but once the sweetness of her intimacy, he could not believe she would reject him, and the more cold she seemed, the more warm grew he. If she had wished to torment him, the queen could not have sought a more clever approach. Now there are those, too, who claim emotion marred the young man's judgment. I do not say that myself, but it might be so. He certainly was not prepared when the queen appeared for the ride in man's attire, as a trooper of her guard.

They say the queen laughed and began to braid her long hair to hide it beneath her cap, with fingers that are longer and more white than any other woman's. "God's mercy, boy," she is supposed to have said, her eyes sparkling at the thought of adventure after so many years of inactivity. "Have you never seen a woman without her skirts? How shall we gallop along if I am supposed to trot sidesaddle on a palfrey? When I went with Louis to the Holy Land, I rode astride, my ladies and I, dressed like Amazons, one breast bare, bows slung across our backs, our legs naked, stuck into boots. Christ's bones," as Hue continued to stare, "so rode your mother once, and not only rode. She lived as man in a camp of men."

Hue did not say another word, went about his business grimly, curtly ordered the march to begin, although he had secretly hoped to be allowed to lift the queen upon her horse and himself adjust her bridle and reins. Perhaps, too, for the first time the thought occurred that if his mother had so ridden when she was young, that must have been a score of years ago, and the queen must be much older than the Lady Ann!

Afterward, in grief and pain, Hue used to admit as much. "The queen rode like a man," he explained, "but she was still a woman and a queen. Every so often we had to stop on some pretext. Either the weather was too hot, or the way was hard, or there was some friend she must greet. Or she was hungry, thirsty, tired. We might have made better time with her carried behind one of us, or in a litter as I had planned. I had intended to have her ride with a group of ladies, surrounded by a phalanx of men, so that we would seem innocent, yet so strongly armed as to make any skirmishers give us a wide berth. She chose instead a way that might not have worked for a girl half her age."

So it was that although Raoul de Faye's men left a trail a mile long, Henry's troops, already out in force, ignored them and were perhaps already scouting for the queen. It was not surprising that they caught her almost without trying. For Henry's men had already come storming into Aquitaine. Even Raoul de Faye's own castle had been seized, and other fortresses of equal note, so that often places where Hue might have found support were occupied before he got there. Twice he was able to change course in time, once warned by a pall of smoke from a ruined tower, once by a band of fleeing peasantry. The third time he could not escape. He described it thus:

"Forced by circumstance to bivouac, we were resting too long at midday at the queen's insistence. Suddenly a group of Henry's men appeared. I had posted guards, without whose warning we would have been overrun. As it was, the few knights we had with us, I myself, were already mounted. The men I had were good, well trained and disciplined; they knew what to do and were prepared to ride out, two abreast, to cut our attackers off before they attacked us. We easily could have sliced a way clear had we been alone.

"But the queen would not mount, nor ride. 'I am queen,' she cried in her imperious way, 'I am Duchess of Aquitaine. They will not dare detain me. Tell them who I am.' And not even waiting, she did so herself. Well, they surrounded us, a small enough group to have captured such a prize, their captain a friendly soul whom success that day made almost tipsy with surprise. To the queen he showed all respect, but let her go he would not. To me he said in private, 'Lad, I've been a soldier these thirty years, not ever taken any lord of note. At my first skirmish of the season, to have a queen fall into my hands like

a ripe plum! And what a queen, whose husband is already scour-
ing the country for her. Now, God be praised, I'll give up
soldiering, marry me a Gascon wench I've my eye on, go back
where I belong. Praise God and the king, say I; they grant me
luck. But how comes it lad,' for in private, as I have said, he
was in jovial mood, 'how come you are in such a state, so
poorly guarded; where are the queen's men? How come you
roam the borderlands like wandering vagabonds?'

"To the queen he was brisk, professional, although still polite
and, in his rough way, courteous. Quarrels between kings and
their wives are not uncommon, nay more common than not,
but seldom last long. A man could lose his head for misspeaking
on poor advice. And Queen Eleanor still was queen, even though
her husband had ordered her brought forth under guard.

"So it was we rode on north as prisoners, toward the Norman
stronghold, the castle of the Norman dukes that they call their
home, at Falaise. The queen's Potivin soldiers were angry at
their capture, not wanting to be held by Henry in his own ducal
lands, angry enough to whisper suspicion of betrayal. Certainly
one of her former friends, William Maingot, might have arranged as much. As we passed by his fort, out he rode to cheer
us on, a maggot, indeed, slimy scum. Full of leers and courtesies
before the queen, full of regrets he could not rescue her; I could
have kicked his teeth in, full of smiles and winks behind our
backs.

"So we came to Falaise in due time. Oh, it was not so bad
at first, as prisons go. We had the run of the place, like to kill
us of boredom; the queen kept to her chambers above, we in
the gatehouse, nothing to do but drink and dice." Hue's eyes
had darkened for a moment in their habitual, angry look. "If
that was prison fare," he cried, "or its foretaste, better death."

But death did not come for Hue then, although it waited for
him. Yet death came for many men that spring, as Henry struck
now here, now there, making those rapid moves, those forced
marches, those lightning sweeps for which he is famed, holding
his enemies back on one side, driving them forward on the
other, until at last he had time to spare for his queen. Henry
and Eleanor had not met in years, and their last meetings had

been stormy affairs. He was in no rush to deal with her. Having her under lock and key in the strongest, oldest of his castles, he was content to let her bide and cool her heels. It was not until full summer, when a lull in the fighting gave him respite, that he bethought what to do with her. And since at the same time worrying reports reached him of a fresh Breton advance cutting across Normandy toward Falaise, he came north himself, on a fine day, to this greatest of all his fortresses, a vast, massive, square block of stone, impregnable, a fitting prison for a queen.

What he meant to do with her is not certain. That she had urged her sons on, that she had planned their rebellion and herself had tried to join them, was unquestionable. Equally without question was that she should pay a queenly price. But what or how taxed Henry's ingenuity. He was in no hurry to go to Falaise, even reluctant to face this woman he once had adored, less anxious than she for an interview. So it came as a great surprise to him to learn that among her entourage was Hue of Sieux. As now his queen let him know.

Queen Eleanor was no fool. To the contrary, she was clever, quick, more shrewd in the early days than her husband had been, used more than he to courts and kings. Better than anyone she knew this episode could not be ignored. This time, indeed, she had gone too far. She had tried his mettle once before, when, as it was claimed, she had supported his brother, Geoffrey Plantagenet. But she had done so in secret, never openly. A reconciliation at that time had been made between her husband and herself, possible only because they both needed sons. Sons she had given him; now she was beyond childbearing age, as he was quick to point out. And those sons were not much to gamble with, already in themselves suspect. Instances of sons who rebel are commonplace, not so open rebellion by a queen. Desperately Eleanor looked for a way to wriggle free from her predicament. What said the laws, she asked of Henry's seneschal, a portly man who held Falaise until the king's return, what was the position regarding rebellion of a queen? Did Henry's lawyers, who blanketed all of England with their laws, have a statement to cover her case? If so, what arguments would be suggested in defense? Back and forth she sent her demands within the fortress of Falaise, as if in a papal court, causing the worthy seneschal to break out in a sweat, trying to find some means of avoiding the consequences of her rashness. For the queen had begun to be seriously alarmed. Henry's ancestors had not been nice in their dealings with recalcitrant wives; one had actually had his wife burned as a witch. Although those days of barbarism were long past, the queen did not altogether trust her royal partner. His anger was legendary, and as her imprisoner, he might do anything at all to her if the mood took him. She was on the point of despair when she bethought of a chance, a victim to offer in her place. Hue provided her with the logical offering.

Perhaps I do the queen injustice; perhaps she was not so clever as I give her credit for; perhaps, in panic, she merely used an excuse that came easily to mind. But certain it is that she herself sent word to Henry, as soon as he had entered in at Falaise, to let him know that among his prisoners was Hue of Sieux.

King Henry was resting after a long, hard ride, boots on table, chatting genially with his men. He had been amused to hear of the queen's scurryings and, well satisfied at these signs of proper fear, is supposed to have grunted, "An old woman, bestride a horse, has other problems than legal ones," a thought to make him laugh. The queen as little liked to be laughed at as he did. Late at night, to stir him into an uneasy fret, a game-fly to torment him awake, she sent her message. They say Henry's boots crashed to the floor, the plates were spilled, the chair up-tipped. "*Jesu*, Mary, Mother of God, Christ's wounds," he swore all at once, "that young whelp who mocked at me!" In the middle of the night he sent his guard, himself came storming into the gatehouse, where Hue had bedded down as he had done these past months, sleeping off a head of wine. That night Hue was dragged out of bed unceremoniously for Henry to get a good look at his prisoner.

Of course Hue fought. Asleep in bed, half drunk, when the guards kicked him in the ribs, he thought at first it was a trick, a spiteful game of his former companions to make him wild, a joke to catch him unawares. Furious in his turn, he attacked, dragging two of them with him, almost crashing into the king himself, wrestling like a wildcat on the floor, until it suddenly dawned on him that the swords were real and the man who wanted him was not playing games. Still bemused with wine and sleep, half dazed from the battering, his red curls grimed with dirt, his face bruised and cut, Hue did not much look like anyone. But when the soldiers dragged him to his feet and held the taper close enough to make him wince, his gray eyes, still unfocused with wine, stared back into gray eyes like his own. Henry the King stood looking at him, nursing the blow Hue inadvertently had given him. Gray eyes to gray, red hair to red, white skin that bruises at the slightest touch, Henry looked at Hue and saw his younger self. I do not know which was worse: a young boy, half asleep, who had mocked a king at Chinon; or a Plantagenet, who was none, who looked like the king's own son. The king was startled himself out of thought; his rage flared. Before the startled gaze of his own courtiers, some of whom he had also routed out of bed, some certainly as drunk as Hue was, all weary from the long day's ride, Henry made the example the queen had sought.

With his own fist he knocked Hue down again. "Traitor," he howled. "Treacherous dog. I'll have you strung up for this, I'll have you hanged and quartered, I'll have your guts." He had his guards clap Hue in irons, haul him below out of sight, throw him into one of those foul cells in Falaise, dug so deep no man knows the way in or out. "Escape from that, Hue of Sieux. Laugh your way out from there," the king is supposed to have cried. "Or get your father to help you, if he can." And there, in truth, Hue would have languished, lost to sight, to memory, until Henry bethought to drag him up for sentencing, had not Gervaise of Walran been there.

And so it was that Gervaise sent a second message, this one to Sieux, in all haste, warning us and bidding us entreat the king for mercy. Gervaise of Walran's story to this point is soon told. He had joined the king as he had planned, had fought with him at the capture of Rouen, with valor, I may add, as became a Norman lord, so that the king had noticed him. But the king's war had not been all that he had hoped. Come north now with

Henry to Normandy, Gervaise had expected to be involved with the campaign against the Breton rebels, not with the saving of an old friend. His dismay that first day at finding Hue in Falaise, a Hue who lounged negligently against the gatehouse door and drank and laughed at Gervaise's warning to beware, was matched only by the shock of seeing Hue so treated by the king. Whatever Gervaise might have felt, he knew an earl's son deserves better care, should not be handled like a common criminal. Word he sent, in that respect behaving like a true friend, to Earl Raoul to save his son. One of his men, for you remember Gervaise still had men with him, rode out before the dawn, posthaste to Sieux. What did the message say? A simple one this time, dictated in a rush, without flourishes: "Henry holds your son, Hue, at Falaise. As your future son-in-law I will act for you until you come. As that son-in-law in fact, I will do the best that I can. But come yourself in any case."

Chapter 12

oes come in threes, beating like ravens before a storm. How did that first grief fall on us here at Sieux, in our little island of calm? Let me pose the question another way—how was it that that evening, almost at dusk, when Gervaise's messenger came laboring up the cliff, lathered, dust-coated, how was it that the Lady Ann was already waiting for him by the gates? Hooded, in her cloak, as I had seen her standing on the battlements at Cambray, why did she wait, her hair unbound, in mourning, her dark eyes steadfast, her face pale as milk, as if she had heard of Hue's death, as if, in her own flesh, she felt the rending of his? *Come yourself.* She already knew before Gervaise's message was read out.

Into our courtyard came the messenger, where the earl but a scant half-hour earlier had returned and was still on horseback himself, much of his time spent out and about in the hope that riding through his lands would keep down thought. I saw how his hands shook as he took that crumpled parchment and smoothed it flat. He did not exchange looks with his lady wife, nor yet his daughter, nor with anyone, merely read the message aloud in a calm voice, from which all emotion had been removed, the bare facts clear: Hue is Henry's prisoner, condemned to a traitor's death unless I intercede for him. And Olwen's marriage to Lord Gervaise the bargain offered for help.

My lord read the parchment, folded it, returned it. Why did his lady look at him with an expression in which pity struggled

with dread? Why did his daughter bend her head as if bowed
beneath the weight of acceptance? Why did the earl himself sit
forward on his horse, his hands crossed in front of him, as he
had sat that day his older son had left? When he spoke, it was
not even to us but rather to himself, far off, reaching back into
those shadows that lay unsleeping, unforgetting, from Cambray. "In Paris," he said, "I looked for my son. All through
the spring I waited for Hue; had he come then, I would have
brought him back here. Before the rebellion was formed, I
would have rescued him. But to Henry long ago I swore that
I should neither be for nor against. And long ago I also swore
that never should I ask aught of him, nor take, unless he begged.
I cannot be forsworn, not even for my son's life. And my
daughter is not to bargain with."

His bleak reply, its tone, could not be argued down. He did
not even try to argue with himself, and his men, who had heard
the first part of the message with mounting anger, they, too,
were silent, no help in them. Well, such are oaths, I repeat,
sworn in their innocence by honest men, who live to be trapped
by them. Not one of the lord's friends who knew his mind
would challenge him; in all other things was he reasonable save
only this, his personal pride, his own honor. That was our
second grief.

Now came the third. The earl turned his horse abruptly. He
did not say anything to his wife, he did not ask for understanding, forgiveness, but spurred out of the gates, between those
towers that Henry long ago had razed and where he had hanged
Raoul's men from their shattered walls. Down the cliff the earl
went at a gallop, a man who had never turned his back on
anything and who feared no one, caught in a trap of his own
making. I cannot say what would have happened in the end or
what Earl Raoul would have done. Flesh of our flesh are children,
remembrance of our youth, our second selves. So do fathers
accept their sons who grow to destroy the men who fathered
them. But for Hue to meet a traitor's death, such as Henry had
planned once for Raoul, who, then, if not Raoul to save his
son? I cannot say that the earl would have let Hue suffer such
a terrible fate without having made his stand against a king

whose hate now revealed itself again. Instead the third grief fell upon us like a thunderbolt, rendering such speculation superfluous.

Some claimed it was deliberate, that a worker overhead in the semi-dark let slip the stone. God knows the earl had enemies enough: two kings, a queen, many barons who would welcome such an opportunity. The master mason, the earl's old friend, swore in the chapel, which he had built, that not one mason was unknown to him, all loyal as was he; and, in truth, I myself think it was an accident. But I see the hand of God in it, to keep the earl from being forsworn but to ensure that Hue should have his chance. The earl, riding furiously, heard the sound of the stone's falling and tried to rein back his horse to warn his men. He had never made a false move on a horse before, he who had been taught to ride by the best horsemen of the time, who, in his youth, they say, rode a stallion more like a human soul than beast. In trying to avoid the stone, in trying to divert the men who followed him, the earl reined back too hard and threw his horse. The stone did not crush him, but the horse did. They fell together in a slide of pebbles, gravel, dirt, broken branches—a small avalanche. On level ground the horse lumbered to its feet. The earl lay on his back, did not move when they ran to him, did not open his eyes.

Only then did the Lady Ann give a cry, one keening note that our women make upon the moors when they sense death. I think perhaps she saw again her brother's murder, when, as a child, she had watched men bear him back, his body wrapped in his cloak, his arms dangling by his sides as now Raoul was brought. Sensing death, she thought it must be Raoul's; I believe she thought his life forfeit to the gods for Hue's.

But Raoul was not dead. Losing consciousness, bleeding from a score of wounds, his right arm (which once had been torn in battle for her sake) ripped apart, he still breathed, although grievous hurt. We carried him into the hall, which his determination and courage had rebuilt. God's will be done.

From her sick lord's side, at first the Lady Ann sent word that she herself would ride to Falaise, but no man would hear of that, each swearing by his sword or whatever thing he held most dear that never should the lady put herself in Henry's power again. Through tears the lady thanked those loyal men. I knew some of them now myself: Dillon, the master swordsman; Matt the Younger, master of the horse, who although he could no longer ride knew every horse in the stableyard; and many others equally famed. Dillon, old and grizzled, notched with scars like an old blade, spoke for them all. "You must not go."

"Dear friend," the Lady Ann told him, "friends all, to whom we owe our lives a hundred times, you have braved this king before. Who then will ride to see that Henry will not rob me of my son?"

"I do not think he would refuse me." Lady Olwen was equally determined. "If Gervaise will help as he promises, I should try. I am the last child of our house." And if she remembered when she had used that phrase, and to whom, she showed no sign. *Loyal are the women of our house.* Steadfast was she now in her turn, resolute and calm, without counting her own personal loss, prepared to beg what her father could not.

On one other point was Lady Olwen equally resolute. "Three men," she said, "I will take only three men. With that number my mother rode to save Earl Raoul. Make ready horses and supplies. Bar well the gates when we leave; let no one in. But choose well those three."

A hard choice it was, more difficult than if none had begged to volunteer. Chosen these men were by Dillon for swordsmanship and by Matt, the horse master, for horsemanship. But also they were men who knew Hue, who knew Normandy and the Sieux borderlands, and, most important of all, who knew King Henry well. But for me, who had no skills of any kind, the Lady Olwen did not even ask, and on my own I prepared to leave. Now was the fulfillment of my childhood dream made true; now was my oath kept that I had doubly sworn. And so it was, come the daylight, when we departed on our quest, I rode, too.

The parting between the Lady Ann and her daughter did not take long. They sat on either side the couch where the earl lay, while Lady Ann gave such advice as she could, what supplies a prisoner would need, what care. With her long, thin fingers she smoothed and resmoothed the coverlets. The earl's eyes were closed; his face had not lost its color nor his hair its luster, but he neither spoke nor moved, not asleep, not awake, as if some hidden wound drained his life force.

"My love." So spoke the Lady Ann to her daughter that night. "I do not wish anything on you, nor beg what you yourself cannot do." She smoothed the coverlets with her hands. "When I was born," she said, "my mother died, and all the grief of the world was due to me. My father never forgave my mother's death, and when my brother was murdered, so died he. And when I was a child, a prophecy was made that in my life I should know much sadness, little joy. High on the moors above Cambray there stands an old, old circle of stones, which all men shun. And there a Celtic witch made her claim on me. 'Many men will woo you,' she said, 'and die for you. And landless will be the man who marries you. Yet in the end, your last child shall heal all wounds.' Dear daughter, when I was a girl, I loved one man, your father, who was my overlord, although I fought against that love. And when Henry's men took him away, I thought that my child, my unborn son, would be the only remembrance I would have left when they had had their will of him. I thought Henry's hate would kill my love and kill my child. Yet God in His mercy spared us then. We came to France, and despite all odds, we survived attack, defeat, and treachery. My dearest friend, who was the queen, turned her back on me and with her friends sought vengeance of her own. To go against king and queen is a grievous crime, and dearly have they made us pay.

"When Hue was born," she suddenly cried, her eyes fierce, "alone, far from home among my Celtic kin, I used to talk with him. Who else in that Welsh hinterland was there to talk to? What Henry the King accused me of had prevented my return, as surely as if he had barred the gates. I did not ask Geoffrey, his brother, to woo me; I never thought Geoffrey would betray me to the king; I never expected Henry to lie to Raoul that I had been his whore. Yet it is true that Henry imprisoned me in the castle of my enemies, the castle of Maneth that used to haunt my dreams. And it is true that there, one night, I swore, and so swore the king, that we two at least would never do each other wrong. How long did Henry keep his word? But I kept faith with him. And when he told your father that I had slept with him, your father swore a great oath himself, by all he holds most dear, that he would help Henry no more, nor aid the king in his Welsh campaign. He would nothing have of the king, or England, or me, who alone had power to do him hurt. A landless knight, he lived, a wandering knight, searching the world for some sign that would render him his honor back. I could not stop him," she said simply, "I could only wait until he and Henry met again, man to man, to fight to the death. I used to tell Hue that. He lay in my arms and listened to me. 'When you are grown,' I used to say, 'your father will come back for you. He will set you on his great black horse, ride far away, and bring you safely back to Sedgemont. He has not forgotten you or me,' I used to say. 'Be patient. One day he will come for you.' Oh, God," she cried, "now he cannot come."

The Lady Ann calmed herself as she soothed the silent earl, with her white hands smoothing his coverlet. "And when Raoul came back to me at Cambray at last, his own quest done," she said, "I thought the world reborn, I thought life returned. Down the hill I ran, the curse broken at last, and when he swept me on his horse and carried me within the walls, I thought happiness was come to stay. I thought to make of you, our last child, the girl of our house, our child of joy, who had been promised long ago to bind both Celt and Norman as once in the past. Your sign was made for happiness, Olwen of the White Way. I put no restraint on it; you are free to choose. You were born to unmake a curse put on me as a child, not live cursed because of us."

"For my brother's life," my lady said, "what choice is there?" They embraced each other then, mother and daughter, alike in looks and thoughts and deeds. Now went forth the younger to rescue her brother if she could, even if her own hopes were lost. So have other ladies, whose names are writ in the chronicles, queens of England, wives of lords, princesses of our own race;

they have not hesitated to lead out men when they must. Among the list, among those Matildas and Adelas, write the names of the ladies of Cambray in gold. And say I went with Olwen of my free will.

It is said, when things look bleak to bring a man against a wall, then even the weakest of us can show determination if we must. All through that night, through the next days, I clung to that thought as we rode north toward Normandy. A traitor's death is death thrice wrought, no fate for any man, to hang you like a side of beef, to tear out your vitals from your guts, to tear out the parts that make you man, to hack, until even crows know not what flesh is. Dear God, I choked on the thought. So had Prince Taliesin's brothers died; so now should Lord Hue. Better any death than that—a clean sword stroke, a dagger thrust in the dark. Without words, without forethought, I knew then why I was come and what the final bond was between Lord Hue and me, what, failing all other hope, my part must be, to ensure him honorable death.

The road to Falaise is rocky at first, leaving the grassy plains around the lake and rising through hills whose flinty stones crumble like shards underfoot. After a while we dipped along the borderlands into the vast forest that stretches toward the castle, the ducal hunting grounds. Here we went along easily and would have made good time, had not the way been blocked by serfs and peasants, even some townsmen, fleeing with their herds and goods. Like mice those peasants scuttled aside, and when we tried to question them, they stood mute; in a country at war any armed knights are a potential threat. Lady Olwen bid us throw them alms to pry out news, and so we heard, for the first time, of a new threat; in this world of armies always on the march, another one approaching fast toward Falaise, all these fugitives looking for safety there.

News of this unrest gave my lady her idea. And so once more I say God works his will of us to his own device. Had we known what army approached, deep into Norman heartlands, or that among its Breton leaders again came Prince Taliesin, would that have helped our cause? Suppose instead Prince Taliesin had tried to rescue Hue; knowing Hue was inside Falaise, would he have succeeded where we could not? Would Taliesin have been killed in the attempt, and we with him? But we did not know what army marched, nor did anyone among those terrified souls, so we did not wait and had not that choice either. Knowing only that fugitives sought refuge within the walls, we went with them. And in this decision, too, I see the hand of God.

Lady Olwen called a halt as we neared Falaise. "The castle guards," she told us, brow furrowed in thought, as brisk as any lordling giving his first command, "will be on the outlook for armed men. Even had my father come, they would not have let him in at such a time. But those serfs, they'll pour in like a flood since the duke bears the responsibility of sheltering them, the more that Henry in his time has put whole towns and villages to the sword. He owes his Norman peasantry some refuge from similar attack. A woman alone, with her page, will have no difficulty getting in."

Of course our men demurred, argued, cursed, shouted, all in vain. My lady was adamant. "We should not go foolhardy into that place," she said. "This is my suggestion. Three men my mother took to save my father, and when she came to Henry's court, she left those three outside its gates so that, in need, she could rely on them. Inside the castle we have Norman help. We leave you here, out of sight; we shall summon you when we must." And she showed them, solemn as a knight, the seal ring of her father's strung around her neck, the maps and charts she had found in his campaign chests, and as a last resort, she reminded them of that fluting bird's call that border men use to communicate.

Finally they smiled among themselves, as men do, persuaded against their will, and she at them, her brother's smile, companions all. Their spokesman, an honest knight, enduring and battle-wise, regarded her soberly. He was dressed for war, his helmet slung at his saddle bow, his lance propped against his boot, and now he pushed back his coif and ran his hand through his thinning hair. "By the Mass, lady," he admitted after a while, "my men and I have been chosen to defend the honor of Sieux. We must do as you bid. Perhaps your idea is sound,

I do not know. To come against a fortress with only three men is like trying to beat down a stone wall with a thistle's head. Before you lies a dangerous place, a mission well-nigh impossible, a cunning foe. God knows I do not shrink from it. All I have to say is this. One day, years ago, the Lady Ann came through the storm to where your father lay. I was a squire then, and guarded him. Dying he was, and so were we. To us the Lady Ann said, 'Take heart. God will succor you, and with His help I will undertake to save my lord.' And so she did." He said simply, "God provided then. I think we must call upon Him today. I cannot say what will be or not be, but in God's name at least this I swear."

He swung himself off his horse, stiffly, for we had been many hours in the saddle, and came up to her. Kneeling in the dust, he and his companions made their oath. "If all the gates of hell were closed, we should break them down at your command."

She took each man's hand between her own, as do lords when they accept fealty. She bid them await her sign and absolved them of all responsibility. Then without more ado she prepared to go on, on foot. I shouldered our bundles as best I could and went with her. When we looked back, those three horsemen, leading our mounts, had already vanished like deer, hidden in the undergrowth where bracken and ferns grew to shoulder height. Ahead, the massive walls of Falaise loomed above the trees, a solid block of stone set on a great outcrop of rock.

I cannot say I felt much or thought much as we now advanced toward its gates, skirting the little village at its foot, where once its duke had spied a peasant girl and on her fathered the child who was to be known as Conqueror. Remembering how that girl had crossed the drawbridge, proudly, my lady held up her head, as proud as her father or his sons, and took my hand to draw me along. "Come, Urien," she said, as if we were children hiding in the straw from Hue's rage, or as if we were planning to outwit Prince Taliesin. Her hand was firm, no tremble now; I told you, in adversity she could be steadfast. And in her eyes the light of battle glowed; her own courage ran high.

As Lady Olwen had foreseen, as could anyone used to war, there was no difficulty being granted admittance. With all the world around Falaise upon the run, the forest athrob with alarm, all we had to do was join another group of fugitives intent on scrabbling for safety while there yet was time. We let them beat upon the gates, and when those gates were opened, in we went, up a narrow causeway winding beneath flanking walls, where the Norman guards hung, stern-faced beneath their heavy helmets. This causeway wound about, crossing the moat, almost like a culvert, the main way in and under guard for all its length.

Of all the Norman castles I have known, Falaise was the strongest and the worst. It smelled of age and decay like that old church undercroft, and when we were let into the first courtyard, it seemed steeped in blood; even the peasants' animals sensed it, straining piteously to break free. But the Lady Olwen was without fear. Had we not found Lord Gervaise or had he not been there, it is more than possible our mission would have ended here. A girl and her page, neither one knowing anything of siege castles or of kings, we were not well provided for such a task as rescuing a king's prisoner or getting free ourselves. A few carefully worded questions, a discreet exchange of coins from the sack I carried, brought us to the main guardhouse in the great square keep at the far end of successive courtyards, where, on an evil night, Hue had been routed up from sleep and where we now found Gervaise.

He started up on seeing us, his fair face flushed. War had broadened his broad shoulders, hardened him. His blue eyes that used to shine so arrogantly were heavier, ringed as if with fatigue, and there were creases of worry where before all had been complacency. He, too, looked older, coarser, all illusions gone. Whatever he had expected of war in a king's company, he seemed not to have found it. And whatever he had hoped of the Lady Olwen and his courtship of her, he obviously had not expected her herself. Seeing her approach, his greeting was less than flattering. He was appalled.

"Holy Christ," he cried, for once saying to her what he truly thought, "Mother of God, what brings you here? Where is the earl, where his troops?" And he searched about him frantically, as if expecting them to spring from the air.

"You do not seem so glad to see me, my lord," Olwen

answered him steadily. She looked at the man who would marry her. "I am come on Hue's behalf."

But when the whole story was told, Gervaise's mood only worsened. "Christ's wounds," he stormed, "I looked for a show of force, such as King Henry would understand, not a mad woman and her, her, her . . ." He mouthed at me, not sure what to call me in his rage and disappointment. "You make me look a fool, to ride in here alone, like a man yourself." He almost added, "As an earl's son-in-law I would have some worth; you, like this, bring none."

"I am come to keep my part of your bargain." Lady Olwen's voice did not change. "So keep you yours. First to Hue, then to the king."

Gervaise, whose face had begun to blotch with rage like his father's, cried, "*Jesu*, he'd eat us alive. We cannot walk up to a king and demand a prisoner. I am but a knight of his guard. And you have come at a most unsuitable time; the king is about to be caught here by an army he did not expect. No danger to us, but for the moment, when all are prepared to resist attack, no time to look for favors. Pray God those Bretons you admire so much begin to squabble among themselves and turn back. As for Hue, I have done what I could, but no sight for you." So he fumed, pacing back and forth. "I do not know which is worse," he admitted finally, "for the earl not to have come, or to have sent you."

As a lover's greeting it was not overwelcoming, the lover torn between his obvious fear of King Henry and his desire not to lose face with the lady he had wished to impress. He must have regretted the message he had sent. Meanwhile, his mention of the Breton army had had its effect. Gervaise did not speak to wound, and my lady, too proud to question him, did not ask, but it must have crossed her mind for the first time how near Prince Taliesin might be and how cruel fate would seem thus to separate them. But she said only, "My lord, as my betrothed, you claimed the right to speak for us, and I ask for an audience with the king. But first I shall see Hue."

Gervaise began to bluster like a man who hopes half-truths will hide his intent. He seemed almost to have forgotten his promise to help his friend, and I certainly had the impression that he did not stand as high with the king as he would have had us believe before. When Lady Olwen persisted a third time, he grew shrewd. "If you will swear to marry me, before witnesses," he began. "There stands the castle chapel; there shall we be wed." He caught at her arm to drag her along. "Before the priest himself shall you swear," he insisted, but she interrupted him.

"No need before anyone, but if it pleases you, I will. Afterward."

Gervaise was forced to bow to her will, although it did not please him. "Come, then," he said angrily, "on your own head be it."

Hue was imprisoned in the depths of the square *donjon*, or keep, the oldest part of Falaise. Its upper crofts are wide, wooden-floored, lit by lamps that burn there constantly. One passes easily from one level to the next, down wood ladders bolted against the walls. The walls themselves are lined with barrels and casks, set up on benches out of the damp and away from rats. The goods of a great fortress are kept there, more than a year's supply, as I can attest; so well victualed is this castle that even with a besieging force on the march, wine was spilled, and grain, as only men confident would dare. Below these levels were the armories; they, too, were neatly kept in Norman style—weapons oiled against the damp, hung with shields and helmets on wooden pegs, all in order for instant use. Beneath them again was disorder, darkness, despair. The steps that led to the lowest levels were foul and damp; a vile smell rose up to choke us. We must have been below some waterline, deep in the rock, for now you could see the green slime of damp upon the stones, all the refuse of a castle thrown therein, privies, offal, the vilest filth. But not all the smells and sights came from rubbish tipped above. The guards who, knowing Lord Gervaise, had let us pass now hurried us, but not before we caught glimpses of souls in purgatory, arms outstretched, bearded faces like animals, eyes that stared from hell.

Before one of the larger cells the guards stopped and motioned Gervaise to step ahead, alone. The door was unlocked. We heard murmuring within, a curse, a scuffle, the sound of a blow. Hue was dragged out. In the dim light I would not have recognized him, his red hair lank, his face covered with bruises, one eye half closed. But it was his hands that were worst. I had not realized what chains can do to a man, for they had fastened him by the wrists to the walls, and once, when he had cursed too loud, strung him up by his thumbs.

"By the holy Virgin, let me pass." Olwen pushed through the guards. She tried to stifle a cry, biting deep into the back of her hand as she saw her brother shuffle toward her.

He cocked his head on one side and gave a grin. Between his bruised lips the blood still showed where they had shoved him with a spear butt. A prisoner of a king counts but little as earl's son. "*Jesu*," he croaked, "by all the saints how came you here, my sister and her hobgoblin? Where is my father?" And he, too, tried to peer around her as Gervaise had.

When she did not reply, I cannot tell you how the light died from his face. Even beaten, in such a dreadful place, even with his hands broken and raw, Hue had kept his spirit high. He could even try to grin; he certainly knew how to curse and shout defiance at his guards. That silence, saying all, defeated him. Our hurried explanations of the earl's fall (for we would not tell him what the earl had said) hardly reached him, I think. Hearing that his father had not come, he blocked out thought, so intent had he been that his father would rescue him. His body, thinner than I ever remembered, seemed to sag. He shivered in his shirt, for they had taken away the rest of his clothes. Too distressed for speech, we busied ourselves with the bundles we had brought; Gervaise knocked the spout off the wine and held the flask so Hue could drink. He downed it in great drafts and, when he was done, set it aside as best he could, stared at us, his eyes too large. "Not come," he repeated.

"Nay." Olwen tried to comfort him. She drew closer so the guards could not hear. "We've friends without," she said, "three of them. And a Breton army on the march. And as your sister's husband, Gervaise of Walran will plead for you."

But even to herself she did not sound convincing, and Hue, looking from her to Gervaise and back, said only, "Friends.

Well, friends or not, I thank you, but let me be." And to Gervaise, suddenly fierce, he said, "Get her away. Never bring her here again."

Olwen picked up her bundles without a word, turned her back, and let Gervaise lead her along, so blinded by tears she scarcely saw where she went. But to me Hue spoke again. "Manikin," he whispered; he raised his chained hands and felt for me as a blind man might, grasping for sight. "Now tell the truth. Why would not my father come?"

It was a cry from the heart. Yet I did not know how to answer him. "Not for lack of love," I wanted to say, "not for its lack, but for some old wrong, of which you, alas, are part." I looked at him. Where was the arrogant boy who used to hurl his boots, whose whip used to strike the wall above my head? Where was that vitality that used to spill over like quicksilver into laughter, eagerness, anger, by turns, taking up the slack of the world, working on our dull selves as yeast, changing us, making the air around us come alive? I could not express those thoughts aloud, but I let them pour out to him, and I think perhaps he understood. His face lightened for a moment. "So be it," he said. Then, after a while, "But they will never let me go." He tried another grin. "Better a quick, clean death than this." And he raised his manacled hands and suddenly with an oath beat his chains against the wall until the blood spurted from his wounds. The guards, hearing him, came rushing to thrust him back inside. I watched for a moment and then on an impulse pulled off my cloak and threw it around him, I who had never been touched by him since that day at Cambray and had never dared touch him but once, when I tripped him in the great hall. In the face of the startled guards I began to sing, a song of love and loyalty; what other weapons has a bard but words? I clung to the bars, and he within his cage listened to me until I in turn was dragged off, pulled out from those lower cells where even death is hope. In Welsh I sang, the second time before him, to give him heart, to give it to myself, until I was sure he knew what I meant, until the walls silenced me and I stumbled up the stairs, wiping blood from my own face.

In the open courtyard Lord Gervaise and Lady Olwen were

waiting for me. Lady Olwen was twisting the rope fastenings around her bundles, back and forth, much as her mother had twisted the coverlets. She spoke tonelessly, a voice in which no color showed, no life, as once Lord Robert had spoken when he faced his oldest enemy. "I swear," she said, white-lipped. "Gervaise of Walran, I swear to marry you; before my page and before the world I give my oath. Why else have I come, my brother's life for myself, what else have I to bargain with?"

It was clearly stated, no pretense. And a hard bargain, I think, for any man to accept. But Gervaise was forced to. I do not think he believed her at first, so long had he wanted her. He swallowed twice, as if his throat were parched, and he ran a finger under his mail coat as if it were too tight about the neck. Twice he tried to speak—a dream come true, and yet even he must have known how unlike the dream he once had had. I could almost have found it in my heart to pity him, a man possessed, who still did not have what he longed for, who, having it, had found it turned to dust. He did not even try to embrace her, he who before had been so insistent in his wooing, but stared at her, his hands slack by his side. "Judas, lady," he tried to say, "you speak too blunt." But she turned aside, for pity, too, I think, pity for him, perhaps for herself. *For a brother's life there is no choice.* Gervaise was as caught as we all were.

"Lady," Gervaise was saying, recovering himself somewhat, hiding disappointment under a more stoic air, "if we are betrothed, I claim the right to order you. The Bretons have broken through the borderlands and are pressing hard upon Falaise. Dear God," he cried suddenly, "this war we make has been hard. Slaughter, revenge, looting, for the most part upon miserable villagers. It is not . . ." He bit his lip. A soldier does not complain of soldiering. "A castle under siege," he went on, "even as strong as Falaise, is no place for you. Christ's wounds, had you come but a scant hour or so late, you might have been taken by those Celts along the road, God forbid." He crossed himself fervently.

I thought, a scant hour late, or a scant hour soon. But there it was, we within the castle, Prince Taliesin without, no way to alter that. Yet God has ways we mortals know not of.

Olwen did not flinch. "I am your betrothed," she said as firmly
as before. "Now I shall see the king."

That was a decision, too, that Gervaise clearly was not pleased
about. In company with an earl such audience would have been
another thing. Alone, himself to take responsibility, it was an
idea that he had not agreed upon. Muttering to himself angrily,
at last he reluctantly agreed to show her where the king kept
state. Well, of course, a young knight, even brave, the oldest
son of a border lord, does not walk up to a king and ask to
speak to him. It began to dawn on me that Gervaise of Walran's
help was not as much as he had boasted of, and the fact of our
suspicion began to work on him. But the Lady Olwen did not
dispute with him as her younger self might have done; she
merely went about finding us a place to bestow ourselves in
company with all those other fugitives; shabby lodgings they
were in a crowded yard, not what a lady of her rank should
have had. Within the small niche of an outer wall I hung a cloak
to give her privacy, and since she had no maids, no help, I will
not deny I did what woman's services I could, straightening
her long sleeves so that they hung to proper length to her
fingertips, fastening the girdle swung low about her hips,
snatching a handful of wild weeds that grew in crevices in the
stones to bind into a chaplet for her hair; flowers there were none,
this being a fortress, not a place for living in.

Nor will I deny that now she did tremble as she prepared to
meet this king whose name had long been anathema to us. And
yet her beauty that day was such that even Gervaise was blinded
by her. He led her along, almost as if in a daze; poor soul, how
he strained to catch what slipped through his fingers, the harder
he grasped, the farther away, a flower that withers, a butterfly
crushed. Myself, I had no idea what she would do or say, but
I felt apprehension rise.

The king had made his quarters in a small tower, added by
his grandsire to the first keep, more comfortable than the rest.
He was lolling at the table with some of his lords, hashing over
plans with his captains, this Breton advance like a fly's bite, and,
like a fly, as quickly to be brushed aside. Although Lord Gervaise
would have waited at the door to have the guard announce him

as was fit, she brushed him aside, glided between the men like a shadow. Her dress swished over the floor where piles of refuse were littered, and as she held it high, for a moment I caught a glimpse of her little feet sliding to and fro. I myself will swear I saw the king start back and cross himself, his prominent gray eyes almost bulging from his head. He stopped talking, a crust of bread halfway to his lips. "By the living Christ," he swore, "what apparition is that?"

From the doorway where the lady had left him, Gervaise tried to speak but scarce had the breath to summon up the words. I think for the first time he realized what sort of lady he was bound to wed, and even he was awed. But Olwen did not heed him now, or anyone. "Lord king," she said, "I am come in my father's stead, to claim his son, whom you have wrongfully imprisoned."

Beside me I heard Gervaise groan, not the way for a suppliant to talk. Henry had recovered from his shock, leaned easily back against his chair, continued gnawing on his bread. I was curious to see him, the second king I had ever laid eyes upon. He was dressed more casually than his French counterpart—his mail coat on, his tunic unlaced—more like a huntsman himself, I thought. As our man had done earlier today, he ran his hands through his hair, cut cross-cropped against his skull, although, at the neck (thick like a bull's), where enough was left, it curled in ringlets. Unlike King Louis he alone in that room wore a sword, although weapons there were in plenty stacked against the door, yet like King Louis (albeit royalty did not sit on him full of pride) a king he seemed when he moved and talked.

"And what," said King Henry of England, throwing out his question as swiftly as he tossed the scraps of bread to his hounds, "should I get in return for all the trouble this young man has caused?"

When my lady did not reply, his face unexpectedly broke into a smile. "Daughter of Earl Raoul," he said, "come, I thought you could do better than that. But in truth, lady, I'd rather you than Raoul himself, breathing fire and gloom. You know, of course, what your brother is accused of," he went on, with a touch of sarcasm. "Assisting my son to escape, helping my

wife, the queen, run from me, setting war in all my lands but
part of it. A nothing to you, I suppose. But all the same, you
are welcome, Olwen of Cambray, in your mother's name.''

He knew her, then, at once. And gesturing, he had her join
him at the table, a place set beside him on his right hand. There
sat my lady, as much at her ease as if she wined with a king
every day. He bowed to her, most courteous, then drank from
a heavy silver cup and had it passed to her so she could drink
to him. She made her curtsy, drank, but did not set her lips
where his had touched. Beside me Gervaise groaned a second
time, not wise to slight a king. I myself was merely stunned.
To think my little lady of the tattered dresses and bare feet
would drink from a loving cup with royalty.

The king leaned back and eyed her at his leisure. He had
pulled a dagger from his belt and was playing with it, twisting
the handle this way, now that, so that the lights from the flares
caught first the blade, then the hilt, sending shafts of brilliance
across the wooden tabletop, for he dined roughly, too, no sign
of feasting here.

"So, lady," he said after a while, "what is your will?" All
the men around him seemed to hold their breaths, as did I. I
had no idea, I tell you, what she would say. Gervaise was already
purple with embarrassment. He had not thought to present his
lady like this, he mute, she alone.

She said quietly, but since everyone was listening the words
rang out, "My father claims back his son. I offer myself as
prisoner in his place."

Henry's courtiers began to nudge and grin among themselves.
Gervaise would have leapt forward in protest, had not I, over-
bold myself, caught him by the tail end of his cloak. The king
eyed her narrowly again, then threw back his head and laughed,
too, a great guffaw that sent the nesting pigeons in the high
rafters fluttering. Hearing him, his lords began to laugh more
openly.

"By God," Henry cried. "I should have known you without
your looks; you have your mother's tongue and your father's
effrontery. Prisoner is it, lady? What should I do with you? Do
you want me to hang you first?"

He leaned forward and regarded her intently. "I warrant you your father does not know," he said, suddenly shrewd. "What put that thought into your pretty head? Christ's bones, we've fret enough without a silly maid playing at heroine. Any moment now those Celts will swarm like a hive of bees. Not many maids walk into such a noose, let alone tighten the rope themselves. Not many would hope to walk out of it." He let that thought sink in. "So what else would you ask?"

"Better treatment for my brother," she said without hesitation. "Surgeons for his wounds. And a promise that you will do him no more harm until my father is well enough to treat for him."

"Which he will never do willingly, if I know him." Henry's voice was silky smooth. "Those requests, then, for a brother whose guilt includes treachery, deceit, revolt. And what do you have to offer me that I do not already have the right to claim, as king?"

He stretched out his hand—a long, fine hand it was, too, for a man who rode and used a sword as much as he did, thin-boned, supple—and took her chin between forefinger and thumb. "Like your mother," he said softly, "in all things, whom all men praise."

She did not flinch or turn away, nor even blush and pretend she did not understand, as a well-brought-up maiden should. "I am betrothed," was all she said. "But my mother sends you a message, too. For the memory of a time you spent with her at Maneth castle, long ago; for the confidences you once exchanged there, let Hue go."

At those words the king snatched back his hand as if it stung and with a curse thrust the dagger point into the tabletop. Curses formed and died upon his lips, even as his companions drew aside, silent before all the signs of a royal storm. Only she did not move. What he might have done or said, or she also, we shall never know. Praise God, say I, for that mercy at least. A clamor arose from the door where I had been hovering; a man burst through the crowds, and outside, high on the battlements, a bell began to toll. Even the king bit his lip and turned expectantly. A messenger came in and fell to one knee. He was

covered with mud, cut about the cheeks as if tree branches had
scored him as he rode, breathless with haste. "My lord king,"
he cried, "I am come from the outposts. The Breton army has
arrived."

Henry pushed back his chair, bounded up light as a boy. "*Jesu*
be thanked," he cried. "Now we will have done with them.
Prepare to mount and ride."

But the messenger did not budge, still kneeling, and I saw
his eyes flicker shut for a second in a private prayer of his own.
A royal messenger does not always get respect, especially if he
brings unwelcome news. "My lord." His voice was cautious,
restrained, scratching at the surface of all he knew. "This is a
large army, no scavenger force, both Bretons and Welsh. Your
captains report they have already seized Avranches, taken it but
not plundered." He hesitated again. "Your outposts here have
surrendered." At last he faltered. "By dawn Falaise will be
surrounded. And the Welsh prince holds their line."

The king's expression changed. He caught hold of his messenger by the hair. "You lie," he shouted, and shook him as a
terrier does a rat. "No one besieges me." But the alarm bell
still continued to ring, and the messenger, although he frothed
with fear, would not admit he was wrong.

Henry's anger veered back and forth like a weather vane.
"That Welsh cub," he snarled, "who outspoke my son. The
only thing of sense Prince Henry did was to dismiss him, his
demands as preposterous as the lady's here. And Raoul supported him. God's wounds, I'll have that Welshman's head,
too, hanged from these very battlements. You, lady, prepare
to sit out a siege; see if that pleases you." He was already striding
toward the door, his men trailing behind him, all signs of mirth
gone. "And you, Gervaise of Walran," the king snapped as he
pushed past, proof that not much missed his eye when he wished
it. "Keep your lady under guard. God's wounds, man, if I were
you I'd knock sense into her, else as wife she'll pin you by
your ears."

The warning bell boomed; the king's companions, knights
and squires, went streaming after him; the castle sprang to alert,

a besieging army no laughing affair. Lord Gervaise fretted again, scarce knowing where to look or what to do. "I warned you," he howled. "Worse than if you had not come at all. Turn the king against us, what hope for any of us." And he struck her deliberately on the face, a Norman knight berating the woman he would wed as sign of strength.

"Lord Gervaise." Lady Olwen sounded weary; she closed her eyes. "Go play the part of knight," she told him. "If fighting you crave, here it is."

"Do not mock me." Gervaise was cold himself now, his voice hard. "This Breton horde is nothing. If this prince of yours," his mouth closed in a sneer, "has kept them together all this while, he has already achieved one miracle. Do not look for a second one. When we have done with him, Henry will do with you. And so shall I." But she kept her eyes closed, would not look at him, and did not acknowledge what he said.

"Get you below," he told her at last, defeated by her silence. "Out of sight. Pray God we win. And when we are wed, then look for comfort where you will." It, too, was a threat, as ominous as the king's. We were left alone, and she still said nothing. But when we came back to our small niche, whilst all about us during the night men ran back and fro preparing for attack, I heard her weeping silently, slowly, despairingly, to herself. A *scant hour more, a scant hour less,* then perhaps she could have turned to Prince Taliesin for help; then she would not have been forced to swear her oath to Lord Gervaise; then she would not have tried to outface this king. But God decides; we within, the prince without, the castle under attack, and at the end, when the king had won, as he was sure to do, death perhaps for all of us, certainly for her the death of her dreams of happiness with her prince.

A castle under siege is the nightmare children of our age live with. Those walls we think so strong can crumble like cheese; those gates we put our hopes in fall apart as a loaf of bread is halved. Falaise was the strongest castle I have ever known, but even it could not take a besieging force as lightly as it wished. Now, as the clamor of a great fortress put on defense ebbed and flowed about our ears, diminishing, for a moment, our little hopes and fears beneath these greater ones, the Lady Olwen and I sat huddled together, two children sitting out a storm.

But the skirmish was not to be so easily won as Henry and his lords had planned. The news the messenger did not give was soon self-evident. This was a disciplined army—as armies go, I mean. And in one thing its leaders showed good sense. Falaise is almost impregnable, a solid mass of stone on rock; where were the engineers skilled enough to undermine its rocky base? It could withstand a siege forever, and so the Celts themselves realized. They did not try to attack the fort, merely surrounded it and waited, out of sight. And they were clever. Using tactics that combined their border skills with Norman ones, they did not try a frontal attack as Henry expected but, keeping under cover by day, harried the castle by night. Hearing of this I was convinced Prince Taliesin was behind their plan. But it infuriated Henry the more. Inside Falaise he knew himself safe. Yet he could not afford to be shut in, safe or not. Time was essential to him. Falaise could outsit a year's siege; a year's delay would lose the king his throne.

As for us, this distraction, if I may term it thus, saved us from the king for the while; saved us from Gervaise, no wedding possible under siege conditions, at least, no opportunity for Gervaise to spend time with us or show his bride what joys lay in store for her, being too occupied with soldier's affairs. Sometimes we saw him on the battlements; once we watched him ride out with Henry's guard to seek the honor his honor demanded; like the rest of the castle he allowed his fury to grow by leaps and bounds that a bunch of vagabonds should hold these Normans to their will. But for once King Henry had met his match; as soon try to trap water in the palm of your hand or catch a shadow as catch these wily Celts off guard.

Hue was moved to a better place; his wounds were bound and the broken bones set, although it was clear it would be long before he could ride or use a sword as he once had. Yet have you seen a wild hawk caged? Either it beats its wings apart, trying to break through the bars, or it sits and pines. So now it was with Hue. I often saw him during these days of wait, although he never asked for me, and seldom spoke, except once or twice his eyes flashed when I told him of the Celts. For the most part he sat hunched in his cell, his hands spread before him on a table, as if he willed them to heal, lost in his thoughts that took him back to what he had been when his hopes ran high, forward perhaps to what he hoped again would be his. And although he never spoke to me, sometimes never looked, the bond between us tightened each day more painfully. *Quick death and clean.* That at least would be my gift to him.

The castle was bewildered; each night a fresh inroad, a new attack kept us from sleep and set us all on edge. One time it was a brushfire, floated against the castle gate, causing us all to splutter and cough; another time it was a flight of arrows released at dawn from the western heights overlooking the keep; a third, the sound of chanting, to make the blood run cold. Henry was beside himself. Twice indeed he did try to break out, the first with all his guard, four abreast, the great gates thrown wide to let him out, himself openly leading his troops. The way was clear; down the rock hill they rode, and at the wood's edge he had his standard bearer advance his royal flag and sound the charge. His Norman knights moved into step, a wall of steel to slice through an enemy. Along the wide grassy paths they moved at a gallop, lances held. But a charge needs an enemy to charge against! There was none. Except, from the trees came a new rain of death, arrows shot high in the air to stampede those horses that were not killed or maimed, to set their Norman riders in a panic; arrows from those Welsh longbows that can drive a bolt through a mail coat. And behind the Normans, moving steadily with their long Welsh stride, spearmen began to pour up the hill, toward the gates, flanked by a group of Breton cavalry, mounted and armed like a Norman troop.

Henry saw the danger at once—the gates left open, himself cut off. "Back," he howled, striking about him with the flat of his sword to turn his men. "Close the gates. Ram them home." His orders could be heard, but no one dared lock a king out of his own castle. While the Welsh archers prevented a forward drive, the Welsh footmen and their cavalry prevented an easy return. Well, in the end the king won a way through, losing half his men, and once indeed having to fight for his own life, a small group of knights, seven in all, pursuing him, and he forced to defend himself against its leader, who almost rode him down.

Inside the castle we heard of this exploit with a mixture of admiration and fear. We had no doubt it was Taliesin; had not he vowed that when he met the king in open fight, he would cross swords with him? But on the other hand, a victorious army, taking a ducal palace by storm, does not stop to inquire politely what race you are before it cuts your throat. For the first time the words "victory" or "defeat" began to be whispered openly, and those who had survived the humiliation of turning tail before a handful of mounted men began to feel the prick of fear.

Gervaise was among the survivors. He drank heavily these days, lurched from castle watch to table in a sullen fit; the more he burned to show his prowess, the more he hated the Welsh who prevented it, the more he swore to himself that one day his chance would come.

The second attempt to break out was different, but showed, I think, King Henry's desperation. A small group, twenty in all, left by stealth, at night, not to defeat the enemy but to escape, abandoning castle, queen, prisoners, and all behind. Again the king was driven back by those unseen archers, whose worth, once sneered at by the Bretons, now openly proved itself. Defeated in this second attempt, King Henry grew sour. For days afterward he sulked, whilst the castle waited with bated breath. Had it been a Norman army attacking, already the siege tower would have been hauled into place, the battering rams, the catapults brought up, the sappers busy undermining the walls, all the signs of siege that strike terror into a beleaguered place. Here there was none, only a silence, and an emptiness, that struck even more fear.

King Henry knew himself outfoxed. I had no love of this king, whose enmity had done the house I serve much harm and whose cunning was about to fall upon us personally. But I did not think him a fool either, although he had been foolish in his dealings with his sons. And no one ever accused him of cowardice. Of all the men who have ruled the world we live in, he was the quickest to manipulate events, the most ready to negotiate without keeping faith, and the most clever to catch whatever means he could. But he knew this silence, this inaction, would lose him his war. It might even have already lost him England, where, on the northern border, King William of Scotland had made good his promise to invade, in return for Northumbria. And elsewhere Henry's enemies outside Normandy, gloating on his predicament, had begun again to attack his lands with full force. At a loss as to what to do, the king at last turned to the one person he knew more skilled in cunning than he was, more devious, and the one, or so it is claimed, from whom he had learned what skills he had.

Queen Eleanor had been kept, or "imprisoned," if you prefer that term, in her own quarters at Falaise without hitherto having had a chance to see the king. But she had not been idle all this while. She knew all that went on in the castle, and all without, and the Celtic siege had thwarted her plans as well. She wanted to be free of this dreadful place, without a creature comfort to its name; she longed to return to Poitiers. Realizing perhaps more quickly than the king that this was no ordinary alliance, the Celtic forces not usually so committed to one cause, she had already begun to think of a way to undo it, thereby releasing herself from Henry's grasp. His gratitude should win her her liberty and, incidentally, achieve the revenge she had first sought. Well, God's will is served in many ways. We in turn were to be released from our predicament, not, as might be thought, by a prince who would have given his right arm to save us had he known us there, nor by three men who had sworn to hew down the gates of hell, nor by a king, nor by that Norman lord, who, too, longed to show his bravery (although each of these in turn played a part). Malice was the way; malice such as the queen would use. Now she turned her skill to good account.

Not all this I know as fact. Silent are the chroniclers, as well they might be, reluctant, as ever, to reveal all the truth in an affair so unsavory. But in a castle where a king and queen are lodged, the very air breathes news; gossip hangs like spiderwebs. And the queen's plan was simple in the extreme. The difficulty lay in persuading the king that it would work without emphasizing her part in it. And here, also, Eleanor was skillful. She knew everything in the castle and all the human emotions bound up there. Her strategy relied on human affairs; let Henry keep to his military ones. And, as in all human terms, she knew there must be a weak link somewhere. From her chambers, set apart, she began to look for it.

Now when she summoned Lord Gervaise, I do not know what he thought. After all, once he had professed to despise her and her lascivious ways. And had I been the one she fixed upon, I do not say I could have withstood her either. She never told Gervaise what she wanted at first, I think; merely turned her charm upon him full, as she once had upon Hue. Less openly, more discreetly—for after all, her husband was the king and she was not in her own palace now—she began to work on the young lord. And I only guess that, drunk with wine and sweetness as a bee is heavy with it, Gervaise gradually began to tell her what she hoped to hear and soon willingly was pouring out his woes: his love of Olwen and her disdain, his hatred of Prince Taliesin, the embarrassment of Hue's imprisonment.

"But the Lady Olwen is your betrothed," the queen must have said, smoothing his blond locks as before she had smoothed Hue's. When she looked at a man like that, her almond-shaped eyes grew light, her face, pale from confinement, drew into a look of concern, and her voice became more husky. "What maiden could resist you?" It was as if she added: "A young man, virile, strong, courageous, a woman could die for you. Show her what you are capable of; willingly will she come to you." I do not know. I do not say that Gervaise left her room drugged with passion for her, on fire with thoughts of chivalry and love, filled with the desire for heroic deeds to make the queen smile at him and to win him Olwen's full consent, but I think so.

And with this knowledge the queen now went about her attempt to persuade the king. She did not have to tell Henry the advantages to him. The advantages to herself she kept private, but they were many: the lifting of the siege to enable her to go home; the end of Hue; the destruction of the house of

Sieux; the death of Olwen's love; mischief whichever way the blow fell; and the return of Henry's dependence upon her—many things, then, for the price of one.

She waited one day more, when she knew inactivity would have driven Henry wild, he of all men the most restless. She also chose night, the hours of dark suiting her ways of thought because she was at an age when her beauty shone best in dim light. Yet she still was beautiful; and when she appeared before Henry in her shimmering white, beaded with her favorite pearls, like a bride, he might well have thought a second time he beheld an apparition. She had made sure that Henry was alone, not too early, not too late, and when she spoke, her voice was deep in the way it is to rouse men. "So, my lord," she said, "since you have not come to me, I have come to you. I have looked for you this long while."

Henry, who had been seated before a fire, brooding, merely grunted and closed his eyes. But he watched her beneath his eyelashes as she put aside the book she had been carrying, as if she had been reading the scriptures devoutly, and bent over to tend the dying embers in the brick hearth, a wifely gesture meant to placate.

"Remember, my lord," she told him softly, "that spring you came to Poitiers for the first time? How you made your horse prance and rear; how lathered were its sides from your spurs?"

"Took three hours to get clean," Henry grunted laconically, but he gave a secret grin. When the queen praised him or was in a remembering mood, when she was amorous, he knew the time was come for her to make demands. In his youth, overwhelmed by her, he had not cared. Now he knew enough of women's ways to be on his guard.

But the queen was not dismayed. She kept her place; her voice did not change, and perhaps, in truth, she did remember. King Henry had weathered more than forty years; beside his sons he was not young. But in himself he was still active, quick; his hair, although thin, did not lack for curls; his gray eyes had not lost their feral gleam. From abstinence and hard work he had kept stoutness, his secret fear, at bay; he was broad but not an ounce of fat, and stripped, he would still make a figure of a man. The queen must have thought of that and remembered what her spies had told her of his speech with Olwen. But most of all, I think, she remembered the youth who at Poitiers those years ago had claimed her body, ravaged it, set his seal therein to make himself the equal of kings.

Henry said lazily, "So, madame, you have been looking for me. Rather I thought you looked for your sons."

"Our sons," she corrected him, "ours."

Henry grunted.

She cried passionately, "Should I be left to rot, should they be set aside, while you bat to and fro the world, great king, here one day, gone the next? How should we hope to match your speed? Once," she grew cunning, her long eyes narrowed, "once you relied on me to be your regent. Once you let me rule with you."

"And once," he told her bluntly, sitting bolt upright, "you tried to supplant me. Regency." He repeated the word contemptuously. "You wanted to be king yourself. I gave you instead Poitiers to rule. Could not that content you that you should let your sons try to oust me from my throne? Christ's balls," he bellowed in rage, "that unbearded whelp of yours has had the gall to take my names; Henry of England, Duke of Normandy, Count of Anjou, he calls himself. Do I look like a ghost?"

And he thrust himself up from his chair so violently that hearing the noise, his guards at the door spun around in alarm. The queen waved them away imperiously. On foot, beside her, the king was not much taller than she, gray eyes to match her blue ones, yet if he were the lion, she was lioness. "This time, Eleanor of Aquitaine," he whispered, full of threat, "you have set all men against me, roused up rebels who never knew they wished me ill, scraped up from the cess pits all the scum of France. By the living cross, I swear no king was ever so tormented in his wife."

"Perhaps you think so." The more he raged, the colder she grew. Rage weakened him and gave her strength. "But think also this. Had you given your sons some part of your time, had you not ignored them, why should they have needed to bring themselves before you in this way? Did not Richard as a child write to beg your return? Did not the archbishop rebuke you for ignoring him?"

As always she found the means to outargue him. He did not reply but beckoned to the page who cowered by the entrance-way, had wine brought, and drank in great drafts to fortify himself.

"You roam the world, great king," Eleanor was saying, "many lords and ladies know you, but not your sons."

"Your son, Prince Henry, liked my company so much," Henry said caustically, "that he fled from it. Your favorite, Richard, is already on the loose in Aquitaine. As for roaming the world, remember your sons need land. Who else will give it to them if I do not?"

It was the chance she had been waiting for. "And what use land," she cried, almost wringing her hands, "if it all goes for naught? Shall a bastard have it?"

"Bastard." He repeated the word sharply. He put down the cup and stared at her. His eyes glared. "What bastard, yours or mine?"

She ignored the cruel thrust. He knew of her amours, of course, and had always shrugged them off, but open adultery was another thing, as was open proof. Yet he also knew she was beyond childbearing age, a double insult, then. But she drew herself upright. Her scorn would have cut through flesh. "Five sons have I given you," she cried, "four living sons. You know full well that they are yours. But there is yet another son who lives to be a danger to you."

"Where?" he said. "I know of none."

She arched her eyebrows and looked at him slantwise. "I thought you knew," she cried. "Why else imprison him? I speak of Hue." The king's look gave him away. Satisfied she had his attention, she hurried on. "He planned your son's escape; he escorted me. Why should he help us except to help himself? Have you not considered whose son he is?"

Henry cried, "Raoul knighted him last summer; he allowed Hue to join Prince Henry's household. Hue is the son of the Lady Ann."

"And the son," she told him quietly, "who would have killed Raoul for not being the father that he claimed. Raoul has not come for him now, has he?" She leaned forward and pulled at his sleeve, twisting the knife that had been used against her, but in reverse. "Son of that virtuous Lady Ann," she sneered, "but by whom? If not yours, then Geoffrey Plantagenet's!"

She let that thought sink in, not the idea of bastardy itself, but the loss of Henry's trust in a lady he had always in his heart believed. "No doubt," Eleanor went on after a while, "Ann hid the real facts from you, as from her husband, no need to boast aloud her lover's name. But think, great king. If Hue is Geoffrey Plantagenet's get, then he is bastard heir to all of Geoffrey's lands in Brittany. Why else," and now her voice did grow low, insistent, "why else, think you, these Breton lords have come to rescue him?"

She looked at him, triumph for a moment darkening her eyes. "Get rid of them, get rid of him; then will your own sons feel safe," she said. "Then will their revolt be done."

And so she told him of her plan.

Chapter 13

he queen's plan was simple, and so she made the king feel. To each of his objections she had an answer pat, so that when he finally said, "But not the little maid, I'll not have her harmed," she knew she had caught him fast. And perhaps it was to the king's credit that at first he demurred, saying he wished to consult with his councillors.

"Very well." Queen Eleanor rose to leave. "Talk all you wish. You'll be here until Christmas before they give an answer straight."

That, too, was true, and so he knew, and since she knew his need for haste, expediency now being the most important thing, she brought him to agree.

First she told him bluntly he would never outfight the Celts; not because he was not strong enough but because shadows cannot be fought with steel. "Bribe the Bretons," she told him. "Offer them gold from the treasury at Falaise. Give them the border castle of Dol in perpetuity. Tell their leaders, the Viscount of Leon, Ralph de Fougères, and the rest, that they can keep the lands they've won—you can always win them back again. And get rid of the Welsh prince who controls them."

At the king's quick, appraising glance, she said, "Offer that prince, also, what he wants—a little sentence or two of apology, some Welsh borderlands, which also you can recover at will. And the three hostages his father claims." She paused for effect.

"Three he wanted, give him three. You have them here: Lord Hue of Sieux, Gervaise of Walran, and the Lady Olwen. And take them back, too. Have them ride under escort, not telling the prince who they are, not telling them why they are being used, and at the time of exchange, plant men before to ambush the prince and seize him with his prisoners."

She suddenly laughed. "A nice touch," she said. "A Plantagenet bastard as bait to catch a Welsh prince, what alliance could withstand that plan? Let none of them leave the place alive, prince and his hostages, have done with them."

That was when the king cried, "I'll not have the little maid harmed."

"No," she soothed. She sighed. "Then let her go. Make it seem as if Taliesin has tricked your men, not you his, and send her at least back to Sieux under escort, as is fit. That way Raoul of Sieux will feel in your debt (if he lives, which I doubt); so shall your promise not to hurt her be kept."

But the king only smiled, and for a moment his eyes gleamed. "No," he repeated softly, "I'll not have her harmed. I've plans for her myself." And he jutted his head forward dangerously, as a bull does, and stared at his wife with his hot gray eyes so there was no mistaking what he meant. Well, there was little she could do about that, then, not having taken his lusts into consideration, save shrug her shoulders and pretend she did not care, but it dimmed her pleasure to be sure. And when after a while he shot his last question at her: "And you, madame, what do you get?" she snapped at him, "Freedom in Poitiers for me and my son," which was a mistake on her part again, to admit to wanting anything.

I do not know that this is exactly what was said or how it was arranged. I do not say Queen Eleanor thought all would go according to her plan. The difficulty with human affairs, as she well knew, was that at the last moment those humans might change their minds, might grow balky or act too soon, but these possibilities she took into account. For although she planned to use Gervaise as pawn, she did not afterward hesitate to give away to him as much of her plan as she thought he should know, working on his jealousy of Prince Taliesin so that to betray the prince would seem a virtue, twisting things enough so that she would appear a saint, a friend, who wanted to make amends for past wrongs by helping him and the Lady Olwen rescue Hue. It was the prince, she cried, who with the king had agreed to a trade, Falaise freed in return for hostages. So she deceived Gervaise until in the end he agreed that his betrothed and her brother should be used to catch a man he had come to hate. He believed her when she told him he alone had best reason for killing the prince. He believed her when she told him the king would honor him. She never told him, of course, that he, too, was to be used as bait, or that she had no desire to save anyone; what she did not tell him was more important than what she did.

I have said Henry was no fool. He saw the sense of her plan at once, and at once he acted on it. But he had an idea or two of his own, and he did not tell his queen everything. Nor did he give the order to begin until he had, in secret, made one last visit to Hue's cell. They say he came without fanfare and stood in the shadows, gazing through the iron bars. Hue sat in his accustomed place, his hands bound and taped in front of him. Eagles or hawks sit with such a look when their wings have been clipped. They say the king kept his face covered with a cloak, so he should not be recognized, and there he stood for a long while looking at the young man whose death he now arranged and who reminded him of his own boyhood, until with a sigh, he spun on his heel and went away. But to the Lady Olwen the king came openly, striding up to her where she sat, listless, by the courtyard wall. He looked down at her, royal then in his red and gold, with the lions of England stamped upon his surcoat, his red hair uncovered. "Your offer that you made, lady, is remembered. Prepare now to honor it." And that, too, was a statement to cause alarm.

The next morning the truce began, a truce flag was raised, and royal courtiers were sent to the Breton camp as had been decided upon. It did not take those Bretons long to accept, the more so that day because for reasons of his own Prince Taliesin was absent from the council, as shall be explained. Over the years Henry had come to know these Breton lords. They were vainglorious, inconsistent, and distrustful, and their weaknesses were such that he could use them. His bribes of gold, of lands, of castles, set their suspicions flaring—after all, who could say which man had captured which castle alone? In good humor they would have admitted that Taliesin's insistence had been responsible for a large part of their success and that they owed much to him and his bowmen. Now they began to let their jealousy of him show, afraid that were he there, he might claim more than anyone. In after years, to salve their consciences, they used to swear that the prince was an adventurer, like all the others Brittany has been cursed with, and their loyalty to him, as his to them, had been suspect from the start. All these hidden conflicts Henry's offer played upon, and since, in the final instance, a fish in a net is worth two in the pond, the Bretons agreed to disband their camp and begin their retreat back to the borders of Brittany and Dol (which many of them now maintained they should never have left).

In this way, shrugging their shoulders over Prince Taliesin's fate and the fate of his men, they left the prince to find his own way home. (And some of his men did reach their own land. But many more died, caught now between these contending treacheries. The remainder, clinging to the hope that Prince Taliesin would be found alive at Falaise, came there looking for him, an opportunity Henry did not miss. He employed them as mercenaries himself, thus making the Welsh bowmen part of the English defense. But those Welsh soldiers never saw their prince again; the Celtic alliance was broken, and the siege of Falaise ended forthwith.)

I have spoken little of Taliesin these past weeks, although he was so close at hand that sometimes if the Lady Olwen could have cried his name he might even have heard her. Deliberately I have not talked of him. What should be said of him, a warrior, engaged in the greatest exercise of the war, all his energies pinned on it, all his abilities at full pitch, either to hold back the temperamental Bretons or urge them on. Wiser than his years in council, he was, after all, a young man, careful not to offend yet in his own way burning to succeed. If he thought at all of Olwen, he must have imagined her safe at Sieux. But perhaps he did not think of her. Perhaps, like my mistress herself, he kept thought down. In the midst of war and death, personal desire seemed painful, too real, to let intrude upon the present world. What then of Taliesin this momentous day?

The prince was well aware of the treacherous nature of the king. He would suspect some trick when the king's messenger arrived, the same who had brought the news of the Celt advance and who now carried the news that would drive them away. The poor man sweated in his heavy robes of purple and gold, fidgeting with his staff of office, surrounded by these wild cut-throats, who, he thought, would as soon gut a man as look at him, while Taliesin had him read aloud, carefully, point by point, what the king's offer was. The message to Taliesin was clear enough. King Henry knew the best way to tell a lie was to speak as much of the truth as can be told, and what he offered must have made the prince feel as if he saw a light at the end of a dark and lonely road. If suddenly he realized that, at last, against all hope, his quest was done, that he could go home honorably to Afron, that he could go honorably to Sieux, well, he may be forgiven his little moment of triumph. And if he never thought ahead—who those hostages were, how he was to get them back, what his father would do with them—having grown used to living day by day, he perhaps had lost the in-clination to search the future as carefully as he should. And knowing, as he did, that the king had to break the siege soon, it seemed reasonable this was the way the king would choose.

To the king's offer then: Henry made no bones that he would not humble himself before a man half his age, for whose country he had only contempt, albeit he had failed to invade it twice. He did admit that his treatment of his hostages had been "over-hasty," a nice euphemism for killing them. He offered border-lands north of Chester (making of its present overlord another enemy), and finally he suggested hostages of his own in recom-pense. He did not lie about their status: offspring of a count, an earl, a border lord. He only omitted to give their names, or to explain that one was the lady whom Prince Taliesin wanted, too. He also omitted two other things. The first was that he had resolved to ride with his men himself, and himself rescue the Lady Olwen. The second, of minor significance—he omitted me.

Now why King Henry chose to go out on an expedition of this kind is hard to explain. It may well be that, fretted by inactivity, the idea appealed to him, the more because it was the sort of venture that in his youth he would have enjoyed. Perhaps he feared his queen and, at the last, could not trust her not to try and cheat (as indeed she did, for if she planned for Gervaise to do the rescuing, neither would Henry have the chance to keep the lady as he intended). Perhaps he simply wanted to ensure there was no mistake and that the two men were taken alive and handed over to him. Perhaps he wanted to impress the lady and ensure no blame fell on him. I think beyond all these reasons lay his simple curiosity to see in action this prince who had almost bested him once before. But most of all, it was a personal challenge, to pit his aging strength against youth, which on all sides now appeared to threaten him.

As for me. When Lady Olwen was told to leave, in haste, hurried along while still dark into the main courtyard, where horses and men were prepared; when Gervaise rode up on his bay horse, his forehead furrowed, his cheeks wet with sweat, although the day was young; when Hue was led out, nay, dragged, toward a horse, how could I be left behind? The soldiers had bid my lady ride astride, no hardship for her, and enveloped her in a long heavy cloak such as soldiers wear, with a hood drawn low to hide her face, so that she was indistinguishable from the men. Gervaise was dressed in the same way, so were all who were to accompany us, we, of course, having no idea of what was planned, and Gervaise knowing only snatches of it. But when Hue was hoisted upon his horse, his half-stifled cry as they thrust the reins into his broken fingers gave me the chance to dash forward and offer to lead him. They laughed, threw me up in front, and told me to ride instead. "God's mercy," behind me I heard Hue groan, part in anguish, part mockery, "the manikin to take me by the hand." But when I leaned against him and he felt the outline of my little sword (which I had thrust, unbeknownst to anyone, beneath my shirt), then he laughed no more.

We clattered out of the main gate openly, a flag of truce borne in front of us, six Norman soldiers in line, all cloaked and hooded over their mail, we in the middle, then six more behind, fitting escort for a delivery of prisoners under treaty. But when we had gone down the steep incline and come within the edge of the woods, where today no one waited for us, the spearmen, bowmen, Celtic outposts, all withdrawn as the Bretons leaders had agreed, in the thick underbrush we found more of the king's men waiting, positioned there secretly, at night, ready to set the ambush that would surround Prince Taliesin.

Behind me in line rode the Lady Olwen, her horse led along by a Norman knight. Terrified at what this activity meant, obviously relieved that Hue was not to be killed on the spot, my lady said not a word, biting her tongue to keep her anxieties to herself, hoping against hope perhaps that Hue would be freed, never for a moment imagining that she would see Prince Taliesin, and never in such wise. But her looks at her brother were eloquent, to comfort and reassure him. She had not ventured into the cells since that first day, not wanting to impose her presence upon him; and the way he threw back his head, as if scenting out the fresh air, the morning dews, all the summer day beginning to brighten around us, made her begin to think her prayers were to be answered. Cruel was that king to have planned such a trap.

In front of us rode Lord Gervaise astride his own horse. Although like the rest of us he wore heavy cloak and hood, I noted his nervousness at once, unlike any I had seen in him; he fingered his sword hilt as if estimating how long it would take him to unsheathe it. What he had been told by then I did not know, but something he knew, to make his round, innocent face withdraw into its hood with a peaked look, and his blue eyes, what glimpse I caught of them, seem hunted, almost furtive.

Hue noticed, too. "What devilry?" he muttered in my ear, and shifted himself so that the blade of my knife was within reach. And well he did. For having advanced out of sight of the castle walls, to the wood's edge, the Norman escort stopped in their tracks. At a sign from their hooded captain, they showed their true intent. Wordless, they bound our wrists and thrust gags into our mouths, efficiently and fast. They did this to all of us, even Gervaise, whom they also disarmed (I suspect he had not expected that), but at least I had time to hiss to Hue to remember the Cambray men still abroad, and to begin to whistle the bird's call, before they thrust the thong into my mouth.

Their captain gave a sign, and again we moved forward, silently now, toward the meeting place. It had been well chosen, for Henry knew Falaise and its hunting grounds. A rocky defile, ridged with trees, it lay east of the castle, on the side where the Celts had previously kept but scanty watch, having judged the spot a barrier of itself. It was far enough from the castle not to seem dangerous, inside the perimeter that the Celts had kept so that we did not appear to be trying to escape, and our main escort was small to be in keeping with its purpose. (And afterward we learned that in his thorough way, Henry had ordered a feint be made to the south by the rest of his household cavalry from Falaise, to draw away what might remain of the Celtic troops and to keep them occupied at this time.)

The path wound in and out, following the course of a woodland stream that presently, as the gulley steepened, began to fall in short cascades, widening at the foot of two ridges into a deep pool. On either side wooded slopes spread to contain a kind of scooped-out hollow, long and flat, although hemmed in with trees. And on the southern rim Henry's ambushers began to filter out, slipping silently among the thick underbrush, waiting until Prince Taliesin appeared. And thither now we descended the rocky path, we four prisoners gagged and bound, almost blinded by those heavy hoods, the bait with which the trap was to be set.

Almost all of us, that is. Beneath the folds of thick cloth, I felt Hue reach cautiously for the edge of my knife. I cannot explain to you with what agony his wrists and hands had already been tied, nor how with exquisite pain he now untied them, rubbing the edge of the thongs back and forth against the knife, the blade itself, by turns, slipping and digging against my backbone, so that in the end we were both streaked with blood from a score of cuts. Nor can I explain with what careful, drawn-out, torturous effort he untied the gag in my mouth. I felt him shake with it, as, at each turn in the path, or curve, he tore at the knots with his bleeding nails, or forced his fingers to bend and move, all beneath that heavy cloak so that no one saw. But it was done; I could speak and yell, and his broken hands were locked about the hilt of the knife, all done before we plunged down that last incline in a slide of stones. And there, at the far end of the open space, Prince Taliesin was waiting for us.

Now the prince had never made a secret of his own personal vow and, ever since the start of this last campaign, had openly spoken of it with his companions. And to tell the truth it was something these fickle Breton lords might well admire, for they held vows of this kind, made to avenge personal wrongs, as most sacred. Feudal vows, Norman oaths of military strategy and policy, they cared not a fig for, but personal honor, that they understood. Taliesin had not thought then to explain to them thoroughly all the details of the king's message to him. What explanations he had sent were obviously lost somewhere in the general confusion of the time, the more so, as I have explained, since the Breton lords, almost at once, had decided to withdraw their troops. But Taliesin had learned a lot from these Breton lords. Honed to sharpness these past six months like Gervaise, hardened by war, he had begun to know how to deal with these wily Normans and had not walked unwarily into their trap. He had brought his own bodyguard, and they worth twice as much as any other men, and as was later proved wise, he had set bowmen in the trees on the opposite side of the ridge from which the Normans should approach. They, spotting Henry's additional troops, began to prepare themselves, at once seeing the sense of their prince's strategy, to expect some underhanded move. And there were still our three Cambray men, somewhere nearby, for I was sure they had not been captured, else would Taliesin have known of our whereabouts. And like all border men, they could move as warily as the Celts when they chose and were worth a dozen Norman knights.

So there we came, the bait. There appeared Taliesin, on his black horse. I caught but a glimpse of him, armed I saw, like a Norman with captured booty and with his six taciturn men at his back. At Hue's nudge I threw back my head, howled out the cry of our house, and as best I could whistled aloud the Cambray call, whilst Hue tried to lift up my sword.

That cry, that painful gesture of defiance, almost cost us our lives. The Norman leader, who had reined up expectantly, either in salute or to signal to his hidden men, at once spun around and with a fearful curse lunged at us. His own hood slipped; I saw the king's face, even as he knocked Hue backward with a blow to his head. Hue fell, the horse startled, plunged forward, the reins slid through my hands, and I fell, too. Together we rolled over and over down the gulley to the edge of the pool, kicked and trampled underfoot as the king gave the signal for his men to charge.

I do not remember much of that initial charge, drifting in and out of consciousness as the air filled and rippled with the shouts and screams of men and steeds, the thudding of hooves, the slice of swords. I remember the taste of blood, the heat of the sun as it beat down between the leaves, the coldness of the water to my waist, where Hue and I lay together, he still half under me, his face a mask of blood. I remember finding and holding on to my knife with some thought of self-defense. I remember seeing the prince and his men stand firm, even as Henry's first charge smashed against their spears, even as down the south-facing slope the rest of the ambushers now appeared, the sun glinting on their lances like a silver line. And overhead, like dark hail whistling, like a wind of steel, I remember how the Welsh arrows fell upon these advancing knights.

Better, I think, not to remember it. Better not to have been forced to watch, bound and gagged but eyes free, as did my little lady. Nor to do as Gervaise, whose bonds had been already freed as the queen had promised, to seize a sword from a fallen comrade and fight, not knowing which was enemy, which friend.

I pieced together what happened afterward. It was a rout that made no sense. Henry's men should have won. For even those arrows, although they took their toll, could not be used when men fight hand to hand. And the king was an old and experienced warrior. He knew how to make best use of men, and even decimated, he had more soldiers than Taliesin's seven. Down the open turf like a tilting field the Normans charged, were beaten against the Welsh shield wall, swept back and forced to charge again, Henry urging them on, himself in the midst of the fray. And riding with him, desperate, came Gervaise, who forced that bay horse of his against the prince, howling what he believed as truth, "Welsh treachery be damned," determined in only one thing, that to him would fall the honor of saving his bride and of killing the man he loathed, as the queen had promised him (although Henry had decreed he wanted Taliesin alive). These were Henry's best men, the ones he relied upon. They had never failed him before, they might not have failed him then, had not in the rear of the king a third force appeared.

A little force it was, a bird's cry in the air, a hawk's cry, and like hawks they swooped, our three men, charging down the gulley path, seeming to multiply to ten times their number, seeming to swell and fill an emptiness. Now it was Henry's men who in turn sensed a trap. Like a wave they had poured down to overwhelm their opponents, like a wave their force was spent. Thrust upon the Sieux guard at one end of that open place, thrust back against the Welsh spears at the other, they began to waver, fragment into groups, hover, despite the king's insistence. And Taliesin took advantage of that hesitation. His own men, who had closed ranks to make their shield wall, began to move apart. From their closed line they started to fan out, their long spears still snaking from their shields, until each one had room to draw his sword, beginning now to hack a way clear toward their Sieux comrades, whom they recognized by the colors they wore. So, gradually, a way was cut through to the place where Hue and I had rolled, where the Lady Olwen waited, guarded by two men.

It must also have been obvious to the king by this time that he had made a mistake. He might even have sensed it from the very moment when he had heard our battle cry and Hue had tried to hoist my sword. He certainly realized it now, the trap that he had so carefully set beginning to shut him in. His own men, those left, were not cowards; they did not try to run but closed ranks, encircling their king, and in a mass sought to cut their way out. But in this, too, they could not succeed. Gasping, grunting with effort, their horses blown with it, in the end they could fight no more, just stood and waited to be worn down.

Then it was that the king called a halt. "Hold," he cried, "hold back. Parley, I claim, in the king's name."

Taliesin heard him, pushed up his helmet, too, had his men lower their swords and shields, glad for a small respite. I cannot tell you if he knew anyone. Certainly he had never openly met this king; he would not have seen Hue in the mud; he did not realize Olwen was there; and he did not recognize Gervaise.

But Gervaise knew him. From beside the king, where he had been fighting with the rest, caught up in the wash of men back and forth, bewildered, the plan the queen had laid for him to rescue Olwen come to naught, Gervaise of Walran gave a cry of pure rage. Like a man run amok, he rode out to break the king's parley, straight at the prince. It was the one thing he seized upon; whatever else not made clear, this was, that the prince would barter for Gervaise's bride. And that was a lie that the queen had told.

"Rot you to hell," Gervaise cried. "By the rood I run you down, treacherous dog." And uncaring that he acted as no knight should, to strike against a foe unprepared, in the midst of talk, he hurled himself and his horse with all his might. His sword came flailing down. The prince had no time to throw up his shield, barely succeeded in parrying Gervaise's sword, caught it full upon his own, thrust up his arm so that Gervaise's hold slipped. And as that bay horse careened past, with his free hand he hit at it to make it swerve. Off-balanced by the blow, Gervaise lost control of his horse, that Norman knight who boasted of his horsemanship. Crazed now with defeat, overcome, I think, with a sense of shame, he staggered in the saddle, tried to turn his beast, tried to run it full upon Taliesin, and almost without lifting his own weapon to defend himself, threw himself with all his weight upon the prince's descending blade. There was a gasp, an inrush of air, like a sigh. Gervaise tried to speak, choked, bent over the saddle as if catching his breath. "Rot you all," he whispered, through lips that had turned red, "kings and princes, both, and your treacherous feuds." He tried to say something else, choked again, toppled slowly to the ground, lay there puddled in scarlet against the green. Well, to die of treachery is perhaps better than to live with it. But so he died, Gervaise of the merry smile and proud look, although I think he first died long ago at Cambray, when he put his hand to war and fame.

All this I was told afterward. I saw it not, nor did Hue, both of us lost to consciousness. But the Lady Olwen saw, numb with horror, unable to cry or make a sound, forced to watch as her betrothed, the man she had promised to wed, died on the point of her lover's sword.

But some of the rest I did see for myself, from the mud banks, when the world came back in sickening waves. Henry was saying, "In the name of England, I ask a truce. Let me and my men withdraw in peace."

Taliesin said softly, trying to recover breath, "I know now what trust to put in you, King of England, whose words are writ in water."

Henry's face was infused with red; he seemed to bloat with it, and his gray eyes, ever prominent, grew hot with temper as they had with lust. He, too, tried to speak, but anger choked him. He tried to argue; shame silenced him. From the water's edge, where I held Hue's body out of the mud, sheltering his head with both my bound arms, I watched the king draw his sword.

"Fight with me, then," he cried. "You claimed it as a right. I give it you." He and Taliesin began to advance upon each other without ado, the king quick, determined, angry but not so angry that he was not in control, Taliesin gone past anger, cold and hard. From their huddle the king's men gave a groan, folly for a king to give combat like this, an honor that was seldom granted ordinary men. But from both ends of this arena, from the southern ridge, where the Welsh bowmen had appeared, there was a cry jubilant; the prince threw up his arm, the gold bracelet gleamed, and he smiled as if he claimed combat as his right.

They say, men say who saw them fight, that the two horsemen spurred together, their breath coming in great gasps, each blow forcing the wind out of them. Shield rim to rim rang until the air was numbed, their swords hammering, hammering, like an incessant drum. They say the king was a canny fighter, deadly quick, full of tricks. His horse carried him unfalteringly; tirelessly the king rode; tirelessly he raised his shield to push and force; tirelessly he used his sword to stab and slash, sweeping right and hacking left, turning his horse in and away from the return blow. But they say that Taliesin was quicker, more alert, making up by practice and courage what the king owed to long experience. And having one advantage, that since he had never held his stallion on the curb bit since that first day he had ridden him, he rode now with only heels and voice, so that he had both hands to lunge and thrust, could turn quicker, make a feint and swerve. And in the end, they say, he pushed back his helmet, laughed, and swept down as he had done at Cambray. But this time it was the king's sword that flew into the air and arched away.

They say Henry, covered with sweat, panting with a sudden fear, shouted, "Kill me, and all of France will hunt you down. A king's murderer, you'd never escape from Normandy alive. But safe conduct I promise you to the coast, you, your men, and your hostages. My life for theirs."

They say the king cried, "Take your hostages and give me life. Or I will kill them first."

They say he snapped his fingers so that the two guards who held the lady pointed their swords at her throat and threw back her hood. For the first time that day the prince and the lady looked full at each other, and the prince knew who she was.

And the king, on seeing their look, whispered, "Let me go; take your prisoner, Prince, as you agreed."

Well, the prince let the king go. Back Henry withdrew, close under guard, his men milling around him, our men opening a path to let him through. Back to Falaise he spurred, where he called out his army, bid them search and kill, set after the Bretons with full force, stormed the castle of Dol and captured it along with the Breton rebel lords. As for his queen, the king bid her prepare to leave. For sixteen years thereafter he imprisoned her, and never saw she Poitiers again. But the stain of that betrayal that he had planned he could not shake; nor the order to take and kill us. So much for a safe conduct. And he ordered no one to write or mention this event, so it never has been writ before. Behind him in that small hollow he left the wreckage of his plans, the dead, the dying, while Prince Taliesin, his sword still red from Gervaise's blood, gazed at the lady who believed she was his prisoner.

The delivery of the hostages had been planned for dawn. It was near midday when I again knew where I was, awareness lurching beneath me like the saddle I was on. I felt as if I had been flogged, my body on fire, and I had only lain still while others fought! The motion of the horse seemed far away, both familiar and strange, not related to me or the man who was riding behind. I remember the sky seemed brighter, the trees more green, even the dust motes dancing in the sun, which filtered in streaks between the leaves, seemed golden bright. We rode on. We rode, rode all day, I think, and at the end of the hot afternoon, when those soldiers of Taliesin put us down, I realized at last we were safe. Safe for the moment, that is, from Falaise and Henry's pursuit.

Little needed to be done for me; a few rough bandages around my bruised and bleeding ribs, a healthy slap on the back to make me sit up, a rough soldier's laugh when I coughed and spat. Lord Hue was a different case. The broken hands and fingers they could reset while he lay in a swoon; the open wound that gaped across his forehead along one eyebrow, that they could pull close, although the bleeding was long done, washed away in the water's cool. But they could do nothing for his lack of consciousness. He lay breathing heavily; the good eye half open, already the sheen of fever on his skin. I suppose it was luck he breathed at all, but it was obvious he was too sick to ride much farther and needed special care and rest. And when, looking around cautiously, for the slightest movement or turning of the head jarred my spine and made me retch, I saw the Lady Olwen sitting apart, head buried in her knees, I felt my spirits sink. The thick brown cloak was thrown over her, as if she still wished to hide behind it, and it, too, was blotched with great dark stains that had stiffened through the folds. I tried to crawl to her, each step seeming to last a year, but she would not speak to me when I came up, lost, I suppose, in her own terrible memories. The marks of the thongs had left welts across her cheeks, and her wrists were raw. But it was the blank stare that eventually she turned on me, the empty eyes, that set my pulse racing with new dread.

Prince Taliesin was conferring with his men. One by one I counted them, taking in suddenly the rips and tears on their mail coats, the bloody rags, the cuts. There were not so many as before, five left of his guard, two men of Sieux, and even as I counted them the Sieux men saluted him, saluted each other, and began to ride away, one heading east, one directly south. Prince Taliesin, too, had not escaped unharmed. There was a dark and bleeding bruise on his face where a shield rim had caught, and along his arm a long open wound where Gervaise's sword had slashed through his mail sleeve. But it was his look that also held mine, stern, unsmiling, no sense of relief, or joy, as he might have shown, only darkness. And I suddenly remembered what the king was supposed to have said, what the lady had heard, "his" prisoners, as "he" was supposed to have planned.

Perhaps he sensed my look. He turned in his saddle and returned it; there was a pride, a sadness, in his eyes that haunted me, and when he came up to my lady, pride and grief were in his voice. Yet he spoke graciously, giving her a choice, allowing her to understand what lay ahead, explaining the predicament, not to alarm but to ensure she knew what was being done.

Taliesin said, "My lady, I fear the road to Sieux is already blocked. The king's troops have come storming out of Falaise, like bloodhounds on our trail. My messenger, whom I sent previously to report to my Breton comrades, tells me they are retreating fast with Henry in hot pursuit. I bade him follow to see if shelter can be claimed among them or if they will honor us. I have sent your men back by stealth to see if they can force a way through to alert Sieux. I do not believe they will succeed." Bleakly he spoke, to have sent men he admired to certain death, but she made no sign she had heard him. "As for your brother, he cannot go on."

She did not reply, simply nodded her head beneath its hood as if the thought of speaking sickened her.

He continued insistently, "A decision must be made. A night in the open is nothing for us, but for you? And for your brother it may be fatal. With your permission I will send someone ahead to scout for a resting place. Somewhere in these hunting lands I have been told there are charcoal burners with their huts; there we could spend this night at least. But if we hide among them, we must go west, not south to Sieux. The king will have put a price upon our heads; every crossroad will be watched; we may not be able to circle back."

Calmly he spoke, in a formal way, with as much regard as if he were discussing a hunting field, west or south, which track the lady would chose. But the lady was the game that was hunted today; so were we all.

My lady's voice was dull, so lifeless, I scarcely recognized her. "As you will," she told him. "We are prisoners in your hands."

I saw the flush that overflowed his face at her charge, one he neither denied nor accepted but suddenly seemed to understand, the accusation that King Henry had thrust on him, the king's last trick. Well, in truth, hostages he had wanted, and now he had them, to his despite, certainly not in this way and not these. And so I thought, in pity for him (for whatever my lady said, that charge I, at least, did not accept), now has his oath come back to curse him.

He gave her his hand, but she did not take it, only swayed to her feet by herself, clinging to a tree bole. He whistled up his horse, but she gestured instead to one of his guard, who, red-faced, at last came forward at his master's nod and took her up instead. Another trooper took up Hue, a third me, whatever spare horses we had brought from Sieux lost somewhere in the confusion of escape. Seeing Hue, Olwen pushed back her hood and took his arm where it lolled across the man who held him. Lifeless, gray seemed his face, except for that matted wound, as if all vitality had drained from him; only the blood still seeped from his fingers. She crossed herself and seemed to mutter a prayer. "As God is my witness." Then she cried for the first time that day, all the pent-up grief and fright pouring out. "Why do you keep him alive, why send away our last men to leave us alone? Hostages you wanted, now you have us. And if we do not suit, why not kill us, too? You have already killed Gervaise; murderer once, why not murder again?"

Taliesin's men, those loyal men who had fought that day for her, yea, and died for her, growled, but Taliesin hushed them. His mouth tightened in a line, the skin stretched thin along the fine cheekbones; you suddenly saw what he would be like in old age, when determination had hardened and deepened. She had not even noticed the state he was in, he and his men; exhausted, wounded, I doubt if they had the energy left for one more charge; their horses weary, carrying double burdens most of them, a pitiful remnant, with all of Henry's army searching for them. He would not dispute with her. But I sensed his thoughts. "Think that of me," he seemed to say, "then I am not worth the ground you walk upon, and you, less to me, to put such shame upon my name."

He swung himself upon his black horse, gathered up the reins, and wearily lifted his arm for the forward march. On we rode, deeper and deeper into those great woods, the hunting preserves of the dukes of Normandy, where now the Normans were hunting us.

I could not have thought Normandy so wide, nor our pace so fast. Out of the five men left, Taliesin posted one ahead to act as scout; another dropped behind to keep rear watch. But Henry's men knew these forests, too, and would follow us. A group of horsemen, even a small group, cannot ride through woodlands and hide their tracks, although we kept to no fixed path and seemed to wind by instinct ever deeper and deeper among these endless trees. Knowing all this, aware of the danger he was in, hampered by his "prisoners" (whom, if my lady had been able to think at all, she would have realized he would have long since abandoned if we were, in truth, his captives), Taliesin now began to show some of the skills that had made his rise so fast among the Breton lords. Turn by turn with his men, he rode ahead, rode behind; wherever he could, taking advantage of the natural lie of the land to push forward; wherever he could, following the course of water beds, running water being a good way to throw hounds and huntsmen off the scent. Once we skirted around some sort of farm; a second time, having come too far south, we doubled back to avoid a village, surrounded by thick thorn hedge, just as the dogs inside began to bark alarm. And perhaps another two, three, hours passed before he again drew rein.

We were still within the forest, the Norman love of hunting that made them leave so much land untilled coming to our aid. The twilight had settled, thick and heavy, the air close and hot, as if all the tension of the day were gathered overhead in a great and heavy knot hanging above us. We had readied a small glade, where there was a ruin of a hut, not one used by the charcoal burners, for they make more comfortable dwelling although their work is hard. This was a woodcutter's shelter, its roof of branches half torn off, its wooden walls gaping, little shelter here, and no defense. But we could go no farther, and that Taliesin recognized.

Inside, under the tumbled roof, there was a dry patch where we could set down the injured man, and in the clearing a small stream from which one of Taliesin's men scooped water in his helmet to bring us. Lady Olwen, seeming to recover somewhat, I thought, less numb with shock, bathed Hue's face and tried to keep him warm, for now he shivered constantly. I remembered how his brother, Robert, had shivered long ago, and thought to myself that fate had certainly repaid him in full.

Myself, although stiff and sore, a mass of bruises, I finally went outside. The two men left on watch barred the way, polite but firm. Their horses were tethered at the edge of the clearing; they themselves, although still full armed, were busy sharpening up their swords, dulled by the morning's work. "Save you, masters," I whispered at them, through parched lips, "what place is this? Where are the rest of you gone?" For it was clear to me at once that they were left here alone.

They nodded in their laconic way toward the stream where

I could wash. "No farther," they warned, "guards beyond." I would not have gone anywhere in any case, but I did not believe them, no sign of anyone, nothing but the dark, ominous woods, green and heavy, stretching for miles. Then I began to wonder where Prince Taliesin was, where the pursuit, where even we were, lost in this maze. Away in the distance there came a sudden rumble, and a swirl of air set the leaves all aquiver, set my own pulses racing, the thickness of the day settling again like a heavy cloak.

Hearing that far-off sound the guards sprang to their feet; one threw back his head and sniffed at the air, like a deer that scents out danger, threat. And again we heard it, growing closer, the foretaste of a summer storm. They beat each other on the backs, those two men, eyes suddenly bright; they straightened themselves, went to their work with new energy. "A storm, boy," one explained, as if to an idiot, as if that word "storm" said all.

"By Saint David," the other cried, "our prince was right. It comes in good time." And in time it came, bursting on us in its fury, ripping through the trees, snapping them back and forth like twigs, turning the stream to a quagmire, pouring down upon us the gathered anguish of the day. For a while I stood out in it to let the rain beat upon me and wash me clean. What is the wrath of man compared with the wrath of God? Only afterward I realized, as those men had done from the start, that this storm would save us. Nothing else could have done. All Taliesin's hunting skills, all his fighting ones, could not have prevented Henry's men from finding us, they were so fast in pursuit, following every sign we left. The storm washed our traces away, as if we had never existed, drowned every sign of us as if, in truth, we had been drowned. And saved the prince.

For, knowing how close the enemy was, how fresh mounted, how wild with desire to wipe their humiliation out in blood, the prince had doubled back to the best possible place for defense, he and three men, to make their last stand, to buy us a few more hours' grace. The storm caught him, but it also caught Henry's knights, in the open, unprepared, such sheets of lightning, such cloudbursts that they faltered and would not go on.

Most of them turned tail, forced to walk or swim to the nearest settlement and wait out the storm there, then slink home to Falaise. The few, those of Henry's own household guard, who hung on grimly, were cut down by Taliesin. Easily caught, blinded by rain, buried in the mud, their honor trampled to bloody shreds, a bitter ending they made, too. God, I think, gave us that storm to save us and save the prince. Yet even now as I give thanks for such mercies, I also pray for the souls of those men whose deaths achieved our gain.

In all other things, though, God was not so gracious. Inside the hut we tried to drag Lord Hue to a safer place, out of the cold. The rain blew in through the ruined walls and roof, and the thick cloaks were not much use, soon heavy and sodden through. Taliesin's men helped us, rigging up a kind of shelter with wet sticks over which they spread their own cloaks, against an inside wall, and while we three huddled within, they crouched patiently outside. But Celts are used to rain. They began to talk in broken whispers, and I sensed in them a hope that had not been there an hour before. I had a memory of them around their campfires at Cambray, how they had seemed prepared to sit and watch forever until their master bid them move. So now they waited for their master's return. There is a story told among the borderlands that in a battle with the Normans a young Welsh prince was killed. His hound, faithful to him, sought him out among the dead, stood on guard, would let no one approach, until in the end death came for him, too. Both were buried in one grave and a marker set above, in remembrance of loyalty. Faithful like that hound, those Celts waited out the storm. And when at last they heard the sound of approaching hooves, they snatched for their weapons and stood prepared, not questioning anyone or fearing anything.

It was Prince Taliesin and his three men, bowed with weariness, scarce able to dismount alone. Their gear was wet, their saddles slippery with mud and slime, the reins black with it, all their trappings so smeared that it would have been hard to tell what color they were originally; only their swords were still sharp and bright. Whatever new wounds they had, they had been washed clean by the driving rain. They took care of their horses first, each man his own; on a forced march no time for ceremony. Somewhere along the way they had found grain for foddering, and there was plenty of grass. On the far side of our shelter they stripped themselves, rubbed themselves dry with handfuls of hay, patched up each other's cuts, pouring over them some sort of liquid that smelled vile but of which they drank gratefully what was left. Later, when the dark was full come, they gathered wood flakes, leaves, a bit of bark, to coax a fire out of the damp, to dry their gear, and hunkered around it, wrapped in their horse blankets, cleaning their soldier's weapons with precise strokes. Under cover of our shelter I watched them carefully. They spoke in Welsh, of course, and strange, even in this dreadful place (what shelter this for an earl's son, an earl's daughter, what shelter for a page who had grown used to finer things?), their voices had more about them of home than any of the fine places or people I had seen. They spoke in fits and starts, as do men who have gone beyond weariness, of strange, unrelated things, unimportant ones, as if this day had not seen them best the greatest king in Christendom, as if in the final count, it is only small, homey things that matter at all. And now they began to speak of their dead friends in matter-of-fact tones; of one's skill with a harp, of the other's love of a certain food, as if, even in this, they had no time for mourning. Yet one thing they did that struck me hard. They could not give their comrade, nor our one man, decent burial, had had to leave them where they fell, but they had brought with them their swords. These now they stuck into the ground so that the hilts made two crosses in a row. And in their talk I at once began to detect their puzzlement and their concern at how this morning's events had been arranged and who, in truth, lay behind the plan.

On the other side of that flimsy shelter, I say, we lay, trying to sleep, without food—for there was none—without comfort—an earth floor that was both damp and hard—with straw for pillows, and a saddle to lean against. But when I tried to tell my lady what I had heard, she pursed up her lips and would not listen, or could not, still numb, bewildered by shock. Too tired to argue, I would have slept myself, had not she, now in turn, begun to speak. So on one side I heard what Prince Taliesin thought, as he talked with his men, and on our side of the curtain I heard my lady, as she told me what she had seen and heard. It was like hearing and seeing the same thing twice. God forgive Henry for his cruelty, God forgive his queen. And God pity my little mistress who had to be the witness of their schemes.

She said suddenly, quietly, so I had to strain to catch what she said, words pouring from her like those sheets of rain, "I saw him die. I held him in my arms until he died, in the mud, like a dog. I held Gervaise's head, I tell you, and heard his last testament." She suddenly gave a cry like the one her mother had made. "I did not expect him to die," she whispered. "I turned aside his love; I did not want him to die of it." Most of what she told me then I have told you before, how she had had to wait there and watch, bound and gagged, so that even her mouth was stopped from crying out, even her eyes were dry. She saw how Gervaise rode against the prince, how he threw himself on the prince's sword, how he fell from his horse. She heard how the king offered her life for his royal one, and how he told Taliesin to take the prisoners the prince had sworn to have. But when her guards were hauled aside, free to ride off with the king, when the prince had slashed her thongs, I did not know that she had slid from her saddle and gone forward among the carnage of that place to where Gervaise had fallen.

"He was not yet dead," she cried. "Although hurt so grievously, he knew me. He tried to smile the way he used." The tears, unshed then, now coursed down her cheeks. "I sat beside him," she said, "and heard him speak. Do dying men speak lies?" She cried passionately, "Would he lie before God? He told me that Taliesin had made a treaty with the king, to leave Falaise in return for hostages. Gervaise was to be one, Hue and I the other two. But, warned by the queen, Gervaise was to be freed in time to rescue me. One of the guards was in her pay and had so agreed. The king's presence almost destroyed her plan." She looked at me, her eyes too large for her white face. "That is why Gervaise rode against the prince," she said simply, "that is why he died, to save me, who had promised to wed with him, I who made him first begin his love." She sat on the ground and picked at the dried blood smears on her skirts. "I am stained with Gervaise's blood," she cried. "What will wash away that guilt?"

I remembered what she had said at Cambray, many lifetimes away: *We are at the start of some enterprise that will destroy us all.* I remembered what her brother Robert thought: *Quarrels should not stretch so far to shadow our lives.* But vengeance lay around us, puddled like the aftermath of that storm. I had no words to comfort her, nor, like Taliesin himself, words to argue against hers. I knew her wrong, but she must find out the truth for herself. *Would a dying man lie?* It was the queen's lies that spoke through him.

So we were stranded, far from any expectation of help; no one knowing where we were; only enemies to ring us round; the prince's own hopes destroyed, save that of his own personal one, and what worth it, to fight against a faithless king? His men scattered or dead, his quest over, for what? To be dishonored in the lady's eyes? I grieved for her; I grieved for him. But there are some things even a bard cannot do. Their differences had to be resolved by them. Somehow Gervaise's love and death had to be atoned.

On his side of the division the prince was speaking more forcefully now, without rancor, although what he said might have embittered many men. For he was speaking again of his dead comrade. "He was of my father's bodyguard," he said soberly, "like you. We were lent to each other, you to guard me, I to guard you, until either death parted us or we returned. Death hitherto has passed us by. It lay in wait for us today. Tomorrow it may lie in wait for the rest of us. I should have killed that king like an unclean beast. I would have done so, had he not held at his mercy the lady and her brother, unknown to us. I could not kill them to kill him."

They nodded, no regret, no bitterness in them either. "So since this lady and her brother and their page are now our charge," he went on, "we cannot abandon them. Henry will not let them go. He may not seek us out immediately, and while we stay here, I think we may be safe. But he will be waiting for us. How shall we break out? I ask you, friends, companions all, what you advise. Your lives, as well as theirs, are at stake." Each man then present spoke in turn, not deferring to his lord but openly, as becomes free men. One pointed out that the Paris road east, back to Prince Henry, which Hue must favor if he could speak, would be impossible for them, the royal lands in any case forbidden them and all of Normandy to ride across. (And in truth I should add that Prince Henry never tried to help Hue.) Another wished to go north, to cross from the Channel ports, but he, too, was argued down, the Channel being the one place the king would watch like a hawk. That left but south and west. South, then, to Sieux.

"Suppose," the third man said (and I must tell you that I never learned their names, these men who to the outside world kept a distance and a silence, as unyielding as their shield wall), "suppose we sit here, or rot here more like," and he poked the dismal fire with a boot, trying to dry it out, "until the Earl of Sieux comes looking for us?"

"Impossible." His companion's answer was direct. "Those men of Sieux, God rest their souls, they ride upon a task impossible. They will never reach Sieux alive; and even if they do, Henry would never let them leave again. Sieux will be the first place Henry will look for us."

Since for clarity it should be known what happened to Sieux, I will tell you that Taliesin's men spoke truth. They never reached the castle, those two brave men of ours, each trying to find a different route back. Dead they were, caught somewhere by some hostile force, robbed of their armor, horse, and gear, left to rot in some ditch, part of the unknown casualties of war. As for the castle, contrary to all his old vows, Henry marched against it. When Henry's men arrived, they found it bolted close, for all that its lord still lay abed. They say Henry sent his feudal levies to besiege Sieux, not mercenaries, whom he could not trust, but men he could rely upon to hold a siege. And they say that when those troops arrived, it was the Lady Ann herself who came out upon the battlements to answer them.

Their captain was amazed. Keeping careful distance, out of bow shot, this officer rephrased the king's message for more delicate ears. His request, then, politely stated in more courteous terms than usually Henry used, asked for the king's prisoners to be given up, or, failing that, for Henry's troops to be allowed in to prepare a welcome for them.

Realizing at once that we must be still at large, the Lady Ann answered him like a man. "I speak for the Count of Sieux," she cried. She wore a mail coat like a knight and had pushed her hair inside a coif. She would have carried a sword had there been one she could lift easily. She spoke so loudly that even her seneschal, Dillon the swordmaster, who knew her of old, was startled that so slight a figure could command such strength. "Tell Henry, your king, as once my husband did, that not one stick, one stone, one life, shall he have at Sieux. We shall not proceed against him, loyal to our feudal oath and his, but tell your king he will never claim another inch of land from us. Make one move, and we smite him body and soul to hell."

Such was the message, it is said, the earl himself had sent to King Henry years ago, when Sieux lay in ruins. They say, too, that Henry's officer was so taken aback, he almost stuttered in reply. "My lady," he said at last, with a reverence akin to awe. "So shall I report to him. But it is not Sieux he seeks, only your sons."

"Then tell him this," she cried, her eyes ablaze. "As he has sons who defy him, how does he answer for them? Will he kill them when he catches them? Remind Henry it is not honorable to seek vengeance of a boy for wrongs that were done before his birth. Nor is it worthy of a king to use a girl to avenge a memory of another girl, years ago. Shame on your king, who has broken faith with us."

So she, too, defied the king, as have done other ladies of these times. And, they say, such was the impression she made that her injured husband, hearing it, cried, "By God, she swore she would lead a charge one day. Take care she does not try." And sitting up in bed, he could scarce be prevented from tumbling out to stop her himself. And, it is whispered, when neither she nor the earl are near, that a song is sung of her in those parts, no doubt a scurrilous one, how the lady of Sieux proved as valiant as a man and, not hesitating to act in her own right, bested men as might another man.

> *Bien fous les soldats du roi,*
> *Qui de la gente dame, dans leur*
>   *émoi,*
> *Croient vaincre les remparts,*
> *Quelle illusion, pour ces*
>   *soudards . . .*

And so on, the rest not suitable for gentle folk. And so Henry, although to his shame he besieged Sieux, did not capture it, and presently, losing heart, he withdrew again. But all this happened later. As we pondered in the forest, we knew only that we could not go there.

Well, the way to Sieux was barred. That left but west, westward through southern Brittany to the Atlantic coast.

Easily said, westward. First there were Henry's men to outwit, along the forest edge; then all of Brittany before us, where Henry's army was out in full force, the Breton rebels for the most part seized, the rebel castles under attack, all Henry's vassals warned to prove their loyalty by catching us. Not one castle, not one town, not one village was safe; already Henry's decree had been sent even to outlying farms where peasants might give us help, and death the punishment allotted for those who dared break his command. And what of us who would make this journey, enough to test the endurance of seasoned warriors? With but five men, one wounded lord, a lady, and a half-size page, how should we endure hardships that would make this ruined hut seem a palace? Where to get food, shelter, supplies? And when we reached the coast, where to go from there? I tell you, my heart sank as I listened to the Welshmen's plans. But so it was decided that night, our fate and theirs. And whether we would or not, we were bound to go with them.

Chapter 14

e stayed five more days in that hut, part hut, part ruin, not the best days I have ever known. Nor yet the worst; anticipation of what was to come might have made them seem an oasis in a barrenness. The weather continued fine after the storm; we had lodgings of sorts, and the following day, when the men were able to set their nets, small game to eat, caught in those sorts of traps that Lady Olwen had loved to set. Heat became more of a nuisance than cold, the canopy of leaves acting as a shroud, a coverlet, to keep it in, so that airless and humid, the little dell became a kind of tepid bath. By noon we were bathed in sweat and plagued with flies, which bred in swarms around the pools of drying mud. In one way the Celts were better served than we; their hours of guard duty done, they could strip down and, free of their weight of mail, lave their cuts or lounge along the water's edge.

Within the hut my lady kept watch of her own, sitting by her brother's side, his head in her lap so she could brush the flies away from his wounds. She seldom stirred, sat patiently, pinned down by his weight and by her heavy, clinging robes, her clothes still bloodstained. As for Lord Hue, he seldom moved either, but his fever did not worsen, praise God, and toward the morning of the third day his eyes flickered open before closing again in what seemed more like a natural sleep.

On hearing of this, Prince Taliesin approached. He had not come near us since that first day but punctiliously, with each changing of the guard, had sent one of his men to inquire for the lady's comforts or had let me run back and forth as messenger. To tell the truth her wants were few; all was for the sake of her brother, who, poor soul, had he but known, would have scorned such favors. For my own part, to act as messenger suddenly became a thankless chore, little to recommend it, certainly bringing nothing but ill will from both sides, so that even I began to balk at a service that offered such scant reward. I even vowed to myself that were we free from here, which, God willing, sometimes I thought we almost might be, the lord and lady could make their own peace without benefit of me.

I noticed at once, that predawn hour, that Taliesin's cuts were healing fast, but although he still wore mail and sword belt like a Norman knight, the hauberk would not last long, so hacked and ripped was it become that even his men's skill could not repair the damage done; an armorer was needed to patch the broken links. He ducked his head with its golden curls under the broken lintel and stood looking down at us in the semigloom, face shadowed. It was not easy to tell what he thought—certainly he gave no indication of feeling anything, no change in expression or voice, merely cold reserve—but I noted how his knuckles had whitened where he grasped his sword hilt hard, and I sensed, not saw, the sympathy that he felt for our predicament.

Lord Hue lay beneath the blanket, his hands stretched in front of him as he used to hold them at Falaise; he appeared asleep again, his long eyelashes, like to the lady's own, fanned across his cheeks. The Lady Olwen was leaning against the rough walls, for a moment caught off guard, her own eyes shut. She looked frail, her bones like sticks—one almost felt pity for her surge through the prince, but he beat it down. He did not speak or look at her but bent instead toward the sleeping man and said something in his ear, the words so shocking loud and bleak that we all started as if an arrow had come whistling viciously into our midst. "Ware arms," the prince had cried, the traditional order of attack. The Lady Olwen sat bolt upright and clutched her cloak. The effect on Hue was even more evident. His eyes opened wide, their grayness suddenly intent and alert, and almost imperceptibly, his fingers inched to where his sword would have been had he one, as if by instinct he reached for it, proof, if proof there was, that at least his soldier's training was intact. Lady Olwen soothed him, her hands soft and cool across his face, until, seeming to recognize her touch, he settled back to sleep again. But her words to the prince were less kind.

"Monster," she hissed at him when Hue's eyes were fast shut, "what do you want of my brother, to mock him thus?"

Prince Taliesin straightened himself up painfully, for a slash across his knee had stiffened and his rib cage was still bruised and raw where Henry's lance had caught. "Lady," he drawled, in that cold and distant tone he used for us these days, "at the week's end the moon will be dark. I hope, nay believe, the rains will return to give us the extra cover that we need. I plan to make a move at that time. But we cannot ride with an unconscious man. Seeing your brother now, I feel sure he will soon regain his wits, perhaps today. I trust you will help him regain his strength. For unless he understands what we do, we cannot move him, to his jeopardy and ours."

She cried, "He can never ride alone. One of you must support him."

"Then Urien must." The prince's reply was bleak. "I need all my fighting men. I cannot spare anyone to act as nursemaid. Arrange it as you wish, but we leave here at the week's end."

She gaped at him, then scrambled upright, her white thighs and long legs gleaming for a moment before she could straighten her skirts, her feet bare, mud-caked, as they used to be when she was a child. She pushed past the prince, her hair flying so that it hooked about the buckles at his belt, but she never paused, simply tore it free and went outside, her back rigid with offense. The prince hesitated for a second before following her, as did I, an air of resignation rather than anger in his eyes. But Lady Olwen was filled with more than a usual rage. Her dark eyes snapped, and her bare feet almost stamped with fury. "You want him to live," she cried, rounding on the prince, a wren fluttering its wings at a hawk's menace, "you want him conscious to know all that you do. What is it exactly you mean to *do* to us?" She emphasized the word. "What is it, monster, you will ask of us to gratify your pride, your revenge? Or am I mistaken, do you want to carry us all back dead?"

He let her talk on for a moment or so, standing nonchalantly in front of her, twisting the golden bracelets he wore, her words like rain to be flicked aside. And when she was done, "Lady," he said, in the same stiff, formal way, his own feelings held in check, "you speak with as little sense as if you, not your brother, had taken a blow to the head. Think. If you were Henry the King, how much longer would you grant us respite before you grew weary of the wait? Henry's men know where we are. It is a simple matter for them. All they have to do is decide which is easier: to let us try to break out or for them to come in. Sooner or later they will come. We have tested their patience long enough, and Henry is not a patient man. A few days more, and they will be on the move. I mean to catch them first before they catch me." He paused. "And not only these woods to cross," he added for her benefit. "We do not make a royal progress, as perhaps you would prefer, but a forced march."

"And if I insist we be left here . . . ?"

"Then you come by force," he said, almost disinterestedly. "You can ride or be carried. Facedown, across saddle, you'd not have breath left to complain. And in such likelihood my men may not be as gentle as I would be. They still mourn their dead companions, who died for you."

"Then send to Prince Henry, let him rescue Hue," she cried. "He is Hue's dear friend; he would reward you well."

A second foolishness that he ignored, although he might have pointed out that it was friendship with that prince that had first got Hue into such a state. Instead he merely said, in his dry way, "Aye so. But that prince would not honor us. Lady, whether you will or not, you must come with us. Remember," and now a bitterness did creep into his voice, "remember you swore once to follow me to the world's end; you wanted to be with me; you begged me not to leave you behind."

She did not know how to answer him. "That was in a different time," she said at last, hanging her head, speaking low.

"Just so." His reply was still dry, but his eyes had begun to smolder, with pain or regret I cannot say. "Just so. And thus in different wise is our leave-taking arranged."

"And what will your father do with us?" she next tried to outargue him, "murder, revenge, rape, which?"

He said, still reasonably, as if he should take her accusations seriously, "Murder and revenge are things all men can answer for; rape is more in a woman's line. What sort of rape would be to your taste, which would suit you best? And how would you have it arranged? Here now, or later, as you will."

She stared at him, her mouth half open, took a startled step back, put out her arms, thin like sticks, to ward him off. It was the sort of jest he might have made before, but there was not a mocking smile from him today, only anger in those dark blue eyes.

"We are your hostages," at last she gulped forth, "treat us with more respect."

"Hostages." He suddenly shot the word out at her, threw his head back, and laughed, not his hearty, boyish laugh but a sound threaded with bitterness to make her start back a second time. "Hostages," he repeated. "God's wounds, lady, you speak like a fool. What hostages? A wounded knight whose wits are gone, a half-pint page like a bag of bones, a sharp-tongued wench whose words would flay the skin from a man's back; a fine idiot I shall look to bring you home. My father's court would laugh me to scorn. Not hostages, lady, for my Celtic pride, but prisoners." He spun around to hurl that word at her. "Prisoners of war for me to do with as I will.

"Aye," he went on when she did not answer him, "aye, to leave you here might make sense, a weight about my neck, an added care. But I could buy my freedom with you if I had to. Have you not thought of that, mistress-know-all? Henry wants you back more than he wants me. A nice fat reward for you, no doubt to slake his royal lusts on you. So I take you for insurance at worst, upon a safe passage out for my men and me. Rape is it?" Again he made another menacing move to make her recoil. "That is a word to bleat about. Celts are not the only men who relish rape. Or do you think Norman knights are gods, accepting graciously what is offered them? Why do you think King Henry wanted you? Do you believe he meant for you to go off freely from Falaise, without even a farewell embrace?" She was silent, remembering perhaps her meetings with that king. "By the living cross," Prince Taliesin swore, truly angry now, "you are more naïve than I thought. He used you as bait, Lady Olwen, bait, as once you said you would never countenance for any living thing; true Norman bait for me and my men. So listen carefully that there be no mistake. You owe your life to us, and you have endangered ours. Yet for pity's sake we will not abandon you. Hue must be made fit to ride, and you, lady, ride with us."

He had crowded right against her, not as he once might have done; words he might have said in love or jest spilling out in bitterness, even little traits of her character that once had pleased or amused him held up for scorn. "Take care," he had told her, "words hurt." Now he showed her how. He looked down at her one final time. "I'll not have you as hostage, Lady Olwen," he told her simply. "My brothers' lives were worth much more." And he turned away from her.

Left alone, she began to follow him, hesitated, stayed where she was, by turns confused, thoughtful, and disturbed. She started to send me after him, then called me back. I soon realized I was useless as a go-between. Each of them felt the other was wrong, each was so convinced of being right that my sympathies were torn between the two. Now, I am honest enough to admit that I knew if they were to be reconciled, they would have to make the effort themselves. She understands her feelings better than I do, I argued silently; let her choose when and how to speak. But that was not quite the whole truth. Although this was not the time or place for such pettiness, I will confess I was mutinous, jealous. I knew the prince did not deserve to be estranged from her, but I felt that I was not obliged to help him back into her favors, which I would have liked to keep for my own. Since this is the only time my vocation failed, and if in the ensuing days I closed my eyes and ears, perhaps I can be forgiven. I could not watch unmoved; I could not spy; better, I thought, not to watch at all. I withdrew into my shell, did what had to be done, suffered for them, suffered myself. For these reasons, then, I shall let her tell her story in her way, as later I came to hear it. Later I could endure the telling; not then.

Twice she heaved a great sigh and looked sideways to see if I would respond, and once again, while Hue still slept, she went outside the hut and stood against the wall, on the side away from where the Celts made camp. But although she did not look at them, she knew of them, was aware of them; the more she looked away, the closer she seemed to lean toward them, as if in her very body she felt confused, as if in every part she was riven in two, longing to believe what her lover said, dreading that what Gervaise had told her was truth; longing to find Taliesin's love, fearful that she had forfeited it. "I did not know what to think," she after said, "thoughts beat in my brain like bat's wings. When I closed my eyes I saw Gervaise's face, a mask of pain; I saw those dreadful wounds, those gouts of blood. All I heard was his whispers, his suspicions, panted out with his dying breath. But superimposed I saw Taliesin. He was wounded, too, and I had ignored his hurts. He had fought with the king and won; to save my life, he had let the king go free, and I had not given him thanks. I could have better understood," she cried, "if Taliesin had disputed with me; if he had argued, shown anger, told me I was wrong. That cold, stiff bitterness, that cold, stiff pride, set up a barrier I could not break down. It reminded me," she dropped her gaze, "it reminded me of my father's pride, my father's way, so unlike my own. Or Hue's. I knew from the start I had done him wrong. But how was I to make amends? How apologize, say to a man, 'Forgive me, my lord, for calling you villain and murderer'?" She almost laughed at that thought, then cried, "I wanted to run and beg his forgiveness. But what should I have begged for? Ahead, such danger lay that even to think of personal quarrels seemed to add to my offense. There was no time to ask him to talk with me; I had forfeited his goodwill, I say, and had to abide the consequence. But even so I could not believe all love was gone, wiped away, lost, although I told myself it must be so. And every time he moved or spoke, once when he laughed (not that hateful, cold laugh but the one I remembered),

I felt desolate, as if that barrier kept us apart, two wraiths who mouth, wordless, across purgatory.

"I have never been so aware of anyone," she said another time, "for when he spoke with his friends (he and his guards were companions, not like those Norman lords who keep a distance between master and men), I have never seen anyone so alive. Life flared in him; I sensed it like a current, a wind, a flame. And, I think, despite his scorn, he was aware of me. Why else, when I looked, was he always looking aside; when I moved, he had just turned his back? Pride, my pride, kept me still in my place. And pride, my pride, kept me quiet. Once I would have dared say anything to anyone. That was before my lover became my enemy." And then she was silent, musing for a long while.

But presently, continuing in a more normal voice, "Well," she said, "it was just as well the weather broke. We could not have endured longer there, not like that, saying, doing nothing, feeling all. But how could the prince have been so sure the weather would change? Urien asked one of the guards, who winked his eye, tapped his nose, and cocked his head heavenward, by which gestures, I presume, he meant by signs: the smell of the wind, the path of the clouds, the feel of the air. And perhaps by prayers to God. I know I prayed. But what I prayed for, God Himself must have interpreted; I did not know myself, for even in my prayers I was confused. But the fine mist, the west country mist that followed, as if by command, was all that we could have hoped—not heavy rains this time to flood the streams and bog down our path, but light, drifting, so that we, like shadows, could drift through the trees, and a heavy sky without even stars to hinder us. We left at dusk. They had brought Hue out earlier and hoisted him on a horse with Urien in front of him. Hue was still weak, but these five days had made a difference. He could move and stand at will, although when he walked, he shuffled more like an old man, one foot slowly making way for the second one. It was not loss of strength that hindered him but loss of—how shall I say?—of will. Strength would return in time, and movement to his broken hands. It was rather there existed a gap, a divide, between what he wanted and what he did, as if a distance separated him from what he was. He could speak clearly enough, but he never began the talk, only replied; questions he could answer but not frame. I sensed it was difficult, nay impossible, for him to think thoughts of his own; and although I tried to conceal that lack, it must have been obvious to us all that not only should Urien ride for him, he must think and act for him, too, Hue who could master any horse that moved. My heart contracted for him, my brother whom I loved and fought and held in my heart like my own life, for whom I had given up happiness. When I saw him thus, led like a child by the hand, uncomplaining, whatever softer feelings I had hardened anew into outrage. And yet, I will be honest, had Hue his full wits, had he had control of himself, he would never have let us leave as we did. Sense would not have quieted him, nor danger, nor even physical weaknesses. And in that perhaps God showed his mercy, to dim for him the understanding, to bank down the fire.

"We started off in single file, Prince Taliesin in the lead on his black stallion, thrusting through boldly under the ranked trees, using his shield to batter through. These past days he and his men had not been idle, I grant them that, each day scouting out a trail and blazing it so that at the right moment we would know which way to go. Close behind him came Urien, with Hue; dear God, had I mirth to spare, I should have smiled to see my page lead out that horse and scramble onto its back, gathering up the reins like a knight new-spurred. Myself, I rode behind one of the guards. I was prepared, too, skirts bound up, knife ready and sharp, my hair tied under a cap, out of sight. I had thought to cut it off, but Urien had begged me not, and for haste as much as vanity I had left it alone. As for the knife, my Welsh rider bid me put it away. 'No need to stab me in the back,' he told me with a broken grin. 'You'll know when to use it if you must.' Behind us in line the other men wound along in their silent fashion, save one, who went at some distance in front, to act as scout on foot.

"The path they had patiently prepared cut straight across the forest wilderness, dipping and rising along the contours of the land so that sometimes we seemed to be plunged into ravines, at others breasting a cliff, but never losing cover of the thickest growths of trees, never following any known way. The summer foliage swung about us thick and damp; the moisture fell in great drops; we saw no one, nothing, save only once, breaking from the ferns beneath our hooves, a deer bounded away, its eyes bulging with alarm, its golden-flecked coat drenched with rain. Toward dawn I began to realize that however much we twisted and doubled around, the trees had begun to thin; once we skirted close to a kind of farm, but we never faltered from our easy gait, not fast, not slow, eating up the miles.

"It lacked two hours to first light when we finally came to a stop. The rain still dripped and blew in gusts, not enough to hinder us, only sufficient to cover our tracks; we had been hugging a long, thin finger of woods and had come to its fringe end. Beyond it stretched a hill of low-lying bushes and gorse, beyond again, an open road, gleaming white. The sight of that white road both startled and repelled, but the Celts were obviously relieved to see it. At this early hour it was still empty, winding along the forest edge before bending out of sight. Around that bend, we now learned, was the border town of Brittany. But how to reach the town, or cross the boundary, guarded here by a bridge that spanned the river whose course I now realized we had been following these past hours? Out of the forest, upon the plains, the river had widened, deepened, too wide or deep to ford, no way through except by this bridge. And athwart the bridge Henry's men had laid their barricade. From our halting place we could not see this, of course; but the prince's men already had, and they explained, with the help of sticks and stones, just how the guard was kept, where housed, when changed, each hour thirty men or more to bar the passage to anyone they were suspicious of.

"Silence followed, not a happy one. Thirty men. That number beat in my brain. I was ready to plead that we should retreat, but my rider bid me be quiet in no uncertain terms. 'On our own,' he told me in his laconic way, 'a river is easy to swim across. Now we must wait.' He meant, of course, 'with you in tow.' He had me dismount, pointed to a kind of gulley running down the hill, where we could hide, and began to lead his horse away, presumably to tether it out of sight. 'What next?' I began to ask but he put his finger to his lips. 'Watch,' he said. We watched. Farther along the hillside, closer to the road, the Celts hunkered down under cover of long grass and scrub. They did not look especially uncomfortable; they might have been sitting around their own campfires, and one was even whistling beneath his breath, a tuneless song, while he sharpened up his sword. As the darkness lightened, some early travelers went by, one or two at first, trotting back from some night adventure of their own—a young man still half drunk from wine or lust, a peasant with a cart of produce, an old woman carrying eggs. These were no use to us. A sudden louder sound made us all look up.

"Along the road, still out of sight, a group of horses was approaching, not fast, not slow, several of them, trotting along in military style, a regular entourage. And this, I think, was what the prince watched and waited for, not this procession in particular, but one like it, any of sufficient size that he and his men could use for disguise. If he had a plan other than this, I could not guess what it would have been, and my spirits quaked to think that he would take such risks.

"We waited. Slowly and steadily the hooves beat up the road until the little band came into sight. It did not seem so little as it began to unfold. Ahead rode the outriders, men-at-arms, resplendent in green and red, with an abbot's miter for their crest, riding fine battle steeds, escort to a most unwarlike group, ecclesiastical, as the six black-cowled monks proved. The sight of those fine horses made the Celts' eyes shine. One whistled again beneath his breath and ran his thumb across his spear; another crossed himself, muttering, 'Praise God from whom all blessings come that He has sent His gifts today,' before he, too, slid closer to the road. There were six mounted men in all, two in front, two more behind, and two on either side a litter, large, hung with leather and silk, swaying alarmingly between the mules who carried it. The riders rode, hands on hips, not especially energetic, not especially cheerful in the rain, not es-

pecially watchful. The monks strode on stoically, either telling
their beads or with heads bent low to avoid the wind. God sent
us His true gifts indeed. We took them with open arms.

"It was quickly done, and professional. Celts make the best
thieves in the world; stealing is but play to them, trained to
pick off a man's sword while his back is turned. They claim
they can unhorse a Norman knight and leave him sitting in
midair before he even knows his horse is gone. Now they
slipped like shadows along the road, two ahead, two behind,
two gone to fetch their own horses and charge. At a prepared
signal those four uncoiled like catapults beneath the very bellies
of the splendid mounts. One each to front and back, one each
to side and side, to tip the riders unceremoniously on the ground;
the last two, mounted themselves, to sweep down from the
woods, driving the frightened monks like autumn leaves. I tell
you, it was in an instant done; six riders sprawled without even
breath to shout alarm; six monks gibbering with fright; the
placid mules already turned toward the shelter of the trees; the
road stretching empty, white, and innocent.

"Within the confines of the litter all was not so quiet. The
leather curtains heaved and shook, and a head stuck out, a sleepy
one, prepared for complaint. 'By all the saints of Christendom,'
a priestly voice began to trumpet, 'by Saint Cyprian of Stefensforth, what goes amiss?' and a most unpriestly string of
oaths poured forth. Urien recognized that priest at once and
nudged me into awareness. We started up at the same time and
together ran down the hill. Who could forget that raucous, oath-
swearing voice, and to whom it belonged, the Abbot of Stefensforth, red-faced and fat, who, already pried out of cover by
the Celts, was shuffling along in his embroidered robes, protesting at his most impious.

" 'We know that abbot,' we cried in unison. 'He is of no
earthly use to us. He has already plotted against Henry last year.
He would have made us part of that plot and ambushed us to
make us join with him . . .' My own voice trailed into silence
as I realized it was the first time I had spoken of my free will
to Taliesin for many days—anything of import, that is—that

was not full of anger, disappointment, bitterness of my own. I owed the fat abbot at least some thanks for that.

"Taliesin was one of those on foot; he was tugging at the horses' bridles to fasten them to our own; some of his men were already gagging and binding the abbot's riders (any left who were not too dazed to move) and were stripping off the monks' black robes before binding and gagging them in the same way. The abbot, seeing what was planned for him, was already begging most piteously, his flesh cringing in anguish. I heard him offer gold for his own skin, nothing, of course, for his fellow travelers. I do not know if he knew us at first, too distraught to think of anything, too intent on saving himself, but we knew him, and so I told Prince Taliesin. I thought to warn the prince; instead he took my warning in another way.

" 'Ambush,' he repeated with a frown, 'trap you into rebellion. God's wounds, rebellion your brothers made soon enough.' Then he laughed. 'No earthly use, I think you said; we'll make use of him unearthily.' His laugh was a genuine one, warm, and full of good cheer. 'We'll have him call on God for help instead. As fellow conspirator, since he's so good at setting traps, we'll use him to walk out of one.'

"He looked at me almost pityingly that I was slow to catch his drift. 'God's my life, do I have to spell it out like a primer book?' But his men had already understood, were grinning among themselves, and Urien, too, had run back to bring Hue down. Thank God Hue at least obeyed and climbed into the litter without argument; wide enough that litter was to hold several men of ordinary girth, and covered with monkish robes, he and Urien were almost concealed. Taliesin threw me a cloak. 'Get you in,' he said as I stood as if rooted to the spot. 'Pull that knife you are so fond of brandishing. Prick it against the abbot's ribs, let him sweat a little lard off, that he do as we bid.'

"I clambered in, hugging to one side. It was warm and comfortable within the tent of curtains; there were rugs and furs, and a jug of wine and fresh white bread with which the abbot had been breaking fast. Outside we heard the prince addressing the abbot in mock reverence. 'My lord,' he was intoning, and there was a ripple to his voice that it had lacked; I only knew its lack on hearing it again, 'my lord abbot, I hear you are so well loved by Henry, our king, that you will speak for us to Henry's men. Tell them you long to visit the king to inform him of those plots you made and make confession to him of your part in the rebellion of his sons.'

"The abbot, caught mid-bellow in outrage, choked and wheezed in a new frenzy of fear as Taliesin's meaning hit home. 'Who are you,' he spluttered at last, 'that you speak of things better left unsaid?' He gave a fearful glance around, as if he expected Henry to appear from behind a tree. 'And who are you to threaten me, a man of God?'

" 'No one.' The prince's reply was cheerful. 'A mere passerby who wants to cross a bridge. You will achieve that for us, vouch for us to Henry's guard, protest your loyalty and ours. And to demonstrate your loyalty, you will offer them gold, all those bags you've tucked away beneath your furs. And prayers, of course, many prayers as you go on pilgrimage to Rennes.'

"The abbot's face grew redder than before; he seemed to swell with rage. 'And if I refuse?' His one attempt at dignity. 'By the holy Mass, shall I be made a mock of by every cheeky rogue? I came in fact on pilgrimage, but not for this. I can shout out truth before you cut me down. Who would then believe you?'

" 'You'll not shout.' Taliesin's voice was brisk. He beckoned to his Celts to push the abbot inside, like trying to bend a bag of grain. 'Not with my men's knives at your back.' He gestured to where we three were hunched together, Hue, hidden beneath a pile of cloaks, almost asleep; Urien, all eyes in a white face; myself, pretending a fierceness I did not have.

"Dear God, I thought, to put such work on us. But the prince was continuing in his mocking way—he was a professional, I tell you; he might have been stealing horses and carts all his life, as I expect he had. 'Besides,' he was telling the abbot, 'if you challenge us, we shall produce witnesses against you. The name of Sedgemont is well known to you. You owe us much for the ambush that you tried against us last year.'

"I could not see Taliesin, but I knew across his face had spread that young and joyful grin, the grin he gave when he saw victory ahead. I remembered how he rode, how fought, with an out-pouring of joy. And I thought, realization breaking upon me like a summer storm, as the abbot heaved and pushed, Dear God, he shows his faith in us; he trusts us to serve him now. But it was his 'us' that finished me. 'Dear God,' I prayed again as I held my knife with grim intent, 'Mother of God, protect and hear. I have been wrong; I have misjudged. And this day's work will prove it so.'

"The litter was being turned once more to face the right way on the road; the patient mules tugged and strained between the traces. We lurched along. The road was rough beneath its slick of rain. Inside the litter the abbot grunted, intent upon hefting his weight into more comfortable place. In stretching out to find room, his fat legs happened on Hue's own. 'What's that, what's that?' he almost screamed. 'Mother of God, what's hid there?' For I think, such was his previous fright, he had not realized there were three of us. I started to mutter about extra baggage, when Urien, fierce as a lion, piped up, 'My master. Treat him with care else we boot you over the bridge.' A threat that made the abbot pale, although the thought of Urien booting such bulk almost made me laugh again. Ahead of us we could hear the prince and his men chattering softly to each other, as much at ease as upon their own high hills. Between the slats of wood through which, on pushing back the covers, we could peer, we could see the white road slipping past. Easily was it done, I say, quickly; the soldiers and the monks left behind, gagged and bound; the horses tied with our own; the abbot's litter, with its abbot installed, rolling merrily along. Henry's men could have taken a lesson in competency.

"I repeat, I do not know what plan the prince had had. I think, like all Celtic warlords, he loved to improvise; a carefully thought-out scheme losing much of its charm, better to take whatever fate or God drops into your lap. And so, I think, are Celtic warlords made, masters or men, the reverse of what more cautious souls call 'temperance,' what those who plan and ar-range each moment's place shudder at for thoughtlessness. But to a Celt such unexpected chance, such unrehearsed plan, gives him a freedom, an ease, an expansiveness that caution does not dare contemplate. And for a moment there, on that wet and slippery road, I knew that freedom, exulted in that expansiveness, shared in its wild grace.

"By now we had swayed around the corner that hitherto had blocked our view ahead and, incidentally, shielded us. Now we could see the rough stones of the bridge's approach, and the horses' hooves began to clatter and clink in new fashion, ringing out hollowly as we came full upon the wooden planks. My palms, my face, were wet, and my fingers slipped upon the knife hilt, for all I held it so tightly that the abbot squirmed. 'Ill-served,' I heard him hiss menacingly. 'Those mercenaries cost me two years' rents.' Beside me Urien tightened his grip on his sword, which he had brought with him from Falaise. 'Ill-served,' he whispered back, 'ill-served, forsooth. Was my lord ill-served at your table, abbot, when you schemed to betray him?' And I felt the abbot's start as he dissolved into a silence, peering at us, curiously, with an avid intensity that I recalled.

"We had come to an abrupt halt. Men's voices were raised in questioning; answers sounded overloud. I nudged the curtains aside a crack. We were halted midspan, the river water lapping green below. Ahead of us the king's guards, some mounted, more on foot, had come spilling out from their guardhouse to bar our advance. I shall never forget the way the river ran fast and deep and green, splotched on its swollen surface with great raindrops, or the way a gaggle of geese had gathered beneath one of the stone pillars, or the way the king's captain pushed forward on his brown horse.

"Taliesin's reply was pleasant, not hurried, passing the time of day—the downpour, the state of the world, all done with courtesy. But the captain did not unbend, nor did his men, waiting for us with weapons drawn on the far bank.

" 'And you, sirs, what do you do? Not many travelers in these parts.'

"The prince's reply was succinct, the sort of answer a mercenary gives. 'The Abbot of Stefensforth, on Church affairs.'

" 'And you as escort?' Henry's captain was not so slow as he seemed. 'A Celt? And a knight? That is a knight's charger there.' And he gestured toward the black stallion.

" 'The abbot,' Prince Taliesin sounded amused, 'like many men of peace, prefers fighting men. Ask him yourself.' At his gesture one of the Celts pulled back the leather curtains so the abbot was revealed. A jab from us made him stretch himself and poke his head out as he had before. 'What, what?' He sounded testy, the more because his anger was misdirected, although anger there was, certainly. 'Make way,' he continued, while we mouthed at him words to fit our needs. 'Who are you to hinder a man of God?' He even managed to trace a tremulous cross, raising his pudgy hands to display his rings.

"The king's captain drew back a step and sketched a brief salute, but his eyes were sharp. He was a short, hard-looking man, comfortably astride a good horse; like all of Henry's captains he was both shrewd and blunt, competent in his way, too, a professional. I thought suddenly, fooling him will not be easy, will not be something he forgets.

" 'My pardon, my lord,' he was saying to the abbot respectfully, but caution, like a thread of menace hung beneath. 'The roads are closed. We look for fugitives from the king's justice: Hue, so called of Cambray, his sister, Olwen, their page, and a Celtic vagabond.'

"I saw the abbot's eyes blink twice as he took in this news, as he looked back and forth, almost counting heads aloud. But he did not dare put suspicion into speech. 'The road to Hell is never barred,' he cried pompously. He bowed his head as if saying his prayers, pressing his pudgy hands together tight. 'Even so, no man would prevent our pilgrimage. I shall pray for your success, Captain.' I gave him another jab. 'As Hell will hold its place for you,' he amended hastily, 'if you hinder a loyal Churchman about royal business. We go to Rennes.'

"At that the captain looked uneasy, knowing that Rennes was a holy place, loyal to the king, and behind him his complement of troops fidgeted in the rain. No soldier likes to meddle with Churchmen; they always have some unexpected reserve of strength, God waiting to back them in the end. To these soldiers it was nothing either way, pass or not pass, as the king commanded them, but God's will was another case. Almost imperceptibly I saw how they began to give ground. But for their captain honor was at stake, and at least he was tenacious. 'And what,' he asked, his question very clear, as if he had been saving the best one for the end, 'and what is that gewgaw at your wrist?'

"He nudged his horse so it bounded forward, and with his mail glove he flicked back the edge of the mantle that covered Taliesin's arm. Under the folds of cloth the golden bracelets gleamed, his own, and the one used to entrap us.

"I held my breath. 'That?' Prince Taliesin laughed again. 'Do not you know Welsh gold when you see it? Why, man, I got them off a border wench, and she no more faithful than any of her kind.' I caught my breath, I say. Those, too, were words to strike like darts, but they made the captain grin. He slapped his hand along the black stallion's flank. 'Ride on, ride on,' he said as the horse pranced and snorted and we rattled past. I slunk back within the shelter of the curtains, but not before I had seen the captain's look. The smile had died, and he was watching us, still thoughtful. Another enemy made, I told myself, and catching sight in the semi-dark of how the abbot eyed us malevolently, I almost crossed myself.

"Well, thus was the bridge traversed, the abbot hastily throwing alms, more pain that than our sword pricks. Thus came we to safety, out of Normandy to Brittany, and now, stepping up the pace, jolting the abbot mercilessly, we trotted on through the town, its cobbled streets slippery with wet, its citizens, on hearing us, coming out to stare and wave. I do not know what plan the prince might first have thought of, I say, but had I been forced to walk or ride through these streets, my legs would have collapsed under me. Not so the prince and his men. One of them was whistling softly again, whatever sign of strain or relief well hid, if felt at all, this but a day's work for them. And when, without further incident, we had got well clear of the town, and we hoisted the abbot down, his part over with, I think only I felt tension break, like sun coming through an overhang of clouds.

"We tied the abbot well and shoved him behind a convenient hayrick, tipped his litter over, and unhitched his mules. The sacks of gold, what was left of them, we strung about our saddle bows.

" 'Rest easily, my lord abbot.' The prince lifted his sword in salute. 'And God be thanked for your help after all. You buy our passage to England with your rents.'

" 'Impudent cur, I'll have your head,' the abbot managed to howl before the gag was shoved in. 'Thief, heretic, God's anathema on you; I excommunicate you.' He lapsed into a muttering. But his eyes were not bound. He saw Hue led out, he saw Urien, and finally he saw me, as we now all took to horse and, leading his as extras for our own, parted with him. And I thought again, a thought to chill, neither will the Abbot of Stefensforth forget.

"Now we rode hard again, all of Brittany to cross to reach the western sea. And behind our backs the king's captain to appreciate how we had cheated him. Yet this ride was easy compared with the one previous, for although Henry's men kept the border firm, in reality they could not hope to be everywhere at once, for all that Henry had commanded it, and each mile that we put between us and Normandy took us farther away from his influence. The Celts, on their own, would have made light of such a ride, nothing for them. Celts live off air and can steal anything, as now was proved, anything that flies or walks or creeps, and failing that will snatch at part-grown crops or weeds, or green stuffs that they pull from hedges or fields. It was a hard ride for me, skirts bundled up, astride a horse too large. At one stop they brought me men's clothes plucked from some wayside line, but I pushed them aside. 'I'll go on as I am,' I said. 'I'll not hide behind men's gear.' They shrugged, but Hue, starting up from his daze, cried, 'So did the queen, rot her soul to Hell.' He subsided back upon his cloak, mumbling to himself, but I felt a flash of hope. It was the first coherent thought he had uttered on his own, and I took it for a sign that gradually, in nature's time, a healing of sorts was taking place. For that reason alone, as thanks-offering to God, I would not imitate that lady's way, to bring more ill luck. But I also would not for willfulness, that Taliesin had sent the clothes.

For although he never since had had speech with me, I still was aware of him, knew every move, every turn he made, even without looking at him. And those jesting words at the bridge had rankled deep; jesting words, or not in jest, I did not know, but I nurtured them in silence and regret.

"We rode for the most part between dawn and dusk, as on that other ride. The daylight hours we spent in hiding, although as we progressed, in rain or mist, we often did not stop at all, changing horses frequently. There was little to eat or drink, of course, no time for setting nets or traps; I learned to sleep for moments at a time, leaning back in the high saddle, rocked by the steady, loping gait. Strange dreams those snatched moments of sleep gave, more vivid than nightmare, making me start awake. And always, it seemed, at our back I heard the sound of pursuit, horses coming ever closer, men's cries. But it was only the pounding of my heart, the catch of my own breath. Even Urien was quiet, lost in his thoughts, and toward the end the Celts no longer whistled their tuneless songs, no energy left for whistling anything. We followed roads that were but tracks, dipping and swaying where, for centuries, farm carts had brushed their way from field to barn; we avoided even the smallest towns, avoided churches, abbeys, monasteries. And presently, as we came farther west, we found ourselves crossing open moors like our own, with granite rocks, hard to ride through in haste yet giving us better cover than farmland. And here the mists came down in true west country style to make us inch our way along. But never faltering, by instinct, I think, those Celtic horsemen led us on; westward we went, toward the sea. And behind us, hearing of our escape, King Henry raged and swore that he would catch us yet.

"I dreamed of Henry sometimes, and sometimes of his lady queen, what their lives might have been had power and greed not made them what they were. I often saw Henry's bold stare and awoke remembering Taliesin's taunts. I thought sometimes of my parents, far away, sometimes of Robert, farther still, in Aquitaine, but seldom now did I think of Gervaise. Although when I did, it was as if I had to search for him through a loneliness, as if he wandered, too, looking for something. These were my thoughts, or part of them. For the rest I concentrated most on keeping alive, keeping awake, caring for my brother, who, day by day, now seemed improved, although he had never yet asked why we rode like this or what we were hiding from. And never did I lose sight or feel of Taliesin, like a fever running through my veins.

"We came to the end of our ride one cold evening, after a day of driving rain. Even the horses were tired that day, plodding slowly on and on; weary were the men. I myself had gone past weariness, and only Hue's training held him in place. Poor Urien, he seemed indeed a bag of bones, shaking with cold. I knew the sinking feeling that we could not long continue like this. Then, somewhere, out of the mists ahead, we heard the sea beating on a shore; we could smell the wrack of weed; the wind that had begun to blow these past hours was flecked with salt, and I sensed rather than saw that we had begun to move across a headland.

"The horses sensed it, too. They picked up their ears at first and broke into a trot over the springy turf. But I cannot pretend I felt relief; rather, uneasiness grew. Soon we all felt it, beasts and men, starting at the slightest sound, wary as if we walked into a trap. But it was not exhaustion or thought of pursuit that smote such fear as then I felt, fear that was not only fear but fear tinged with awe. It was the stones. They came looming out of the mist in lines, rank after rank of them, sentinels keeping watch in parallels or splayed out like finger bones clutching at the bare earth. We picked our way among them carefully, the horses shying at their own shadows, the surging of the waves a dirge, almost beneath our feet. It was a desolate place, I say, a place for men to shun, yet Taliesin moved forward easily, urging us on, never hesitating. I think now he had chosen this as his destination from the start; it held no fear for him, only familiarity, gratitude, a relaxing of weight that we had safely arrived. And these stones, they were but that, old stones, worn and aged, smothered in places with vines and thorns, in others brushed clear, the ground around them swept clean. For me, they were man-made, cruel, seared with old and terrible histories, and I had to close my eyes to force myself to go on, apprehension rank and cold.

"We were to spend the night in a kind of tumulus, or grave, underground, scooped out beneath a ring of stones and faced with them, a long stone tunnel, then, damp and dark even at noontime. Fugitives from a king's justice might well have felt safe there; no king, no law, no time came there, a secret place, hidden from the world. Even Hue entered it uneasily, and when he slept, he twitched and fidgeted like a hound. Urien retreated against the farther wall, backed into a corner, crunched up, his arms wrapped around his chest as if to fend off ghosts. He neither spoke nor looked, nor moved, not even his thoughts to keep him company. As for myself, I could not have stayed underground, like being buried in a living tomb, older by far than what Urien had known in any Viking vault. I crawled out into the open air, feeling my way with my bare hands. Prince Taleisin was not with his guards; I noticed that at once. And even the guards tonight were uneasy, nervous, pacing back and forth. Celts live on air; sometimes I thought they were of air, to ride and watch and ride again, unceasingly, without sleep. But there was something else tonight that kept them awake, a tension, like an outburst of storm although no storm was threatening. On seeing me they nodded among themselves and jerked with their thumbs. At first I did not know what they meant, only gradually came to realize they were pointing out where was their prince. I pushed through the knee-high grass toward the headland, drenching my skirts for the hundredth time, my boots crunching over the wild mint and sage. Our horses had been hobbled for the night, but they, too, moved uneasily, snuffling at the wind and pawing at the turf as if it tainted them. The wind tugged at their manes and tails, reminding me of Cambray when the Celts had come through the pass; it tore at my braids, too, breaking them loose, making my gown billow like a sail. The smell of the sea, the salt air, sent shivers running down my spine, and behind me those long gray lines of stones settled down to brood another night away.

"I wandered at random for a while, listening to the wind and surf—familiar sounds these, causing no harm—tasting the salt upon my lips, and presently I caught sight of Taliesin close to the cliff edge, partly hidden by a great boulder that stood apart from the other ones, a giant stone that surely must have been used as marker of great significance. He turned his head as he heard my approach, then leaned back again, half sitting, half leaning against the stone, which on the seaward side sloped under an outcrop of cliff like a granite chair with its own canopy. And there he stayed, boots propped up on a ledge, arms crossed behind his head, as much at ease as if before his own hearthside. I saw at once he had shed his hauberk, the first time free of it in days, and although his sword was laid close to hand, he had unbuckled his belt and thrown it over a bush.

"From where I stood I could look down at him, toe to head: long legs stretched out, leather jerkin unbraced, broad chest and shoulders in a shirt that had once been white, bright hair whipped into snarls, as was my own. He did not speak. In truth, I repeat, we had had but little speech, almost none since the crossing of the bridge, when he had put his life once more into my hands and I had put mine into his. I had not even shown gratitude to him for that, nor for bringing us here with such care. Yet neither had he praised our work. And those last words, 'faithless wench,' had left their poison in my mind.

"I said, too quietly for him to hear, for the wind snatched the words away, 'My lord, I am come to give you thanks,' for that at least seemed just, but he still stared outward at the sea, and I felt foolish to start again. The dark was soft, as if it glowed beneath the mist and rain, and the sea was shimmering, white-flecked, vast. Westward it stretches, the western sea that circles our world, where no man has gone and returned, not even those Celtic missionaries. Tomorrow or the next day we would embark upon it. Whither would that sea take us, where should Taliesin order us to go? I said again, more urgently, 'My lord, I must have speech of you—' when he interrupted me, almost speaking to himself, so that I had to crouch forward to listen.

" 'Off shore, where I come from,' he began, 'there is an island sacred to our race, the most holy place for all the western Celts, Mona, the Holy Isle, our Earth Mother, it is called. The longest place name I have ever heard is found there, encompassing within its many syllables all the mysteries of the Celtic faith. There are rocks on the Holy Isle, like to these stones, so old they have magic qualities. One stone is shaped like a thighbone and is believed most venerable. An enemy who invaded us tried to hurl that stone into the sea. He loaded it with chains to make sure it would sink, yet by daybreak it had returned to its own place. You should not fear these stones of Carnac. They are as old, as sacred, to our kin.'

"I had never heard him speak so seriously before of sacred things. 'And do you hope to return to that Holy Isle?' I ventured next, eyeing him nervously when I thought he would not see.

"He stared ahead again, his mouth clamped up tight. He had a sensuous mouth, curved at the edge with its mocking smile, and the long, dark eyelashes fringed his dark blue eyes. There was a faint stubble of beard across his chin, and where the iron of his harness had chafed at neck and wrist, marks were scored into the skin. I could see how the fabric of his shirt rose and fell as he breathed, and the way his arms stretched into the sleeves, long brown arms, and strong, with hollows at elbow and wrist like boys have. I remembered how those arms had held me once, those hands.

"He said, 'I shall go back to my father's house.'

" 'And I?' I cried. 'What of Hue, Urien, and me?'

" 'Why,' he said, as if surprised, 'I bring you back to England, of course.'

"It was what I had wanted to hear. I suppose it was what he should have said. But another cloud of disappointment settled on me. He said, 'Tomorrow we take ship, a small, fast fishing smack. Breton-manned, bought for a price. The abbot's gold has served us well.'

"He stretched himself, long like a cat, and put out his arms. The golden bracelets were gone from his wrists. He must have sensed my look, for he flicked one glance of his own at me. 'They, too, will buy us passage,' he said, mocking me.

"I could not prevent myself from saying it. 'Those bracelets were a pledge,' I cried, 'a pledge, my lord, between us both.

For life, or death, as that she who planned our deaths would have lured us on. And for love.'

" 'Love.' He almost shrugged. 'That's a word you have not lectured on this while.'

"He did not sound bitter, only older, dispirited. I said, and again I could not hold the words back, 'I have not thanked you, Prince of Afron, for my life, my brother's life. I have not thanked you for the pains you took. I have not thanked you for the love you offered me.'

There was a silence for a space. Presently he said, still not looking at me but I saw how his breath had quickened as if against his will, 'I, then, shall thank you for your courtesy. But, God's wounds, we have shared such ventures, surely formality has long been gone. Come down out of the rain.' He gave my skirts a tug as he might have pulled at a companion's cloak. 'Else you be blown over the cliff, to waste so much effort on our part.'

"It was not the most gracious of invitations I have heard, but I scrambled down as best I could, my boots slipping on the wet grass. He let me come as I might, who once would not have let me move alone. Beside him I remembered again how he had held me, drawn me close; that, too, was gone, all gone.

"I lay beside him under the outcrop of stone, my legs not long enough to reach with his, the surface of the stone not rough, as I had thought, but smooth, almost warm, as if the heat of many summers lay trapped beneath. We were in a sheltered place; the wind could not reach us, nor the mists; the bracken rose on either side like coverlets, and the cliff did not fall off sharply, rather sloped gently like a hillside toward the sea. He had moved slightly to make room, and we lay side by side.

"He said, 'This is a holy place, Olwen of the White Way. And this an altar made by holy men.' At my start, 'Do not be alarmed. I do not speak of newer Druid rites. I speak, I tell you, of Celtic ones, long ago, when the Celts were masters of the world. Fire they worshiped, and flame, and all the elements of air and wind, and this was an altar to the gods they loved.' I tried to speak. 'Hush, Olwen,' he said. 'Be quiet. Put fear aside. Listen to the sea, the rain, the wind; listen to the promptings of your own heart.' He had not called me by my given name these many days; he had not spoken to me like this. 'Listen, Olwen,' he said a second time, 'my task is done. I do not boast, but I have bested a king and had him beg to me for life. I granted it. That is a thing my father will not accept, who lives his days in shadow of death. But I have lived my life, too, in shadow of a worse thing, a hateful thing, called revenge. When I return, I shall tell him so. Then will my work be through. Once,' and now his voice had grown softer; I thought I remembered the way it used to sound. 'Once I asked you what you would say when it was over. I had not thought to have it end in such bitter wise.'

"Now I could not say anything; my heart pounded in my breast; my lips were dry, salt-caked. I felt the length of him along my side, like flame.

"He said, 'You are wet. God's wounds, you'll die of cold. Take off your skirts.' With calm hands, those long, strong hands, he helped me untie the knots. I knew it was not cold he thought upon, nor yet did I, and yet I trembled as if I were cold. I laid my rags aside, for they were only rags; under cover of the cloak I felt his hand rest nonchalantly, casually, close to my body, naked beneath my shift.

" 'I told you once,' his voice had taken on an intensity of its own, 'I told you that I would claim your lips, your flesh, white and soft as the name you bear. I told you no man would have you unless I did. A thousand times, then, for your naked breasts; a thousand times for your mouth, sweet it is when it does not cry your wrongs at me. And but once, I said, for your maidenhood. Are you still a maid, Olwen the Fair, that you should think to cry rape at me?'

"He said, his fine supple hands where they belonged, curved about and between, 'I must have all, dear heart, no space, no room for anyone else, no holding back. Thus was our pledge, and thus I set my seal.'

"Long, supple hands he had, with wrists like steel to work their cruel, sweet will on me, and hard I felt him surge, with cruel, sweet pain, that makes a woman of a maid and turns a man into a god. Together, then, no space between, my bare back against the stone, and his bare skin upon my own; beneath us beat the western sea."

Chapter 15

o passed the night, the shortest night of all the year. It was too short for us. And when the sun came up, that fickle west country sun, suddenly rearing through the mass of clouds, starting up on our left side out of the milky sea, he held me on his lap, fingers twined about my hair, and swore that he would return to me. 'When you are safe at Sedgemont,' for so he promised, 'I shall come there for you.' He twisted each strand into ringlets and smoothed them into place across my breasts. 'Long have I wished for this,' he whispered. 'Long wanted to touch your hair, your skin, ever since you rode against me as a child. How you challenged me, how you threw down your gage, how you teased me out of mind. And at Cambray, when you swore your blood oath to me! Not look for you in France, Sweet *Jesu*, what else should I look for? As you teased me, shall I tease you, shall I ride you.' His mouth covered me, breath, tongue, lips; who was to say which were his, which mine, out and in, and so out and in went his hands below, so went his flesh. 'By all the Celtic mysteries,' he whispered again, as the sun's rays mounted and spread. He drew aside the cloak that covered us; the heat moved from toes to ankle bone, up each inner leg. 'Thus do I offer you as sacrifice; thus in my own fashion do I seal our vow, your blood for mine, as now.' And the sun beat down like a benison.

"Too short the night, too many things left unsaid, some things not even spoken of; we felt God had given us all the time left in the universe, no need for words. And when the morning was full come, we dressed ourselves, slowly, lingeringly; came down from that high and magic place, to the real world of men, horses, gear, boats. There were the Breton sailors to cajole, more suspicious, if possible, than our Irish ones at Cambray, although we paid them well. And while we waited for the tide, lacking three hours to high watermark, the village, with its scattering of huts around a central space, seemed as familiar as that at Cambray, the same smell of fish and brine, the same wash and rush of waves along the sandy cove, the same small boats, beached like colored whales, for the sea to float upright. The fishermen sat blinking in the unaccustomed sun, mending their nets, hiding their thoughts, and while I sought shelter in one of the huts, Hue and Urien waited on the shore, backs to the land, against a boat, dozing in the warmth.

"Taliesin and his men were gone to arrange the disposal of their horses. They rode around the cliff head, but a short distance off, leaving a guard, seeking themselves to find a better place to sell their mounts, no use at all to fisherfolk. Good battle destriers are hard to find, command their own price, and that black stallion had been a gift, which in due honor Taliesin felt he should return. The monies from these transactions would furnish us with comforts, and, of more import, equip the Celts when they landed on the English coast. As I have explained, my brother, Urien, and I were bound for Sedgemont, the largest and most secure of my father's lands in England, safe for us; while, true to his bond, Taliesin and his men would ride westward to his homeland. A parting, then, but not for long; his quest done, he had promised to come for me. Sweet, then, was that morning in Carnac, in that little hut, a fortress it seemed after all those nights on the road—a peat fire, smelling, if truth be told, of cattle dung and fish, but comfortable; and water, tepid but clean, in a crockery bowl to wash, a strip of sacking to dry myself; I might have bathed in milk and lavender. I let the water drip upon my skin, aware of each drop, each inch, each pore; a thin trickle of water between my breasts. I had never thought myself anything but what I am, thin, small, red-haired; that morning I felt beautiful. My clothes were spread out to dry on a stone before the fire; a fisherwife had promised to mend the worst rips with her sailmaker's thread; I stood there on the earth floor, felt the dirt, cool and black between my toes; felt my hair spring from my head, happiness tangible, within our grasp. When Taliesin's shadow darkened the threshold, I said, not turning around, spreading my tresses apart with my fingers as I had no comb, 'Come, love, help me unsnarl this.'

" 'So should I be glad to do.' The voice was hard, strange, a soldier's voice, and the man who spoke did not move.

"I twirled around, already feeling for my little knife, horror like cold water flung. But the knife was too far away, and the man between it and the door. On foot he was shorter than I had thought, travel-worn, his boots mud-splattered, as was his cloak, but the sword he held unsheathed was bright, battle-honed.

" 'So, lady,' he said softly as I looked at him, hearing his men behind him in the square; how had I missed their horses' approach? 'So,' he said, the captain of Henry's guard at the bridge, 'we meet again. Did you think I was left behind? A long chase have I had, and hard. But here I am.' He suddenly let a smile break across his harsh face. 'You did not trick me, Olwen of Cambray.'

"For a moment, I think, all went black, a moment only, for my mind was already working faster than it had ever done. Behind that darkness I saw Hue and Urien, dozing in the sun; I saw Taliesin striding back over the headland, on foot; I saw the trap set for them. Perhaps my eyes closed for that second, I do not know; perhaps it seemed like a blink of surprise. When sight returned, certainly the captain had not moved, and his men outside in the square had not finished riding in. And clear as a bell came the thought, they have me, but not the others yet. And he does not truly know who I am.

"I said, my voice stronger than I would have believed possible, not taking my gaze from his brown, square face or his hard, knowing eyes, 'How do you know what name to put to me? And who or what are you looking for? There is some mistake . . .'

"He did not reply, his gaze neither leaving mine, his naked

sword catching at the sun and glittering. Then he took a step forward, his spurs grating over the threshold, and behind him his men stilled and watched him intently. He did not have to reply, he did not need to. In his other hand he held proof, those armbands of Taliesin's with which we had purchased the help of the Breton fishermen. *Do you not know Welsh gold?* Henry's captain knew it as well as I did.

"I said, breathlessly, as if I had been running, as if I had no control over my voice, even to myself it sounded strange, husky, heavy, 'Those are mine. And he who took them as pledge is long gone, sailed away, sod him, he and his men. You'll not find them.'

"He listened to me without moving a muscle of his face, not even a grin of derision.

"Now some god helped me I think, and I cried, 'Do I look as if I minded to be left? Why should I concern myself about a man who deceived me? Fickle, he called me, false, why should I be loyal to him? I know the way they've gone; for a price of my own I'll tell more than those Breton fools. Give me back my bracelets, I say.'

"He did not contradict, listening to my Celtic lies without comment. A captain of the king's guard is used to lies; how many had his duty bid him listen to, how many lies turned truth when the king's will had been done?

"I cried again, letting anger show, woman's anger, petulant. 'Should I wish to protect a man who made a fool of me? I should have asked for help before. Your help.' And for the first time I, too, moved, slightly, letting the sacking slip.

"I do not know where my words came from. It was a frantic attempt, little else, that somehow there would be a chance to warn the rest; no escape for me, but for them at least a hope. Nor did I even think these thoughts clearly, although that was what I must have intended. Blunt was that captain, and shrewd; I played shrewdness and bluntness, move for move, calculatingly. I remember thinking again, he cannot be sure where Taliesin is, he will be wary of him. . . . Yet even as I spoke, and God forgive me, smiled, even as I picked up another piece of sack to dry my hair, I thought I heard above the stamp of horse and the wash of the sea the sound of men, coming from a distance, around the cliff's point.

" 'Do I look like a girl men spurn?' I now cried, willing him to look at me. 'There are others where he came from. You or your men perhaps? Please me, and I will tell you where they are.'

"For the first time I saw a small cloud of hesitation, a suspicion of a frown, gone in an instant. He said evenly (a captain is used to his prisoner's chatter), 'They purchased passage, that I know. Breton sailors can be easily bought. Easily bought, easily persuaded to talk. As can you. No need to pay for what we can take.'

"I gave another smile such as I have seen women give; I moved my hips as do those Paris whores. 'Ah, so,' I breathed, 'but taking is not like the giving I could give, if you pleased me. And you might please.' And for a moment, God forgive, it might have seemed so, that short, blunt man with a man's hard body and a man's hard eyes, staring at me, sword in hand. Fresh from my first game of love, I baited him. *Do not wanton with me.* Now I should.

"He said, fingering the armlets, rolling them round and round with his left hand before tossing them aside, 'If a passage was purchased with these, then where else should my prisoners be but waiting for the tide?' He was sharp; he missed little, that captain, so certain of himself he named us prisoners, already sure of us. 'And my men and I, we can wait. Here we bide until I give the order to ride out. But,' and now his eyes narrowed, his voice dropped, 'if in truth they have already sailed, and perchance they have, as you insist, why, they are dead men anyway, all of England closed to them by Henry's express command, the ports all closed. And the Abbot of Stefensforth, when he found breath to speak, has ordered all the church doors barred, no sanctuary for those who misused him, no place left to succor them.'

"Speaking of the abbot almost made him grin, but horror rose in my throat to choke. Nowhere safe, then, this not the end, happiness still an illusion far away. And from around the headland, rising green and smooth, clearer now, I thought I caught snatches of laughter, talk. Surely all there must be hearing it, listening; was I the only one to sense Taliesin's return? And hearing, were they waiting to strike?

"Moving myself as a woman does who has not time to waste, as in truth I had not time, although not in that sense; letting the sacking slip deliberately; thinking despairingly even as I flaunted my nakedness, how little to offer a man who must be used to women, certainly knowing them, long accustomed to harlots of camp and field. I said, 'Be quick.' I breathed. Beautiful this morning had my lover called me, and beautiful had I been; now I prayed for what beauty there was to attract his enemy.

" 'Do not keep me waiting,' I panted, biting my lip, moving my feet, white they looked against the earth, 'you or your men. Six of you for the price of one. But first I'll have my bracelets back.'

"He looked me up and down, a man bargaining for a horse, estimating its value, its use; a king's captain might not pleasure with a king's prisoner, but if she insisted, if he thought her of no worth, he might; that might be his gain. I swayed my hips and smiled; the sacking fell to the ground; I tossed my hair; now I had his attention sure. But to give me those bracelets he must stoop to fetch them forth from where they had rolled.

"He said, 'Quickly, then, before my men know what they miss.'

" 'First my gold.' I insisted as a harlot would, the Celt's approach so loud in my head that it was rather like a drum, a drum to summon them all to attend. He gave a whistle himself, half a whistle, half the sound men make when they cannot believe their luck, and shouted over his back for his men to dismount, never taking his eyes from me. The noise they made, grumbling as troopers do, cursing, would surely drown every other sound, and on foot whatever advantage they had would be lost. But they would see Taliesin and his men when he saw them, and mounted again, they could ride the Celts down, however well Celts can run. A warning, then, still to be given. But fast.

" 'By the rood.' The captain had turned back to me, almost

laughingly, beginning to unbuckle his belt, hefting his sword from hand to hand, 'whatever your crime, and whether the king will have you swing for it, who am I to deny your wish? The Abbot of Stefensforth warned that you were red-haired and wild, Olwen of Cambray, a witch, he said, to entice men.'

" 'The abbot judges women as he does men. Red-haired, hot blood, isn't that what all men think?' I did not even bother to deny the charge, neither yea nor nay, let him decide, but I stirred with my foot again and smiled.

"He moved briskly, then, ripping open his steel corselet with one hand, stripping off his spurs, one by one, never dropping his gaze, never giving up his sword (but even a king's captain cannot make love with a sword in hand). He came toward me purposefully, a short man, compact, tough, hardened by campaign like old leather, but not unjust, professional, knowing pleasure and savoring it. He would love a woman well.

" 'First my fee.' I marvel that I was so cool, for my part edging to keep us face to face, his back to the door. He paused in his stride and laughed outright, the sort of laugh men give when they are alone, a solid laugh from the chest. 'God's my life,' he swore, 'lady or not, the king has got a prize in you. Here, then.' He propped his sword against the wall, stooped to look for the golden circles where they had fallen. That was my chance. In a flash I had slid past to the open door. I could not escape, all his men staring at me, but the others could.

" 'Ware, ware,' I screamed, 'Henry's men.' And I gave the battle cry of my house, a high, loud shout.

"He was on me fast, arms about my waist, bowling me to the floor, hand to mouth. But not before I had seen Urien start awake, seen Hue. That was all I cared about. And in the silence that followed, I heard no sound from the cliff. Taliesin must have been warned, too.

"We clawed along the floor, knocking over stool, jugs, sword. I bit and scratched, the more he tried to quiet me. 'Vixen,' I heard him shout, 'bitch. The abbot warned that you were sly.' He gave a great heave that sent me tumbling against a wall, followed with hand raised to slap my head upon the ground.

'Make a fool of him, make a fool of me,' he gritted out between his teeth. 'Damn your eyes. You'll rue this day; you'll wish for death.'

"Spitting blood, I cried, 'So be it. Escape is worth the price.'

"His sword was in his hand again; he raised it, pointed it. I suppose I was as close to death then as any man, anger overwhelming him. But he was an old campaigner, too; killing could wait. Recollecting himself, with a mighty effort he scooped up his gear and leapt for the door, bellowing to his men. They started toward him, started back. 'Mount, mount,' he was howling, 'arm yourselves.' And to those who in panic would have struggled inside the hut, 'Get out, out, too late for that.' For it was already too late, and so he knew, and so with a rush of gratitude I knew also; Hue and Urien disappeared, slid along the boat's side, the sea licking at their heels; the Celts vanished likewise, the cliff path empty. That moment's hesitation had cost Henry's captain his command, perhaps his life.

"Even as he ran to his own horse, yelling for his men to throw up their shield wall, the arrows hissed among them, scattering them. Two died upon the spot; a second flight caused a horse to squeal and kick the others loose; a third took the captain in the arm. He clutched the shaft, trying to break it off, still shouting orders, mostly ignored as his men struggled to get away.

"From the floor I watched all this, unable to move, my head aspin. I saw the Celts swarm down from the headland, seeming almost double their number, so fast and furious they came; I saw Urien, with Hue close behind, make their way along the beach. Then Taliesin was in the hut, crashing through the door, sword swinging dangerously, eyes lit with battle rage. He scooped me up, bore me outside; the last of Henry's men speared through, only the captain left upright, cornered, his teeth bared like a wolf's. I clutched at Taliesin's arm. I could feel the sheen of sweat, like satin on the skin, and the muscles taut with strain. 'I am not harmed,' I told him, still spitting blood. 'No more killing; let that man go.'

"Taliesin snapped his fingers for a cloak and wrapped it round.

He must already have seen the purple bruises, the cuts, the weals. He put me aside; his hand tightened for its final thrust. I clung to him so he could not move.

" 'No more,' I cried, my voice surprisingly firm although in my body I trembled like a leaf. 'Have done. Let us away as soon as we can.' When he still hesitated, I whispered in his ear, 'As betrothal gift, a life. His. I beg. I owe him it.'

"Well, Taliesin, too, was a fair man. He did not question or refuse, simply nodded. As swiftly as the attack began it ended, nothing but dead men left, the villagers cowering at their doors in fright.

"The Celts began to carry things down to the boat; saddles, bridles, packs of food, the reverse of their departure at Cambray. I counted them. But four men left, this the reason the guard had not cried alarm, and I crossed myself to pray for yet another dead soul. Urien and Hue had begun to climb on board, Hue still laboriously, yet I had heard him shout, one shout only, but in his old voice. The tide was running fast, the little cove almost awash; the boats were bobbing on their mooring lines, and the waves beginning to pound into surf. The fishermen, those who had betrayed our whereabouts and who had promised to sail the ship for us, reluctantly came forward, driven like sheep, protesting, arguing in true Celtic style, their women screaming outrage. They had not thought of Henry the King when they took our gold; they had not been frightened of retaliations then. I gathered up my cloak, and with escort, went back into the hut to claim my clothes; sadly burned and scorched they were, when they had fallen into the fire. Beyond them gleamed the armlets, where they had been kicked. I gathered them up, slipping them above my elbows on either arm. Outside, the dead had been dragged apart; the captain, leaning on the wall, blood dripping down his arm, watched in silence, sword still in his hand. He turned his head when I went by, watching me now with his hard eyes. He said suddenly, cried out, almost puzzled, almost beseechingly, 'Why so? What, lady, did you want from me?'

"We looked at each other, nothing to say. He was a professional I tell you, he knew what should, what could, what must, be done. In silence, then, I passed, but I tore off a length of ragged hem from my skirt and tossed it to him.

He caught it to knot around his wound. Well, I thought, he said he would not forget, and he never will, a man bested by a girl who has turned her first day's loving into its parody. But when I had gone most of the way down to the cove, he shouted at me. 'I liked you better as strumpet,' he cried, 'than lady, with your head in air. But you gave me life. I give you yours.' As we all looked at him, 'You did not expect me to ride alone, not with only six men.' And he cocked his head toward the eastern cliff, not the one Taliesin had come from, but on the other side. It was bare, nothing to see, only a sparkle where the sun's rays caught some bright thing. Some bright thing, a shield rim perhaps, a helmet crest . . .

"We dropped our bundles then, and ran, no time to wait for reluctant fishermen; we struggled into the sea, knee-deep, trying to push the boat out through the surf. It answered sluggishly, the tide not yet turned, veering broadside to the waves, shipping water so that slowly it began to fill. Those on board fought to break out the sail, tried to keep us on even keel, tried to bail the water with helmets or even their bare hands. Along the cliff edge, to the east, there was a shout, the sound of hooves; mounted men began to appear, pointing, spurring furiously toward the village, Henry's men, the captain's rear guard. Taliesin had thrown his mail coat off; it dropped into the sea like stone. Waist-deep, shoulder-deep, he and two companions were swimming us out, while two others, standing firm on shore, beat back the fishermen. For they, recognizing our predicament and assured of help, miserable knaves, had come rushing forward to hinder us. Half over the gunwales I wrestled with the ropes that held the sail, trying to bite them through with my teeth when nails broke; we still drifted helplessly within spear range. Then Hue, without speech, calm, picked up a knife, cradling it between his crooked fingers, and sliced through the knots; with a rattle the sail, a small, square sail, unfurled. It was small, but it was enough. A gust of wind off the headland caught it full, and we began to move. I pulled myself on board; Taliesin and his companions did likewise, dragged through the water, breathless, waterlogged. Not so fortunate were the other men. Helpless to turn back, too far for us to tender aid, we saw one of them go under, overwhelmed by the fishermen; the other, trying to shuck off his harness and swim at the same time, threw up his arms, sank beneath the waves, and disappeared. The wind filled the sail and bore us away.

"We were afloat, out of reach, all of us wet and gasping like netted fish. *I give you life.* That was all we had; three men with only their unsheathed swords, a wounded man, a page, and a naked girl, little food, less water, no place to sail to even if we could. Yet Taliesin threw back his head, when he had breath, his brown throat gleaming in the way it has, and cried, 'So, gods, I defy you, wind and waves.' He began to laugh, choked, water streaming from his hair, plastered to his skull, running from his eyes and mouth, 'Sweet *Jesu*,' he cried, 'back to Cambray, then, as we left.' But beneath the laughter for a moment was defiance, desperation perhaps, perhaps even fear. We were afloat, and little else.

"Soldiers are not sailors, that's a truth, and the ship was a sorry hunk of wood, worm-riddled, small, splitting at the seams. But we made it sail. Or rather Hue made it so. He could not work the ropes nor man the oars, but he could advise us which to use and when. Hue knew how to swim; he had been well trained in seacraft at Cambray; even better than Taliesin he understood boats. Gingerly, headland by headland we edged along until, more confident, we left the shelter of the frowning cliffs that rose up steeply north of Carnac and began in earnest to strike out to sea. This stretch of water is the roughest in the world, the western sea, shunned and feared by experienced mariners. Ignorance made us brave. I cannot say either that this was the best time I have known; we lived off fish when we caught them, Urien and I being good at that. When we could, we hugged the coast; a deserted stretch of land, it seemed, with little to recommend to anyone. Once we had to go on shore to fill our water casks. I told you that Celts can steal anything, but there was little there to steal, some half-ripe apples and a goat. The goat was tough, but we ate it down to its hooves, its toughness spread over several days, and we stilled the pangs of hunger with green fruit. But we never spoke of that day at Carnac or our losses there; it seemed drowned, too, sunk from sight. And yet for all our grief, for all our loss, I cannot say it was the worst of times. We had each other, Taliesin and I. And when the long twilight came and we drifted with the currents north, we would come together in the rear of the ship. The sea was calm, praise God for that, the nights and days continuing fair, and our wake was like a ripple cut across a millpond, such as small water insects make, scrabbling with their legs. There was a place under the stern where fishermen coil their nets, and there we made a sort of bed, spread with cloaks. I spent much of the daylight hours there with a fishing line; it was of a size for Urien and me, but Taliesin had difficulty fitting in his long legs. He looked thin, as did we all; the wind and sun had burned his skin to a golden brown, and his blue eyes by contrast were almost black. The nicks and ridges of old scars showed purple, and I longed to cover them. Urien used to sit against the sail, for the first time in weeks, it seemed, he had begun to sing, and one of the Welsh soldiers had brought out his stringed harp; that, too, I had not heard in months. I said suddenly to Taliesin one night when we sat there, looking at the stars, the half-moon rising clear (hard to believe that the moon had grown so fast since the night of darkness when we had left the forest of Falaise), 'When we come to Cambray, what will you do? Will you stay there with me?'

" 'Perhaps,' he said. 'If Dylan will let me in. Will he give me and my men horses to ride, armor, weapons, so that we do not have to come begging at your gates? Will he render me my own horse back?'

" 'Your horse!' I mocked him. 'It is but part yours, horse thief.'

"He pulled my hair. 'Take care,' he said. 'Your tongue grows sharp. I told you what I do to sharp-tongued wenches when I am crossed. Let me show you since you forget.' Afterward he said, 'You smell like clover and honey; you remind me of a clover field' (a lover's exaggeration, I think; I smelled more like seaweed and stale fish, my skirts in shreds). And so I told him, but he closed my mouth. 'No need of clothes,' he told me with a grin. 'But there is a field of wild clover I will show you, close by a stream. The banks are shady, where kingfishers breed, and trout for the catching in the shadows under the stones. Shall we ride there together one day?'

" 'And would your father accept me,' I asked, 'of Norman kin? Perhaps you had better face him first!' But he did not hear me, far away among his northern hills. 'Not hills,' he corrected, 'mountains, capped with snow, where eagles and hawks abound, the best hunting lands on this earth.'

"He stretched and sighed. 'I have been gone too long,' he admitted, 'I should bide at home. My father is old; he needs a son. He needs a son who takes a wife. And that also I mean to tell him.' I let him speak, happy in his happiness. 'Then I shall bring you to those fields of clover, where the bees hum all day long,' he said, a boy who suddenly thinks of home. 'Olwen of the White Flowers, no fairer maid in all of Afron.'

" 'So you have said to many maids, I have no doubt,' I told him tartly, to hide my pleasure in his compliments, and smiled to myself as he argued me down; well, princes, even in the northern mountains, are men, with all of their princedom to choose maids from. It was not disagreeable to be proved wrong. And you see that not everything was misery as we rocked steadily toward Cambray. And one day I dared to tell him what also was in my heart. 'I cannot forget Gervaise of Walran,' I blurted out, 'although I did not want to be his wife. Long are the prayers I make for him. But, my lord,' for I spoke seriously, 'if, in my turn this past week, for honor, love, what you will, I could have sold myself, so perhaps did he.'

" 'He is dead, Olwen,' he said soberly. 'God rest his soul; I meant him no ill. Nor do I think he meant wrong to you. But if he had lived, then would I be dead.' He suddenly took my palms and pressed them together as once he had done before. 'And if you had not deceived that man,' he told me softly, 'then we should all be back in Henry's power. I can only thank God that he did you no harm. No harm, that is,' and he began to smile, 'as now I mean to do to you.'

"Fickle are the Celtic gods, inscrutable, smiling fair, bringing

grief, death, and joy like clouds that shift, like mists that gather
and dissolve upon a summer's day. They gave us a following
wind, calm seas; they brought us back to Cambray. A second
time we tasted hope; a second time they snatched it from our
lips. Listen now, my part is almost done. Easily we crossed
open sea; we rounded the Cornish peninsula where the rocks
that form its western tip are spear points, stabbing through to
air. Up the northern shore we beat, sailing in the shadows so
that even from a cliff we could not be seen, hidden during the
day by the heat haze. Relying on Hue and Urien, who claimed
they best knew the coasts about Cambray, we put into shore,
our voyage done.

"The evenings were still long, the nights short; it was semi-
dark when we came to that headland where Urien and I had
brought the fishing fleet. We shipped the oars, for we had thought
it better not to use a sail, and ran the boat right up onto the
beach, expert now in handling it, knowing all its weaknesses
and quirks. The tide and current brought us as easily as a piece
of driftwood; we did not even have to wet our feet when we
stepped out. Anticipation had made us look our best. At least
I felt clean, saltwater clean, although my gown was so sun-
faded where it was not torn, I think even a serf at Cambray
would have turned her nose up. The men had washed, no way
to shave, no martial gear, only their swords, kept rust-free
somehow.

"It was strange to stand again at Cambray and look up at the
cliffs; high they reared above our heads, green and dark against
the night sky. I swear I could smell the heather on the moors
and hear the dry rustle of the wind through the grass. The Celts
made great show of stretching their arms and flexing them, row-
ing not being much to their taste, and they stamped their feet
back into their boots to show their pleasure in dry land. One,
for a jest, even offered to race his fellow up the cliff and back,
a test of endurance such as Celts love, although I think he made
the wager more to show exuberance, a thing to marvel at; I had
never heard them jest before. We watched them almost indul-
gently, older men turning themselves to youths at the thought
of that border a few miles away. They bounded from tussock

to tussock to show their skill, leaping, where Urien and I had crawled, and soon were gone from sight. Urien himself was in brave mood, too. He stamped and stretched with the others, swore like a man, braced his shoulders against our slaps of brotherhood; well, he deserved to crow a little, come back triumphant to his own yard. Only Hue, poor Hue, who daily had improved so he knew where we were and who he was and what had happened to us, only Hue hid his feelings, a fugitive returned after setting off with such high hopes. But once he was safe within Cambray's walls, then Henry could whistle in the wind himself. In high spirits we unloaded the ship, not much left to unload, the bilge water for the last time unbailed. The thought of hot food and wine, of fires and friends and tale-telling to pass the hours suddenly seemed real, and their reality a fitting end to so many hardships. I remember thinking this must be a dream and thrusting my arms in up to the gold armlets to test the cold of the sea, whether I dreamed or not; I remember wondering, God forgive such foolishness, if I had grown and if the castlefolk would notice how I had changed. They say lovemaking turns a woman sleek, soft as a cat; had I been a cat, I might have purred. I remember, too, watching the way the little waves eddied up and down, sinking into the sand in a swirl of foam; cool and sweet that water was, the air crystal clear, the scent of it like the touch of silk . . . Down the cliff the Celts came at a run, in a slide of stones, reaching the shore together in a single leap, landing on their heels. Our hand claps, our bravos, died away as we saw them, white-faced, panting, breathing in ragged gasps. It was not the climb that had winded them. 'My lord.' They spoke in unison, for once not mincing words. 'My lord, turn back. The way is barred, the castle under siege from Henry's troops. The cliff paths watched. Odo of Walran waits there for us.'

"They thrust us under the shelter of the beetling rocks, making us hug the side of the cliff. Face pressed to the wet stones, my heart pounding with shock, I waited for a shout of alarm to come. But minutes passed, our breathing eased; for the moment, then, we had not been seen. But what next? Gently had the Gods brought us home; now they let their furies loose.

"We were all huddled against the side of the cliff, the men's swords already out, their backs braced to take the shock of attack. The little boat lay innocently on the sand, but soon, when the tide was in, there would be no beach left. And even if we were to push off, where should we go? At sea, unprovisioned, how much longer could we trust to luck? Taliesin summed up our position clearly enough. 'Not worth a tinker's cuss, that boat,' he said. 'A good fortune not to have staved its keel open; a sudden squall, a rainstorm, we'll split in two or flood. As soon go to sea in a sieve.' And he beat his bare hand on the rock as I had seen him do once before. But he was still able to think, and his ability to improvise now stood us in good stead. First he listened to what his men had seen, certainly not good news. Soldiers, a score or more, Walran men, along the cliffs, stationed at intervals as Robert had placed his men. Odo of Walran had not forgotten his threats. And now he had a dead son of his own to avenge. Closer to the castle was a ring of campfires, revealing the presence of troops about the walls, not clear from here how many but a large force, King Henry's answer to our defiance. No way into Cambray, then, no way out for the Cambray men, and the road west blocked. And even if it were open, all about us only open moors, where a man can be seen for miles. Yet in this cove nothing had changed; the little beach in shadow, the waves idling in, the boat drawn up to reveal our whereabouts. Of all the plights we had been in, this was the worst; to feel safe, to feel home, and to have that hope dashed to bits. Like waifs we crouched against the cliff face, happiness turned to gall. Fickle are those Celtic gods, like their fickle land, their fickle weather, their fickle folk, smiling fair, bringing woe, harbingers of storm when they seem most calm.

"But Taliesin would not let us be found like sitting hares. Action he could arrange, could handle, not hopelessness. We dared not sail, then we must go by land; we could not walk, then horses must be found; if the open moors would reveal us, then we must find a place to make a stand and arm ourselves to fight. The darkness would hold for another hour or so; we must act soon.

"Celts can steal a horse from under a man and leave him sitting in midair. Now Taliesin and his companions proved how easily it can be done, practice having made them craftsmen, showing, if nothing else, why Normans fear the Celts more than any other foe, able to strike and disappear without anyone seeing them. The three Welshmen swarmed up that cliff as if on ropes, taking advantage of every cover, every bush and rock, sliding through the bracken with a ripple such as the wind makes. We came after them, climbing slowly, having to help Hue at every step. 'Useless, useless,' I heard him groan as he forced his fingers into handholds. I wanted to comfort him, but what comfort was there? We were all useless; we three 'prisoners,' another time a burden to our rescuers to imprison them. Without us, perhaps, they would have had a chance to escape; with us, there was no chance at all.

"On the path at the cliff top the Celts slithered through the grass so close to the mounted men I thought they must be seen, although had we not known where they were, we would not have seen them. They made their move seem easy, having practiced it often enough, a stone thrown, a pebble to the landward side to cause those horsemen, three men of the Walran household, bored, no doubt, cold, almost asleep, to lean out and peer into the darkness. The Celts rose up, one by one, to unseat them, as simply as they had unseated the abbot's men. But this was not an abbot's entourage to jest about. This was war. Stripped of their armor, their throats cut, the Walran soldiers were dragged over the cliff. Quickly the Celts mounted, throwing on as much armor as they could so that they had some protection, so that at least they would be armed. Those three horsemen had been placed athwart the road, to guard it going west. Now that they were gone, the road lay deceptively clear, except for a last fourth man, a bow-shot farther on, who was stationed on the road itself. We rode openly up to him, hailing him. Perhaps he took us for friends, perhaps he expected someone to relieve him soon, he never raised a hand in self-defense. But he did not die as quietly or as quickly as the others had. 'Curse you,' he cried, 'I know you. My master has sworn revenge, and revenge he'll have.' He died so, with a curse, more horrible than silence. Yet there was not even time to pray for him. We mounted up, Hue and Urien together for the last time, I in front of Taliesin. The road ahead of us lay straight, and we stole along it softly, in single file. Behind us was left all the evidence that we had no time to hide if we were to reach the pass before the dawn. And as the road rose up from the coast, on looking back I could see the little campfires of Henry's men, glowing like watchful eyes.

"Against my ear I could hear the beating of Taliesin's heart, steady and strong; beneath my shoulders feel the breadth of his; his bare skin was warm where he had not had time to lace the steel corselet close. Under my fingertips those ridges and scars I had longed to touch rippled and knotted about his ribs, along his arms. Each of those hid a wound that had caused pain; each one had been a vicious cut into bone and flesh; blood had flowed from them, living blood. And his hands about my waist pressing me to him, they were warm, alive hands, their fingers, hard and gentle, miracles of life. I thought, this is flesh joined to flesh, not in lust but in love, this is what life celebrates; Mother of God, do not let it be lost to us. But even prayers seemed useless, Odo of Walran's vengeance allied with the king's, both waiting for us. I think the most I could pray for was that they would not take us unless dead.

"Soon we were come to the familiar track that Urien and I had taken years ago when, for a child's whim, I had schemed to ambush a prince. Did I know then what fate had in store; did I sense then what I wanted? Did Taliesin? *No love lost between my house and a Norman one.* Not love lost, but lost love, thrown away uselessly, for other men's vengeance. What I wished as a child I cannot say. I only can tell you that the worst thing I could ever know was about to happen here today. The path had not changed; it had not changed in a thousand years; there stood the same ruined walls, the same old fort along the cliff crest, the same broken watchtower at the western end of the pass. Our horses picked their way along gingerly, Norman steeds these, bred for weight, not for speed; no hope of running far on them. Here was where we must make our stand, the western end, where the pass was narrowest, under the shadow of the watchtower where Taliesin had come charging down to outwit me. Here it would happen, that worst thing.

"The Celts knew the place instinctively. They backed their horses into the gap, turned them to face the way our enemies must come. Practical to the end, they shortened their stirrups, they being smaller than the Normans whose horses they rode; they tightened the girths, prepared to withhold a charge. They checked the arm straps of the Walran shields, with their wolf's crests; they tested the spear points on the rocks and loosened their swords, working them back and forth in the scabbards so they would not catch. Then they leaned forward as I had seen them, expectantly. All this they did dispassionately, not one word of distress or regret, only two of them left; they would die together, side by side, never leaving their master until he, too, died. But they did not whistle today, no time left for whistling.

"Taliesin had spurred his horse up the cliff path to the highest point. He needed a place for a lookout, so he could have warning of the numbers and time of attack. He was gone longer than I thought; by moments now the light was coming fast, and soon the sun would rise in its haze of red. But when he returned, he did not ride alone. Beside him, cantering over the grass with a springy stride that was recognizable, came a gray stallion, Taliesin's own, the horse that he had been forced to leave behind. 'Look,' he said, his voice almost cheerful, his smile its most joyous. 'I saw it running wild with a herd of Cambray grays. No hope of catching them, but it came to my call. It remembers me.' He slid off the other horse, letting his own nuzzle his arm, pulling its ears as he used to, talking to it. It was a moment's work to strip off a saddle and bridle and harness it, although it moved restlessly, used this past year to running free. 'There,' he said, almost triumphantly, 'now all is well.' He turned to us. We had dragged ourselves out of the way behind a pile of boulders and had been sitting, silently, against the stones. There was nowhere for us to go, nothing for us to do, useless. For Hue that waiting had been hardest of all. I saw tears steal down his wasted cheeks as he tried to force his hands to obey him.

Useless, aye so, a wounded soldier is worse than none at all. But he had managed to pull a dagger from its sheath and held it across his lap. He, too, must have prayed to his gods that he should not be taken alive. The sun had almost come up in its crimson round. Pitiless it would rise, pitiless would it set. 'Come, Olwen,' Taliesin said, and I knew already what he meant. 'Come, my love. No Norman horse can catch mine.' He almost laughed. 'It will bear you safely away. So once your mother rode,' he cried. 'Go north to Afron. Tell my father I wish him well; remember me.'

"I told you my tale would be soon done. Here was its end.

" 'And you,' I whispered, 'what of you?'

"He tried to jest. 'It is not a horse magical,' he said. 'It cannot carry all of us. We must wait our turn.'

"Well, I said this was the worst thing in my life, to bid my lover, brother, companions farewell, not even time for long adieus, no words to say them if there were. And they, my lover, companions, brother, to die that I might live. No choice for them, no choice for me. The fates willed it so. '*I had not thought,*' said Taliesin, '*to have it end in such bitter wise.*' Bitter in truth that red day dawned.

"" 'Live or die,' I said, 'I live and die here with you. What would there be left without you?'

"The gray horse stood almost reluctantly, eager to be off, not exactly patient, not exactly mollified. The veins in its neck and legs stood out; it rolled its soft, intelligent eyes and snorted, laid back its ears. Taliesin soothed it, gentled it, as if he gentled me; a second time he held out his arms to help me mount. Beneath our feet, from the bracken where he had thrown himself, head locked in arms, Urien suddenly rose up. A bag of bones, a thing of skin, his black hair on end, his dark eyes lustrous. Up he rose as if he were a messenger from the gods. 'No,' he cried, and the wind took his words and blew them away, 'no, stop. There is yet another way.'

"I told you my tale would soon be done; let Urien the Scribe, Urien the Bard, tell you the rest."

Chapter 16

, Urien, known also as the Serf, bondsman to the lords and ladies of Cambray, sworn to cherish them while breath lasts, I stood up from the bracken, right under the feet of that gray horse as I had startled its master in this same place. "No," I cried, and the vast expanse of air took my words and flung them wide. I stretched out my arms and felt the wind surge through me, blowing off the moors as it does at dawn. In it were all the echoes of another time, long ago, when a woman of our race, immovable as stone, ice-cold for grief, bid her lord, her lover, farewell and saw him ride out to battle and death. About me were the forms, the spirits, of those long-dead heroes and kings; red ran their spears, sad were their eyes, to have life snatched from them in their youth. How could my lady and her prince know what I saw, what felt? Those figures, who burned like flame to brand themselves upon my sight, a beauty about them such as never exists in the real world, seemed superimposed upon the present here to make it and the past as one, making the past repeat itself unless I forced my will to alter it. How could they know? But Hue sensed it. "Do as he bids," he said.

"Lady," I said, "take your brother; hide in that cave where we used to go; you remember where, buried beneath the bracken where the foxes den. You, my lord prince." I turned to Taliesin. "Station yourself up there along the crest, in the fort where long ago we set an ambush for you. I will lead the enemy to you."

They might have argued, protested, but the words were not mine. Fickle and cruel are the Celtic gods, but some other, kinder ones put the thoughts into my mind, for pity or for recompense. "Leave me your skirts, Lady Olwen," I said. "Mount me on the gray horse, tie me on. I shall be your decoy."

We clasped each other's hands, a little band of brothers, one last gamble of the dice, one last throw. My lady, never taking her eyes from me, stripped off her ragged gown and her shift. She gave me the golden bracelets she had worn since Carnac. I had never seen her naked before, the sun coming up fast through the haze to outline her white shoulders, the pink-tipped breasts, the pearl-lustered hips and loins, the long, slender legs. I threw her my dirty tunic, almost too short for her, a belt, a pair of worn-out boots, but my little sword, half knife, half sword, I gave to Taliesin, and he put it in his belt. No one had seen me naked before, a boy's body, child's body, not fitted to a man's age, never to know a man's size or the weight of a man, or man's parts; never to sow man's seed.

They tied the skirts about me, gathering them up decorously at the waist in a bundle of cloth, and with my sharp knife cut off the tresses of my lady's hair to pin inside the hood of a cloak. They heaved me up on that horse and strapped me on, binding my knees with leather thongs; no way to fall off unless the horse fell. With clever knots they tied short the reins so that when the time was come, I could jerk them free, my hands too weak to hold on in any other way. The lady and her brother, arms entwined, crept out into the morning mist, she supporting him, he comforting her. She knew the way, the hare's track, the secret threads that wind between the gorse bushes, through the gullies and crevices. Safe underground she would wait for us, safer there than above. Together with Taliesin and his men I went up to the top of the hill. I remembered it well, stone by stone; how should I forget where my lady and the prince met? *My horse can outrun the world.* Now it must. By this time the mist was rising; straight up it poured in columns, like incense smoke. The wind that blows at daybreak had died down into a whisper, a warning. Far below, the dark blue of the horizon rimmed our world; before us, all the purple moor. "Not yet," I said, "they have not come together yet. When they are all there, let me go."

From this high vantage point we could see the gathering of Walran men, like small clusters of blue and gray, blending into the morning mist, but as daylight brightened, they burst out clearly, as if their very accoutrements had caught on fire. The household guard they were, Norman knights, born and reared, proud of their Walran arms and their Walran crests. They were grouped around a thing, a heap, that lay sprawled on its back upon the road, and as we watched, another cry went up, the shout of discovery; a second body, perhaps, or our beached boat (its timbers more like, where the incoming tide had dashed them apart upon the rocks). But "Wait," I said.

Farther beyond, from where the Walran watch had spent the night, the siege fires we had seen were doused. Coming in gusts, sometimes faint, sometimes loud, the stir reached us from Henry's camp, where his soldiers, his most highly paid mercenaries this time, kept close watch themselves. We could hear the trumpets and drums, the bustle of men waking up; their Angevin colors, silver and blue, made a large circle around the castle walls. The camp watched at a safe distance, though, Henry's new siege tactics in force, borrowed from the Celts, who had used them with such success against him. As at Sieux his men had not been ordered to attack, but (keeping within the letter of his oath to Earl Raoul) merely to hold the castle firm, no way in or out. Cambray itself was not visible, hidden behind the folds of hills at the water's edge, but I could well imagine how it looked on this summer day, small itself, stout-built, made from these very stones where we stood, dragged there in ones and twos. And like the man who had built it, dour and resolute. And as was Henry's camp at this early hour, so was Cambray, already ahum with gossip and suspense. But "Wait," I said.

A Walran messenger was riding full tilt back to the camp. We could mark his progress as he rose and dipped across the moors. We could guess the message and judge by the sudden flurry of activity what effect it caused. For Henry's troops now began to run and crisscross back and forth, all orderly watch forgotten in the excitement of a chase. Some brought their horses out and saddled them; others let loose their hounds and ordered their huntsmen to track the game. A good number of Henry's men, mounted and equipped, began to clatter off to join the Walran men. *I shall hunt you down.* Now we could see how the hunt began. But still, as the clamor and bustle spread, as Henry's troops spilled out fast, two-thirds of them sweeping out from their camp, "Wait," I said.

The noise, the racket, of their departure must spread to Cambray walls. We could not see the castle from where we stood, but Dylan could hear the noise. Night and day he would have been patrolling those walls, waiting for such a chance. The sight of that withdrawal, for whatever cause, was all he needed to make his break. "Mount," he cried, taking the steps in his stride, running like a young man again. "Open the gates." Down he swept from Cambray with the castle guard, who, like him, had been awaiting such an opportunity. They caught the remainder of the besiegers in the rear, rammed them down, cut them apart, all those left in the camp to guard, all who, forgetting their real purpose, had turned away from the castle side to watch. There were still too many Angevins left for Dylan's troops to break right through their line, and he was too wise to risk such a foolishness. Besides, he did not know that we were there, merely that something had distracted Henry's men. His charge demoralized the rest of the enemy force so that it returned to camp as quickly as it had left. So, although the Cambray guards were driven back inside their gates, and although the Angevins renewed their siege with such determination that we could not hope to force a passage through, Dylan's attack prevented help coming to the Walran troops at a crucial time. That gave us a chance. But "Be patient," I said to the waiting Celts, and smiled at them. "The time will come."

The Walran soldiers were still grouped beside the cliff, milling back and forth, expecting reinforcements that never came. Back and forth they surged, Norman knights, ready for a hunt, the hounds baying long and insistent, blood lust running hot. Their huntsmen were binding their spears, testing the wind, pointing the way they must take, a special game today, and we were it. Into their midst rode Odo of Walran, bestriding his war-horse. He was armed with sword and shield, and even we could distinguish his broad frame and feel, from here, hate burning in him like a second sun. He raised his arm in its mail coat to give command. I took a great gulp of breath, gripped with my knees, twined my bound fingers into the horse's mane. "Now," I cried.

Taliesin had been standing by our side, speaking into his horse's ears, telling it what to do; it seemed to listen, its large, liquid eyes wide with intelligence. He released it, stepped aside, and smote it on the flanks. "Run with God," he cried, and his men lifted their spears in silent salute. Down from the old fort we floated, moving on air, along the moor, like a wave unfolding across a shore, like a wind rippling through the grass, barely touching the ground, tail spread in a great arc, head high. So I rode, Urien the Serf, who had never ridden battle charger on his own, who cannot ride, a thing of reed and straw. And, of all men, most like to woman, to deceive an enemy.

They saw me come—I meant they should—for we followed the track openly, not riding fast, for the reins were tied, skimming the ruts, barely touching the turf. I needed to be seen, no concealment necessary for me, the decoy. I let the cloak fall back a little to reveal two copper-colored braids, pinned on either side, and let the sheen of the gold armlets be seen. And they were silent, those Walran men, struck dumb themselves. Whatever game runs toward the huntsmen to spoil their sport?

The reins had been knotted short in a clever way, so that by the slightest tug that great beast, which could have unseated me with one toss of its mighty head, would be forced to slow or veer aside as I wished, trotting now easily so that all gathered there could see who I was and recognize me for what I pretended to be: the Lady of Cambray, Olwen the Fair, come back from France to flaunt herself. We stopped in good time, in front of them, out of bow-shot but close enough so that I could see Lord Odo's prominent eyes bulging with anger and surprise. When the rest of his men had looked their fill, chattering together like magpies, I shouted, my voice as high and reedy as a girl's although muffled by the cloak, "Odo of Walran. I know you. I would speak with you."

He pushed back his coif so that there should be no mistaking who he was, but I knew him long before, his face a mask of hate.

"Peace," I said, "I come in peace. Let my brother and me go freely into Cambray; you are sworn to be my father's man, and as warden of the marcher lands he orders you. It is your oath to help, not to hinder, us."

I thought he would choke with venom at those words. "By Christ," he roared when he had speech, "the whore of Cambray returned, who took my son's life, who planned his death. Come down, mistress, and I'll give you peace. You and your paramour will scream for it before I'm done. And so your brother, a traitor sworn, who even his father would not help. And so that mis-shapen imp, your devil's twin."

A second and a third time I cried, "Odo of Walran, keep to your bond. If not to Cambray, then let us cross the border freely, without let."

Then he did give a bellow of rage and shouted to his men to ride after me and take me alive. "I knew," he howled, "that you were in league with those Celtic scum, scavengers of the earth, carrion. Go where you will, we follow you. The border does not protect you, nor them, this time."

His men gave a cry, as huntsmen do when they sight their prey. "Ho, Olwen of Cambray," they mocked. "Wait there for us, little one. Fall in our arms, we beg." And other such things too obscene to mention here. They began to gallop toward me, Lord Odo in the lead, fanning out to hem me round. For a second I watched them, terrorized, until the gray horse, scenting battle, began to sidestep and prance, throwing its head from side to side. In panic I spread my hands apart as far as I could, jerked them down with a violent twist so that the knots parted as they were meant and the reins slid free, although my hands were still shackled to them. I twined my fingers once more into the mane, and kicked with my heels. "Run," I shouted, "now run."

Taliesin's horse, which had never felt the touch of spur or

whip or needed them, half reared, to toss such impudence from its back, laid its head low, flattened its ears, began to move. Back it went, the way we had come, snaking in and out of rocks, taking bushes at a stride, pounding out the heather beneath its flailing hooves so that clods shot behind us in showers of mud. Almost jerked out of place by that first lunge, I flopped in the saddle like a rag doll. But it could not toss me off, too well tied on for that. So, bearing me, a nothing, on its back, it ran free.

That horse knew every inch of the moors, and so did I. When I had recovered breath enough to haul myself upright, a cut streaming blood where its head had knocked mine, my eyes so water-filled I could not see, lips dry, heart pounding in my ears, I leaned forward over its neck as Taliesin used to and spoke to it; I gathered up the reins, which were bound to my wrists in such fashion that, although I could not stop or hold the horse in any way, I could still guide. Back and forth it swerved, almost prancingly, sometimes doubling around to pass through the Walran line, plunging through with a sweep of hooves and teeth that caused many riders to go down. Soon those Norman knights were jostling each other, fumbling for foothold at the gaps, running foul. Bunched together or spread out, they could not hope to catch us, nor could they control their mounts. Some fell at rocks; some stumbled at the ditches hidden by the gorse roots; some tried to jump the bushes; their horses were too heavy for jumping. At every pass they lost a man, their numbers openly diminishing. An unhorsed knight is useless, too; back he had to limp on foot. But Odo of Walran was a good horseman himself. He saw his men running wild; he called the remainder to heel. "A gold piece," he told them, frothing with rage, "a sackful of my treasury, for the man who catches her, alive or dead. Death for him who lets her escape."

Now danger ran close and hot. Those still left hefted their spears to hurl and unplucked their bows. They had no breath to gloat but came on more cautiously. The Lord of Walran leveled his lance, threw up his shield with the wolf's head. He spurred his own destrier forward so that it, too, advanced, fighting mad. Once more I leaned in the saddle, breath gone, vision gone, my voice hoarse, hands and legs wrenched apart, jarred by every raking stride. Now would the last ride of all be run. "Come, my lord," I whispered through cracked and bleeding lips, for a beast can be as noble as a man, "come, my lord, show your speed."

I felt his muscles tense, his hooves spread; the heather ripped and fell apart. Back toward the pass we came, across the open moors. And following as fast as they could, the remainder of the Walran force persisted in their pursuit. Some threw their shields and helmets aside to reduce the weight; some even let their sword belts fall to give more speed; so ride huntsmen when they have their quarry within their grasp, so flees the terrified prey. Except suddenly terror was gone. Never in my life shall I ride like that again. Strength flowed from that horse to me; I was a god of air myself, and he had wings. The open moor flowed past as if it were unrolled on either side, and before us the hill fort waited patiently.

Down the track our enemy came, not twenty men left now, perhaps not ten. And of those some were unarmed, some willfully riding to win the gold that had been offered them, some almost forgetting that I was also an enemy with friends of my own. Along the track, then, beneath the fort, toward the ruined tower at its western end; the border almost reached, one by one those Norman knights pushed ahead for place, those a length behind whipping their horses along furiously. Down from the fort, cutting down from the high path that Taliesin had used those years ago, the three Welsh horsemen plunged, in front and behind, to catch the Normans as they rode.

At the ruined tower I swept past, not on the track but across the moor with its deadly scatter of stones and rocks. Taliesin had not fallen here, neither should I. But the Normans could not make the turn. Trying to wrench their horses to a stop, trying to force them around, a maneuver impossible, they spilled and tumbled; so much for Norman skill. A broken back, crushed ribs, and Celts at hand to finish them. "Sa, sa, sa," beat the Celts upon their shields. "Sa, sa, sa," they sang. Rising in the stirrups as one man they hurled their spears, brought their shield rims down hard, hacked with their swords, hewing a path of their own. No Norman afterward left horsed, they say, the moor littered with dead or broken men, except Odo of Walran and his body-squire, both trapped against the ruined tower.

They say, too, that Taliesin reined up, his hair blown golden until it looked like summer grass, his eyes like the distant sea. "Yield," he cried, "you and your man. Safe conduct promise me and mine; safe conduct I give you."

But, they say, that Norman lord, maddened beyond hearing or thinking sense, wild with fury as his own son had been, cried, "I fight on," although his horse was foundered and he had but one frightened boy to back him.

And they say, too, those who relish this tale, that Taliesin replied gravely, like a graybeard in council, "I give you life. Would you have given that much?" And when Odo did not reply, "Then fight. But since your horse goes lame, fight like a Celt, on foot with knives."

And they tell how Taliesin threw his sword aside, and his armor and his shield with the Walran crest, which he had taken and used—the last time he ever did such a thing, for pride and arrogance, and for something else, youth's exuberance perhaps—and leapt off his horse. He sprang on foot over the heather clumps, lithe with youthful grace, and in his hand he held that knife of mine which was neither knife nor sword. "Here I am, Odo of Walran," he shouted. "You swore to take me, I think. Now try."

Odo of Walran, seeing the advantage that impetuosity had afforded, gave a laugh of derision and scorn. A fool, he must have thought, a simpleton, a barbarian untutored in knightly ways. Ignoring the challenge that the prince had made, he spurred his horse into a charge, flailing down with his sword for one last lunge. And they say Taliesin never moved, his feet planted on his own ground, bowstring taut, but determined not to give way.

When the horse and horseman were upon him, the horse laboring mightily, its rider bent over to run him through, he hurled himself against its lame side, rolling away from the churning hooves but dragging hold of the reins and stirrup irons. The sword edge hewed through his leather coat, but that was the last thrust Odo made. Man and beast went crashing to the ground, the rider caught beneath.

They say that Taliesin was the first to rise, one hand held to his ribs where the sword had ripped, the other still clasping that little knife with its sharp blade and its handle worn right through to gold. They say he cried to Odo, who lay half stunned, "Catch," and had his men throw a second knife so that it slid along the grass within Walran's grasp. They say that that Norman lord heaved and pried with both hands, trying to lug his massive weight upon its feet. But there was no one to help him, and his own horse had him pinned, its neck snapped.

And they say, too, that the prince watched him strain for a while, neither moving toward nor away, not even seeming to notice that his own wound was bleeding heavily. And when the struggle was done, and Odo was spent with fear, he walked up to him, almost strolled. Odo's head rolled back; he tried to twist himself around—so looks a hare caught in a net. But Taliesin made no move to harm him, merely beckoned to the squire. A young boy he was, fresh from home, and this his first taste of war. "Here, lad," Taliesin is supposed to have said, his breath coming in gasps, "bear your master home. As he has other sons, bid him cherish them. I never sought to kill the oldest one. And as I have a father whose life has been destroyed by hate, bid your master not let hate destroy him. Life I grant. Let him savor it."

They say he called to his men to lead up a horse, and never taking his gaze, dark and thoughtful, from Walran's face, grown gray itself, all blood drained from it, he heaved himself into the saddle, motioned to his men to ride on. They wheeled as one, rode up the cliff path toward the fort. And when they had quite gone and he was sure it was no trick, they say the little squire came timidly out from the wall where he had crept, dismounted on that scuffed and bloodstained track, and stood gazing around him in complete amaze. So long he looked after those three horsemen that he almost forgot to help his lord. But they say Odo of Walran as silently allowed himself to be helped, and when at last he was freed and could speak, as Taliesin and his men had long since gone, he went back to Walran in silence, too.

That is what they say, all those who remember the crossing of the pass and the encounter there. I never saw what happened, nor did the Lady Olwen, waiting for news herself, hidden in the foxes' lair. She and Hue stayed there until the prince returned. The wait was not as long as they feared; first they heard the sound of horses trotting over the grass, and then, in the distance, that Celtic whistle. Out she darted, a strange-looking boy with her hair cropped short and her dirty boy's clothes, and ran toward them bare-footed, since my boots did not fit. When she came to them, she looked at each carefully, and each in turn nodded at her as if to say, "It is done." Only the prince added slowly as if his voice came from far off, "Now we can go home."

Well, they got him off his horse before he fell; they tied him up, a deep and raking wound but not one to hinder him. They mounted again, two by two for the last time, the lady behind him to steady him, the single man who could have carried me riding as guard. And since Henry's men still encircled Cambray, too many in number for the Celts to break through, too few to watch the castle and pursue, the five fugitives had no alternative but to cross the border and continue on.

And what of me, where was I? Who knows where the wind blows or where wild birds fly. We ranged the open moor, the horse and I, all through that long and vicious day, as fleet as cloud shadows that sweep down from the hills and ripple past. But there was no cloud as shield that day; the sun beat down without restraint. Thirst bothered me at first, but afterward even thirst was gone. Bound to that saddle, hands still tied to the reins, fingers latched about the mane like thorns, I remember thinking, we shall ride like this until I die and he can find some way to rub me off, or until he dies, and I with him, no way to untie myself, no way for anyone to approach us, not even when he tires of galloping. When once he halted by a moorland stream, ice-cold it trickled beneath the fern, I could almost taste its peaty water on my tongue, but never a way for me to drink. We splashed through boggy patches, where gnats rise in swarms, and strayed among the meadow-sweet and parsley flowers, brushing heavy and dew-laden about my knees, no way to reach and pull at them. Toward nightfall, I know, we came up onto the highest part of the Cambray hills, where stands an old circle of stones, leaning together like ancient men discussing the state of the world. Once, long, long ago, a prophecy was made there to the Lady Ann. Grief was in it, and joy, and hope, that perhaps one day the rift between the two races, Norman and Celt, might be bridged. I turned my head stiffly and watched those stones as we sped by, until they sank over the crest of the hill. Fickle are those Celtic gods, promising fair, showing foul, never gift without due sacrifice. And we journeyed on.

But you see I live to tell this tale. The gods had not yet had their will of me. The second, third day, what matter, dark and light as one, the night bringing relief from heat, the day swelling those leather thongs to eat into the tender flesh, so that I knew in part what torture Hue had known, I felt the horse start, flick up its head, catching me anew where I dropped upon its neck. It laid back its ears, listening. I thought I heard, far away, across the hill, mindless as a fluting bird, that Celtic whistling.

Perhaps I heard it, perhaps I dreamed, perhaps so dreamed the horse. It moved into its flowing gallop once again, heading away from the coast, inland, across the border, straight to where its master rode. And so it is that I, Urien the Bard, the horse master, tell the end of this tale. We were caught easily, the horse happy to have its real rider returned. The Celts untied me, carried me in a litter slung between their two mounts. Surely the Lady Olwen was at wit's end at first, three sick men, each trying to cheer the other on. Christ who reigns in Heaven, never was such a pitiful group, as we wound our way north to Afron. And in truth only the survivors of the princely guard, their duty almost done, began to speak, freely allowing themselves to talk of family and friends, each day another tale of new delight and gossip to encourage us, such memories of green fields, vast stands of oak and birch, such horses, sheep, and womenkind, until even their prince threw up his arms in protest, as if to say, "Is that truly as it was when I left?"

"But look you, masters," one said in his shy and gentle way, his cunningly entwined Celtic thought lacing his cunning Celtic words, "on my travels I have seen Englishmen who speak and talk and think like French, and Frenchmen, born and reared, whose greatest wealth lies in England. Back and forth that channel sea those lords bate, like hounds, as if water were a hunting field; how can you know or love any land since you are pulled between the two, since you own properties in both? Afron men live and die in Afron, or should; that is where our roots are." A truth in that, for sure, and so it was, I think, for their prince. And when I heard those Welshmen sing, as now they did, epitaphs for their fallen companions, denied a fitting burial, their song were marvels of intricacy to praise and honor dead friends.

We did not hurry; no need for haste. We had food in plenty, the weather continued fair, and although we avoided any place of note where the prince might be recognized, there was no enemy left to harry us. Nor did haste best suit our needs; how many weeks now upon the road, what matter if a few more passed? And it may be that in my lady's mind there was more than one reason for loitering, not least, the knowledge that at our journey's end there was yet the Lord of Afron to be faced.

The high pasture air gave Lord Hue new heart. He still was slow of speech but could feed and dress himself, and, praise God, could ride, taking turn and turn about. To see him astride a horse, you would not think he had ever lacked the skill, his hair grown long to cover his scar, his training in horsemanship so ingrained as to give him back his old fire. And in good time he learned to draw and wield a sword as well as any mounted lord, giving him the nickname of "Hue Crook Thumbs," which title he did not scorn. I learned to walk myself, my bones so wrenched apart, my joints so racked with fever fits, I half believed I would end more twisted than nature meant.

And what of the prince and his lady love? Taliesin, too, would bear a scar all his life; an inch closer in, so much for pride! But his wound did not hinder him or hamper him in his loves. Wherever he and the lady went, sensuality seemed to flow from them; they seemed to move as if still joined. He could not keep his hands from her nor she from him, so that when he lifted her on his horse—for he let no one touch her but himself—his hands felt beneath her short boy's tunic; and when he helped her off, she slid down his full body's length; and when he mounted behind, he kept his hand low on her waist to pull her down upon himself; and when he rode, by turns, in front, she pressed her breasts against his back and breathed softly in his hair, crisped long around his ears. And nightly, or in noon heat, when they moved aside and we heard him cover her, the incaught breath, the sob of lust, was as natural as any sound in those wide hills. I accepted it, God's gift to them. So may it be to all mankind.

We came to Afron's castle at dusk. I think the prince had planned to make his entrance without all the ceremony of midday, or perhaps he merely wished to round off his journey in fitting wise, the day's work done, the restful night ahead. Or perhaps I imagine this, and he merely lingered for a few more hours among those clover fields he had described. The scent of them, the sound of bees humming all day long, was enough to drug any man out of mind. I lay in the clover myself, upon my back, and held the gray horse to graze, while its master was pleasure-bent. It was hobbled tightly, to be sure, but it snuffled, as if to show it bore no ill will; nor I to it, although I will confess I never asked to ride it again, nor any horse, if there were some other means. Yet that day I lay between its great forefeet as nonchalant as if it had been a hound.

And my little lady, leaning back against the prince, tried to pull her tunic down (for women's skirts we had none left, her own past repair, and I was sewn into a spare shirt). With her long fingers she plaited flowers into her short hair and tidied straight the prince's curls. "Let be," he told her lazily, his eyes closed against the sun, "no need to worry how we look. They must take us as we are." And that, too, I think was what he meant.

The news of the prince's arrival had been spread abroad; these last miles we could not ride unseen, and everywhere, from field and cottage, men and women came running to point and cheer, their prince returned. "Hail, Prince of Afron," the children piped, and he smiled at them, taking these signs of favoritism with as much grace as he had those of the French queen. And so it was at nightfall, when the wood fires were sending up their pale blue haze and the sheep came down in flocks from the pasturing, that he led us to his father's fort.

Not a Norman fort, not stone-built, but of huge earth ramparts, bristling with wooden pallisades. As we rode up the steep causeway, members of the household lined the sides to stare, and the watch saluted smartly as to a royal progress. We came within the massive timber gates, as once the Lady Ann had described, where the women of the court were gathered. Dressed in their Welsh robes, their Welsh headdresses, they certainly were comely folk, and one, a tall and slender lady, with eyes like the prince's own, dark-haired, wrapped in a cloak, her face beautiful, if some secret care had not eaten hope away, surely she must be his kin. But she did not move from her place beside the gate, merely looked at him with his own grave look. And he and his men raised their shields and spears in salute, honoring her, lady wife to the High Lord of Afron.

A strange group I suppose we must have made: Hue and I creeping along (for these days he supported me), strangely fitted as companions in truth we were, and yet the gods had willed it so; the prince's two companions, sole survivors of his father's guard, their grins breaking out despite themselves; and the lady, almost defiant in her boyish clothes, sitting on the gray horse, where the prince had set her. But once we had dismounted within the inner yard, the guards of the royal household did not hold back. Although none acknowledged the prince openly by name, many clasped him wordlessly in their arms, as they did the returning veterans. And a little maid, not more than a child, darted out between the ranks, weeping for happiness, so like the prince you knew she must be one of those sisters he had talked about. He put her gently to one side, lifted down his lady, drew us on. And so we came into the hall of his forefathers.

Wide and long was that hall, dim with smoke, smelling of sweet fruitwood; the floor littered with straw and herbs; hounds trailing underfoot. Along the walls were tattered flags from old campaigns, and old weapons, battle-axes, hunting spears. At one end, on a wooden platform, in his carved oak throne, seated like a king, Taliesin's father awaited him. He was a tall man with iron-gray hair, hawk-nosed, showing, if truth be told, signs of age in the way his hands were hooked about the chair edge, as if to hide a nervousness, a trembling. Yet not one smile lighted his somber looks, not one word of welcome came from that imperious mouth, and his dark blue eyes, piercing against the wind-browned skin, looked out as proudly as ever the prince's did. He did not speak or acknowledge his son, but waited for his son to begin.

"Greetings, my lord father." Taliesin spoke easily; he did not kneel to kiss his father's hand, although I think the older man expected it, and his voice rang out in its young and jubilant way. "I hope I see you well. It has been a long while since I rode into my father's house. I hope I am received."

The older man said never a word, leaned forward in his oaken chair, waiting for the news he wanted to hear. What news does revenge want, what does death wait for, but news of other deaths?

"My lord," said Taliesin, and now you saw what pride was; now he bore himself as does a prince, heir to a long and royal line. Before his father he neither blinked nor looked aside, he neither boasted nor explained. *They shall accept me as I am.* "I am returned, if it pleases you, to stay. And if not, then I claim a just part of my inheritance and will seek my fortune elsewhere in the world. But first I present to you my dear and loyal friends, Hue, Lord of Cambray, the page, Urien, also of that house, and most dear of all to me—"

Before he could finish, his father had snapped his fingers for silence. "Normans," he grated out. "What use to us are loyal ones? What of our request to the man who calls himself England's king?"

Then Taliesin did hesitate, not from fear but from respect. He wanted to express clearly, I think, the ideas that had been growing in his own mind, to give them form the older man could accept; he wanted chance to show his father honor without dishonor to himself. He wanted most of all for his father to honor us.

His hesitation told the older man all that he needed to hear. The Lord of Afron drew himself to his feet; tall and active he must have been before old grief had burdened him, as handsome as his son now was. I wondered suddenly, with pity's pang, what his other sons must have been, to destroy him with their deaths. And my heart contracted with pity for this youngest son, who in no thing ever would or could please a man whose revenge was fathomless.

"Three sons I had," the father intoned; his voice keened on one note low, vibrant; so sing the Welsh bards when the gods inspire; so speak the Welsh wise men when they prophesy. "And only one son left to pay respect to their memory and revenge our house. Must I ride forth myself to achieve what justice demands? Shall I have no son to my name?"

Taliesin would not answer him; what should his pride say except those bleak words that would end all reply: "If my father wishes it." But his father must accept him as he was or not at all. This was Taliesin's true answer, as a son to a father who had long commanded him. But he would not explain, even if silence cost him his patrimony.

Silent were we all in that hall, in the presence of that old and stubborn man, only one person able to break the impasse and say what Taliesin would not. And so my lady did.

She let go of Taliesin's hand, which she had been clutching, almost childlike in her intensity, and advanced boldly, as is her way when she senses an unfairness. "My lord," she cried in her high, sweet voice, impetuous, too, forgetting the way she looked, "you do your son grave injury. A soldier he has been, and bravely fought in all the wars against your enemies. Two kings has he challenged in their courts, and the greatest king of all of Christendom defeated in open fight with his own hand. Three things you asked for; three things he brings. King Henry was forced to beg for life; my father will restore you your lands; and here we be, three hostages to do with as you wish."

If his hound had leapt and bitten him, or a cat had been given tongue to speak, the Lord of Afron could not have been more taken aback. He did not answer for a while, not now because of pride but because he did not know what to say. "By Saint David," he finally brought out, "what is that . . . that . . . that changeling, wench or knave, to challenge us?"

His description was not flattering, but my lady had looked for no better, and she began to laugh. "Why," she cried, "my lord of Afron, you are at fault. I am no changeling, nor wench, nor knave. Olwen am I, granddaughter to Efa of the Celts."

The older man sank back into his chair as if arrow-shot. "Efa of the Celts," he almost whispered, "beloved by all men, whom Falk of Cambray stole from us. Then you must be daughter to Ann of Cambray and Raoul of Sedgemont and Sieux, sister, then, to this young lord." And he looked from Hue to me and back as if gradually taking in what he saw. "By Christ," he swore, "whoever you are, or what you claim, who are you to dispute with me? My vow was made long ago. No son I have unless my sons are revenged. Thus have I sworn, and thus my oath stands."

"Well," she said, in her way as proud as any man, "here we are. We have come of our free will. Without your son would our lives be lost, and without us so would his. We are bound by vows of our own. But if you would stand by an oath that was so long made—" She suddenly smiled at him. "Remember my grandmother," she cried. "Falk thought she was a boy at first. 'Give me that lad as hostage,' Falk said, not knowing who she was. So now you have mistaken me. Would not your son's wife be the best hostage for peace, as Falk's wife was?"

There was an inrush of breath from where, in the distant corners of the hall, all the world of Afron was listening, not daring to reveal itself, not daring in any way to give approval or deny. No one spoke thus to this old man, certainly no woman had. And hearing her, with less amaze than his father had shown but still surprised, Prince Taliesin suddenly laughed himself. I think it was the first time for laughter in that hall in many years. "There, father," he cried, as a young son might, "have not I brought you home a prize?" He took the lady's hand as if to lead her forward. "A little the worse for wear, I admit," he jested in his open way, "a little worn. Nothing that clean water and fresh clothes will not mend. Then even as Norman she might grace your hall and fill my bed." He smiled down at her his sensuous smile, was as suddenly serious himself. "Of all women else," he said, "I cleave to her. If I have her not, then no man shall. If she have not me, then wifeless shall I remain. So has our own oath been sworn."

"Without consent." There still was stubbornness in those fine old eyes, still strength. "I sent you forth to wage a war against the Normans, not to pleasure them. Keep her as harlot in your own hall, not mine."

Again there was an inrush of breath; dismay and anger were in it, and despair. Hue's face grew hot. But I held him tightly to hold him still. This was not our quarrel. And the Lady Olwen was not yet done.

She had paled, then flushed, but she did not flinch. "You put no shame on me," she cried. "Harlot I am not nor never will be. Yet willingly I admit that I am lover of your son and he lover of me. Willingly I came of my own accord, to ask for shelter in your house. But if you will not accept me, or a son who has achieved more than any man, then in that, too, are you forsworn. For you will lose not only him but your son's sons. Your line ends here. You forgo the son I shall give him."

A second time the Lord of Afron was silenced by her. But Taliesin had turned to her and swept her up into his arms. "Is that so, dear heart," he cried, "is that true?" And he held her as if we were not there, as if they were alone. She looked at him proudly again and nodded. "It is so, my lord," she said.

He gave a great shout to make the rafters ring, and from those distant corners, one by one, then altogether, those men and women of the royal court took up his cry, and the soldiers beat upon their shields. "Father," Taliesin said when there was time to speak. "Then am I returned with honor's gage. My dear brothers are at rest at last. Life for them we give you, my lord, new life. In my son shall your dead sons be restored to you." And he held out his arms to his father to be embraced and to embrace him, the first sign of affection ever to be exchanged. And slowly the Lord of Afron came down to greet his son and honor his wife.

And they say, that night, when all the household slept, after

feasting such as had never before been known, such rejoicing
after so many barren years, the Lady Olwen rose from her place
beside the other ladies of the royal house. In her long Celtic
gown she went up the high wooden steps, past the guards
outside the door, without a word, but they saluted her with all
respect and let her by. The chamber where the prince lay was
old, ill-lit, a faint fire burning on the neglected hearth, the
walls and floors hastily swept, the great bed strewn with linen,
fresh-laundered and dried in the sun, smelling faintly of clover
and mint.

Taliesin sat before the fire, in a high carved chair such as his
father used. His face was in shadow; only the crest of hair
showed its copper gleam in the firelight. He leaned back when
she came in, never turning around, stretching his feet upon the
worn hearth, never speaking until she came up close to him.
Her head scarcely reached the top of the carved oak frame, and
the flickering flames etched a pattern on her white gown, curling,
twisting, like dragon's breath.

Nor did he touch her, nor hold her hand as was his wont,
staring in front of him as if searching in the fire for some sign.
"This was my oldest brother's room," he said, "he who was
heir. When I was a child, he slept here. I used to hear his
footsteps after dark, when he and his companions had been
drinking below. And in the morning, when he and his brothers
went forth to hunt, they used to bound down those stairs three
at a time, their hounds barking, their huntsmen laughing. Once
my brother dropped his spear. It slid down the steps in a great
clatter, making the girls in the hall scream. He followed it,
laughing, too, crying that he wished his reach so long. This is
the room of the heir of my house. When my oldest brother
died, it should have passed to the second, then the third. I, the
fourth, came scant behind." He paused, a long, hard pause in
the semi-dark. "I never looked for it to be mine," he whispered,
"God knows, I wish it never had been so."

Now she did reach for his hand and took it without answering, running her fingers along the back, finger by finger,
as if assuring herself it was real, and like him she looked into
the fire. Old fears, old thoughts burned there; sadness burned

there, and prophecy. She said in a voice that seemed not hers, timeless it was as the matriarch's, and yet was hers, with the same ripple of intensity, "Dear my lord, your grief becomes you well, better than any feat of arms, since you hold it in your heart. But in your heart your brothers ever remain, and in your memories, as for all men. Long ago it was foreordained. Who knows what God has in mind for us; from the day of our birth is our death written there. But the dead look to us to give them life, and so it was foretold for us, long ago, by Efa of the Celts, that one day all would be joined in us and made most fair. We, as little as they, can avoid the fate that God ordains."

She stirred after a while, shivering slightly, for the fire was small and the room large. "My lord," she told him now, simple as a child, "they wish us well. They loved you, the little one, as you loved them, the elder and strong. I know. I, too, have brothers whom I love. I, too, have honored them and they me."

Then he did turn to her, and touched her face with wondering fingers along the luminous skin, wrapping his arms about her to keep her warm. Their heads were close together, bent with sudden intent, as he loosened her gown and she his, both of them moving now with the same accord. He undid slowly, lace by lace, the white linen gown of Celtic weave, fine as a cobweb, and she unbuckled his sword belt, her hands deft with the heavy leather and ornate fastening. She laid her hand upon his heart, hearing its beat against her palm as the sound of her own blood. His fingers traced a path between the budding breasts, across the delicate skin, until she brought them lower down, surging to him as a wave upon a shore.

"Hold me," she cried, "fill me, love me, until I die of love."

And "Hold me," he cried.

He caught her up, in one stride came to the bridal bed, laid her down, and covered her. So was the heir of Afron made welcome, so did his lady comfort him.

Well, thus it was that the prophecy was fulfilled which had been made many years ago within that circle of stones at Cambray, that in God's time peace should be made between Norman and Celt, that they should come safely home. And so was the marriage arranged between the Lady Olwen and Prince Taliesin of Afron; so was she a hostage to accord as had her grandmother been. And their child, their firstborn son, grew to resemble both his Norman and his Celt grandsires.

Hue lived with his Celtic kin, happier, I think, where he was born, and married among them in time, although the old wildness was not completely lost; and there were days still when he would leap upon his horse as if riding away from or toward something that he could not even give a name. I stayed with him for a while, and learned what I could of Celtic ways and Celtic songs. I told you bards were considered here in high repute, more honored among them than any lord, and words as highly valued as deeds. The Lady Olwen, the Fair, ever held me a beloved friend. And when, as happened in due course, I, too, left, I never was far from her thoughts, nor she from mine, my love whom God both gave and took away. *Ora pro nobis.*

Note From the Author

Like the first two books of this chronicle (*Ann of Cambray* and *Gifts of the Queen*), *A Royal Quest* is based upon history, as far as possible. Where there is a doubt, or where "the chronicles are silent," I have tried to give reasonable explanation within the historical setting. However, since a novel is not a factual account, it can at best serve only to illuminate or give the impression of past times. The castle at Falaise may not have been besieged by the Bretons and Welsh in 1173, nor is there any proof that the castle was chosen as a prison for Queen Eleanor when she was captured for her part in the Great War of Henry's reign. As the greatest of Norman castles, it well may have been; and in the end, King Henry certainly used Welsh mercenaries. The fictional characters in this book act according to their own dictates, but their actions are based upon those of real people, who often did what they do and suffered similar fates. As Ann of Cambray says in her first chronicle, "Write swiftly, scribe, before this year draws to a close and these last days of sun are gone. Soon all about us will be dark and cold, and no one will be left to speak for us, or care if we speak at all." It is to give voice to those long-past times, those long-gone people, that this book is written.

I should like to thank my family and friends, old and new, who have given me encouragement and help, especially the many who have written to me. To my editor at Warner Books, Fredda Isaacson, and to Elise and Arnold Goodman, my agents, my thanks and appreciation again for their help. And to all of you who have not minded my retreat to the twelfth century, my gratitude.

As historical background for this book, I have relied mainly upon contemporary sources, a good general book being *English Historical Documents, 1143–1189*, edited by D. C. Douglas and G. W. Greenaway. Specific writers I found useful include Roger of Howden, Walter Map, William of Newburg, Robert of Torigny, and Gerald of Wales.

General books on the period include *Le Gouvernement d' Henri II Plantagenet* by J. Boussard, and *Henry II* by W. L. Warren. Specialized books include *France in the Middle Ages* by Paul Lacroix, *English Medieval Castles* by R. A. Brown, *The Military Organization of Norman England* by Warren Hollister, and *A History of Wales* by J. E. Lloyd.

In addition I have made several trips in the past two years to the major sites mentioned in this book, mainly to the Welsh border; have visited various castles in England and France, especially in Normandy; and stayed in Paris, Poitiers, and Rouen. My thanks to friends and hosts who helped me on these journeys.

copy 2